Molly and Joe
sweet, chuggin
wherever they
were both very disconcerted, for Molly had given
birth not to a baby girl or a baby boy – but to a
chicken.

This was a fully grown chicken, same size as a lusty
new-born human baby, an eight- or nine-pounder
with feathers of buff gold, still slicked and matted
from birth. Already it was fluffing these out to dry,
flapping the crooked arms which were its wings as it
perched at the bottom of the bed. Its beady eyes
shone bright and prominent as it gazed at its human
parents.

"My God, what'll we *do*?" asked Joe. "It isn't as if
it's a freak or a monster! It looks perfectly normal. It
just isn't human, that's all. It's a blithering chicken.
You just gave birth to it. We both made it together,
didn't we?

"In that case it's a *human* chicken," gasped Molly.
"It's our child."

by the same author in VGSF

THE JONAH KIT

THE MIRACLE VISITORS
(VGSF Classic)

THE EMBEDDING
(VGSF Classic)

THE FLIES OF MEMORY

IAN WATSON

STALIN'S
TEARDROPS

VGSF

VGSF is an imprint of Victor Gollancz Ltd
14 Henrietta Street, London WC2E 8QJ

First published in Great Britain 1991
by Victor Gollancz Ltd

First VGSF edition 1992

ACKNOWLEDGEMENTS

"Stalin's Teardrops" first appeared in *Weird Tales* 1990; "Gaudi's
Dragon" first appeared in *Isaac Asimov's Science Fiction Magazine*,
1990; "In the Upper Cretaceous with the Summerfire Brigade" first
appeared in *The Magazine of Fantasy and Science Fiction*, 1990; "The
Beggars in our Back Yard" first appeared in *Colours of a New Day:
Writing for South Africa* edited by Sarah Lefanu and Stephen
Hayward, 1990; "From the Annals of the Onomastic Society" first
appeared in *The Gate*, 1990; "Lambert, Lambert" first appeared in
Fear, 1990; "Tales from Weston Willow" first appeared in *Dark
Fantasies* edited by Chris Morgan, 1989; "In Her Shoes" first
appeared in *Fear*, 1988; "The Human Chicken" first appeared in
Tales from the Forbidden Planet 2 edited by Roz Kaveney, 1990; "The
Case of the Glass Slipper" first appeared in *Gaslight and Ghosts* edited
by Stephen Jones and Jo Fletcher, 1988; "The Pharaoh and the
Mademoiselle" first appeared in *The Book of Ian Watson*, 1985;
"The Eye of the Ayatollah" first appeared in *Interzone*, 1990.

A catalogue record for this book is
available from the British Library

ISBN 0-575-05281-3

Printed and bound in Great Britain
by Cox & Wyman Ltd, Reading

Contents

For George and Pam

Stalin's Teardrops

PART ONE: THE LIE OF THE LAND

"This is the era of *clarity* now, Valentin," Mirov reproved me. "I don't necessarily like it, but I am no traitor. I have problems, you have problems. We must adapt."

I chuckled. "In this office we have always adapted, haven't we?"

By "office" I referred to the whole cluster of studios which composed the department of cartography. Ten in all, these were interconnected with archways rather than doors so that my staff and I could pass freely from one to the next across a continuous sweep of parquet flooring. In recent years I had resisted the general tendency to subdivide spacious rooms which, prior to the Revolution, had been the province of a giant insurance company. For our drawing tables and extra-wide filing cabinets we needed elbow-room. We needed as much daylight as possible from our windows overlooking the courtyard deep below. Hence our location here on the eighth floor; hence the absence of steel bars at our windows, and ours alone. Grids of shadow must not fall across our work.

On hot summer days when breezes blew in and out we needed to be specially vigilant. (And of course we used much sealing wax every evening when we locked up.) In winter, the standard lighting – those big white globes topped by shades – was perfectly adequate. Still, their illumination could not rival pure daylight. We often left the finalization of important maps until the summer months.

Mirov's comments about clarity seemed spurious in the circumstances; though with a sinking heart I knew all too well what he meant.

"We have lost touch with our own country," he said

forlornly, echoing a decision which had been handed down from on high.

"Of course we have," I agreed. "That was the whole idea, wasn't it?"

"This must change." He permitted himself a wry joke. "The lie of the land must be corrected."

Mirov was a stout sixty-five-year-old with short grizzled hair resembling the hachuring on a map of a steep round hillock. His nose and cheeks were broken-veined from over-indulgence in the now-forbidden spirit. I think he resented never having been attached to one of the more glamorous branches of our secret police. Maybe he had always been bored by his job, unlike me.

Some people might view the task of censorship as a cushy sinecure. Not so! It demanded a logical meticulousness which in essence was more creative than pedantic. Yet it was, well, dusty. Mirov lacked the inner forcefulness which might have seen him assigned to foreign espionage or even to the border guards. I could tell that he did not intend to resist the changes which were now in the air, like some mischievous whirlwind intent on tossing us all aloft. He hadn't come here to conspire with me, to any great extent.

As head of censorship Mirov was inspector of the department of cartography. Yet under my guidance of the past twenty years cartography basically ran itself. Mirov routinely gave his imprimatur to our products: the regional and city maps, the charts, the Great Atlas. Two years his junior, I was trusted. The occasional spy whom he planted on me as a trainee invariably must deliver a glowing report. (Which of my staff of seventy persons, busily drafting away or practising, was the current "eye of Mirov"? I didn't give a hoot.) As to the *quality* of our work, who was more qualified than myself to check it?

"What you're suggesting isn't easy," I grumbled. "Such an enterprise could take years, even decades. I was hoping to retire by the age of seventy. Are you implying that I stay on and on forever?" I knew well where I would retire to . . .

He rubbed his nose. Did those broken capillaries itch so much?

"Actually, Valentin, there's a time limit. Within two years – consisting of twenty-four months, not of twenty-nine months or thirty-two; and *this* is regarded as generous – we must publish a true Great Atlas. Otherwise the new economic plan . . . well, they're thinking of new railway lines, new dams, new towns, opening up wasteland for oil and mineral exploitation."

"Two years?" I had to laugh. "It's impossible, quite impossible."

"It's an order. Any procrastination will be punished. You'll be dismissed. Your pension rights will diminish: no cabin in the countryside, no more access to hard currency shops. A younger officer will replace you – one of the new breed. Don't imagine, Valentin, that you will have a companion in misfortune! Don't assume that I too shall be dismissed at the summit of my career. My other bureaux are rushing to publish and promote all sorts of forbidden rubbish. So-called experimental poetry, fiction, art criticism. Plays will be staged to shock us, new music will jar our ears, new art will offend the eye. Happenings will happen. Manuscripts are filed away under lock and key, after all – every last item. We only need to unlock those cupboards, to let the contents spill out and lead society astray into mental anarchy."

I sympathized. "Ah, what we have come to!"

He inclined his cross-hatched hill-top head. "*You*, Valentin, *you*. What you have come to." He sighed deeply. "Still, I know what you mean . . . Colonel."

He mentioned my rank to remind me. We might wear sober dark suits, he and I, but we were both ranking officers.

"With respect, General, these – ah – orders are practically impossible to carry out."

"Which is why a new deputy-chief cartographer has been assigned to you."

"So here is the younger officer you mentioned – already!"

He gripped my elbow in the manner of an accomplice, though he wasn't really such.

"It shows willing," he whispered, "and it's one way out. Let the blame fall on her if possible. Let her seem a saboteur." Aloud, he continued, "Come along with me to the restaurant, to meet Grusha. You can bring her back here yourself."

I should meet my nemesis on neutral territory, as it were. Thus Mirov avoided direct, visible responsibility for introducing her.

Up here on the eighth floor we in cartography had the advantage of being close to one of the two giant restaurants which fed the thousands of men and women employed in the various branches of secret police work. The other restaurant was down in the basement. Many staff routinely turned up at eight o'clock of a morning – a full hour earlier than the working day commenced – to take advantage of hearty breakfasts unavailable outside: fresh milk, bacon and eggs, sausages, fresh fruit.

As I walked in silence with Mirov for a few hundred metres along the lime-green corridor beneath the omnipresent light-globes, I reflected that proximity to the restaurant was less advantageous today.

At this middle hour of the morning the food hall was almost deserted but for cooks and skivvies. Mirov drank the excellent coffee and cream with almost indecent haste so as to leave me alone with the woman. Grusha was nudging forty but hadn't lost her figure. She was willowy, with short curly fair hair, a large equine nose, and piercing sapphire eyes. A nose for sniffing out delays, eyes for seeing through excuses. An impatient thoroughbred! An intellectual. The privileged daughter of someone inclined to foreign and new ways. Daddy was one of the new breed who had caused so much upset. Daddy had used influence to place her here. This was her great opportunity; and his.

"So you were originally a graduate of the Geographical Academy," I mused.

She smiled lavishly. "Do I take it that I shall find your ways a little different, Colonel?"

"Valentin, please."

"We must mend those ways. I believe there is much to rectify."

"Are you married, Grusha?"

"To our land, to the future, to my speciality."

"Which was, precisely?"

"The placing of names on maps. I assume you know Imhof's paper, *Die Anordnung der Namen in der Karte*?"

"You read German?"

She nodded. "French and English too."

"My word!"

"I used my language skills on six years' duty in the DDR." Doing what? Ah, not for me to enquire.

Her shoulders were narrow. How much weight could they bear? Every so often she would hitch those shoulders carelessly with the air of an energetic filly frustrated, till now, at not being given free rein to dash forth – along a prescribed, exactly measured track. There lay the rub. Let her try to race into the ambiguous areas I had introduced!

I covered a yawn with my palm. "Yes, I know the Kraut's work. He gave me some good ideas. Oh, there are so many means for making a map hard to read. Nay, not merely misleading but incomprehensible! Names play a vital role. Switch them all around, till only the contour lines are the same as before. Interlace them, so that new place names seem to emerge spontaneously. Set them all askew, so that the user needs to turn the map around constantly till his head is in a spin. Space the names out widely so that the map seems dotted with unrelated letters like some code or acrostic. Include too many names, so that the map chokes with surplus data."

Grusha stared at me, wide eyed.

"And that," I said, "is only the icing on the cake."

Back in cartography I gave her a tour of the whole cake. In line with the policy of clarity I intended to be transparently clear.

"Meet Andrey!" I announced in the first studio. "Andrey is our expert with flexible curves and quills."

Red-headed, pock-marked Andrey glanced up from his glass

drawing table, floodlit from below. Lead weights covered in baize held sheets of tracing paper in position. A trainee, Goldman, sat nearby carving quills for Andrey's later inspection. At Goldman's feet a basket was stuffed with an assortment of wing feathers from geese, turkeys, ducks, and crows.

"Goose quills are supplest and wear longest," I informed Grusha, though she probably knew. "Turkeys' are stiffer. Duck and crow is for very fine work. The choice of a wrong quill easily exaggerates a pathway into a major road or shrinks a river into a stream. Observe how fluidly Andrey alters the contours of this lake on each new tracing."

Andrey smiled in a preoccupied way. "This new brand of tracing paper cockles nicely when you block in lakes of ink."

"Of course, being rag-based," I added, "it expands on damp days by, oh, a good two per cent. A trivial distortion, but it all helps."

The second studio was the scale room, where Zorov and assistants worked with camera lucida and other tricks at warping the scales of maps.

"En route to a final map we enlarge and reduce quite a lot," I explained. "Reduction causes blurring. Enlargement exaggerates inaccuracies. This prism we're using today both distorts and enlarges. Now *here*," I went on, leading her to Frenzel's table, "we're reducing and enlarging successively by the similar-triangles method."

"I do recognize the technique," answered Grusha, a shade frostily.

"Ah, but we do something else with it. Here is a road. We shrink a ten kilometre stretch to the size of one kilometre. We stretch the next one kilometre to the length of ten. Then we link strand after strand back together. So the final length is identical, but all the bends are in different places. See how Antipin over here is inking rivers red and railway tracks blue, contrary to expectation."

Antipin's trainee was filling little bottles of ink from a large bottle; the stuff dries up quickly.

Onward to the blue studio, the photographic room where Papyrin was shading sections of a map in light blue.

"Naturally, Grusha, light blue doesn't photograph, so on the final printed map these parts will be blank. The map, in this case, is correct yet cannot be reproduced – "

Onward to the dot and stipple studio . . . Remarkable what spurious patterns the human eye can read into a well-placed array of dots.

All of this, even so, was only really the icing . . .

Grusha flicked her shoulders again. "It's quite appalling, Colonel Valentin. Well, I suppose we must simply go back to the original maps and use those for the Atlas."

"What original maps?" I enquired. "Who knows any longer which are the originals? Who has known for years?"

"Surely they are on file!"

"All of our maps are in a constant state of revolutionary transformation, don't you see?"

"You're mocking."

"It wouldn't be very pure to keep those so-called originals from a time of exploitation and inequality, would it?" I allowed myself a fleeting smile. "Nowadays all of our maps are originals. A mere two per cent change in each successive edition amounts to a substantial shift over the course of a few decades. Certain constants remain, to be sure. A lake is still a lake, but of what size and shape? A road still stretches from the top of a map to its bottom; yet by what route, and through what terrain? Security is important, Grusha. I suppose by the law of averages we might have returned to our original starting point in a few cases, though frankly I doubt it."

"Let us base our work on the first published Atlas, then! The least altered one."

"Ah, but Atlases are withdrawn and pulped. As to archive copies, have you never noticed that the published products are not *dated*? Intentionally so!"

"I must sit down and think."

"Please do, please do! I'm anxious that we co-operate. Only tell me how."

My studios hummed with cartographic activity.

★

Finding one's way to our grey stone edifice in Dzerzhinsky Square only posed a serious problem to anyone who paid exact heed to the city map; and which old city hand would be so naive? We all knew on the gut level how to interpret such maps, how to transpose districts around, and permutate street names, how to unkink what was kinked and enlarge what was dwarfed. We had developed a genius for interpretation possessed by no other nation, an instinct which must apply anywhere throughout the land. Thus long-distance truck drivers reached their destinations eventually. The army manoeuvred without getting seriously lost. New factories found reasonable sites, obtained their raw materials, and despatched boots or shovels or whatever with tolerable efficiency.

No foreigner could match our capacity; and we joked that diplomats in our capital were restricted to line of sight or else were like Theseus in the layrinth, relying on a long thread whereby to retrace their footsteps. No invader would ever broach our heartland. As to spies, they were *here*, yes; but where was here in relation to anywhere else?

Heading home of an evening from Dzerzhinsky Square was another matter, however. For me, it was! I could take either of two entirely separate routes. One led to the flat where tubby old Olga, my wife of these last thirty years, awaited me. The other led to my sleek mistress, Koshka.

Troubled by the events of the day, I took that second route. I hadn't gone far before I realized that my new assistant was following me. She slipped along the street from doorway to doorway.

Should I hide and accost her, demanding to know what the devil she thought she was doing? Ah no, not yet. Plainly she had her reasons – and other people's reasons too. I dismissed the speculation that she was another "eye of Mirov". Mirov had practically dissociated himself from Grusha. She had been set upon me by the new breed, the reformers, so-called. Evidently I spelled a special danger to them. How could they create a new country while I held the key to the old one in my keeping?

I had not intended a confrontation quite so soon; but she

was provoking it. So let her find out! I hurried up this prospekt, down that boulevard, through the alley, over the square. Workers hurried by wearing stiff caps. Fat old ladies bustled with bundles. I ducked down a narrow street, through a lane, to another street. Did Grusha realize that her gait was springier? Perhaps not. She had not lost her youthful figure.

At last, rounding a certain corner, I sprinted ahead and darted behind a shuttered kiosk. Waiting, I heard her break into a canter because she feared she had lost me. By now no one else was about. Leaping out, I caught her wrist. She shrieked, afraid of rape or a mugging by a hooligan.

"Who are you?" she gasped. "What do you want?"

"Look at me, Grusha. I'm Valentin. Don't you recognize me?"

"You must be . . . his son!"

"Oh no."

The distortions wrought by age, the wrinkles, liver spots, crows' feet and pot belly: all these had dropped away from me, just as they always did whenever I took my special route. I had cast off decades. How else could I enjoy and satisfy a mistress such as Koshka?

Grusha had also shed years, becoming a gawky, callow girl – who clutched my arm now in awkward terror, for I had released her wrist.

"What has happened, Colonel?"

"I can't still be a Colonel, can I? Maybe a simple Captain or Lieutenant."

"You're *young*!"

"You're very young indeed, a mere fledgling."

"Was it all done by make-up – I mean, your appearance, back at the Centre? In that case how can the career records . . .?"

"Ah, so you saw mine?" Despite the failing light I could have sworn that she blushed. "Make-up, you say? Yes, *made up*! My country is made up, invented by us map-makers. We are the makers of false maps, dear girl; and our national consciousness is honed by this as a pencil is brought to a needle-point against a sand-paper block, as the blade of a mapping pen is sharped on an oilstone. Dead ground occurs."

"I know what 'dead ground' means. That merely refers to areas you can't see on a relief map from a particular viewpoint."

"Such as the viewpoint of the State . . .? Listen to me: if we inflate certain areas, then we shrink others away to a vanishing point. These places can still be found by the map-maker who knows the relation between the false and the real; one who knows the routes. From here to there; from now to then. Do you recognize this street, Grusha? Do you know its name?"

"I can't see a signpost . . ."

"You still don't understand." I drew her towards a shop window, under a street lamp which had now illuminated. "Look at yourself!"

She regarded her late-adolescent self. She pressed her face to the plate glass as though a ghostly shop assistant might be lurking inside, imitating her stance. Then she sprang back, not because she had discovered somebody within but because she had found no one.

"These dead zones," she murmured. "You mean the gulags, the places of internal exile . . ."

"No! I mean places such as this. I'm sure other people than me must have found similar dead zones; and never breathed a word. These places have their own inhabitants, who are recorded on no census."

"So you're a secret dissident, are you, Valentin?"

I shook my head. "Without the firm foundation of the State-as-it-is – without the lie of the land, as Mirov innocently put it – how could such places continue to exist? That is why we must not destroy the work of decades. This is magical – magical, Grusha! I am young again. My mistress lives here."

She froze. "So your motives are entirely selfish."

"I am old, back at the Centre. I've given my life to the State. I deserve . . . No, you're too ambitious, too eager for stupid troublesome changes. It is *you* who are selfish at heart. The very best of everything resides in the past. Why read modern mumbo-jumbo when we can read immortal Turgenev or Gogol? I've suffered . . . terror. My Koshka and I are both honed in the fires of fear." How could I explain that, despite all, those were the best days? The pure days.

"Fear is finished," she declared. "Clarity is dawning."

I could have laughed till I cried.

"What we will lose because of it! How our consciousness will be diminished, diluted, bastardized by foreign poisons. I'm a patriot, Grusha."

"A red fascist," she sneered, and started to walk away.

"Where are you going?" I called.

"Back."

"Can't do that, girl. Not so easily. Don't know the way. You'll traipse round and round."

"We'll see!" Hitching herself, she marched off.

I headed to Koshka's flat, where pickles and black caviar sandwiches, cold cuts and mushroom and spirit were waiting; and Koshka herself, and her warm sheets.

Towards midnight, in the stillness, I heard faint footsteps outside so I rose and looked down from her window. A slim shadowy form paced wearily along the pavement below, moving out of sight. After a while the figure returned along the opposite pavement, helplessly retracing the same route.

"What is it, Valentin?" came my mistress's voice. "Why don't you come back to bed?"

"It's nothing important, my love," I said. "Just a street walker, all alone."

PART TWO: INTO THE OTHER COUNTRY

When Peterkin was a lad, the possibilities for joy seemed limitless. He would become a famous artist. He dreamed of sensual canvases shamelessly ablush with pink flesh, peaches, orchid blooms. Voluptuous models would disrobe for him and sprawl upon a velvet divan. Each would be an appetizing banquet, a feast for the eyes, as teasing to his palate as stimulating of his palette.

Why did he associate naked ladies with platters of gourmet

cuisine? Was it because those ladies were spread for consumption? How he had lusted for decent food when he was young. And how he had hungered for the flesh. Here, no doubt, was the origin of the equation between feasting and love.

Peterkin felt no desire to *eat* human flesh. He never even nibbled his own fingers. The prospect of tooth marks indenting a human body nauseated him. Love-bites were abhorrent. No, he yearned – as it were – to *absorb* a woman's body. Libido, appetite, and art were one.

Alas for his ambitions, the requirements of the Party had cemented him into a career niche in the secret police building in Dzerzhinsky Square; on the eighth floor, to be precise, in the cartography department.

Not for him a paint brush but all those damnable map projections. Cylindrical, conical, azimuthal. Orthographic, gnomonic. Sinusoidal, polyconic.

Not Matisse, but Mercator.

Not Gauguin but Gall's Stereographic. Not Modigliani but Interrupted Mollweide.

The would-be artist had mutated into an assistant in this subdivided suite of rooms where false maps were concocted.

"My dreams have decayed," he confided to friend Goldman in the restaurant one lunchtime.

Around them, officers from the directorates of cryptography, surveillance, or the border guards ate lustily under rows of fat, white light-globes. Each globe wore a hat-like shade. Fifty featureless white heads hung from the ceiling, brooking no shadows below, keeping watch blindly. A couple of baggy babushkas wheeled trolleys stacked with dirty dishes around the hall. Those old women seemed bent on achieving some quota of soiled crockery rather than on delivering the same speedily to the nearest sink.

Goldman speared a slice of roast tongue. "Oh I don't know. Where else, um, can we eat, um, as finely as this?"

Dark, curly-haired, pretty-faced Goldman was developing a hint of a pot-belly. Only a proto-pot as yet, though definitely a protuberance in the making. Peterkin eyed his neighbour's midriff.

Goldman sighed. "Ah, it's the sedentary life! I freely admit
it. All day long spent sharpening quills for pens, pens, pens
. . . No sooner do I empty one basket of wing feathers than
that wretched hunchback porter delivers another. Small
wonder he's a hunchback! I really ought to be out in the woods
or the marshes shooting geese and teal and woodcock. That's
what I wanted to be, you know? A hunter out in the open
air."

"So you've told me." Peterkin was lunching on broiled
hazel-hen with jam. However, each evening – rain, snow, or
shine – he made sure to take a five-mile constitutional walk,
armed with a sketchbook as witness to his former hopes; rather
as a mother chimp might tote her dead baby around until it
started to stink.

Peterkin was handsome where his friend was pretty. Slim,
blond, steely-eyed, and with noble features. Yet all for what?
Here in the secret police building he mostly met frumps or
frigid functionaries. The foxy females were bait for foreign
diplomats and businessmen. Out on the streets, whores were
garishly painted – do-it-yourself style. Slash lips, cheeks
rouged like stop-lights, bruised eyes. Under the evening street
lamps those ladies of the night looked so lurid to Peterkin.

Excellent food a-plenty was on offer to the secret servants of
the State such as he. Goose with apples, breaded mutton
chops, shashlik on skewers, steamed sturgeon. Yet whereabouts in his life were the soubrettes and odalisques and
gorgeous inamoratas? Without whom, how could he really sate
himself?

"So how are the, um, projections?" Goldman asked idly.

"Usual thing, old son. I'm busy using Cassini's method.
Distances along the central meridian are true to scale. But all
other meridian lines stretch the distances. That makes Cassini's projection fine for big countries that spread from north to
south. Of course ours sprawls from east to west. Ha! Across a
few thousand miles that's quite enough distortion for an enemy
missile to miss a silo by miles."

"Those geese and turkeys gave their wings to shelter us!
Gratifying to know that I'm carving patriotic pens."

"I wonder," Peterkin murmured, "whether amongst our enemies I have some exact counterpart whose job is to deduce which projections I'm using to distort different areas of land . . ."

Goldman leaned closer. "I heard a rumour. My boss Andrey was talking to Antipin. Andrey was projecting *the future*. Seems that things are going to change. Seems, for the sake of openness, that we'll be publishing true maps sooner or later."

Peterkin chuckled. This outlook seemed as absurd as that he himself might ever become a member of the Academy of Arts.

Yet that very same evening Peterkin saw the woman of his desires.

He had stepped out along Krasny Avenue and turned down Zimoy Prospekt to enter the park. It was only early September, so the ice-skating rink was still a lake dotted with ducks: fat quacking boats laden with potential pens, pens, pens. The air was warm, and a lone kiosk sold chocolate ice creams to strollers; one of whom was her.

She was small and pert, with eyes that were brimming china inkwells, irises of darkest brown. Her curly, coal-black hair – not unlike friend Goldman's in fact – made a corona of sheer, glossy darkness, a photographic negative of the sun in eclipse; the sun itself being her round, tanned, softly-contoured face. From the moment Peterkin saw her, that woman suggested a sensuality bottled up and distilled within her – the possibility of love, lust, inspiration, nourishment. She was a liqueur of a lady. She was caviar, licking a chocolate cornet.

Her clothes were routine: cheaply styled bootees and an open raincoat revealing a blotchy floral dress. Yet Peterkin felt such a suction towards her, such a powerful current flowing in her direction.

She glanced at him and shrugged with what seemed a mixture of resignation and bitter amusement. So he followed her out of the park, across the prospekt, into a maze of minor streets which became increasingly unfamiliar.

Some empty stalls stood deserted in a square which must serve as a market place, so he realized that he was beginning to tread "dead ground", that unacknowledged portion of the city which did not figure on any plans. If inspectors approached by car they would be hard put to find these selfsame streets. One-way and no-entry signs would redirect them away. Such was the essence of this district; impenetrability was the key that locked it up safely out of sight.

Of course, if those same inspectors came on foot with illicit purposes in mind – hoping to buy a kilo of bananas, a rare spare part for a washing machine, or a foreign pornography magazine – they could be in luck.

Subsequently they wouldn't be able to report where they had been with any clarity.

The moan of a saxophone assailed Peterkin's ears; a jazz club was nearby. Rowdy laughter issued from a restaurant where the drapes were drawn; he judged that a heavy drinking bout was in progress.

A sign announced Polnoch Place. He had never heard of it. How the sky had darkened, as if in passing from street to street he had been forging hour by hour deeper towards midnight. At last the woman halted under a bright street lamp, her ice cream quite consumed, and waited for him, so unlike the ill-painted floozies of more public thoroughfares.

He cleared his throat. "I must apologize for following you in this fashion, but, well – " Should he mention voluptuous canvasses? He flourished his sketchbook lamely.

"What else could you do?" she asked. "You're attracted to me magnetically. Our auras resonate. I was aware of it."

"Our auras – ?"

"Our vibrations." She stated this as a fact.

"Are you psychic? Are you a medium?"

"A medium? Oh yes, you might say so. Definitely! A conduit, a channel, a guide. How else could you have strayed so far into this territory except in my footsteps?"

Peterkin glanced around him at strange façades.

"I've heard it said . . . Are there really two countries side by side – one where the secret police hold sway, and a whole other land which is simply *secret*? Not just a few little dead zones – but whole swathes of hidden terrain projecting from those zones?"

"Why, of course! When human beings yearn long enough to be some place else, then that somewhere can come into being. Imagine an hourglass; that's the sort of shape the world has. People can drift through like grains of sand – though only so far. There's a kind of population pressure that rebuffs intruders. For the second world gives rise not only to its own geography, but also to its own inhabitants."

"Has anyone mapped this other terrain?"

"Is that what you do, draw maps?" Her hair, under the streetlamp! Her face, like a lamp itself unto him!

His job was a state secret. Yet this woman couldn't possibly be an "eye" of the police, trying to trap him.

"Oh yes, I draw maps," he told her.

"Ah, that makes it more difficult for you to come here."

"Of course not. Don't you realize? Our maps are all lies! Deliberate lies, distortions. In the department of cartography our main brief is to warp the true shape of our country in all sorts of subtle ways."

"Ah?" She sounded unsurprised. "Where I come from, artists map the country with kaleidoscopes of colour. Musicians map it in a symphony. Poets, in a sonnet."

It came to Peterkin that in this other land he could at last be the painter of his desires. He had never believed in psychic phenomena or in a spirit world (unless, perhaps, it was the world of ninety-proof spirit). Yet this circumstance was different. The woman spoke of a *material* other world – extending far beyond the dead ground of the city. Peterkin knew that he must possess this woman as the key to all his hopes, the portal to a different existence.

"So do you despise your work?" she asked him.

"Yes! Yes!"

She smiled invitingly – and wryly, as though he had already disappointed her.

"My name's Masha."

*

Her room was richly furnished with rugs from Central Asia,
silverware, onyx statuettes, ivory carvings. Was she some
black marketeer in art treasures or the mistress of one? Had
he stumbled upon a cache hidden since the Revolution?
Curtains were woven through with threads of gold. Matching
brocade cloaked the bed in a filigree till she drew back the
cover, disclosing silk sheets as blue as the clearest summer
sky. Her cheap dress, which she shed without further ado,
uncovered sleek creamy satin camiknickers . . . which she also
peeled off carelessly.

"Take fright and run away, Peterkin," she teased. "Take
fright now!"

"Run away from *you?*"

"That might be best."

"What should frighten me?"

"You'll see."

"I'm seeing!" Oh her body. Oh his, a-quiver, arrow notched
and tense to fly into her. He laughed. "I hardly think I'm
impotent."

"Even so." She lay back upon the blue silk sheets.

Yet as soon as he started to stroke her limbs . . .

At first he thought absurdly that Masha had concealed an
inflatable device within her person: a dildo-doll made of
toughest gossamer so as to fold up as small as a thumb yet
expand into a balloon with the dimensions of a man. This she
had liberated and inflated suddenly as a barrier, thrusting
Peterkin aside . . .

What, powered by a cartridge of compressed air? How
risky! What if the cartridge sprang a leak or exploded? What
if the compressed air blew the wrong way?

The intruder had flowed from Masha in a flood – from her
open and inviting legs. It had gushed out cloudily, spilling
from her like pints and pints of leaking semen congealing into
a body of firm white jelly.

He gagged, in shock.

"Wh – what – ?"

"It's ectoplasm," she said.

"Ectoplasm – "

Yes, he had heard of ectoplasm: the strange fluidic emana-
tion that supposedly pours out of a psychic's nostrils or ears or
mouth, an amorphous milk that takes on bodily form and a
kind of solidity. It came from her vagina.

Pah! Flimflammery! Puffs of smoke and muslin suspended
on strings. Soft lighting, a touch of hypnosis and auto-
suggestion. Of course, of course. Went without saying.

Except . . .

What now lay between them could be none other than an
ectoplasmic body. A guard dog lurked in Masha's kennel. A
eunuch slept at her door. She wore a chastity belt in the shape
of a blanched, clinging phantom. Peterkin studied the thing
that separated them. He poked it, and it quivered. It adhered
to Masha, connected by . . .

"Don't try to pull it away," she warned. "You can't. It will
only go back inside when my excitement ebbs."

And still he desired her, perhaps even more so. He ached.

"You're still excited?" he asked her.

"Oh yes."

"Does this . . . creature . . . give you any satisfaction?"

"None at all."

"Did a witch curse you, Masha? Or a magician? Do such
persons live in your country?" Perhaps Masha belonged to
somebody powerful who had cast a spell upon her as an
insurance policy for those times when she crossed the in-
between zone to such places as the park. If composers could
map that other land with their concerti, or painters with their
palettes, why not other varieties of magic too?

She peered around the white shoulder of the manifestation.
"Don't you see, Peterkin? It's you. It's the template for you,
the mould."

What did she mean? He too peered at the smooth suggestion
of noble features. His ghost was enjoying – no, certainly not
even enjoying! – Masha. His ghost simply intervened, another
wretched obstacle to joy. A twitching lump, a body equipped
with a nervous system but lacking any mind or thoughts.

"And yet," she hinted, "there's a way to enter my country.

A medium is a bridge, a doorway. Not to any spirit-world, oh no. But to: that other existence."

"Show me the way."

"Are you quite sure?"

How he ached. "Yes, Masha. Yes. I must enter."

As his thoughts and memories flowed freely – of old desires, of canvases never painted and bodies never seen, of stuffed dumplings and skewered lamb and interminable cartographic projections – so he sensed a shift in his personal centre of gravity, in his prime meridian. He felt at once much closer to Masha, and anaesthetized, robbed of sensation.

His body was moving; it was rolling over on the bed, flexing its arms and legs – no longer his own body to command. Equipped with the map of his memories, the ghost had taken charge.

Now the ghost was making Peterkin's body stand up and put on his clothes; while he – his kernel, his soul – clung against Masha silently.

That body which had been his was opening and shutting its mouth, uttering noises. Words.

"You go along Polnoch Place – " Masha gave directions and instructions; Peterkin couldn't follow them.

He himself was shrinking. Already he was the size of a child. Soon, of a baby. As an Arabian genie dwindles, tapering down in a stream of smoke into a little bottle, so now he was entering Masha.

"I shall be born again, shan't I?" he cried out. "Once you've smuggled me over the border deep into the other country, inside of you?" Unfortunately he couldn't hear so much as a mewling whimper from what little of him remained outside of her. All he heard, distantly, was a door bang shut as the phantom left Masha's room.

Warm darkness embraced his dissolved, suspended existence.

Only at the last moment did he appreciate the worries of the persons in that other, free domain – who had been forced into existence by the frustrations of reality and who depended for their vitality upon a lie, which might soon be erased. They, the free, were fighting for the perpetuation of falsehood. Peterkin had been abducted so that a wholly obedient servant might be substituted in his place in the cartography department of the secret police.

Only at the last moment, as he fell asleep – in order that his phantom could become more conscious – did he understand why Masha had trapped him.

PART THREE: THE CULT OF THE EGG

Church bells were ringing out across the city in celebration, *clong-dong-clangle*. The great edifice on Dzerzhinsky Square was almost deserted with the exception of bored guards patrolling corridors. In the mahogany-panelled office of the head of the directorate of censorship, General Mirov rubbed his rubicund boozer's nose as if an itch was aflame.

"How soon can we hope to have an accurate Great Atlas?" he demanded sourly. "That's what *I'm* being asked."

Not right at the moment, however. The six black telephones on his vast oak desk all stood silently.

Valentin blinked. "As you know, Comrade General, Grusha's disappearance hasn't exactly speeded the task. All the damned questioning, the interruptions. Myself and my staff being bothered at our work as though we are murderers."

The ceiling was high and ornately plastered, the windows taller than a man. A gilt-framed portrait of Felix Dzerzhinsky, architect of terror, watched rapaciously.

"If," said Mirov, "a newly appointed deputy-chief cartographer – of reformist ambitions, and heartily resented because of those, mark my words! – if she vanishes so inexplicably, are you surprised that there's a certain odour of rats in your offices? Are you astonished that her well-connected parents press for the most thorough investigation?"

Valentin nodded towards the nobly handsome young man who stood expressionlessly in front of one of the embroidered sofas.

"I'll swear that Peterkin here has undergone a personality fluctuation because of all the turmoil."

Clangle, dong, clong. Like some mechanical figure heeding the peel of a carillon, Peterkin took three paces forward across the oriental carpet.

"Ah," said Mirov, "so are we attempting to clear up the matter of Grusha's possible murder hygienically in private? Between the three of us? How maternal of you, Colonel! You shelter the members of your staff just like a mother hen." The general's gaze drifted to the intruding object on his desk, and he frowned irritably. "Things have changed. Can't you understand? I cannot suppress the investigation."

"No, no, no," broke in Valentin. "Peterkin used to be a bit of a dreamer. Now he's a demon for work. That's all I meant. Well, a demon for the old sort of work, not for cartographic revisionism . . ." As if realizing that under present circumstances this might hardly be construed as an endorsement, Valentin shrugged.

"Is that *thing* supposed to be a sample of his most recent work?" The general's finger stabbed accusingly towards the decorated egg which rested on his blotting paper, geometrically embellished in black and ochre and yellow. "Reminds me of some tourist souvenir on sale in a foetid East African street. Some barbaric painted gourd."

"Sir," said Peterkin, "it is executed in Carpathian *pysanka* style."

"You don't say?" The general brought his fist down upon the painted egg, crushing the shell, splitting the boiled white flesh within. "Thus I execute it. In any case, Easter is months away."

"You're unhappy about all these new reforms, aren't you, Comrade General?" Valentin asked cautiously. "I mean, *deeply* unhappy. You hope to retire honourably, yet what sort of world will you retire into?"

"One where I can hope to gather mushrooms in the woods to my heart's content, if you really wish to know."

"Ah, but will you be allowed such tranquility? Won't all manner of dark cupboards be opened?"

"I'm busy opening those cupboards," snapped Mirov. "As quickly as can be. Absurdist plays, concrete poems, abstract art, economic critiques . . . We scurry to grease their publication, do we not? Grow faster, trees, grow faster! We need your pulp. Bah! I'm somewhat impeded by the sloth of your department of cartography. I demand true maps, as soon as can be." With a cupped hand he swept the mess of broken boiled egg into a trash basket.

"Those dark cupboards also contain corpses," hinted Valentin.

"For which, you imply, I may one day be brought to book?"

"Well, you certainly oughtn't ever to write your memoirs."

"You're being impertinent, Valentin. Insubordinate in front of a subordinate." The general laughed barkingly. "Though I suppose you're right. The world's shifting more swiftly than I imagined possible."

"We aren't safe here, in this world that's a-coming."

The bells continued to ring out cacophonously and triumphantly as if attempting to crack a somewhat leaden sky, to let through rifts of clear blue.

Peterkin spoke dreamily. "The egg celebrates the mysteries of birth and death and reawakening. Simon of Cyrene, the egg merchant, helped Jesus to carry his cross. Upon Simon's return he found to his astonishment that all the eggs in his basket had been coloured with many hues."

"I'll bet he was astonished!" said Mirov sarcastically. "There goes any hope of selling my nice white eggs! Must I really listen to the warblings of this tinpot Dostoevsky? Has the cartography department taken leave of its senses, Colonel? Oh I see what you mean about Comrade Peterkin's personality. But why do you bother me with such nonsense? I was hoping to catch up on some paperwork this morning and forget about the damned – "

"Ding-dong of rebirth in our land?"

"Carl Fabergé made his first imperial Easter egg for the Tsar and Tsaritsa just over a century ago," said Peterkin.

"Please excuse his circuitous approach to the meat of the

matter, General," begged Valentin. "Almost as if he is circum-
navigating an egg? I promise he will arrive there sooner or
later."

"An egg is like a globe," Peterkin continued. "The department of cartography has never designed globes of the world."

"The world isn't shaped like an egg!" objected Mirov, his
cracked veins flushing brighter.

"With respect, it is, Comrade General," murmured Valentin. "It's somewhat oblate . . . Continue, Peterkin!"

"Fabergé cast his eggs from precious metals. He inlaid them
with enamelling, he encrusted them with jewels. He even kept
a special hammer by him to destroy any whose craftsmanship
fell short of his own flawless standards."

"What is this drivel about the Tsar and Tsaritsa?" exploded
Mirov. "Are you preaching counter-revolution? A return to
those days of jewelled eggs for the aristocracy and poverty for
the masses? Or is this a metaphor? Are you advocating a *putsch*
against the reformers?"

"Traditions continue," Peterkin said vaguely.

"Yes," agreed Valentin. "We are the descendants of the
secret police of the imperial empire, are we not? Of its censors;
of its patriots."

"Bah!"

Peterkin cleared his throat. He seemed impervious to the
general's displeasure. "The craft of decorating eggs in the
imperial style continues . . . in the dead ground of this very
city."

"Dead ground?"

"That's a discovery some of us have made," explained
Valentin. He gestured vaguely through a window, to somewhere beyond the onion domes. "The wholesale falsification
of maps produces, well, actual *false places* – which a person in
the right frame of mind can genuinely reach. Peterkin here
has found such places, haven't you, hmm? As have I."

Peterkin nodded jerkily like a marionette on strings.

"You're both drunk," said Mirov. "Go away."

"I can prove this, General. Comrade Grusha strayed into
one of those places. She was following me, acting as an amateur

sleuth. Ah, the new generation are all such amateurs compared to us! Now she haunts that place because she lacks the cast of mind that I possess – and you too, General."

"What might that be?"

"An instinct for falsification; for the masking of reality."

"I'm charmed at your compliment."

"You'd be even more charmed if you came with me to visit my darling young mistress Koshka who lives in such a place."

One ageing man regarded the other quizzically. "*You*, Valentin? A young mistress? Excuse me if I'm sceptical."

"You might say that such a visit is a rejuvenating experience."

Mirov nodded, misunderstanding. "A youthful mistress might well be as invigorating as monkey glands. Along with being heart attack territory."

"To enter the dead ground is rejuvenating; you'll see, you'll see. That's one frontier worth safeguarding – the border between the real and the ideal. Perhaps you've heard of the legend of the secret valley of Shangri-La? The place that features on no map? To enter it properly, a man must be transformed."

"That's where the egg crafters come into this," prompted Peterkin.

"*Internal exile*, General! Let me propose a whole new meaning for that phrase. Let me invite you to share this refuge."

"You insist that Comrade Grusha's still alive?"

"Oh yes. She walks by my Koshka's apartment at nights."

"So where does she go to by day?"

"I suspect that it's always night for her. Otherwise she might spy some escape route, come back here, stir up more trouble . . ."

"Are you telling me, Colonel Valentin, that some zone of aberrant geometry exists in our city? Some other dimension to existence? I don't mean the one advertised by those wretched bells."

"Exactly. Just so."

Mirov stared at the portrait of Dzerzhinsky, who would

have answered such an eccentric proposition with a bullet, and sucked in his breath.

"I shall indulge you, Colonel – for old time's sake, I'm tempted to say – if only to study a unique form of psychosis which seems to be affecting our department of cartography."

"It's best to go in the evening, as the shadows draw in."

"It would be."

"On foot."

"Of course."

"With no bodyguard."

"Be warned, I shall be armed."

"Why not, General? Why ever not?"

But Peterkin smirked.

So that same evening the three men went by way of certain half-frequented routes, via this side street and that alley and that square until the hollow raving of the bells was muffled, till distant traffic only purred like several sleepy kittens, and a lone owl hooted from an old-fashioned cemetery amidst century-old apartment blocks.

As if playing the role of some discreet pimp, Peterkin indicated a door. "Gentlemen, we shall now visit a lady."

Mirov guffawed. "This mistress of yours, Colonel: is she by any chance a mistress to many?"

"My Koshka lives further away," said Valentin, "not here. Absolutely not here. Yet don't you already feel a new spring in your gait? Don't you sense the weight of years lifting from your shoulders?"

"I admit I do feel somewhat sprightly," agreed the general. "Hot-blooded. Ripe for adventure. Ah, it's years since . . . Valentin, you look like a younger man." He rubbed his hands. "Ah, the spice of anticipation! How it converts tired old mutton into lamb."

Peterkin admitted them into a large foyer lit by a single low-powered light bulb and decorated by several large vases of dried, dusty roses in bud. A faint memory of musky aroma lingered, due perhaps to a sprinkle of essential oils. A creaky elevator lifted them slowly to the third floor, its cables

twanging dolorously once or twice like the strings of a double
bass. Valentin found himself whistling a lively theme from an
opera by Prokofiev – so softly he sounded as though he was
actually labouring up marble stairs, puffing.

The dark petite young woman who admitted these three
visitors to her apartment was not alone. Mirov slapped the
reassuring bulge of his gun, as if to stun a fly, before relaxing.
The other two occupants were also women, who wore similar
cheap dresses patterned with roses, orchids, their lips and
cheeks rouged.

"May I present Masha?" Having performed this introduc-
tion, Peterkin slackened; he stood limply like a neglected doll.

"This is my older sister Tanya," Masha explained. Masha's
elder image smiled. If the younger sister was enticingly lovely,
Tanya was the matured vintage, an intoxicating queen.

"And my aunt Anastasia." A plumper, far from frumpish
version, in her middle forties, a twinkle in her eye, her neck
strung with large phoney pearls. Absurdly, the aunt curtsied,
plucking up the hem of her dress quite high enough to display
a dimpled thigh for a moment.

"We are chief Eggers," said Anastasia. "Tanya and I
represent the Guild of Imperial Eggs."

The large room, replete with rugs from Tashkent and
Bokhara hanging on the walls, with curtains woven with thread
of gold, housed a substantial carved bed spread with brocade,
almost large enough for two couples entwined together, though
hardly for three. All approaches to it were, however, blocked
by at least a score of tall, narrow, round-topped tables, each
of which served as a dais to display a decorated egg, or two, or
three. Some ostrich, some goose, others pullet and even
smaller, perhaps even the eggs of canaries.

On gilt or silver stands, shaped as swans, as chariots, as
goblets, these eggs were intricately cut and hinged, in trefoil
style, gothic style, scallop style. Some lids were lattices.
Filigree windows held only spiders' webs of connective shell.
Petals of shell hung down on the thinnest of silver chains.
Pearl-studded drawers jutted. Doors opened upon grottos
where tiny porcelain cherubs perched pertly. Seed pearls, lace,

gold braid, jewels trimmed the doorways. Interior linings were
of velvet . . .

To blunder towards that bed in the heat of passion would
be to wreak devastation more shattering than Carl Fabergé
could ever have inflicted on a faulty golden egg with a hammer!
What a fragile cordon defended that bedspread and the hint of
blue silk sheets; yet to trespass would be to assassinate art – if
those eggs were properly speaking the products of art, rather
than of an obsessional delirium which had transfigured com-
monplace ovoids of calcium, former homes of bird embryos
and yolk and albumen.

Aunt Anastasia waved at a bureau loaded with egging
equipment: pots of seed pearls, jewels, ribbons, diamond dust,
cords of silk gimp, corsage pins, clasps, toothpicks, emery
boards, a sharp little knife, a tiny saw, manicure scissors, glue,
nail varnish, and sharp pencils. The general rubbed his eyes.
For a moment did he think he had seen jars of beetles, strings
of poisonous toadstools, handcuffs made of cord, the accoutre-
ments of a witch in some fable?

"Aren't we just birds of a feather?" she asked the colonel.
"You use the quills of birds for mapping-pens, so I hear. We
use the eggs of the birds."

"I've rarely seen anything quite so ridiculous," Mirov broke
in. "Your eggs are gimcrack mockeries of Tsarist treasures.
Petit bourgeois counterfeits!"

"Exactly," agreed queenly Tanya. "Did not some financier
once say that bad money drives out good? Let's suppose that
falsity is superior to reality. Did *you* not try to make it so? Did
you not succeed formerly? Ah, but in the dialectical process
the false gives rise in turn to a *hidden truth*. The map of lies
leads to a secret domain. The egg that apes treasure shows the
way towards the true treasury."

Tanya picked up a pearl-studded goose egg. Its one oval
door was closed. The egg was like some alien space-pod
equipped with a hatch. Inserting a fingernail, she prised this
open and held the egg out for Mirov's inspection.

On the whole inner surface of that goose egg – the inside of
the door included – was a map of the whole world, of all the

continents in considerable detail. The difference between the shape of the egg and that of a planetary globe caused some distortion, though by no means grotesquely so. Mirov squinted within, impressed despite himself.

"How on earth did you work within such a cramped volume? By using a dentist's mirror, and miniature nibs held in tweezers? Or . . . did you draw upon the outside and somehow the pattern sank through?"

"Somehow?" Tanya chuckled. "We *dreamed* the map into the egg, General, just as you dreamed us into existence by means of your lies – though unintentionally!"

She selected another closed egg and opened its door.

"Here's the map of our country . . . Ours, mark you, not yours. If you take this egg as your guide, our country can be yours too. You can enter and leave as you desire."

"Be careful you don't break your egg." Aunt Anastasia wagged a warning finger.

"The same way you broke the *pysanka* egg," squeaked Peterkin, emerging briefly from his immobility and muteness. "Most of those eggs are technical exercises – not the one you hold." (For Mirov had accepted the egg.) "That was dreamed deep within the other country." Having spoken like a ventriloquist's dummy, Peterkin became inert again.

However, he left along with his two superiors – presently, by which time it was fully night.

"Maps, dreamed on to the insides of eggs! Deep in some zone of absurd topography!" Mirov snorted. "Your escape hatch is preposterous," he told Valentin, pausing under a streetlamp.

"Actually, with respect, we aren't *deep* in the zone at all. Oh no, not here. But that egg can guide – "

"Do you believe in it, you dupe?"

"Why didn't I receive one for my own? I suppose because I already know the way to Koshka's place . . ."

Mirov snapped his fingers. "I know how the trick's done. They use transfers. They draw the map on several pieces of paper, wet those so they're sticky, then insert them with tweezers on to the inside of the shell. When that dries, they use tiny bent brushes to apply varnish."

Mirov removed the map-egg from his overcoat pocket, knelt, and placed the egg on the pavement under the brightness of the streetlamp. Was he surprised by the limber flexibility of his joints?

"I can prove it." Producing his pistol, Mirov transferred his grip to the barrel, poising the handle above the pearl-studded shell. "I'll peel those transfers loose from the broken bits. Ha, dreams indeed!"

"Don't," said Peterkin in a lame voice only likely to encourage Mirov.

"Don't be a fool," said Valentin.

"A fool, is it, Comrade Colonel?"

"If you're told not to open a door and you insist on opening it – "

"Disaster ensues – supposing that you're a child in a fable."

Valentin knelt too, to beg the general to desist. To an onlooker the two men might have appeared to be fellow worshippers adoring a fetish object on the paving slab, cultists of the egg indeed.

When Mirov brought the butt of the gun down, cracking the egg wide open and sending tiny pearls rolling like spilled barley, a shock seemed to ripple along the street and upward to the very stars, which trembled above the city.

Although Mirov probed and pried, in no way could he discover or peel loose any stiffly varnished paper transfers.

When the two sprightly oldsters looked around again, Peterkin had slipped away without a word. The two men scrambled up. Night, and strange streets, had swallowed their escort utterly. Despite Valentin's protests – which even led the men to tussle briefly – Mirov ground the shards of egg to dust under his heel, as if thereby he might obliterate any connection with himself.

Eventually, lost, they walked into a birchwood where mushrooms swelled through the humus in the moonlight. An owl hooted. Weasels chased mice. Was this woodland merely a park within the city? It hardly seemed so; yet by then the answer scarcely mattered, since they were having great difficulty remembering who they were, let alone where they were. Already they'd been obliged a number of times to roll up their floppy trouser legs and cinch their belts tighter. Their sleeves dangled loosely, their shoes were clumsy boats, while their overcoats dragged as long cloaks upon the ground.

"Kashka? Kishka? Was that her name? What *was* her name?" Valentin asked his friend.

"I think her name was Grusha . . . no, Masha."

"*Wasn't.*"

"*Was.*"

Briefly they quarrelled, till they forgot who they were talking about.

Through the trees, they spied the lights of a village which strongly suggested home. Descending a birch-clad slope awkwardly in their oversized garments – two lads dressed as men for a lark – they arrived at a yellow window and peered through.

Beautiful Tanya and Aunt Anastasia were singing to two huge eggs resting on a rug. Eggs the size of the fattest plucked turkeys, decorated with strange ochre zig-zags.

Even as Valentin and Mirov watched, the ends of the eggs opened on brass hinges. From each a bare arm emerged, followed by a head and a bare shoulder. The two women each grasped a groping hand and hauled. From out of each egg slowly squeezed the naked body of a man well past his prime, one with a beet-red face, though his trunk was white as snow.

"How did they fit inside those?" Mirov asked Valentin.

"Dunno. Came out, didn't they? Maybe there's more space than shows on the outside . . ."

The two newly-hatched men – who were no spring chickens – were now huddling together on a rug by the stove, modestly covering their loins with their hands. Their faces looked teasingly familiar, as if the men might be a pair of . . . long-lost uncles, come home at last from Siberia.

By now the two boys felt cold and hungry, so they knocked on the cottage door. Aunt Anastasia opened it.

"Ah, here come the clothes now!" Anastasia pulled them both inside into the warmth and surveyed them critically. "Oh what a mess you've made of those suits. Creases, and mud. Never mind. They'll sponge, and iron. Off with them now, you two, off with them. They're needed. Tanya, fetch a couple of blankets for the boys. We mustn't make them blush, with a chill or with shame."

"Do we have to sleep inside those eggs?" asked Mirov, almost stammering.

"Of course not, silly goose! You'll sleep over the stove in a blanket. Those two other fellows will be gone by the morning; then you'll have a better idea who you both are."

"Koshka!" exclaimed Valentin. "I remember. *That* was her name."

"Now, now," his aunt said, "you needn't be thinking about girls for a year or two yet. Anyway, there's Natasha in the village, and Maria. I've kept my eye on them for you two. How about some thick bacon broth with a sprinkle of something special in it to help you have nice dreams?"

"Please!" piped Valentin.

When he and his brother woke in the morning a lovely aroma greeted them – of butter melting on two bowls of cooked buckwheat groats. The boys only wondered for the briefest while where they had been the evening before.

Tanya and Anastasia had already breakfasted, and were busy sawing ducks' eggs.

Gaudí's Dragon

When Johnny Butler and his sister Martha arrived in Barcelona, buses were decked with Catalan flags, office blocks were draped with banners. Thin red and yellow stripes hung everywhere. Women of all ages clutched single red roses and stems of green wheat. Police wearing riot gear sat like black robots in armoured vehicles, watching the Sunday crowds.

"What a shame the sun isn't out!" exclaimed their escort, Salvador Miravell, a tubby whiskery fellow in his thirties. "Those Spanish cops would roast. They would bake." Salvador cast a malevolent glance towards the chill, leaden sky of late April. Climatic change was playing games with the planet. "There'll be deaths tonight," he assured Johnny and Martha. "Still, we'll be independent soon."

Angelica Bonaventura, Salvador's girlfriend who was doing the driving, laughed and wagged a finger. "Just as soon as we finish building Sagrada Familia.'

"But we *have* completed Gaudí's temple! Right *now*, thanks to software and holography! Haven't we, Johnny? We just need to iron out our little bug; then all is perfect. How else could we have ever finished such a crazy place?"

"It isn't genuinely finished," insisted Angelica. She was tiny and ebullient, boasting a mass of blonde hair which was perhaps bleached. Forever laughing, smiling. She liked to tease.

"And never *could* be finished!" vowed Salvador.

Angelica glanced back at Martha, grinning. "We make a pretence. A fashard." Martha realized that Angelica was lisping the word "façade". She was making a joke about FaCADes, Inc., which had despatched brother Johnny from California to troubleshoot the little bug in question.

Taxis buzzed the smart Citroen, black and yellow wasps. Avenues stretched to forever, broad noble dead-straight canyons lined with what Martha took to be plane trees. Lopped, still leafless, those were leprous assemblages of dinosaur bones. Parked cars crowded every free space. The Citroen crossed a square; palm trees arose fifty feet high and more. Roses and Catalan flags, everywhere.

"Scotland might soon be independent within the Euro community," said Salvador. "Likewise Bavaria. Catalonia also; you'll see. Gaudí's ghost will rest easy."

"Inside a ghost building?" Angelica smiled brightly. "Salvador means that Gaudí is a symbol of Catalonialism. We like to argue in English, Señorita Butler – Martha. It's a more assertive language than Catalan. Our own little country, independent? Ah, Spaniards will control the situation, as ever."

"The Spanish bombarded our city from the hills during the Franco war," Salvador said offhandedly. "Some shells fell inside Sagrada Familia."

Old wounds, old grievances, thought Martha; ghosts of the past. To shed their jet lag before catching the Barcelona shuttle, she and her brother had stopped over in Madrid for a couple of days; and Johnny had spoken about the political side to Gaudí's architecture. Gaudí was the luminary of the Catalan Renaissance which had bloomed in the nineteenth century: artistic, political, religious too.

Politics wasn't Johnny's strong suit, but he had spent ten days in this city last year setting up the Sagrada Familia project. Even he had gathered that completing the great church (albeit in phantom, holographic form) was a political act, an act that crowned the sense of national identity, completed it. In Johnny's opinion, the citizens of Barcelona should have been worrying more about the sea level than about nationalism.

Angelica detoured to show off the tree-clad Ramblas, the long streetmarket of flowers, birds, and books. Crowds, red roses, banners. Placards: communist and socialist, anarchist and linguistic-nationalist. Martha spotted her first whore, a tough hatchet-faced woman in black biding her time by the kerb.

"A *rambla*," Angelica told her, "means a gutter, for draining water down from the hills. You were never here before?"

"No, I've never been abroad. Except Mexico, once. Johnny thought I might like a holiday; the software problem can't be too serious. And I wanted to see how Gaudí uses ceramics."

"You're Johnny's twin, of course?"

Of course. Tall, red-headed, freckled twins; just a little gawky. When they walked somewhere together, unconsciously falling into perfect – if angular – step, they were like the advance guard of some clan of clones. Martha didn't like going round with Johnny too much. He was wearing chino trousers, a cord jacket, and cream leather shoes, so she had opted for blue jeans, trainers, and a dark purple sweater.

From a holog Johnny had brought back, she recognized the column ahead, atop which the bronze statue of Christopher Columbus pointed out to sea. Angelica slowed to a crawl. High tide! The risen Mediterranean flooded over the esplanade, lapping the very base of the column. Columbus' gesture seemed not one of expansion but of exasperation, to ward off the waters. Down at the harbour end, this particular *rambla* was trying to run in reverse, channelling the sea towards the hills. Perhaps the world-wide rise in sea level had already stabilized, and this city needn't fret. Perhaps. Martha made a joke about gondolas.

"Ah," said Salvador, "but imagine the parking problems!"

"At least the sea food is closer to us these days." Angelica steered in the direction of the promised restaurant, which proved to be miles away. After reaching their goal, she had to cruise for fifteen minutes more to find anywhere to stick the Citroen. Martha's stomach was grumbling. Johnny had warned her that Catalans ate late, though lavishly. Half-three for lunch, ten or eleven at night for dinner.

Over a shallow black soupy cauldron of giant prawns, mussels, and crayfish, all in their shells, and baby octopus, Johnny and

Salvador discussed the real problem while Angelica chatted with Martha.

Neither Salvador nor Angelica were in the least religious. Elektronika, Salvador's company, simply set up and maintained the holographic projectors at – take a deep breath – the Expiatory Temple of the Holy Family, owned and run by the Spiritual Association of the Devotees of Saint Joseph.

Gaudí had been a true visionary, whose buildings were enchanted wonderlands. Angelica surmised he was also probably crazy. In 1883, at the age of thirty-one, he was commissioned to build Sagrada Familia. By 1910, the bachelor-for-life moved on site. Abandoning all other commissions, he lived as a recluse in his workshop, growing ever more pious, ever more wrapped up in the elaborate symbolisms of his building, which was slowly, slowly rising. When Gaudí was seventy-five in 1926, he was killed by a trolley car while on his way to vespers. Buried in the crypt beneath his largely unfinished creation, Gaudí took the exact details of his plans to the grave with him. Eight belfries soared skyward. Still absent: the central spires which would have dwarfed even those.

Ever since, work had proceeded in fits and starts, accompanied by fierce disputes about what the final design should actually be. Would the church ever be finished? In time, say, for the Barcelona Olympics of '92? No way. In time for the next millennium? Not very likely.

Enter FaCADes, Inc., and brother Johnny.

When Johnny and Martha were kids, he wanted to be an architect, while she wanted to be a potter; she had accomplished her ambition, he had not. Electronics sidetracked Johnny. Or maybe he knew that he possessed no truly original vision, the way a Gaudí had; and the way Martha felt she had with pots and plates and pitchers, pardon the immodesty. Johnny went into CAD, computer assisted design; and the upshot was his Big Idea. Alas, his insight into money matters matched his lack of political savvy. Skipping over GMO (Great Missed Opportunities), the result was a company which he hardly held any equity in, specializing in the "wrapping" of people's homes and business premises in simulations of historic buildings. The Kinkakuji temple, Anne Hathaway's Cottage, Notre Dame (scaled to size, and perhaps deformed in shape to fit the site). A craze began. Buyers could change their façade as they pleased. Façades might be the shape of the future, if real wealth dried up: utilitarian boxes enveloped in holographic magnificence, beauty, charm.

Architects would have hated Johnny if he had been more prominent, say the president of FaCADes instead of an employee.

Then came the prestige call from the Spiritual Association of the Devotees of Saint Joseph to complete Gaudí's masterpiece holographically. Those mighty spires must tower over Barcelona *immediately*. FaCADes rejoiced. Johnny set to work.

Several interpretations existed of the finished building. Any of these could be projected; *all* could be, in turn. At last the bickering could cease. Aficionados would be able to assess the impact of several possible solutions on a real-life scale. Mondays, the projectors could conjure up Cunchillos' version. Tuesdays, a subtly different rendering. Why, the central spires could be made even taller than Gaudí ever intended! Sagrada Familia could become a skyscraper of a church! Yet that might spoil the proportions, making the whole ensemble resemble a giant fanciful rocket-ship designed to reach the nearest star, with the authentic belfries reduced to the status of mere strap-on fuel tanks.

Perhaps the appearance in phantom form of the full church would hasten its actual fulfilment in stone, the filling in of the semblance with substance. Whether so or not, the great work would be complete, at least psychologically.

For the best part of a year, tourists had flocked to Barcelona to stare at the reality, and at the image – the images – that transcended it. Yet now seemingly something was roaming loose *inside* the holographic spires, a free-ranging image which wasn't part of anyone's design.

Salvador shrugged. "It's certainly something. We thought it might be a flicker effect in the holog. Even ball lightning, attracted by the aerial display, the laser activity. But when we switch the holog off, the ghost doesn't linger."

"Most likely it's false data in the control program," said Johnny. "A redundancy. A bug. How reliable is the power supply?"

"That's fine. The holog holds utterly steady. Looks solid as rock. Internal details likewise, as if you could actually climb inside those spires. All that climbs is the ghost. Okay, I shall call it a ghost! To me it's more like a wayward cursor on a computer screen, but one of the Devotees speaks of a ghost up there."

"Does he think it's the architect's ghost?" Johnny asked whimsically. "Summoned by the completion? Rejoicing? Discontented? The Devotees aren't thinking of terminating the project, are they?"

"Nothing so drastic. Even looking from high up one of the real belfries it's hard to make out what's there. You glimpse it behind one of the air vents. Then it's behind another. It's in the main spire, it's in a side tower. The shape? Not a man's, I don't think. You can't notice it from ground level, so there's no flapdoodle in the media, not a word. The Devotees have shut the real belfries temporarily to tourists."

"Lots of disappointed Japanese!" said Angelica. "Japanese love Gaudí."

"Isn't that suspicious?" asked Johnny.

She grinned. "That Japanese love Gaudí?"

"No, shutting the belfries."

Salvador shook his head. "You know how the real belfries interconnect by means of little bridges. Two of the hologs have those same belfries bridging to the towers and spires as well. Can't have tourists stepping out on to nothingness, can we? So the belfries are closed pending the installation of safety barriers, the work to be carried out . . . *mañana*. Needless to say, the Devotees already had safety barriers in place. We simply removed those. No one noticed. Most natives of Barcelona climb up the belfries once in a lifetime, if ever." Salvador glanced at his watch. "I'm taking you to meet with the Devotees at seven – "

"Just to say 'Holo!'" quipped Angelica. "I'll drive you both to your hotel first. Check in, and shower? Do you wish to come along and see Sagrada Familia too this evening, Martha?"

Martha contemplated a last juicy mussel afloat in the giant pot of *zarzuela*. She felt bloated, OD'd on the fruits of the sea, as if she had consumed most of the aquatic population of the Mediterranean.

"I'm a bit bushed," she admitted. "I think I'd like to work myself up gradually to the church."

"Fine." Angelica lit a filter cigarette. "Tomorrow I'll show you round Gaudí's city. We'll walk or we'll use taxis. The parking, you know!"

Martha inhaled the rich odour of dark tobacco drifting into her face. "Powerful incense," she remarked.

"No, these are low in nicotine and tar. They just taste good."

Oh well, thought Martha, she was in a smoking country now.

When they left the restaurant, Salvador bought Martha a red rose and stalk of wheat from a wandering vendor. Later, in her room in the Cristina Gran Hotel, glowing from a bath, she heard the chatter of a helicopter. From the window she watched the chopper slide overhead, playing a searchlight down upon the streets. Presently she thought she heard in the distance the crackle of gunfire.

"So the Devotees took you out to *dinner?*" Martha asked over coffee and rolls in the hotel restaurant. "What time was that?" She felt she had missed half a day somewhere.

"Mm, 'bout eleven."

"I went to bed early." She remembered: "I heard shooting."

"Didn't see any trouble myself. Don't worry, Sis, national day's over. Passions will have cooled. This devotee, Montserrat . . . he was fretting about how our holog of Sagrada Familia may be cheating God. Being a short-cut to the expiation of sins." Johnny gulped some black coffee. He always gulped coffee, usually when it was already cold. "On the other hand, oodles of churches nowadays favour plastic cases full of electronic candles. Drop your pesetas in the slot, a bulb lights up. Even flickers convincingly, and no smoke to stain the décor. Same principle with Sagrada Familia, I'd say. Our blip can hardly be a sign of God's displeasure . . . unless God can't cut the mustard any more, compared with the days of Sodom and Gomorrah!

"I guess," he went on, "Dr Rubio's the mystic among the Devotees. He says Gaudí was searching for a higher geometry that underlies the universe and signifies the sacred. We've sure increased the geometrical complexity of Sagrada Familia. Could something sacred be leaking through, attracted by the architectual equation we've written in light in mid-air? Could a miracle be impending? A vision of the Virgin? Oh, here's Angelica."

Salvador's girlfriend bustled effervescently into the restaurant, smiling, waving.

Catalan flags had vanished from the buses. Some red and yellow posters lay as litter. Business as ever; traffic poured through the wide, deep streets.

A taxi ride along the Diagonal took them to the Güell Pavilions. The financier Güell had been Gaudí's greatest patron. The blue and green mosaics of the rooftop ventilators and dome inspired Martha with ideas of pots made of checkerboards of tile. If only the sun were shining, reflecting luminously from the glazed ceramics. However, the dragon gate made her stand still for minutes on end. A fierce prehistoric flying reptile, fossilized not to stone but to metal, splayed across the gate. Indeed it *was* the gate: wing bones, great coils of vertebrae, giant scaly clutching claws, the gaping toothed mouth, the blade tongue curving out like a twisted yucca leaf . . .

"Wow," she said after a while.

"Do you like it?" asked Angelica. "Gaudí used dragons a lot when he was young. Kind of pagan, don't you think? Perhaps he got the theme from the peasants. Fossil of some old cult."

She also saw the dragon as a fossil, a fossil that was somehow still . . . alive.

"Are there any similar dragons on Sagrada Familia?"

"There's just one, amongst all the other sculptures. A type of dragon-demon is presenting a bomb to an anarchist. As Gaudí grew pious, so the dragon became, what's the word, submerged. Come, I'll show you it submerging – "

A taxi returned them to the heart of town, depositing them outside the Battló house. Gaping stone jaw bones framed the lower bay windows. Balconies of the upper windows were lunatic dentures for a small whale that sucked and filtered its food. Along the rooftop sprawled a dragon's knobbly backbone; tiles were scales. Far from submerging, it seemed to Martha that the dragon was emerging from the very fabric of the house, roosting on it, about to take flight over the city.

As they walked away up the wide Passeig de Gràcia through a stream of people, Angelica cocked her head. "Can you hear the difference between Spanish and Catalan yet?"

Like the *zarzuela* they had feasted on the day before, it was all one big soup of language to Martha. Was this prawn Catalan, was that octopus Spanish?

A few hundred yards further on, the apartment block called La Pedrera wrapped an undulating cliff with windowed caves around a whole street corner. The serpentine rippling of stone suggested that a giant snake had seized the building in tier upon tier of coils.

"This may be the masterpiece," Angelica said.

"Must cost a fortune to live in."

Angelica grinned mischievously. "Oh no, these flats weren't popular. No way to hang out bedding to air or dry your washing. Balconies are the wrong shape, see? The crazy wrought iron would tear linen to ribbons. So the rents are cheap. A big bank bought this place to turn into a cultural centre. They can't get the tenants out. They have been trying for years now."

"So is La Pedrera popular or isn't it?"

Angelica chuckled. "I'm just *yoking* – about the bedding, Martha."

When the American woman looked blank, Angelica repeated, "A *yoke*. I was making a *yoke*. Come, we can go up to the roof. That's open to the public."

Monster figures guarded the rooftop, where a maze of steps circuited round two plunging courtyard pits. Alien stone robots, some with ceramic saurian skins, others helmeted like knights: such were the chimneys, the ventilators. Did those move about at night? Did they stomp ponderously around the flights of steps, playing an eerie slow game of chess in which the rules of geometry had altered?

"Look!"

Far over the other rooftops, Martha saw for the first time the closely grouped slim belfries of Sagrada Familia. Honeycombed with air vents and tipped with bobbly stone flowers, those tall rough-textured spindles appeared to have *grown*, organ pipe cactus style, rather than to have been built. Johnny was out there now, checking the programming.

At that moment, apparition-like, the greater church switched on.

A cluster of higher towers now dwarfed the belfries. Some were slender, two were of ampler girth. Martha christened the two main spires Big Boy . . . and Biggest Boy. If the sun had shone, might there have been a hint of unreality? Looming against a grey sky, the phantom church appeared utterly solid and tangible. And utterly strange. She visualized that whole great assembly rising into the clouds on tongues of Pentecostal fire, seeking heaven . . . "Organ pipes," she murmured.

"Yes, it's designed as a musical instrument, too." Angelica explained how the belfries would act as resonance boxes for tubular bells. Air vents were stone sound-boards. Huge organs should have played counterpoint to the carillon. The voices of bells and the deep drone of organs should have resounded throughout Barcelona, making the whole city ring with sacred melody; such had been Gaudí's hope.

Back down on the Passeig de Gràcia, Angelica led Martha to a café to tempt her with hot chocolate and croissants.

"So why did you become a potter?" Angelica asked as she

dunked her pastry into her cup. Martha followed suit; sweetness overwhelmed her taste buds.

Laying her croissant in her cup, Martha kneaded her strong hands by way of demonstration. "I can't put it into words. It's physical. The inner eye, the fingers . . . I know a blind Zen potter – called Ray. Ray empties himself of sight, sight that he never ever possessed. His fingers achieve . . . enlightenment."

"Is Ray your boyfriend?"

"Partner . . ." His touch enlightens me, thought Martha. His fingers know me more surely than eyes that look at me and see only: the female Johnny.

Reading her expression, Angelica nodded. She dipped and sucked, licked her lips. "My body has a will of its own. It lives its own secret life. After Salvador and I make love, I often sleepwalk. I cry out, I laugh, I sing. He has to watch that I do not tumble from our balcony."

"Johnny's buildings are such abstract conceptions," Martha said. "Switch 'em on, switch 'em off. Sagrada Familia looks solid enough while it's switched on."

As the chocolate cooled it became glutinous. Soon the butt end of Martha's croissant was locked in position in her cup.

Angelica lit a cigarette. "I'll show you round the Gothic quarter. We can grab some *tapas* for lunch. A light lunch. This and that. Do you fancy hotly spiced octopus? Then, after, we'll go to the Güell Park."

Martha thought about schooldays. Before she insisted on attending a different school from Johnny, their apparent sameness – at first such a source of conspiratorial joy – had become embarrassing, a cause of social, even sexual confusion. When dating began, girls had accosted Martha – in shadows, or at twilight – before realizing their error, reacting furiously, as if she was making a fool of them by deliberately posing as straight A's, basket-ball heaving Johnny. Why shouldn't it have been the other way round: why shouldn't he have felt insecure in *his* identity, rather than her? If ever boys accosted him by mistake, he didn't seem to care. He wasn't too interested in girls; the design of different sorts of bodies loomed in his head. Sometimes Martha had burned with the

desire to touch and be touched. Did boys avoid her because
they felt they might be lured into displaced gay activity?

"Johnny screwed up," she told Angelica. "He ought to have
owned FaCADes. He wasn't enough in touch with the real
world."

In a narrow lane near the Cathedral, they passed a toyshop.
The window exhibited an eighteen-inch-high holog of the
"basic" Sagrada Familia beside a somewhat larger plastic
model. The porch beneath the belfries was the maw of some
sea-monster with multiple mouths. A tiny hunched demon
made of painted lead wielded a cudgel in the entry. An army
of miniature trolls and werebeasts occupied the checkered
floor of the roofless nave within. Similar little creatures strode
about the holog. These models of Sagrada Familia were
scenery for a role-playing game!

"What's this?" gasped Martha.

"It's called the Game of Good and Evil. Just new in the
shops. The Devotees are very annoyed. They say it's blasphemous. They're trying for a court injunction. They're suing the
manufacturers. I think it's funny.'

The outer façade was rough and smudged, as if chocolate
had melted, then set into teeth and foliage and figures.
Trumpeting angels and saints were the rock climbers here. By
contrast, the inner façade was starkly geometrical: ledges,
niches, and balconies where pterodactyl-like demons roosted.
Martha's fingers itched to swoop a herald angel down from
outside, a pterodemon from its ledge within; to pit them in
combat on the board of the nave, trumpet against talons.

"The whole thing's inside-out, isn't it? Surely the forces of
righteousness ought to be *in* the church, and the forces of evil
outside attacking it? The church is full of demons!"

Angelica peered. "Maybe the shop owner is an atheist? So
he chooses to set the figures out that way, to be naughty. I saw
the manufacturer on TV last week. He argued that this shows
kids the eternal guerrilla war between the Devil and the Angels
for control of the cosmos, so it raises kids' spirituality. Or
something. I hear the plastic version's better, less limiting. As

well as cheaper. The game comes with all sorts of rules and
dice and cards."

"People must be focusing a whole lot of attention upon
Sagrada Familia these days."

"Sure. Of course. But *this*," and Angelica gestured at the
window, "is a rip-off."

Martha had been toying with the notion of buying the Game
of Good and Evil, plastic version – not holog, oh no. A bulky
item, in its box. Ultimately vulgar. She discarded the idea.
They walked on.

Presently they reached what appeared to be a memorial site,
of concrete, wedged between buildings and sheltered by a lone
mulberry tree.

"See the plaque on that wall there? It translates, 'No traitors
are buried here.' Here's where they put the corpses of Catalan
patriots who were killed when the Spanish took over. We dug
up the old bones for reburial. We hold masses for them in this
church." A church façade towered over the narrow street.
"Typical Catalan Baroque."

Martha was unsure whether Angelica was alluding to the
architectural style or to local behaviour.

"Hey, see *him* – ?" Two sombre men in dark suits were
quitting the church. "He's the leader of the Catalan Communist Party. The other guy, with the moustache: I recognize him
from his photo. He's the boss of the Italian communists."

"Communists going to church?"

"That's nationalism for you."

After some paprika-spiced octopus, fried potatoes, and beer,
they caught a taxi uphill to the Park Güell overlooking the
city. Disney gate-houses frosted with ceramic icing gave entry
to a mosaic staircase. Curving side walls were tipped with
jutting vertebrae, or were the spare ribs of a dinosaur.
Roaming amidst shrubs, opuntias, and palms, Angelica coaxed
stray scraggy tom-cats whose elevated tails revealed big balls.

"Another masterpiece, another failure," she said. "This was
intended to be a garden township. Only a couple of plots were
ever sold, and Gaudí bought one himself. So it's a garden

instead . . . I often take a stray cat to the vet's. I have it patched up and injected and given vitamins."

"Does it get neutered too?"

Angelica disregarded the question. She had spotted another battlescarred mog, which they followed under a cavernous viaduct. Up top the roadway was lined with urns. Agaves were succulent green flames rising from those flambeaux. In the sloping interior below, columns leaned in a long row like trees half blown over. Stone facings were scales which overhead became great jagged teeth hanging in defiance of gravity. Martha and her escort could have been walking through the gullet of some fossil beast with a vast neck, a gullet crowned with hundreds of fangs. The tom-cat hissed and eluded Angelica.

Out in the open once more, Martha admired the mosaic benches until their sinuosity reminded her of the writhing of a serpent. Afar below, the enhanced completed church reared. The Mediterranean beyond didn't look at all menacing, as though it had never moved an inch from where it had always been.

Five o'clock. "Time to meet the big one," said Angelica. Did she mean the church, or Martha's brother?

By the time their taxi had scooted straight as a bobsleigh among dozens of others down the Carrer de Sardenya to deposit them outside a turnstile gate, the greater church was switched off. The last tourists of the day flocked out to waiting buses. So many Japanese faces! Somebody had spray-painted a black slogan on the nearest wall: BAJAD EL VOLUMEN DEL CARILLON.

"Lower the noise of the bells," Angelica translated. "If Gaudí's dream of giant organs had come true, what a concert for the neighbourhood!"

Martha gaped up at the belfries while Angelica was phoning from the concierge's hut.

When Johnny and Salvador rendezvoused with the two women inside the gaping whale-mouth, Johnny was dressed in jeans and a black sweater. Not what he'd been wearing at breakfast! She hadn't even known that he owned a dark sweater. Had he changed as soon as she left the hotel with Angelica? How dare he? Brother and sister were almost wearing clone clothes.

"Bit of daylight left," he said breezily. "Anyway, the floodlighting and the holog will illuminate everything just fine. I'm going hunting. Want to come? I could use a spotter or two. Salvador needs to stay below to operate the controls."

Both men had mini radios clipped to their pockets. Johnny, who was also armed with binoculars and a camera, offered a spare radio to his sister. She stared pointedly at his garb till finally he cottoned on, at least to a certain degree.

"It's chilly. Salvador leant me a sweater. Come on inside . . ."

Accepting the radio, she followed him past plaster of Paris models and displays of postcards. Inside, naturally, was also outside, since no roof existed. Half of the interior space was a warren of stacked dressed stone, scaffolding, huts, lifting gear, all seemingly abandoned. Masonry must be a dusty occupation. She noticed the pavilion-like altar, and some of the holography equipment, whatever it was. Techno stuff. Whatever cluttered the ground was of no importance. Her gaze drifted up the inside of the shell. How faithful that plastic model had been: all those ledges, niches; yet not a single pterodemon in sight.

The four people crossed to the base of the far belfries. Johnny stared upward critically, as he once had assessed the hoop at basketball. Still annoyed at how alike she and her twin were clad, Martha shuddered more with irritation than anxiety as she looked up again. Oh yes, Johnny would shin up inside these fluted belfries, just like an action-man doll dressed for the part. It was all just an idea to him, anyway, a schematic. Probably he saw himself as a mouse on a computer screen chasing the errant blob of whatever, to delete it. Competent, competent.

The run-up to the FaCADes fiasco had been a different story. But would she have really wanted riches for her brother? Would she really have wanted for Johnny to be in a position to patronize her? Literally patronize: pumping an injection of capital into her pottery business, lining up publicity and buyers, marketing her, giving the nod or the thumbs-down to designs. Maybe it was just as well that he hadn't managed to market himself, only sell himself off.

Frankly, she and Ray were poor, but they still got by in their partnership up in Marin County. The blind man, and the duplicated woman: a Xerox of her brother, as if Mom and Dad hadn't enough genetic coinage between them to afford two separate individuals. Mom and Dad had dressed the twins alike for years, in a unisex economy drive. For a while, way back when, Martha had taken to following three synchronized steps behind Johnny. He had been born first; *he* was the original. Could she help it that her body language or her liking for caramel chip ice cream were the same? Blame the genes. Did she and Johnny dream the same dreams? Did they think in tune? What went on in her head was her *own*. The pressure of the outside world imposed upon her, nevertheless, urging her always to react as he did. After they went to different schools, life had improved. Ray valued her for what he *couldn't* see. Zen love.

Johnny was Spain, she thought, and she was Catalonia. So how could he possibly understand this temple of Gaudí's? She was here at his expense, otherwise she would never have got to Barcelona at all. She was enjoying the crumbs of his crumbs. Johnny seemed unaware that he only had crumbs. It would be cruel to enlighten him. She would be kicking an eager puppy in the face.

A sign pointed towards an elevator. So they wouldn't need to climb the entire way. At the doorway to the belfry, another sign pictured a savage black hound leaping away from a snapped chain. From six P.M. till six A.M. the beast was let loose. She imagined that the ghost that people had been seeing was the black hound roaming up aloft. Of course the animal couldn't have trodden on air.

"No guard dogs on site tonight," Johnny reassured her. Salvador departed to whichever shed housed the controls. "You coming up top?" Johnny asked Angelica.

"Why not? I have never actually – "

"Been up there! That's how it is when you live near somewhere famous." Chuckling, Johnny led the two women up some steps to the little elevator and tugged the grille door open.

Quiet terror beat its wings within Martha. The narrowest of stone stairways spiralled upwards, affording barely enough space for people to pass each other if one breathed in and hugged the wall. An inner balustrade gave on to a plunging well. Eyes of floodlights looked straight up from the bottom. Since Martha was tall and skinny, it seemed all too conceivable that she might lean between the stone uprights and plunge down the well. Mouths in the outer wall, the air vents placed every yard or so, were drooping lips of stone easily large enough to slide through. Those vents were very similar in fact to the start of a slide, the first two feet of a slide – followed by emptiness, then by the ground far below. Should she stick her head and shoulders into a mouth, should she push with her feet . . . she would fly down; she would die.

She was trapped in a sieve, tapering upwards towards the slimmest of cones. How could these stones hold together? Why didn't those lips fall from the vents? Why didn't the stairway collapse inwards down the shaft? The wind blew through the walls, pushing at her.

As they mounted in single file, Johnny setting the pace, Angelica began to whimper.

They reached an open-air bridge leading to an adjoining belfry. Below, displayed all around, was Barcelona. Very much below. Martha noticed a rooftop swimming pool. The lake in the Plaça de Gaudí looked so shallow, only inches deep. Everywhere else: relentlessly hard surfaces . . . She gazed from the bridge up at the tips of the towers, at the bobbly alien flowers, the faceted, tilting planes of fractured tile. Even in the dying grey light, she responded to their luminosity. If this edifice was a tree, ceramics were the flowers and fruit of the tree, the aim, the pinnacle. Descending mosaic letters spelled the words *Hosanna* and *Excelsis*. Little nubs of stone jutted as if to provide footing for suicidal steeplejacks.

Angelica clung to the bridge wall. "Vertigo," she moaned, half humorously, half desperately. "My legs are giving way. I haven't felt like this for years."

"You're using muscles you aren't used to using," explained Johnny. "There's some distance yet to climb. You okay, Sis?"

"Why shouldn't I be?" Martha had also been climbing awkwardly, as if drunk, bumping against a wall, stumbling over steps. In the core of her being the fear still fluttered, but numbingly so. It anaesthetized her, detached her.

"This isn't my muscles," Angelica insisted, "it's *vertigo*."

"Maybe you'd better go down?"

"Yes! Yes!" Angelica fled back inside the belfry.

Johnny unclipped his radio. "Salvador, let's have the floods."

Blue light filled the belfries, as if the contents of a tropical lagoon had welled up. A remote squeal of surprise reached their ears. Angelica, suddenly illuminated. Quitting the bridge, Martha and Johnny wended upwards through blue air, higher, higher inside the other belfry. A shorter bridge – a bond between Siamese twins – led to a further belfry. They descended for a few circuits till another short bridge took them – surely back into the previous belfry? Or was this another one? Martha was lost. She had no idea of the route back to the elevator. How could there be so many stairways, bridges, all so similar? Was Johnny leading her up and down and up because he wasn't too familiar with this maze either? He hummed to himself, pausing to check his bearings via the air vents.

"Here will do fine." He addressed the radio: "Okay, Salvador, switch on number three holog." He told Martha, "Number three's the most interconnected. Why don't you watch from this vent? I'll nip over to the next belfry."

"You're leaving me here?"

"Two points of view!" He demonstrated how to operate the radio.

A vaster church shimmered into being, outside and above,

spires aiming to cleave the clouds, dwarfing their belfry to a foothill. The new edifice, aglow, was perfectly convincing: giant veined towers with half-hooded vents, linked to the original mass by arching bridges. Johnny hadn't yet had the opportunity to abandon her. "Look, Johnny, look there!"

Something golden had crossed behind an embrasure in a phantom spire. It passed another vent, descending. Lining up his camera, Johnny clicked it rapidly as again the target partly revealed itself. Partly. Martha couldn't identify the golden ghost. What on earth *was* it? But then, it wasn't *on* earth. It was treading unreal holographic stairs.

"You're my luck, Sis. Let's head closer."

"Don't call me that. I use *your* name, Johnny."

"You nervous?"

"Oh, forget it."

Johnny rushed ahead, careering down steps. No, not *ahead*, but around and around. By the time she came to a junction, he was out of sight. The flood of blue radiance pouring up from the well stopped her from seeing if he was lower down the stairs. She couldn't hear the thud of his shoes. She shouted, "Which way, Johnny?"

His answer came through most of the sound-boards of the next belfry. "This way! Hurry!" He must have crossed over the bridge, so she did likewise. Did he then descend or ascend?

"Johnny?" she radioed. "Up or down?"

"I'm heading up." He was panting. So she climbed.

She hesitated at the portal to another bridge. The brightness of the greater church blinded her. Night air buffeted her. Floodlighting in the next belfry transformed its vents into windows of turquoise stained glass.

She screamed. In the doorway beyond the humpback of the bridge: a dragon. Golden-scaled, gilded pterodactyl wings, claws like the buckled tines of a fork left to rust in a field, a long rattlesnake tail . . . Amber eyes glinted. Wings rustled and twanged. A mouth of nail-teeth gaped. A blade of a tongue licked out, tasting the breeze, and her. The dragon hopped out on to the bridge. It was approximately Angelica's size.

When Martha ducked back inside the belfry, she clearly heard the metallic scrabble of the creature crossing the remainder of the bridge. She fled up, round, up again. How far did she flee? She halted breathless, forced herself to listen.

Scritch, scratch, clack-clack, thump. A loud hiss, as of steam escaping below. The spook was in the real building with her! The black dog was loose! But this wasn't any dog. This was a dragon, Gaudí's dragon. The primeval image impaled on the pavilion gate, roosting on the Casa Battló, submerged in the park – it had gathered, it had emerged.

"Johnny," she whispered into the radio.

"Can hardly hear you, Sis! I lost the darn thing." His electronic words echoed loudly in the confined turret. *Hiss*, below.

"For God's sake keep your voice down. It's in this belfry with me."

"Can't be, Sis. It lives in holograph land."

"I tell you, it's *here*."

"Where's here?"

"I don't know." *Rustle, hiss*. She must escape: up, over a bridge, down, around up.

"Hey, Sis, come in will you?' blared the radio, pinpointing her. Furiously she pitched the wretched thing over the balustrade. Johnny's voice fell away down the well. Maybe the dragon would follow that noise instead. If she and Johnny had been together, they might have confused the creature by brother going up, sister going down, then ducking back to tantalize it before one headed left, the other right, running interference for each other. The dragon might have assumed they were both the same person, and wouldn't have known which to chase. A person who could appear and disappear at will. She and Johnny had played that trick whenever a new kid moved into the neighbourhood; until the game sickened her. Johnny wasn't here to play. The night breeze plucked at her, fingers reaching through stone. *Hiss*. She fled.

*

She was gasping as though she had climbed so high up a mountain that she couldn't drag enough air into her lungs. Her ears rang. Her legs ached now with a jellifying ache. Johnny couldn't have kept up such a pace. His basketball days, when he could dance around a court, were long past. Too much time spent sitting in front of VDUs. But she'd kept in trim. Not just her hands by pummelling clay. Her long legs by jogging – in her hunter-red tracksuit up and down roads lined with redwoods between drippy foggy sixty-degree hill-sides. So steep that homes on stilts cantilevered out among the crowns of redwoods, seeming buttressed by tree trunks.

None of which had really prepared her muscles for this flight through Sagrada Familia, pursued by the hiss, the clack of claws, rustle of wings. Leaning into a vent to support herself while she sucked oxygen, she gazed out and thought she had gone insane.

She was looking down upon the cruciform ceramic flowers that tipped the tops of the belfries. *Down* upon them, *down*. And those belfries were the highest peaks of the real Sagrada Familia, of the actual church!

The staircase where she now found herself spiralled less tightly, the wall curved more gently, embrasures were further apart. She wasn't in any belfry at all. Hurrying round a quarter circuit and clinging to a different vent she gaped: at twin spires. She was high up Biggest Boy, the tallest holographic spire of all . . .

"No," she whispered. "No . . ." Briefly the stone seemed to weaken under her hand, the step to soften beneath her trainers. Sickeningly, she imagined herself sinking down through stone which suddenly turned to water, to air, releasing her to fall from a vast height.

"No!" she cried. This was a different denial, a refusal to let the spectral stone betray her. Gaudí's whole church was in existence now, all of it. What had that Devotee told Johnny? About a higher geometry which underlay the universe, which was the quintessence of reality? All around her unfolded Gaudí's master equation of spirals, funicular arches, revolving parabolas, internal counterpoises, axes of symmetry, connections. It didn't matter if this was inscribed in stone or in light or a blend of both. She had trodden most of the route through this equation obliviously, chased by the dragon. So long as she didn't deny her position now, it would sustain her, hold her up. She dared not deny it, or she would fall.

Could Johnny spy her even now with his binoculars, as she ranged through the holographic church? Could he spy the monster that hunted her? A golden power with claws and teeth, the dragon from the heart of reality. The dragon . . . of death?

Hiss! Sssss. She staggered upwards. Walls were pinching in. No more bridges, no more alternatives. A final turn. The steps stopped at a grille. Beyond that grille: only the top of the spire-well, summit of emptiness, a final cone of roof above. In any case the grille was locked. She backed against it. *Iss. Sissss.*

"Hosanna!" she cried defiantly. "Excelsis!" So like some fundamentalist fanatic that she felt ashamed. How could *slogans* save her from the dragon? – which even now rounded that final bend, tiptoeing on those cruel clutchy claws, wings flapping limply against wall and inner balustrade to help lift it, that blade tongue questing for her, *ssss.* How its eyes glared! Despite herself, she admired it. The dragon lunged at Martha.

Somehow she was alive; somehow she *was* the dragon. Exaltation filled her. She thought of angels with their radiance and their many shining wings. She thought of grimacing batwing devils. A dragon wasn't a demon *or* an angel. It was a being which had arisen from the earth, not descended from the sky. Even devils once hailed from the sky, from the immaterial geometric realm, the domain of theology, cerebral cybernetics. Whereas a dragon arose from rock and soil and ore and clay. Its vertebrae were the backbones of hills, its ribs defined valleys, its mouth was any cave. A dragon arose from the same clay out of which the human race came, if archeozoic clay had indeed printed out the first primitive matrix of reproduction, as some scientists said. The same clay which made pots.

She knew that in a sense the dragon had not been chasing her. On the contrary, she had been luring *it*. By fleeing from the dragon, forcing it to follow her through the geometries of the church, she had compelled it to come all the way, to herd her upward, hissing, *sissing*. The dragon existed to panic her into forgetting that these spires did not exist. To turn a thought into a substance.

She was wandering, wandering, down, around, across and down, letting her aching legs guide her. She had been as high as she could go; nowhere was higher. Now she returned. Now she descended. She recognized her surroundings. She was in a belfry again, a belfry built of stone. Solid, albeit honeycombed by holes.

At that moment the greater church switched off; the holog vanished. Through a vent she regarded the abyss lit by blue seepage from the belfries, black bumps of masonry and machines at the base. She was near a familiar grille door. She pressed a button to summon the elevator from below. She rode it down.

To where Johnny waited, with Angelica.

"Where did you get off to, Sis? Soon as I lost the bogey I looked everywhere for you."

"You couldn't have looked where I went."

"I swear I checked all the belfries. Why didn't you use your radio?"

"I dropped it."

"Shit. You might have shouted."

"It's rude to shout in church," said Martha.

"I get it. You were playing hide and seek, like when we were kids."

No, that wasn't the game they had played all those years ago. His memory was false. Why seek someone who looked so much like yourself? They had both played at foxing some naive stranger. For that matter, why *hide* from yourself? Ah, that was different . . . And at last she had been found, by a wild vigour that had been awaiting her, awaiting *somebody*, anybody suitable, so as to discharge itself like lightning surging down a conductor from the abstract sky where it had been conjured, back into the clotted, fertile, tactile soil, its element. But first, the chosen host must elevate itself – herself – as high as could be. By learning to walk on air. Now that her feet were on the ground, she viewed the dragon in a new light.

"What do you suppose the photos will show?" asked Angelica.

"We'll develop them pronto tomorrow. Computer-enhance 'em, if necessary. Me, I couldn't make out what it was supposed to be."

"But it was real?"

"Real? If it isn't a bug in the program, then at most it's an electromagnetic hallucination."

"A what?"

"I guess there's an electromagnetic field associated with the holog. Maybe under special atmospheric conditions. All this cloud cover, freak weather . . . well, you know, if you induce a small electrical current across a person's scalp, they start to see things."

"Really?"

How smug Johnny looked. "The bit of the brain called the hippocampus is very unstable electrically. The hippocampus is an important part of the emotion and memory systems. Tickle that with electricity, and you might see all kinds of deep images that otherwise are suppressed from your consciousness – except in dreams."

"I don't know what *I* dream. But it sends me on journeys!"

"Monsters, archetypes . . . ghosts. They'd seem as real as your hand. We haven't had this problem with other façades. No Shakespeare's ghost haunting Anne Hathaway's Cottage, no, no, no way. But Sagrada Familia is the big one. There's more power involved here. Salvador and I will do some testing tomorrow, check out any electromagnetic fields. If that's the explanation, I'm hardly surprised I didn't see anything clearly. Me, I'm not much into the writhings of the subconscious."

Angelica cocked her head. "So if the camera captured an image, you're dealing with a bug. If it didn't – " She tapped her scalp, beneath her blonde bush of hair.

Martha had listened in disgust. "Did you suspect this brain electricity thing before we flew out here?"

Johnny grinned. "It was a possibility. FaCADes needs to know. Can't have our customers spooked. Personally I rate this as a low possibility, but I did think about it on and off while I was busy, you know, researching the concept in the first place."

While you were failing, she thought, to keep financial control of the concept. You were bothering your brain about electromagnetic ghosts. Not *authentic* ones, of course.

"I ruled it out," said Johnny.

An electromagnetic ghost could *not*, she reminded herself, cause a human being to walk in the sky.

"And you did need a vacation, hmm?"

No, Johnny, you didn't see anything clearly. Least of all me in any of the belfries – because I simply wasn't there.

Salvador was bustling towards them across the littered nave, miming the act of hoisting a beer glass . . .

On the Pan-Am clipper flight back home a week later, Johnny said, "'fraid it *wasn't* much of a holiday, Sis, with you moping most of the time in the Cristina Gran. Even when the sun came out."

The day after she climbed those belfries, the weather had relented. Spring – no, full Summer – arrived. Barcelona began to bake and broil. Drains started to smell.

"I wasn't moping. I was . . . centering myself."

"Is that what it was? First I've ever heard of centering. Poor Angelica thought you were sulking; decided you didn't like her. I told her you caught a bug; probably from the sea food. Ah, what a waste of time."

"I saw all I needed to see."

His photos had come out crap. They might as well have been shot into the sun. Not even a computer could make head or tail of them. As for electromagnetic fields, maybe the abrupt meteorological shift had swept those away – till another season? Johnny and Salvador had detected nothing untoward.

Johnny had climbed the church on five further evenings, in vain. The problem seemed to have disappeared.

"You didn't even visit the Picasso museum."

"When I wasn't centering, I walked a bit."

"Poo. Did that tad of gunfire scare you? Was being in a foreign city such a shock?"

"I saw, Johnny, believe me. I *saw*."

Her brother writhed to adjust his knees behind the backward-tilted seat in front of him. The hotel had been four-star, but this flight was economy. Martha centred herself and didn't worry about cramp.

She carried the dragon within her. When she got back among the misty redwoods, she would show the beast to Ray in such a way that her blind lover would know it too.

In the Upper Cretaceous with the Summerfire Brigade

Rain drenched England's second city. The forecast was a wet one for the whole southern half of the country. What would the weather be like in the Upper Cretaceous era? I hardly cared. Sue's farewell to me after toast and coffee had been lukewarm. I hadn't told her the whole grim truth about our finances. She viewed this trip to my publisher as a frivolity, a piece of self-indulgence, and a humiliation. Juliette had badgered me yet again. Why couldn't she go on the school trip to Italy this summer?

"To see all the Leonardos and things, Dad."

"Which particular ones?" I felt tempted to ask. Why couldn't Juliette content herself with a day trip to London by way of what amounted to the Garden of Eden? People quickly became blasé about the technological miracle. It was yesterday's doughnut; and yesterday's doughnut was stale – just like my *Springdew*, already out of print pending the "long-awaited" sequel.

On the platform at New Street Station a brown-skinned girl with a Brummy accent asked me, "How long does the journey to London take?" She toted a heavy-looking holdall, which she didn't put down. Was she pure Pakistani, Bangladeshi? Or part white, fruit of a mixed marriage? Really, her accent said who she was. She was British, from Birmingham.

She was beautiful, with a trim figure, slim features with a mass of raven hair, wild coaly eyes. She wore jeans and a green anorak. Since she seemed to be testing my attitude, I made sure I smiled.

"Eighty million years. Of course the timetable says eighty minutes."

"So much time! All the time in the world."

She was seventeen or so. Just starting out; so long as the British Government didn't send her "back" to some ghastly fly-blown village she had never seen in her life, by the Indus or the Brahmaputra. Surely they would never do that.

She glanced along the platform, where a couple of hundred other people were waiting, making eye contact with a bearded Asian youth dressed similarly to her. I noticed a score of young people from the sub-continent scattered up and down, with duffels and zipped bags. Nothing unusual. Still, they generally clustered together, didn't they? As the girl's hair swirled I saw the vertical scar on the side of her cheek. The slash mark of a Stanley knife?

She regarded me again, and what did she see? While teaching at college I had cut a dash: dapper, trimly bearded, given to bow ties, my thick chestnut hair receding in orderly rank back over a polished half-dome of scalp. A few of my girl students had quite fancied me. Now here was a second-hand, gone-to-seed, middle-aged fellow, balding and muffled in a beard; attired in loose damp mackintosh, best tweed jacket, checked slacks, wet scuffed suede shoes. I resembled a crooked antiques dealer. "I'm robbing myself, Madam, but I'll give you a tenner for that teapot."

"You really mean eighty million years *twice*, don't you?" she said. "The train goes back in time then it has to come forward."

I nodded affably. Anything to distract me from journey's end.

"I hope we'll see a Triceratops," I told her, though I couldn't have cared less. "Everybody ought to see old Three-Horns. Almost the symbol of our city, hmm?" Our city; hers and mine.

She laughed. "You mean because of the Bull Ring sculpture?"

The mascot of Birmingham's old shopping centre was a bull with lowered horns. Even after demolition and swanky high-tech redevelopment, the emblem was still on display. That bull bore a striking resemblance to an irate Triceratops. Triceratops was rhino-plus: seven metres long, weighing in at a ton per metre, its triple horns sweeping forward from a great frill of bone, its lizard tail a giant rudder. A couple of years ago I watched film footage on TV shot from the Intercity train. I had little time for TV these days.

"Maybe this time we'll see a whole herd," I encouraged the girl.

"Maybe!" Her eyes gleamed. She harboured a fire within her. Why couldn't Juliette nurse a similar flame instead of whining selfishness? Probably my daughter's selfishness was a reflection of her father's self-involvement, a self-centredness which arose of necessity otherwise I would never have enough hours in which to finish *Summerfire*.

"Here it comes!" The Intercity train was pulling in, doors swinging open. Passengers from London jumped out: so many suits, so many black document cases, in such a hurry. The girl followed me into the same carriage and sat directly opposite by the window, blocking the rest of the seat with her bag. Testing my racial tolerance? Daring me to notice her scar? I was facing London; she was facing Birmingham.

"I'm called Anita," she confided.

"I'm Bernard."

"So what do you do in life, Bernard?" This seemed a deeper question: what had I done to help her and fellow Britons of Asian or Afro-Caribbean descent in their hour of stress? Why, I had written a novel to fire the imagination, to let readers escape into wonderful times.

"I'm an author. Bernard Kelly. I wrote a novel called *Springdew*." When Anita looked blank, I continued: "Oh, about Renaissance intrigue. Art, love, death, revolution. With a fantasy twist, with Neoplatonic magical elements out of Pico della Mirandola and Marsilio Ficino . . ." No, she wasn't one of my bygone students; now wasn't the past.

"Revolution," she repeated.

"I'm trying to write a sequel called *Summerfire*. That's one word . . ."

The train jolted into motion. Our carriage trundled through the dingy brick tunnel beneath Moor Street Ringway to emerge briefly into a deluge. Ten seconds later we went through the entry gate to the time-tunnel, a boiling compacted thundercloud sustained by the generator-arch spanning both railway tracks – through into sunlight and Cretaceous scenery bare of any trace of the human race. No urban megasprawl, no factories, car parks, canals or waste dumps, no abandoned detritus of Victorian enterprise where gangs might roam.

Anita breathed in deeply as if she could smell the cubic miles of unpolluted air beyond the window glass and beyond the shimmery translucence of the Swanson field.

"All looks so pure, doesn't it, Anita?"

"Pure?" Her hackles rose. She stared hard at me, assessingly. Might her travel companion be alluding to racial purity? Whatever *that* meant, in this country of mongrels! Mongrels with white skins, to be sure . . .

"The air must taste so sweet out there."

She grunted as though such a possibility hadn't occurred to a city girl. I decided that she had breathed in with relief. She'd been holding her breath prior to passing through the Swanson gate – safely as always, routinely so. Why had she felt anxious? Was this her first such train trip? Yet she chose to sit with an anglo stranger . . .

Rather than beside one of "her own kind"? Why on earth should she know any of the other Asians on this train? My reaction to her, I decided, was patronizingly racialist: see what a tolerant liberal chap I am.

To distract Anita and myself, I pointed. "Look, hadrosaurs!"

Cretaceous *landscape* wasn't too dissimilar to that of uptime Britain, except perhaps that there was so much of it; that everything was landscape. Flowering plants had already evolved, likewise familiar trees such as pine and oak and poplar. Also, more exotic species: figs, magnolias, tulip trees. By a small lake a herd of the tall duck-billed dinosaurs were ripping at vegetation. Their helmet-crests jutted like absurd weather vanes. A few feathered birds fluttered about. Up aloft a solitary pterosaur cruised, a demon from medieval art. *Those* were the differences.

Businessmen glanced out, then buried themselves back in

documents. To them a pterosaur was no more than a big bat. The hadrosaurs were a sort of lunatic cattle draped in green crocodile skin. Had it not been for Anita I might also, plunged in melancholy, have disregarded those.

"They're extinct," I told her. "They failed, and they were replaced."

The train sang as it raced along the rails. The locomotive hauling us was a diesel. A power supply to feed the pantograph of an electric loco couldn't be pushed through the time-gates. This glassy corridor, this hundred-mile-long soap bubble, was a function of the modest deployment of tuned power at both ends, which brought the Swanson tunnel into existence between its terminals. A *modest* injection of power; the Swanson effect was remarkably inexpensive to sustain. The driver could stay in radio contact with Birmingham and London; aerials poked through gates.

Our diesel was fitted with a smoke trap, filters, and a waste gas compressor otherwise the tunnel could soon have resembled the worst of Victorian smogtowns. Exhaust from the engine couldn't puff away into prehistory because we were just out of phase with the Cretaceous. I wasn't exactly in the distant past, though I could see it clear as could be. The past couldn't see me or the speeding train; its creatures remained oblivious.

In Swanson terms "out of phase" meant that if a dinosaur crossed the tracks ahead of us, loco and carriages would zoom right through, and the saurian would lumber on its way, neither past nor present affected by the encounter. Imagine the evolutionary consequences if the roamings of the big lizards had been baulked by implacable invisible barriers scores of miles long networking the archaic countryside, penning species into great separate wildlife parks for however long us twentieth-century travellers continued to journey in this style! Enough to drive the big stupid lizards, the almighty Cretins, to extinction? No, Swanson tubes hadn't zapped the dinosaurs.

Long thin tubes, minimum length thirty miles, Intercity length. And only functioning eighty million years ago, a resonance effect due to where the Earth and the Sun had been in spacetime at that earlier date. Only termini and gates existed on the ground in the uptime. The former railway tracks had been converted to high-speed motorways, which of course weren't suitable for Swanson travel. Too many vehicles to fit with exhaust traps. Car drivers might swerve instinctively to avoid the phantom wild life or might brake to gawp at a rampaging carnosaur; causing crashes and tailbacks.

Nor could the time tunnels be inflated into city-size bubbles in the Cretaceous. Homes and factories couldn't be shifted into the past. But rail travel the Swanson way did relieve some of the strain on Britain's overcrowded environment. Especially in the freight department. Any contribution had to help. I hadn't been paying too much attention to the activities of the forced-repatriation fascists, the fire-bombings of mosques and Halal butchers' shops, the rapes, the beatings-up. Recently I'd had other worries on my mind. But pressure was bringing the pot to a boil, a very ugly boil.

"Hey, cheer up. Every dog has its day." Anita's grin enchanted me, though there seemed to be a zany edge to it. "*Summerfire*! I like that name, Bernard. It grabs me."

"Thanks." In fact, I felt seriously out of phase myself.

On the night before this trip to London I suffered another anxiety attack. Waking in bed beside comatose Sue, I felt my hands and legs twitch uncontrollably. Legs wanted to be on the move. Hands tried to do something, flapping like butter-flies caught in spider's web. Once again the *albatross* was to blame.

Springdew was my third novel, the brick, the breakthrough, written in between teaching classes about the Renaissance. In that first flush of hysteria three and a bit years earlier I quit my job as a lecturer in art history. Unicorn Books gave me a contract and what seemed a fat advance for the as-yet-unwritten *Summerfire*. *Springdew* did well enough, yet never as well as hoped for. What a fool I was to forsake Giorgione and Botticelli for freedom, which so soon became a cage. *Summer-fire* was still hanging round my neck as we sank into debt. Of course the sequel must needs be finished, unless I wished to repay the advance. With what? I was overcome with amnesia as to who all the characters were and exactly what events had happened. Periodically I forced myself to re-read *Springdew* and the wretched printout to date; which wasted more time. Of Leonardo it was said, "the way to perfection is through a series of disgusts." I only experienced the disgusts.

Twitch, twitch. Such hands did not write assured narrative. Time was floating by. Not enough was happening, except in the debit department which was always busy and punctual. Unless I scribbled notes to myself to trip over on the stairs I even forgot whatever I promised Sue or sixteen-year-old Juliette in the way of house maintenance or help with exam revision – because I didn't want to steal the time from myself. Nor could poor Sue go out to work. For the past eighteen months she'd been suffering a crippling post-viral fatigue, one of the new breed of illnesses.

I could see no way back to what I'd been; none. I was becoming a pinched, frantic person. How could such a one kindle the blaze of *Summerfire*? Why was I forgetting what it was supposed to be about? Because that book had become simply another duty, heavy as lead. Lying from four in the morning till six in a state of utter nervousness, shivering, I wondered how long till us Kellys were forced to sell our home.

As daylight filtered through the curtains I watched our cat Ben (short for Benvenuto) sprawled asleep on a chair. The ginger mog spent so much of every day in the land of Nod. Its luxurious laziness used to comfort me. Secure in its home and its world, Ben wasn't worried about a bean. Now the sight provoked panic. Why couldn't I borrow some of Ben's unused, wasted time? Time enough to finish *Summerfire* quickly but surely, while the demanding world stood still? So I lost sleep, and tired myself. In a few hours I'd be travelling to London to beg time.

Really, I thought, it's the end of my life. What would the exact mechanism be? An overdose of barbiturates, towards the end of the summer? Falling in front of an underground train in London? Sue could collect some insurance. How I feared waking up injured – a failure, and an invalid too.

Maybe my forgetfulness might intensify until I simply walked away from everything. To where? How?

The passage of a train on the up-line jerked me back into myself. A continuous blur of windows without apparent occupants raced by, a horizontal hurricane. Anita was frowning, checking her watch.

"Look there!" I pointed. More duck-bills grazing by a stream. The tallest reared high and began to hoot or bellow.

Quickly the duck-bills' fellows followed suit, their weather vanes all swinging alertly in the same direction. Out of a poplar grove there burst a great flesh-eater, its tiny forearms wagging, its mouth agape, full of teeth. Though I pressed my nose to the window, and Anita her cheek, the train whisked us away from witnessing the outcome. Briefly her cheek looked bruised from the pressure of the glass, as if I had slapped her.

"What a monster!" She brushed her hair back into place.

"I think it was a Gorgosaurus . . ." That beast's gaze could turn anyone to stone. "Would you like a cup of coffee from the buffet car, Anita? Or a lager? I don't know if you drink . . ." I shouldn't waste money on anything at railway prices; but nevertheless.

"No thanks, let's not squander . . ." She clammed up.

"I don't suppose us travellers get to see many of those big carnivores. They'll be rare."

She grinned ferally. "An omen. Death the destroyer."

Time passed. The land grew scrubbier, barer. A few trees still reared; also clumps of cycads, fern-tipped hairy grey pineapples. A pair of snake-necked lizards which looked like plucked ostriches were racing side by side, their beaked heads held high, slim, three-fingered arms cocked upright mantis-fashion, long tails tapering straight out behind them. Sprinters for survival from the reek of some carnosaur? Competitors in search of a mate? Hungry to find a meal of eggs somewhere? How far I'd come since leaving New Street Station. Yet in a sense I'd come nowhere really remote. London, rain, and

Unicorn Books awaited me in, what, forty minutes. Those sprinting ostrich-lizards had sunk out of sight. Passengers rummaged in their document cases, consulted personal organizers, rustled pink pages of the *Financial Times*.

The train squealed, and I pitched forward. Luggage, macs, umbrellas skidded along the overhead racks. Some items tumbled on to seats, into the aisle. The Intercity wasn't just slowing; the driver was braking in emergency. Braced for the sudden deceleration by her own backward-facing seat, Anita tore at her holdall, and pulled out a pistol. Pushing me aside, she hauled her way to the interior door and turned to face the carriage. The train had stopped. I was thunder-struck.

"Everyone listen to me," Anita shouted. "Shut up and listen. This train is being hijacked. Sit still and you shan't be hurt. Leave your seats without permission and I'll shoot you, I promise. We have armed people in every carriage. Right, you hear?" Muffled by the two intervening doors I detected a similar harangue in the next carriage.

A burly young business type with eyebrows like big hairy caterpillars half-rose. "*Who's* hijacking the train?" Anita gripped her pistol in both hands. "Sit, or you'll be the first!"

"The first?" bleated a middle-aged lady in deep blue twin set and pearls. "How do you mean, the first?"

"Anita . . ." She was only six feet away from me. My tone pleaded that she should continue whatever relationship we had had, that she should not become an utter alien. She favoured me with a tight smile.

"Don't worry, *you're* okay." Raising her voice: "Listen, all, we're the Friends of Asia."

"Who's she when she's at home?" cried a wit.

"Some friends," sneared somebody else. A woman was sobbing.

"We'll be radioing our demands to London. When those are met, our friends will tell the authorities a code phrase to radio to us; so we'll know."

"What demands, miss?" enquired a bespectacled older man. "I mean, are your demands easy to meet? Are they possible?"

"If people who demand the expulsion of immigrants are

listened to, then all demands are possible – " A gunshot firecrackered elsewhere. A death, or simply a warning? How easy to be killed here. Barbiturates? No, a bullet. Acting the hero, I only needed to launch myself at Anita. I couldn't do it. I would be exploiting her, staining her hands and her mind, making her a murderess. I would need to assault a different hijacker.

From halfway along the carriage a suave voice spoke up. "Listen to her, everyone, and be cool. I'm an officer in the SAS. I'm willing to be your special hostage if – "

"You're all hostages!" Anita screamed.

"Quite. But a surplus of hostages is a nuisance. You'd be best advised to hang on to a token number, disembark the majority from the rear of the train as a sign of good faith, let them walk away. I assume regular services will be cancelled. A relief train will come to evacuate the people you set free."

"What's your name?"

"Jones. Andrew Jones. Call me Andy."

"Listen, General Jones, we're keeping all of you. We'll be moving you into the three rear carriages under guard. What sort of hijack lets half the hostages stroll off at the start?"

"An efficient one, miss. For goodness sake let's be efficient. I'm no general, by the way. Nothing quite as grand."

"Stand up, let me see you. Don't step into the aisle."

A tall lean man in his thirties with short sandy hair made himself evident. He wore a safari suit as if bound for the tropics.

"Identify your luggage. Lift it down with one hand."

A smile played round Jones' lips as he obeyed. "That's good thinking. You're the organizer of this, aren't you?"

"People: pass that suitcase back here hand to hand. Don't anyone lift it high so it can be thrown." When the suitcase, initialled ARJ, arrived Anita shouted, "Key!" Jones bowled a ring of keys underarm. Anita let these rebound from the door behind her before kicking them forward in my direction. "Kneel, Bernard, please. Shuffle to the suitcase. Empty it on the floor then resume your seat."

Jones was eyeing me keenly. Ah, he was wondering how

Anita knew my name. If I tackled her from this position she might fire over my head and miss me.

"Though," drawled Jones, "would I have identified myself if I had a shooter in my luggage?" I emptied out shirts, underwear, aftershave, the usual paraphernalia, and a soft porn magazine. Sorting with her shoe, Anita glared at that last item. "Too many mouths to feed," said Jones. I was taking a dislike to him.

"We'll be provisioned," Anita assured the carriage at large. "They'll bring up another loco with supplies."

"But not too close?" asked Jones. "I expect you'll be mining the track front and rear with explosives. Oh, half a mile from here so there's no chance of a gas attack."

"That's right, clever clogs. You can stop fishing for details. Park yourself *now*. Ladies and gentlemen, welcome to the most efficient spot in the world for a hijack. No security checks on the way in. Nobody can storm our train from the Cretaceous period."

A lanky young Sikh, turbanned and scrappily bearded, hauled open the far door. He cradled a pump-action shotgun. "Anita! We read your first script over the radio." His accent was pure nasal Birmingham too. "Shall I take over here?"

"Yes. And watch out for *that one*. One of the 'Who Dares, Wins' squad. He'll try to soft-talk you."

"It's rather a shame," observed Jones from his seat, "that you can't conduct your private affairs in Punjabi or Bengali. Are you so much of a cross-section?"

"That's because we're British," said the Sikh youth.

"Ah, but you'll need safe conduct out of Britain afterwards. You can never come back. Don't you feel this rather defeats your purpose?"

"We're willing to sacrifice ourselves. And *you* too." The Sikh glowered. Someone whimpered.

"There'll be a change to our second communiqué," announced Anita. "We're the Friends of Asia, but this particular action team," and she smiled acknowledgement at me, "will be known as the Summerfire Brigade. The long hot summer, hmm?"

I heard myself groan. "No, you can't – "

"Why not? It's an honour."

How could I explain the impossibility of ever publishing a book with the title *Summerfire* if terrorists had made the word notorious, infamous? No other title could suit so well; none. That word was bound up with the whole essence of the sequel; was even foreshadowed in *Springdew*.

"Please – "

Anger clouded Anita. "Might you feel identified as a supporter of Asians?"

"Honestly, it isn't so – " What did the fortunes of one novel matter to people who were willing to lose their homes, even their lives, so that their kin could live securely, in safety? Needless to say, hijacking a trainload of other citizens was utterly the wrong way to improve conditions, almost guaranteed to provoke a backlash, to set racial hatred on the boil instead of quenching it (unless of course it shocked the country and the Government towards sanity). Anita and her friends couldn't see that far. I squinted at the scar on her cheek. Instead of merely subsisting in fear and despair, Anita and company acted out of that despair. Theirs was a big despair; mine was a small despair. Yet my small despair was everything to me: my special misery, mine – just as its source had once been my joy.

How exalted Sue and I had been just three years earlier. The fine reviews, the prize, the promises. How full of the future, how confident when I quit my job. "You'll starve," warned my colleagues; and I grinned. They only had narrow horizons. How quickly the money went; then Sue's health had decayed after that terrible bug which never really left her. Insidious new bugs were mutating all the time these days, educated by the antibiotics in food, in so many people's bodies. Allergies were rampant. Britain's farmers were busily breeding diseases. Oh no, we didn't starve. This was Britain, the society of debt, which now I couldn't repay. Oh Renaissance, oh world of *Summerfire*, where had you gone to?

Outside: the Cretaceous wilderness. Inside: terrorists with guns. Events had overtaken. I laughed, surrendering myself and *Summerfire* with relief. Anita regarded me quizzically before heading down to the front of the train.

True to promise, all passengers were herded into the hindmost three carriages, which we occupied to capacity. A member of the Summerfire Brigade stood guard within each; a couple more patrolled the track on either side of the train, with binoculars and walkie-talkies; occasionally we heard footsteps on the roof. A lanky, armed girl called Indira acted as toilet escort. "At least we have an Indian waitress to show us to our seats," said the wit, to chuckles, followed by a stream of threats from our guard, Rajit. No toilet for two hours! The wit became unpopular. And no, Indira wasn't a waitress. No food or drink was served.

Jones had contrived to sit beside me; and it was possible to whisper. He thought I might be of use as a kind of perverse mascot. If only I could put myself in Anita's way, she might give me a guided tour. But she didn't reappear. Our carriage, with its great expanse of glass, didn't become a hothouse. Maybe the Swanson field filtered the sunlight. Thank God no babies or young kids were present. Towards evening billows of cumulus rolled across the west to become a palette for the sinking sun. As light failed, Rajit withdrew to the vestibule between carriages, leaving us hostages alone.

"I'm awfully thirsty – "

"When are they going to feed us – "

Jones stood up. "My name's Captain Andy Jones. I'd advise you all to exercise in moderation. Stretch your legs. Take turns to walk around, but don't crowd the aisle. Be ready to sit down immediately. Don't talk much. I presume our Summerfire friends brought drink and food for themselves, though first they'll be using what's in the buffet car. *We* have to wait for whatever the authorities send down the line."

"How soon – ?"

"Tomorrow maybe. Try to avoid drinking from the faucet in the toilet. It isn't drinking water. Don't want to upset our tummies, do we? Exercise a bit, then try to sleep."

"Aren't we going to try to have a go, Captain? Overcome that Rajit chap? Sneak off up the line in the dark?"

"These people might be amateurs, but they aren't acting stupidly . . . yet. Half will have rested while others are on duty. I estimate there'll be at least twenty terrorists. We could stir up a hornets' nest. Get killed. So stretch your legs then sit tight."

Torchlight glowed intermittently in the vestibule. Now and then a powerful beam flooded through the glass in the partition door, sweeping our carriage, a minor searchlight. I snoozed and woke, snoozed and woke. But I didn't shiver, I didn't twitch.

In the morning my throat was dry and my belly grumbled. Day dawned bright, the Cretaceous uninviting hereabouts, even to its denizens so it seemed. Rajit returned, looking chirpy; must have kipped in first class style while a replacement stood guard.

"Shut your mouths!" he shouted. "You sound like a nestful of little birdies all squawking. I'm the hawk; so watch it."

At noon it happened . . .

Our carriage sagged, groaning and squeaking. The sun beat warm through my window. Outside the vista was startlingly clear; the faint intervening membrane had gone. Voices were shouting. Rajit turned his head; Jones tensed but relaxed. "Oh sod it," he said mildly.

"What is it?" I whispered.

"Swanson field's been switched off somehow. We're in phase."

"What – "

"We're in the Cretaceous. The train, the tracks. They've cut us loose. No giving in to terrorism, eh? We're really here, we're in the past." His voice rose. "They've ditched us."

"What are you saying?" cried Rajit.

"We need to speak to your boss, to Anita. This man and myself."

"Me too?" I asked.

"You're the mascot," muttered Jones.

An hour passed before we were summoned to the driver's cab.

On the way, Jones scrutinized each brown face we passed. No hijacker was asleep now. In the foremost prison carriage an Asian businessman sat beside a black Caribbean: both hostages, eyeing other prisoners nervously. The Asian looked bruised and shaken; I spotted dried blood on his lip. Had his fellow travellers given him stick during the night? Jones noted the litter of empty drinks cans and sandwich wrappers in the buffet as we headed through; he didn't beg for a drink. He was obliged to wear handcuffs for this visit up front. Not me, though. Maybe the Friends of Asia only brought two sets of cuffs in their kit-bags. The other was shackling the driver, a grizzled stocky fellow in his fifties who squatted on the floor of his cab.

"My friend Bernard," Anita said softly. "And the general." She did her best to look nonchalant as she pointed her pistol at him. Including our escort, three other hijackers crowded the cab, one of whom looked sick with worry. He'd been prepared to die; but not for what occurred.

"Captain, actually," said Jones. He introduced himself to the man on the floor. The driver grimaced.

"I'm Dave Cray. They said this could never happen. Fact is, they said it was impossible. A train in the time-tube is a *mass* belonging to the present. Track too; the track anchors us. That's what they said. Said you'd have to take up the track before you could turn the field off. That's how it uses so little power. Once something's in, it sort of sustains itself."

"The field may have a minimum strength it can't fall below, Dave. It might also have a maximum value. Push beyond that, and . . . here's the result. I did hear how some of the research was classified. Obviously it didn't deliver anything very practical. Not much point in dumping people eighty million years in the past if you destroy the transmission system and can never bring them back."

"Never?" grumbled Cray. "This'll be the most overdue service in history."

"Won't it just! Not even the rust will arrive anywhere." Jones turned to Anita, whose face was beaded with sweat. In fact the whole interior was warming up. "Look outside, it's semi-arid. Ten or fifteen miles back, there's water, there are animals. We'll starve and die of thirst unless we all leave now."

"Leave the train: is that what they want us to do? We mustn't do what they want."

"Why should they *care* what we do? We've been abandoned, damn it! The Government refuses to be blackmailed. You know the policy on airline hijacks. Delay, and your hostages will be too weak for the trek, Anita. Stay here and die, or head back to where there's life: it's that simple."

"Surely they wouldn't sacrifice a couple of hundred people – and a train, and the whole track! Just toss it all away! Write it off!"

"I think they might. You'd be to blame, not them. I'm loyal, but . . . the truth wouldn't get into the media. They could open two new Swanson gates to link Birmingham to London. Lay new track. Business as usual in a few months, sealed off from the Cretaceous. They wouldn't put the new line where you could see the old."

"Nobody would travel by Intercity again," protested Cray, "not if you can be lost out here."

"The public wouldn't find out! I know how the news is filtered. The Summerfire Brigade damaged the gates; made the field break down – that's what they'd say. In future there'd be security checks at Intercity stations; screening of luggage, as at airports. You need to get all these people out of here as soon as can be, Anita. I know survival. It's possible fifteen, twenty miles back. You have your guns. There's big game to shoot."

"You suggesting we eat dinosaurs?" asked Cray. "We can't eat bloody dinosaurs."

"They're protein, same as ourselves. There'll be fish, fruit, eggs, nuts." Jones licked parched lips. "There'll be water. You need to form us up and march us, Anita. Forget about the Friends of Asia and all such future trouble. That's millions of years away. We're all in the same boat now. True, there'll be resentments and bitterness. You'll need to remain a brigade till people adjust their thinking. Yes, a brave brigade."

"Commanded by you?" said Anita.

"Advised, only advised."

She grinned as if she had caught Jones out in a fib. "Mr Cray only needs to reverse the train. This is diesel, not electric."

"Didn't you hear the rails buckle as we settled?"

"I did," agreed Cray. "They'll be buggered up. Weight of this train on them, with no proper underpining? Sand and hollows."

"You could drive slowly."

"Naw, we'd derail."

Anita was thinking rapidly. "Why should we lumber ourselves with all of you? Tell me, Bernard, tell me."

I too thought for a while. "Because we're fellow human beings."

This provoked a bitter laugh. "What drove us to hijack you, hmm? Was it was all the fellow humanity we experienced in our own country?"

"You might have firearms," said Jones, "but can you aim straight enough to kill an animal?"

"Maybe we'll take *you* with us. You want to save your own life, eh? As for two hundred people who hate us . . ." She touched her scar. "Why, we'd be murdered one by one. Isn't that likely, Sanji?"

Our escort, Sanji, nodded.

"And we might take Bernard to tell us stories. The tale of *Summerfire*. We can find him a Triceratops to eat."

I was remembering my glimpse of Gorgosaurus. Could pistols or shotguns stop such a monster? Ah, the brigade possessed explosives. Why should Anita invite me to come along? Because I'd been decent to her on the platform, in the carriage? Would I become a kind of jester?

"If it's all right with you lot," said Jones. "I'd prefer to stay with the hostages. Since you won't take responsibility, they'll need a spot of advice."

That was a mistake. "A spot of organizing into your own little army? You're certainly coming with us, Captain Jones. Sanji, tell Abdullah to disarm the explosives; pack them up. Mr Kelly here will carry them. Pass the word that we're heading north."

"Hey, what about me?" said Cray.

"You're the skippr. So you're in charge of your passengers."

"They won't understand any of this. They'll want to stay put."

"Let them. Let them wait for as long as they like. Just don't head north, Mr Cray. We wouldn't welcome seeing that mob again."

I trudged a clear two hundred yards behind the brigade as befitted a bearer of explosives in hot sunshine. Anita didn't want me any closer, but nor must I fall behind or I'd be screamed at. The straps of the heavy bag cut into my shoulders; its bulk banged my spine. This was preferable to carrying my burden by hand for mile after mile. I staggered, slipped in the sandy soil. Summerfire had baked me for a couple of hours as we followed the guideway of the railway northward. Rather than stumbling over sleepers we preferred to keep parallel to the track. At least I wasn't thirsty or starved. Before departure Jones and I received a blessèd Coke and a can of cold baked beans each. We had halted for drinks and chocolate biscuits since.

Loaded with a backpack, handcuffed Jones marched with the main body of the brigade, whose identities still mostly eluded me. Sanji, I knew, and Rajit. Indira, and Abdullah. Oh, and Anita of course. Counting her and Indira, four of the twenty-two-strong brigade were girls. Most members remained nameless faces, me being so far to the rear. What would be happening back at the train itself? How was Cray coping with a couple of hundred thirsty, hungry passengers, who really had no hope of survival whatever? Would they try to straggle south, or just stay where they were? Cruel fate, cruel.

A rushing shadow jerked my sweat-salty gaze aloft: a

pterosaur the size of a vulture drifted overhead on leathery wings, alert for carrion. Well, *this* item of carrion was still moving! Soon there'd be carcasses enough beside the Intercity . . .

Vegetation was growing lusher. Stands of trees, flowers, herbage. Clouds were massing, grey with rain. We didn't need a soaking at this stage. I thought I recognized the poplar groves from which the Gorgosaurus had erupted; and there was a duck-bill, its weather-vane swinging!

Ever so faintly I thought I heard the humming of a train.

Out of absolutely nowhere two grey helicopters appeared. They hovered motionless just above the track, one behind the other. The rowdy growl of engines and swishing thrash of rotors erupted into the silence. A cannon barbette jutted beneath the nose of each, minigun pods under the wing stubs. Rotating towards the brigade, the two choppers surged. Fire raked the hijackers. Dirt exploded upwards, all within seconds.

Throwing myself flat, freeing my shoulders from the bag, I rolled over and over into a dip. I could hear the choppers banking, returning, laying down another hammering of fire. Did a solitary pistol shot crack in reply?

"Anita!" I screamed. For in my mind's eye I had seen the Gorgosaurus of the future snatch her in its jaws, spit her young body out as gobbets.

I lay frozen till silence descended again. Both gunships had landed; then I peered.

By this date, I'm fairly sure what had happened, though naturally the procedures were never explained to me. Over the radio the brigade had already specified the whereabouts of the train – based, I don't know, on the loco's mileage gauge? Thus the relief train, bearing food and drink to the hostages, would halt well short of the booby traps. So as to maroon our train and the track, apparently forever, the Swanson gates were overloaded. Psychologists must have worked overtime predicting what the hijackers would do next. Up-time, doubtless while New Street and Euston Stations were cordoned off, new Swanson gates were hastily installed: gates with a difference, which researchers had devised. As soon as the field was restored those two choppers flew through to follow the time-tube with absolute precision. Unseen from the Cretaceous side, the choppers hunted for the hijackers. Finding us, they hovered; for the pilots could see into the past as clearly as through a window. The command pilot radioed to switch off the field, by whatever new unorthodox means, for a specified length of time. Possibly the fact that the helicopters were airborne, floating free, allowed them to be released then snared again subsequently? The gunships emerged right beside the brigade; and destroyed it.

Including Captain Jones. His misfortune to be in their midst.

Raising my face from the grass to peer, I thought for a moment that my "rescuers" weren't from my uptime Britain at all. Two armed grey creatures with snouted and goggled heads stood examining the carnage. Why were they wearing protective suits? The air was fine to breathe, almost dizzying in its purity. Scrambling up, I hoisted my hands and called out, "I'm a hostage."

Snouts swung in my direction, but I guessed they wouldn't shoot me. While waiting to pounce, they had ample time to suss me out, a white face limping in the rear. Obviously I was with the Summerfire Brigade, yet not of it. And besides, they would need information.

One of the choppers stayed behind in the Cretaceous, no doubt to take command at the train. For the flight back to the present day along the rekindled Swanson tube in the other helicopter, *I* had to wear a protective suit.

Were the biological contamination suit and subsequent sterile quarantine a mere pretext, or a vital precaution? I don't know. Eighty million years is a long time. Viruses and bacteria which were thriving during the Cretaceous could have died out, disappeared, mutated and evolved into something more familiar during all those intervening millennia, just as the dinosaurs died out, just as other creatures evolved. An original Cretaceous bug might wreak havoc in the modern world.

Scores of mice and guinea pigs and monkeys were exposed to the blood of us who returned. So my new captors insist.

I'm ignorant of any details of how the Intercity passengers were rescued, though I'm assured that they *were*. Maybe that's a lie; but I presume that small helicopters carried water and rations to the train, then in threes and fours over several days the hostages were ferried to London and Birmingham wearing those special suits, to be debriefed in isolation and observed . . . and finally released, back to their families?

I was less lucky.

"Now why did these terrorists really name themselves the Summerfire Brigade, Mr Kelly?" asks the intercom for the umpteenth time. Various voices interrogate me from behind the one-way mirror; this one I know all too well.

"I've told you till I'm blue in the face."

"Don't go blue in the face, Mr Kelly, or we'll suspect the worst. Why did you go along with the brigade? The real reason, this time."

"I didn't *go along* with them – I didn't agree with them at all!"

"So why did you accompany them?" Most of the time this is a kindly, patient voice; it can also shout.

"Why was Captain Jones accompanying them?" I ask.

"He was handcuffed; you weren't."

"I'm astonished you could tell *who* was handcuffed, the way those cannons tore the bodies apart!" Oh, I can be defiant, a little of the time; I can also be reduced to begging.

"Do you have many Irish family connections, Mr Kelly?"

"Don't you know already?"

"So why did you visit Caithness three years ago?"

Up at the flat, empty top of Scotland . . .

"We had spare money. Decided to hire a car and drive all the way to John o'Groats." Squandering money on a whim, because the cornucopia had opened – only a small cornucopia, soon empty. Caithness must be where experiments into new applications of the Swanson effect are carried out; hidden away, classified. In the eyes of the authorities maybe I'm not just a sympathizer with Asian hijackers and a possible accomplice of Irish terrorists, but also a spy. Hardly very likely, given my background; though perhaps ever since the Anthony Blunt scandal all art historians are suspect. Questions circle round and round. I know that I've brushed against the edge of something highly secret – and military? – to do with time travel, I presume. Travel, not restricted to the Cretaceous? The Swanson effect must have other possibilities beyond mere Intercity tube travel. Unobvious at first, now of desperate interest.

"When can I speak to my wife?" I ask.

"She's ill. Her nerves. Don't worry, she's being taken care of."

"My daughter?"

"When you've answered all our questions adequately. You might tell Juliette something unwise. So for your daughter's own sake – if you take my meaning . . ."

"I want to talk to my daughter."

"Why such concern? You seem to have lived with them during the last year or so, more as a cover than *en famille*."

No! Juliette had never really whined at me, or been selfish – not excessively so. I thought now of her kindnesses and humour, her *esprit*. The strain I'd been under had been warping my own personality, distorting my vision. I had wronged her. Why should I let some plausible swine tell me that I didn't love Juliette deeply? Or Sue? In ultimate *extremis*, one learns love, and loyalty. Perhaps when it's too late . . .

So I might tell Juliette something unwise?

I'm a writer, aren't I? Supposed to be. When I first returned to Birmingham my grief for *Summerfire* knew no bounds. My own small despair, my special misery, remember? I supposed that I would be released from quarantine within a few days. What else could I do but climb on to my treadmill again, to wear that albatross which had almost fallen from my neck in the Cretaceous; almost turned into a pterosaur and flown away? – except that a novel with such a title had become virtually impossible to contemplate. Oh I grieved, furiously, for Anita. But I'd lost my pet word too, my wretched talisman, which had come to represent the whole book.

Then I decided otherwise. Maybe Anita had given me the greatest of gifts: publicity and stimulus. I must write an account of the hijack: *With the Summerfire Brigade in the Upper Cretaceous*. An utterly honest, writerly account. What other author had walked through that landscape of eighty million years ago, amidst such dramatic events? Surely this would be published world-wide in many languages. Injected with money and energy, I would finish *Summerfire* itself. That novel would soar into orbit on the booster of the memoir.

First I must leave this sterile suite of rooms. Next I need to escape from Britain; but how can I? I'm a hostage still, to the rescue itself; about which I know too much, not least the way the Asian brigade were mown down in cold blood. Even the little I know casts a very long shadow. So how can I be set free?

"Let's give it another spin, Mr Kelly. How did you dream up the word Summerfire?"

Abruptly, as if a light has switched on in my brain, I understand. The questions are clues; discard the redundant, nitpicking ones, and the others fit together neatly. The Government are thinking of offering our immigrant population a journey back in time, a new start, maybe not in the age of the dinosaurs but in some period more recent, say five or ten million years ago if research has made the Swanson effect more flexible.

That won't be repatriation. The people will still all be in Britain! The immigrants will be safer in the past. They can build new live, with aid and supplies. What strains will be relieved! If the Government wasn't thinking along these lines prior to the hijack, surely now it is. The Summerfire Brigade has shown the way.

If the Government had been so thinking, could the Friends of Asia conceivably have got wind of the scheme? Am I a link between Caithness and the brigade? I have no idea what Anita's demands were. Does anyone among the general public know? Maybe the brigade can be presented now not as villains but as heroes, martyrs to this very cause – tooting their kin back in time the way that the Pied Piper tootled the rats of

Hamelin. Presented so, by some ingenious writer? Who knows how the news can be twisted? And after the transfer of population, the Swanson field won't be switched off finally, oh no. Not unless some strange ten-million-year-old bug makes such draconian action necessary.

I feel sick. Oh Sue, oh Juliette, oh *Summerfire*. Oh Anita, oh rediscovered loves and loyalties.

"Well, Mr Kelly?"

"It all started with *Springdew*," I say cautiously. "That was my third novel, the brick, the breakthrough. I wrote it while I was teaching classes about the Renaissance – "

The Beggars in our Back Yard

When I was a little lad, Eugenia Mansion seemed to contain more rooms than I should ever be able to count in a lifetime. Indeed our mansion consisted of a sprawl of some fifty interlinked dwellings of assorted sizes, some modest, some vast. Several centuries had passed since many-times-Grandpop Ebenezer Eugenia raised the first part, constructed of plain timber. Subsequent builders had used stone and brick and marble in a rich variety of styles. Here was a manorial farmhouse tiled with slates adjacent to a chapel with a squat, stumpy tower. Over there, stood a barrack-like basilica accompanied by a soaring campanile. Further along, rose the serried cone-capped towers of a castellated habitat . . .

Paved courtyards, cloisters, and walled gardens punctuated the mansion, but internal corridors also gave access from one structure to the next. Should weather be foul, you could range throughout our whole mansion from end to end on a grand circuit without once setting foot outdoors, and always discovering new rooms, or so it seemed.

Some rooms were tiny and meanly furnished, but many little chambers were far from demure. Other rooms were so large that they had been subdivided. Screens, bookcases, or towering sideboards enclosed extensive rooms within a room. The grandest chambers of all were simply enormous; the Yellow Rose Ballroom could host a gathering of our entire clan, with space left spare. What an adventure for a young boy to scamper through such immensity! What games we juniors played: hide and seek, blindman's buff, colonels and ladies, spook, smugglers, treasure hunt.

Out front, lawns dotted with magnolia trees stretched halfway to the horizon before yielding to a fuzz of hedged kitchen gardens, many of which were whole farms in themselves. In Eugenia Mansion we dined well on bacon rashers fried in sunflower oil with rings of pineapple atop and buttered corn on the side. We ate best bread, hash potatoes, burgered beef. We drank fine aromatic coffee sweetened with brown sugar. It was a blessèd place to dwell, even for poorer cousins.

Beyond the horizon was where our swarthy labourers and house servants hailed from. We employed hundreds of these at the mansion alone. They mowed the lawns and cooked and waited on us and laundered our clothes and kept the many rooms clean and tidy. We didn't pay these servants much heed – they lodged in the attics – and certainly gave no thought to their distant mothers, cousins, sons, or aunts who grubbed a living on remote humble homesteads way beyond the horizon of our lives. We might simply remark with amusement or annoyance on how fazed some newly-arrived servant seemed when faced by the commonest domestic amenities such as lighting or plumbing. We were much occupied with our own family affairs.

And what a family we were! I could pen a saga.

Ebenezer had been such a rough, tough, hard-drinking, quarrelsome critter, though deeply devout on Sundays. Then there were roustabouts such as Diamond Jim Eugenia, and wild ladies of the stripe of Dancing Lil Eugenia. How about financial wizards of the calibre of Rocky Eugenia? Innovative inventors like his son, Ed Eugenia? What famous romances and feuds happened in our house! One notorious quarrel set the entire northern part of the mansion hopelessly at odds with the south for several years till a bloody bare-fist battle on the back lawns settled the affair, though ugly bruises remained. Another colourful epoch dawned when the then-head of the house, "Steady" Eugenia, prohibited the drinking of any intoxicants. Our wine cellar was padlocked for fourteen years; several secret passages were tunnelled so as to supply scandalous parties held in locked rooms.

As the years rolled by and the family prospered, comfort and elegance became a keynote. Adulteries and conspiracies were conducted more subtly and discreetly. Yet the vital, individualistic energy of old Ebenezer always remained in the blood line and forever formed our backbone. That quality, supplemented by his devotion to the principles of honour, loyalty, and good housekeeping. Plus of course, there were our staffs and our wealth-stars.

Let me recall my early schooldays . . .

Thirty of us were seated at little desks in a panelled room. Dust motes, chalk motes drifted visibly where sun beamed through the leaded windowpanes. Some sparkling specks might be pollen from the tall cups full of flowers which we had plucked to decorate the shelves.

"So what is the name for the flag of our house, Eugene?" Miss Mary Eugenia, our teacher, asked me. I had been making eyes at dimpled little Jennifer Eugenia. Long before I grew up tall and passably handsome, already the sexy itch was in me.

"The Stars and Staffs, Miss," I piped. Why, that flag flew from all our tower tops on fête days.

"What is a wealth-star, Eugene? And what is a staff?"

We saw actual stars and staffs every now and then. A banking member of the family might be hurrying along a corridor, clutching some new wealth-star, ferrying it to the treasury. Some house guardian or labour supervisor might be off to sort out a spot of bother, staff of power in his fist. A child took such sights for granted. Facts of life, like the sun and the sky.

Thanks to my favourite uncle, Sam Eugenia, I knew the exact answer to Miss Mary's questions.

"When Eb-en-ezer Eugenia first came here, Miss, there was only a, uh, grove of trees. He cut 'em down, trimmed 'em to logs to build his cabin. The wood was magic wood, Miss, and he'd, er, cornered the market for us all." At that age I didn't quite understand this bit. What was a market without any corners like? Didn't it have any edges? Was it round? I parrotted what Uncle Sam Eugenia had told me. "The wood still sprouted, Miss, 'cause it was power-wood. Staffs grow out of Eb-en-ezer's walls. You can snap 'em off when they're long enough. You use 'em to, uh, hold power over people who ain't Eugenias. The wealth-stars, Miss, they come out of the ends of those staffs now and then – I mean, out of the ones as are still growing. They float off like dandelion clocks. That's to say, they try to float off, 'cept we got nets rigged up to catch 'em. Sometimes a star gets away, an' we lost it. Stars is what makes us rich. It's the bas-is of our econ – econ . . ."

"Very good, Eugene!"

Miss Mary proceeded to repeat the whole caboodle all over again at much greater length; this was the lesson she had prepared. Jennifer gaped at me, and I smirked at her then stared at her chubby knees which didn't really look so different from my own knees except that I knew somehow hers were special, leading to other exciting, only half-imaginable things.

Yes, I could pen a saga. However, while I was growing through boyhood, a strange alteration occurred which couldn't be explained by the changing horizons of a child. The broad wilderness to the rear of Eugenia Mansion began to shrink physically, cramping our back lawns. I remember my Mom and Dad discussing this phenomenon in worried tones one day while the lustres of our chandeliers tinkled.

We lived in a large and elegant room, being direct descendants on the distaff side. "We" was Mom and Dad, my big sister Alicia, and my kid brother Thomas. Dad had screened off a private bedroom for Alicia, another for himself and Mom. Till Thomas came along I had bunked down under the grand piano. Having outgrown that roomy nook, I yielded it to the new baby and transferred to sleeping on the *chaise-longue*. I remember the thrashing I received after Dad caught me peeping through a little hole in Alicia's screen, which I had bored with one of Mom's darning needles so as to spy on my sister at her toilet. I was twelve then, and Alicia was sixteen: a stout girl, overfond of pancakes with maple syrup. Through my peephole I saw her thighs as trunks of white softwood, her breasts as white melons with big squashy pink buttons. It was Alicia who played our piano, sweetly and sentimentally. From earlier years I remember her practising of an evening while I lay beneath the instrument pretending to be asleep, a vain endeavour when the tinkle of notes might become an irritated cloudburst if she hit the wrong keys. I stared up her skirt and petticoats, a little way, in the hope that her footwork on the pedals might hitch those garments higher. I set my sights higher still when later I squinted through the screen.

After Dad had thrashed me I protested, "Aren't we Eugenias all members of one family?"

"What do you imply by *that*, boy?" he demanded.

I should explain that Dad was one of our family doctors. We Eugenias were a hardy breed. Serious illnesses were rare. The last epidemic had been ages ago. Still, old folk die, and babies are born, sometimes with complications. Accidents occurred; somebody might fall downstairs, requiring Dad's bone-setting skills – which was why I felt such a sharp irony, as well as other acute sensations, at his apparent attempt to dislocate my hindquarters. Dad was a great believer in preventive medicine, which explained my thrashing. He inspected and injected all new servants who came to work for us lest they spread any poor person's type of infection. To assist him, Dad could call on two nurses and a midwife as well as the experienced counsel of old Doc Warren Eugenia who had trained him. Dad must soon take on an apprentice doctor to train in turn, just as our midwife, Eulalia Eugenia, was bringing on one of those nurses in the skills of midwifery. I never expected, or hoped, to be Dad's apprentice. A hereditary doctorship wasn't necessarily the best route to public health, as I had heard Dad saying to Mom behind their screen. Certainly the human body interested me, though only certain parts. I always felt squeamish about guts when passing through our kitchens and noticing chickens or rabbits being drawn and quartered, tasty though the resulting fries and pies might be.

Dad's assault had ruffled my pride. True, I felt guilty at being caught out. I experienced a certain moral miasma of shame – had I not dishonoured my sister? – yet I resented what in my boyish way I regarded as an element of illogic.

"What's your meaning, *son*?"

"'Well,'" I snivelled, "everyone in this house is called Eugenia, ain't they? There ain't any Garcias or Fernandos in *our* family." Those were common servant names. "So we're all relations, ain't we? Cousins," I hesitated, "or closer."

Alicia had put in an appearance, robe flung round her, to

see what the thumps and squeals were all about, and why Dad's voice sounded heated. She looked flushed, which lent a rosy glow to an otherwise milk-pudding-like complexion. Perhaps she suspected.

"Don't says 'ain't'," she chastised me. "It's vulgar."

Now Dad really took me down a peg.

"There are medical reasons, Eugene!" His voice became like that of our pastor, Abraham Eugenia. "Reasons why mother shall not marry son, nor father daughter, nor sister brother! What perturbs me is that you should possess so little *initiative*, so little capacity to seek your enlightenment as to these facts outside of this room of ours!"

He meant from other boys, whom I knew to be as much in the dark as myself, on the whole. Dad hadn't troubled to further my own physical education much. Too much of a "busman's holiday" for him? Could it be that he was . . . shy? Aha, the inhibited physician! I visualized Dad requesting a female patient to drape a sheet over herself from face to ankle for decency prior to an exploration of her anatomy. This idea excited me, suggesting to my twelve-year-old mind a way – perhaps – to carry out the vow which I now made.

Right, I said to myself, I shall take your advice. Somehow, some time. I must seek experience. But not in this room of ours, not with you as my mentor nor Alicia as my anatomy lesson.

"Think of your *name*, Eugene!" growled Dad.

One mustn't dishonour the family name. On that score I was then, and continued to be, sincerely adamant. We were respectable nowadays, no matter what capers and antics old Ebenezer and Diamond Jim and Dancing Lil may have got up to. Indeed, the Jims and Lils were part of our legend and thus were respectable too.

"I *am* proud of my name, Dad."

He tutted. "I refer to the meaning of the word 'Eugene'. Good breeding, boy, good breeding! We Eugenias form a big gene pool, quite satisfactorily self-sufficient unto ourselves provided that we obey the Biblical injunctions against . . . against. Against homogamy." This peculiar word stuck in my mind. To this day I'm sure it could only mean "marrying yourself" – an unlikely proposition – so it was hardly a very apt choice. Perhaps Dad presumed that a girl of sixteen would understand less in the way of technical vocabulary than a boy of twelve. By this contrivance he avoided uttering such a blatant word as "incest" in Alicia's hearing.

"Homogamy was the curse of the Pharaohs of Egypt," murmured Dad. "Our dynasty shall not wither nor grow imbecile through homogamous practices. Dr Warren Eugenia has made a deep study of our blood. We are unthreatened provided that young would-be fiancés accept medical guidance, prohibition if need be in rare cases. When your time comes, boy, you should interest yourself in a distant cousin such as, say, Rachel-Jane Eugenia."

I slapped my brow. "That scrawny urchin?"

"Mind your manners, boy! She's a couple of years your junior. Surely she will fill out."

Yes, I thought, to become a beanpole.

"Two years younger," Dad repeated. "The ideal gap. A man should always take the lead."

Hearing this cryptic wisdom, Alicia enquired, "And why is that, please?"

"A question of experience," Dad muttered ambiguously. He eyed me solemnly, man to man, his recent thumping of me temporarily in abeyance.

To an impatient lad of twelve it seems that everything important ought to happen tomorrow or next week rather than years in the future, which was to be the actual chronology for losing my virginity. How does one seek experience in such matters when domestic morality is strict? No doubt this was a perennial problem. Most people contrived to solve it by some clumsy expedient or other, counting themselves thereafter as experienced when they had only, in effect, scratched the surface. And so, inexperience perpetuates itself from generation to generation. Concurrently, awkward love is made and babies inevitably are born. New Eugenias.

Circumstances may have been different in the days of Dancing Lil and other adulteresses! Nowadays our house was circumspect. Not that we boys failed to talk to one another about the mystery of the three-letter word beginning with an "s". Did we not indeed? Thus I soon suggested to my peers, Buddy and Luke Eugenia, the Scheme – which in retrospect seems such a ridiculous charade, yet which may have predisposed me erotically to the world beyond Eugenia Mansion.

Many of our house servants were women: cooks or maids. Some were fat and ugly. A few were younger and darkly glamorous if you put your mind to thinking of cream-chocolate skin and tangles of thick black hair as attractive. We Eugenias ourselves were a fair breed. We were also notably fair as employers, pledged never to exploit a servant beyond the terms of indenture. We boys remained innocent of the unspoken implications of this pledge, concerned as those were with safeguarding our family purity and preventing outsiders from smuggling a moiety of our strength away inside their bodies.

One afternoon, about three months later, Buddy Eugenia, Luke Eugenia, and I crept upstairs to the attics. New servants had arrived that same morning and would be settling in, in the wake of medical inspection by Dad and instruction in their various duties by the house manager, Ezra Eugenia, prior to commencing work early the following morning.

Several circumstances combined that day, akin to a favourable conjunction of the planets. Not that we Eugenias were superstitious – no, we were God-fearing. Yet our family had benefited by seizure of a kind of magical power, the staffs and wealth-stars. Our farm managers generally kept a discreet eye on the placement of planets and stars in the zodiac with regard to planting and harvesting. This rule of thumb percolated elsewhere. The blessing of a wedding would hardly take place on a day deemed inauspicious. When a child was born Doc Warren Eugenia would cast his genetic horoscopes.

Buddy's dad was a house guardian, who happened to have taken to his bed that day, groaning at an unaccustomed and fatiguing grippe. He had placed his staff safely at the back of the wardrobe. While he was snoozing, Buddy borrowed it. I had filched a fairly clean sheet from our own laundry basket, and was waiting in the corridor while Luke acted as look-out. Quickly Buddy and I wrapped the staff in the sheet.

We had seen the new servants: three of them. A wiry, weather-stained little man in raggy trousers and shirt. A tub of a woman squeezed into a ghastly bulging black frock. And finally a barefoot young "beauty" who wore a dress apparently of sackcloth, cinched at the waist by a rope. Slim waist, swelling flanks, slim legs. She was moist-eyed and simple-seeming as a calf is simple, in obvious awe of Eugenia Mansion. By tomorrow the trio would look so very much smarter in their house uniforms. Meanwhile the young calf was naïve.

A few explorations in earlier years, of a daytime when servants were busy downstairs, had taught us the general layout of the attics, and we knew that all males were billetted in the northern sector, females in the southern parts. Each servant enjoyed a private cubby-hole big enough for a mattress and a few personal necessities; quite an improvement on whatever crowded huts they had known previously. It wasn't too long before we tracked down the calf, aided by her door standing open.

She sat on her mattress, playing with her tangly black hair before a looking glass. Smartness in servants was important. A mirror, a comb, a brush, and other toiletries were standard issue. Outside of her little dormer window a white dove perched on the gutter. Was the woman cooing to herself or to the bird?

As we three slipped inside and closed her door she asked us, "*Kay kee-airy oostayd?*" Or something of the kind.

"*Medico extra!*" Buddy announced, amazing us with his smattering. "*Necesario!*" He unveiled the staff and her eyes widened. She knew the meaning of it and could only disobey us at her peril.

While I held out the sheet, Luke mimed how she should take her clothes off behind it then lie down upon the mattress with the sheet over her. I had become fixated on the image of my dad examining female patients blindly beneath a sheet. It seemed to me, when plotting our scheme, that the presence of

the sheet might soothe our own chosen patient in the initial
stages.

Eyes downcast, she did as Luke bid. Screened by the sheet,
she shed rope and sack and lay back with only the sheet for
cover. Buddy used the sprouty tip of the staff to smooth the
linen out then laid the staff behind her, a six-foot ruler.

Kneeling side by side, we three explored her with our
hands. She gasped. She giggled. I encountered what to my
mind was a hairy tarantula spider – which moved. She
squealed.

The door opened. The tub-woman stood there.

"*Basta! Marchesy! Socorro!*" she shouted at us as if those
were our names. Spying the staff, she advanced no further.
Turning, she ran off, calling out incomprehensibly but noisily.

"We better skedaddle," urged Luke.

"Yeah." Buddy snatched up the staff.

His action seemed to release the woman, who dragged the
sheet tightly around her. I tried in vain to pull it from her
grasp. Mustn't leave that. It had our laundry mark on it.

Luke was already out of the room, but Buddy in his haste
had crashed the staff across the doorjamb. I leapt after him,
grappled.

"Touch her, Buddy! Touch her so I can get the goddam
sheet back!"

"Okay, okay." He swung the staff, almost beaning me, and
brought it down on the sheet-clad body. The woman's arms
flew apart. Her legs kicked. I grabbed up the sheet exposing
her.

"Gosh," said Buddy, "look at all of her."

Spreadeagled on the mattress. Her breasts, her loins, her
cleft. My cock was stiff.

"Come on, Eugene! Gotta go!"

Yes, yes . . . Somewhere in the distance the fat woman was
bawling raucously for help.

Within a few hours, needless to say, we three were brought
to book for our misdemeanour. A guard hauled us before the
house manager himself, the snowy-bearded patriarch Ezra
Eugenia.

"Stealing a staff is a serious offence," he lectured us. "You diminish the power of our house. Using that staff to exploit members of a lower class gratuitously for personal pleasure is just as disreputable. I shall leave it up to your fathers to reckon with you privately . . . As to my official punishment, this may strike you as an unusual one. It may seem no punishment at all. Yet it is, it is! To anybody of moral worth it is a harsh punishment. That young woman servant and the older female will both be dismissed from our service instantly. Their simple hopes and ambitions are now dashed. This is what you have done to them by your stupid, selfish action. Think of this, think of this deeply."

I did, oh indeed I did. As did Luke and Buddy. For months we felt like shits, perhaps for years. Long after the memory of our fatherly thrashings had faded, we did our utmost to be moral, sincere in prayer, respectful to sisters and female cousins. We craved all the qualities which made Eugenia Mansion great.

Aside from giving a big nod to Ezra's theory of character formation, I must admit – looking back – that our house manager's harsh justice also served the purpose of ridding our mansion swiftly of two outsiders who, by spreading their story, might have focused discontent amongst the other servants, even hatred. Experienced in handling them, Ezra may have detected early symptoms which he wished to nip in the bud. After all, he had troubled to learn their tongue quite fluently. Consequently I became a laudable adolescent, a rising hope of the house; though in dreams I still saw the big black spider perched where that woman's legs forked, and I itched.

This brings me back to the tinkling of our chandeliers, and the scaring change in our circumstances. This blessèd area of ours was cramping up, to the rear at any rate. The wilderness out back was swallowing itself. What had once been on the horizon was visibly closer. A new horizon had heaved into view.

A strange geological contraction was occurring. The process proceeded gently enough, so that our lustres merely tinkled from time to time. Our walls weren't riven. Plaster didn't crack into patterns of fork lightning. No slates slid from the roofs. Nevertheless, the creepage continued determinedly, dragging the carpet of distance ever nearer. To the rear of our mansion lay a fault line into which the wild backwoods scenery we had formerly known now disappeared, to be replaced by a similar but different topography as the land was sucked under itself.

Our premier egghead, Carl Albert Eugenia, described the process as "plate tectonics" and reassured us that our mansion was in no danger from this geological peculiarity so far as the fabric was concerned, and the gardens and farms out front. Yet there existed a different species of threat to our well-being. Where once open vistas had stretched, now shacks and shanties dotted the fringes of our domain. Increasing numbers of raggy, sunburnt paupers – apparently distant relatives of our servants – took up residence, scratching out strips to plant potatoes and pulses and raising a few scrawny chickens. Their land moved nearer to us. Within a mere couple of years, as Dad had surmised to Mom, we were seeing poor folk, even beggars, ensconced within a few stones' throws of Eugenia Mansion. Those beggars were subsisting on rubbish cast out from our house.

Our pastor Abraham spoke darkly about a "geology of the spirit," whereas Dad was more concerned as to the possible medical consequences.

"What we'll need," Dad said to Mom that day early on in the rolling, slow disaster, "is a sanitary cordon to guard our backside."

Ezra Eugenia advocated far more positive action. He favoured using our power and wealth directly. He led a party of guards and bankers and others out to the fault line which we all referred to by now as "the Lips". Dad was present as medical attaché on account of his views and in case of accident. As reward for my upright demeanour during the years of remorse in the wake of my misconduct Dad invited me to carry his doctor's bag. Indeed, a fair number of spectators tagged along.

This was no long-range expedition. No way was it. Once we

had all assembled at the rear of the mansion five minutes' walk
brought us to the fault line.

Imagine two lips of grassy soil resembling enlarged human
lips (smeared with a green lipstick such as had been fashion-
able for a while a year or so earlier) but extending as far as the
eye could see to right and left. The lower lip, further away
from the mansion, rubbed gently underneath the upper lip,
disappearing softly. All the while new lower lip formed from
the flesh of scenery. Big bushes were swallowed within a
matter of hours; two or three days saw a whole tall tree
dragged down – the rate of suck was greater than the pace of
creep.

At a sign from Ezra, four guards stepped forward. The
guard captain was Buddy's father, Oliver Eugenia, who had
definitely not invited his own son along. I gathered from
Buddy that his dad was still residually sore at the way his son
had filched his staff years ago while he lay sick. On such an
important occasion he wouldn't wish to remind old Ezra of
that unfortunate lapse.

"Let these staffs be planted now," cried Ezra, "to stem this
malign tide in the world!" His voice quavered. He was getting
on in life, though Dad assured our house that the old man was
as sound in wind and limb as a fifty-year-old.

"Thus far," declared Ezra, "and no further! Let the world
roll back to where it was before!"

Pastor Abraham sketched a blessing. The officers tapped
their staffs together to ignite more power; two were already
ribboned in our house colour, silver. In pairs they thrust these
into the lips. The writhing leaves reared out, connected,
formed a sunken bridge of greenery under which a short fellow
could easily have walked. If seen by an eagle high in the sky,
a quartet of toothpicks had been stuck into this thin, never-
ending mouth of the world.

Beggars were peering from the distance, their stance furtive,
faces expressionless. Captain Oliver gestured at them to back
right off, to scoot, take a running jump at themselves.

Slowly the four staffs were swallowed between the lower
and upper lip. They did not withstand the suction, though

they remained upright in their descent. This failure was to extend our expedition far beyond expectations, so what should have been a morning's jaunt became an all-day vigil. As if the earth was consuming their substance, the staffs lost height.

After an hour or so of waiting for this situation to reverse, Ezra conferred with his advisers, Captain Oliver, Pastor Abraham, and a reluctant Carl Albert. Police, Church, and Science. I crept close to hear their debate.

"When the very last inch enters the Lips," stubborn Ezra insisted, "*then* the process will turn the other way."

"Does a child return to the womb?" asked Abraham. "Or a chicken to the shell? Does excrement reform itself into food?"

"We don't wish to lose four good staffs for nothing, Sir," urged Oliver. "Not with that rabble creeping closer every day."

"Fresh new staffs still grow out of Ebenezer's cabin!"

"Not quite so many as used to, Sir; nor so fast. Maybe we're approaching our allotment of, um, this particular resource. Not immediately. Some time in the foreseeable future. A generation or two?"

This was news to me. Dad might already know, but so far as I was aware he hadn't mentioned anything about it to Mom. Other senior members of the family might know. Women and juniors ought to remain innocent of such information. They might fret or panic, even if a generation was ample leeway to come up with a whole range of alternatives. I felt a shudder of responsibility and knew that I mustn't blab about this.

Ezra's next words heartened me.

"Don't forget the large stock of staffs we have in store, Captain."

"May need 'em all," replied Oliver tersely.

Ezra shilly-shallied for another half hour before he gave the order to withdraw the staffs.

How our four guards tugged! Those staffs wouldn't budge. No force could pull them back out of the soil, though the strongest of the guards exerted himself till he fainted and had to be treated by Dad, for exhaustion. The staffs continued their ever-so-slow descent.

At this rate we would need to wait around until late afternoon before the final sprouting inch of each was ingested by the Lips; whereupon Ezra's "last inch" hypothesis would indeed be proven or disproved. Stomachs grumbled. A celebration might have been in order, had all gone well. The outing might have been a picnic, only we hadn't thought to bring any hampers. Finally Ezra detailed *me* to dash back to the mansion and organize packed lunches.

"Bring the food and drink back personally, boy! No servant shall be privy to today's proceedings."

"No Sir, I understand."

Of course, a maid might be peeping out of a rear-facing window right now, aware that something important was afoot. By tonight when our tired employees gossiped in their espagnol, conceivably a garbled version of events could be current in the attics. Conceivably not; Eugenia house affairs were hardly the concern of domestics. But of course we also had beggarly witnesses.

Within thirty minutes I staggered back burdened by chicken on rye, pickles, cold weenies, spare ribs, and lemonade. The picnic which got under way was a solemn affair. Eventually, as the sun dipped lower, the Lips swallowed the last nubs and leaves of our staffs. We waited. No reversal occurred.

"Bankers to the fore," ordered Ezra.

Wealth-stars were produced from satchels. As the bankers flourished those discs enclosing stars, these glowed a ruddy gold in that late afternoon light.

"Wealth-stars concentrate our vitality much more pungently than staffs," declared Ezra. "In smaller compass! Let a star be placed in those wicked lips."

A stooping banker did so. The Lips ate that wealth-star imperturbably and blindly. No aftermath ensued. No convulsion, no belch of wind from the earth.

"Another!"

"Now another!"

"Feed another one in!"

"We're simply stuffing wealth down a hole," protested

Bertram Eugenia, a stout banker approaching middle age. "We're tossing it away uselessly."

"Let this cease, Ezra," counselled Abraham. "It resembles a pagan sacrifice. Next thing, we shall be slaughtering lambs to drip their blood through these lips. When that fails, shall we kill a servant? Finally will we vent the blood of our own girls or boys?"

This shook old Ezra, and he called a halt. Abraham's words about the blood of our boys were to prove prescient in a year or so more . . . We abandoned the attempt, and retired. Yet why should we be downcast? Eugenia Mansion was in no geological danger.

Two consequences stemmed from that day. Ezra soon retired, yielding his position to his deputy, Melvin Eugenia. Servants grew subtly impertinent and a shade assertive, a little too big for their boots. This latter was no real problem. Under Melvin's leadership we were able to dimiss any uppity servants wholesale and hire less expensive labour from across the Lips. What's more, it transpired that we could obtain fresh eggs and peas and watermelons, a whole larder-full of produce, from that direction more easily than if we farmed the stuff ourselves. The better behaved homesteaders in the distance were happy to remain skinny while selling us their crops; though we weren't so foolish as to become dependent.

Brawly beggars continued to be a problem. To keep order along our rear flower border, we bred fierce dogs. For a while we hired the handlers from amongst the beggars themselves on the principle that well-fed ex-beggars made the best moti-vated, most vicious of guards against other beggars. Unfortu-nately these beggarly deputies weren't always too competent. Naturally we didn't dare entrust any staffs to them. A staff might fall into the wrong hands, uneugenic hands. Besides, only we Eugenias possessed the right spirit for handling staffs.

All too soon it became necessary to station a few younger sons of the house on the boundary to advise and organize; then more of our boys, and no longer supervising but running the show themselves. During their tour of duty our boys lived

in tents at the bottom of the lawn. Such service to Eugenia
Mansion – leaving our home rooms, camping out in discomfort
– was compensated by esteem and some privileges on completion. But also . . . ah, my itch . . . the black spider!
Rumour spread of exotic sexual perquisites. Beautiful daughters of the paupers would offer themselves virtually for a song.
Here was a way in which I might combine honour – and a
scratching of my itch.

I must broaden the canvas somewhat. We Eugenias did not
brood overly about distant parts of the planet, but we did have
certain obligations. Away in other lands stood various other
mansions which our ambassadors visited by flying machine,
invented by Ed Eugenia. Those other mansions had in most
cases been founded hundreds of years earlier than our own.
They were more than a little decayed and their families lacked
the vigour of our own clan, not to mention our easy access to
wealth-stars. Uncle Sam Eugenia told me in confidence that
we actually *owned* a number of the best rooms in those other
residences; we had invested in their renovation and refurbish-
ment. The extent to which we had become financially involved
through our ambassadors came as a real surprise to me.
Nowadays we even supplied those foreign houses with puppy
dogs to keep their own neighbouring paupers in check, as well
as to protect our refurbishments.

An obvious career option for such a son of our house as
myself was to become a roving ambassador to those other
mansions. This was no soft option. Aside from the requirement of absence from home for long periods, I would need to
be both ingenious and thick-skinned in order to deal with
r presentatives of those older houses. Such people accepted
our assistance eagerly enough, but they could be pretty
ungrateful about it. Apparently they considered themselves of
superior culture and laughed at our Diamond Jims and
Dancing Lils, usually behind our backs, though sometimes to
our faces. In fact, they were effete hypocrites whose smiles
masked jealousy and ill-will. Supposing that our own beggars
ever became a menace, those elder, allied houses – who were
in their minor way our rivals – might prove totally unreliable.

Here was a disincentive to gadding off to foreign lands in one of Ed Eugenia's machines. Yet I was swayed towards the idea of such service to our house. Sam Eugenia was persuasive. My Dad thought the prospect potentially sick-making.

While I was teetering – still teased by my vision of the spider – two critical events occurred one after the other.

A cousin by the name of John Eugenia was stabbed to death in cowardly fashion while he lay asleep in his tent down at the bottom of our rear lawn. As a result, Melvin Eugenia decided that in future such service on our border should no longer be voluntary. Boundary service must be an obligation shared, though at random, by any younger son of the house. A horoscope machine must be built to select certain birth dates. Boys born on the chosen days would be sent to do beggar duty.

John's sneaky murder appalled me. The possibility of hesitating any longer, and perhaps being ordered to the Lips instead of going of my own free will, pricked my pride. The image of all those available, dusky beggar girls flitted through my mind intriguingly if imprecisely. My uncle had a word in Melvin's ear. Thus I became the last volunteer before the inauguration of the new system. This made me something of a celebrity, at least with the older generation. I might be cut out for great things: a future manager of the house, perhaps. My exact contemporaries, such as Buddy Eugenia, all of whose horoscopes were currently being collated in the new machine, unfortunately viewed me coolly. Thanks to Melvin's edict our younger generation had suffered a souring of the traditional Eugenia *esprit*. Perhaps these once adventurous boys had become scared! I still thought of Thomas as my kid brother although he was into his own scraggy adolescence, by a hair's breadth. Thomas sneered at me, which reduced my Mom to sniffles.

Nevertheless, I enjoyed a fabulous send-off party in our room: me with my newly-entrusted staff of power and my bedroll. On that occasion Thomas contrived to behave decently towards me. Mom had baked her best apple and cinnamon pies. Wine flowed, on doctor's orders. Two score relatives met in the room, and Uncle Sam hung all his attention on my obligatory speech – about duty and such – assessing my diplomatic potential once the present tour of duty had ended. The festive mood was truly capped when sister Alicia stepped forward to say, "I also have a little announcement to make."

Mom and Dad exchanged covert smiles. Bertram Eugenia advanced and slipped his hand into Alicia's.

"Bertram and I are engaged to be wed!"

We all applauded, except Thomas who stared at the fat, balding banker in disbelief. My own heart went out to Alicia in happiness. She was no longer a spring chicken, and perhaps never had been. From so much sitting on the piano stool her bum had swollen to the extent that, if unkindly prankish, you could have attempted to balance a full wine glass on the ledge of her behind. Now Alicia would be fulfilled, and filled with child.

Bertram tilted his glass at me. "Here's to the Lips!" he toasted. Smirking, simpering, he added, "And to other lips too!" and kissed his fiancée fulsomely.

Ah, yes, I thought, to other lips indeed . . .

Blushing pink, Alicia fled to plump herself on that piano stool and launch into our house anthem.

Next morning I departed, staff in hand, sleeping gear bouncing on my back.

Conditions at the border weren't quite as I'd been led to expect. Recently returned veterans must have known that they couldn't tell the whole truth, and be believed. I had imagined myself marching to and fro bold as brass along those Lips with staff held upright. I would mainly be concerned with checking on incomers to our lawns: new servants, or bringers of watermelons. I might escort the garbage detail out into the wilderness and back, ready to apply the persuasive power of the staff if beggars tried to waylay the convoy so as to ransack the rubbish prematurely, or supposing they tried to interfere with our watermelons or new servants. Yet why should they interfere? Wasn't greater prosperity for paupers in the beggars' own best interests too? Didn't wealth filter through to them, if only in the shape of garbage they could find a use for? Of an evening – in my imagination – a maiden (perhaps not exactly a maiden) would creep into my tent. Though I would stay vigilant I would take my long-awaited pleasure, the due wind-down from a day on patrol. Some weeks I might need to patrol of a night accompanied by a trusty colleague, our staffs of power glowing to light our way.

Since John's murder the situation had degenerated sharply.

"Light your way, indeed? Light yourself up, you mean, Eugene!"

I was hunkered near the Lips with Lieutenant Mike Eugenia in a muddy hole deemed an "observation post". Through a magnifying monocle – let's give a nod to Ed Eugenia – Mike was scanning the outlying territory.

"They used to hide and chuck pebbles. Now some of 'em use catapults they've made out of our rubbish. Fancy being hit in the teeth by a stone? Or in the eye, should they be so lucky?" I noticed a purple bruise on Mike's cheek in the shape of a heart. "Boy, when we go out at night we rub mud on our faces, and we don't light nothing." He did look dirty. Ingrained. His fair features were webbed with dirt.

"Tell you another thing: these days we *burn* all our rubbish out there. We conflagrate it. Way out beyond those trees, where the folks back in the mansion won't notice too much smoke."

"If you stop the beggars from laying their hands on useful items and food scraps, doesn't that annoy them?"

"Exactly! Drive the buggers back. Staff ain't much use close up against a little bitty knife blade, as you might have heard." He carried on scanning. "More buggers today than ever."

"Buggers, or beggars?"

"Buggers is what I said, an' what I mean. Can you see 'em?" He passed the glass to me. "Their filth camouflages 'em."

Blobs of mud moved here and there. Some blobs were close.

"They're waiting for our rubbish sortie. Got some kinda elementary organization. That's why we torch the rubbish. Sometimes we torch a shack that's been put up a bit close for our liking, just to show 'em."

"What, even if the occupants are growing watermelons for us?"

"Think you can trust any of 'em? Could be there's a beggar skulking in that shack. We gotta raid shacks, snatch any beggar we catch to tell us some answers, right? I'm talking deep penetration."

A while back I myself had been thinking penetration. I couldn't quite stop myself from asking, "How about the beggar girls?"

"Strip 'em stark first, then you can be sure they ain't hiding no broken glass." Mike was rather an uncouth poorer cousin, though on such one can come to rely.

"I meant the arrangements for, er, entertaining beggar girls."

"Oh we entertain 'em when we catch 'em."

"I mean in one's tent."

"We use a special marquee. An' we keep it guarded. You'll pull guard duty for the brothel tent."

"We're wasting duty hours on guarding girls?"

"*Wasting*? Where you come from, fellow?"

"Eugenia Mansion, same as you."

"No. Not the same as me, not the same at all. I've been here seven months, not seven minutes. D'you even know what a brothel is?"

"I've read family history. Dancing Lil and the roustabouts."

Mike laughed at me as if I was a fool.

A while later I said, "Seems peaceful here at the Lips, doesn't it?" Chirping sparrows were hopping from one lip to the other heedlessly.

"We found the start of a tunnel the other day. Guy fell in an' twisted his ankle."

"Fox hole? Rabbit hole?"

"Yeah. Fucking rabbit." This time Mike's laugh was harsh. "Only good thing about that damn fault line! Buggars can't burrow through the Lips. They'd get sucked under. Gotta cross in plain view if they dare."

"So what was the tunnel for?"

"Ambush."

Next day, I was part of the rubbish convoy escort. As we were heading through shrubbery our point man took a big ball bearing in his forehead. The missile bore a striking resemblance to those from the pinball tables in Diamond Jim's Saloon. Thousand-to-one unlucky chance! – unless the beggars were indeed becoming more organized, more accurate. I heard later how the poor guy, Vince, died in Danny Eugenia's arms. Immediately Lieutenant Mike had half of us plunging through the bushes thrashing about with our staffs till we started a beggar like a partridge. The raggy runt failed to outrun us.

"Okay," panted Mike, "we'll take him to the tool shed. You, Eugenia, Seth, and me."

Our destination was a gardener's shed hidden behind the massive grouping of yews known as the Elephant Hedge. Last century those yews had been trained and clipped, topiary-style, to represent a chorus line of elephants. The bushy beasts were losing their identity, sprouting leaves amorphously. We were too close to the Lips to let our gardeners wander around here keeping the hedge in trim. The shed still contained shears and clippers. Once inside, Mike stroked his staff, making it glow to light the hut. The walls were hung with layers of black-stained sacking.

The beggar stank of sour milk. Mike and Seth tied him backwards over an encrusted wheelbarrow. Mike unhooked a pair of pruning clippers and demonstrated their action on a piece of stick, then he seized one of the beggar's thumbs.

"Hey, Mike!" I protested anxiously.

"Can the shit, cousin. We need some long-term answers." Grinning at the beggar, he applied pressure across the thumbnail. "*Nombre, hombre?*"

The beggar spat at him. I'd never seen or imagined such hatred.

Very soon I had to go outside and vomit up my rations. I could still hear the beggar screaming.

When Mike and Seth emerged they both looked pale beneath their dirt. Blood had sprayed their clothes.

"Senior Sylvano was *el kee-tay*. Diversion, decoy. Lead some of us on a goose chase, leave the others exposed. Didn't

think they were up to such games, fuck it! I guess the rest of
the boys walked into whatever was waiting. Better call everyone out! Lay down some cover beyond the Lips."

"Hey," said Seth. "Double diversion? Swarm over the Lips
soon as we leave off guarding 'em?"

"Hell, I dunno." Mike jerked a thumb at the shed. "You,
Eugene, deal with this, 'bout midnight."

"Take the beggarman into the mansion to stand trial?"

"Senior Sylvano's dead, dummy. Tonight just untie him,
heap him in the barrow, and wheel it to the Lips. Make sure
you squash him in sideways. Don't feed him in feet first or
you'll be there all night. Got it? Now, let's go!"

We went.

Captain George Eugenia called all available guards into the
wilderness to protect the retreat of the garbage detail. In fact
this was already under way. Servants raced the empty garbage
carts along while our boys shoved the servants pell-mell with
their staffs. I saw bruises and a few bloody slash wounds on
our boys. We met up.

"They were hiding in holes with cardboard lids!" reported
Abel Eugenia. "Soon as we dumped the rubbish the buggers
caught us off balance. No chance to set fire to none of it."

"Right," said Captain George. "Back to the Lips at the
double. Get your wounds seen to. Pray the buggers didn't
wipe shit on their knives."

The beggars weren't swarming across the Lips – not this
time, anyhow. Once we were safe I requested permission to
speak.

"I've an idea, Sir. Why don't we use one of Ed Eugenia's
flying machines to give cover for the garbage sorties? We could
drop burning oil from the sky on the rubbish, and on the
beggars too."

"Ed's marvellous machines fly too fucking fast, Sonny. We
might drop oil on ourselves."

"Oh," I said.

"You give me an idea, boy. Next time weather's dry and
wind's from mansionwards we go out with torches and burn a
wide break through the wilderness all the way to the dump."

"Yip-pee!" cried Seth.

"Fire could spread a long way, Sir," said Abel. "Could burn the shanties of the good buggers."

"Tough."

"Teach 'em to organize some fire drill," sneered a voice. "Get a decent water supply on tap."

"*That*", said Abel, "would worry me, Sir. Make 'em even more organized, it will. Not just the buggers but the home-steaders too. Could drive those into the buggers' arms."

Captain George brooded.

"Sir," Abel continued crisply, "I should feel that today's sacrifices had been contemptuously devalued – if we could have travelled open ground all along. I'd remind you, Sir, that the buggers are using catapults now. We need that veg for shelter. We got to learn how to slink through it just like a bugger. I'm talking special operations, Sir. I'm volunteering."

"I'll think about it," said George. "Meanwhile don't start no fires, 'cept at the dump."

With a hideous sense of unfamiliarity I remembered my send-off party, Alicia playing our anthem. Already Eugenia Mansion was a foreign world. In the course of a few days it was is if I had become another person. This eruption of memory made me feel as if I had been possessed momentarily by a stranger. That domestic reverie was brutally erased by a different memory, of pruning tools, and of the task I must carry out that night with the wheelbarrow behind the Elephant Hedge.

Midnight finally came.

Sylvano had mainly had his fingers and some toes pruned by Mike and Seth before they gave him the *des-kabel-yo* across the throat; for that, they'd used a grafting knife. I could imagine worse mutilations. Yes, now I could begin to imagine worse. Untying Sylvano, I pretended he was a pig. Upending the barrow, I tore down some of that supposedly soundproof sacking as a shroud, and heaved the wrapped pig in. I had to pick up bits and pieces of his little trotters. Laying my illuminated staff alongside the bundle, I wheeled the barrow out unsteadily into the night.

At the Lips, I spilled the barrow on its side, dumping the pig lengthwise; then I pressed down with all my weight. *Don't get your hand caught*! I thought to myself a hundred times. *Don't*! Press the pig down gently, firmly.

The process took about an hour, then I scooped out the scattered trotter pieces and dropped them through the Lips, which were still open.

Hardly had I trundled the empty barrow thirty yards in the direction of the shed than a voice cried out behind me. Ice clawed my groin. Somehow the butchered body had crawled out! A dark shape lay twisted. It jerked, scrabbled, clawed. The voice whimpered. Surely that of a girl, not a man? Snatching my staff, I sprinted back.

A beggar girl had been sneaking across the Lips. In the dark she hadn't seen that the Lips were parted. Her foot had plunged between them. A raven-headed beggar girl, dressed in her best, her gladdest rags. Was she sixteen, seventeen?

"Please help me!" she pleaded. "I'm trapped." She spoke our language well, though with an accent.

Her skin smelled of soap and perfume. Violets, I believe. Scavenged scents! I tried to pull her clear but tug as I might I couldn't release her foot. She babbled briefly to herself in her own tongue. Prayer? Curse?

Should I use my staff for leverage? You can't lever open the earth. I'd snap the staff. She couldn't be in too much pain, otherwise she would be screaming. Imagine a leg, a living body pulled through the rollers of a mangle. She was certainly in panic, clutching at me now, begging.

Run for a doctor? Fetch Dad from the mansion, and a saw? Cut off her leg at the knee? That would be . . . the betrayal of young beauty. Better to be sucked down entirely till even her thick tresses of hair vanished like some exotic black fern withdrawing underground. In the wake of the corpse of Sylvano, sharing the same earthy tomb! How long would she coexist with the dead beggar until she stifled? Abominable.

A wedge, a wedge . . .

"Let go of me," I ordered.

"Daren't," she moaned. "Don't want to drag you down, Sir. Listen: cut off my foot. Save me."

Better, kinder to wriggle my hands around her throat and throttle her first.

A wedge.

I *had* a wedge nearby. The wheelbarrow was made of stout metal. It tapered at the front.

"I can stick something in the Lips to widen them! Ten seconds to fetch, that's all. I promise."

Her hands relaxed. "So I trust you. Be true." How brave of her.

Quickly I fetched and upended the barrow, began thrusting it down alongside her leg with my force. The Lips distended to incorporate the barrow too. As this bulked larger in the gap, within five minutes I was able to haul the girl free. By now sweat dampened her skin and lanked her hair. The smell of soap and violets was accompanied by that of fearful, urgent flesh, sweetly acrid. Her rag skirt had ripped.

I supported her weight.

"Can you stand? Can you walk?"

"Not easy . . ."

"Where were you going to, *Sin-yor-eeta*?"

She told me that she had been heading for the brothel marquee to offer herself for service.

"What else can I do?" she asked me. "I say to myself: maybe I can snare the heart of a good man. Maybe I can be adopted and cross over for good! How I hate the life back there. What future, what hope of joy? My heart is snared now, by you who saved me. So brave, so generous, so strong. I can be generous too, not reluctant. You have my heart."

"What's your *nombre*, *Sin-yor-eeta*?"

"It is Conchita."

"Listen, Conchita, forget the brothel." As yet I hadn't brought myself to visit that place. "Let's hobble to my tent. I'll take a look at your ankle." Oh yes, oh yes indeed.

Strip 'em stark, Mike's voice nagged in my mind, so you'll know they ain't hiding no broken glass.

It proved unnecessary for me to strip Conchita. Murmuring thanks, she discarded all her rags inside my tent. I let my staff of power stay aglow till morning. As for my own stubbier staff of flesh, that only wilted the better to spring tall again. With it, at last I plumbed the spider till I knew it utterly, and yet knew that I still had more to know.

Maybe I exaggerate. After an hour of passion I was exhausted, utterly emptied out. When I woke at reveille, Conchita was sleeping warmly against me. Maybe she too was worn out, by the peril at the Lips and then by my lips. She certainly hadn't stolen my power-staff and run away. Nor had she finessed a knife or shard of jagged glass.

I tried to imagine last night's uninhibited amour in the context of Bertram and Alicia, or myself and cousin Rachel-Jane, or most any Eugenia, and failed. How to preserve Conchita for myself? For her own sake too? How, as she quaintly put it, to adopt her?

As I got dressed, fancies ran through my mind. I would beg permission to visit Eugenia Mansion briefly to fetch a fine, stylish dress for her to wear. I would request a compassionate furlough to escort Conchita to our room to meet Mom and Dad. Now that Alicia had gone to live with Bertram, her area was vacant. I would tough it out! I wouldn't be ashamed. Perhaps a less formal solution might be preferable: a token job for Conchita, a cubby hole in the attics, with myself as her visitor. After kissing her while she slumbered – and stirred and turned – I headed out for chow and duty.

". . . So what should I do?" I asked Mike as we were tucking into hash browns and bacon in the mess tent. I felt ravenous.

"That's why we have a brothel tent," he said derisively. "That's why we take our turns with the girls. Keeps your sense of reality, boy. Keeps you from foreign enchantments. You should turn her over to the brothel. We'll see what she's like."

"I'll kill anyone who – "

"Oh shut up. Passionate, is she? Where did she learn? Don't tell me you taught her last night, eh?"

"She must come from crowded circumstances."

"Ha! D'you suppose she watched you get rid of the body? Pretended to stumble? Made believe she was trapped – so as to trap *you*?"

"She was stuck! She would have died."

"Shit, just what we need. Your very own pet bugger girl. Better keep her out of sight, Eugene. Better take her lots of chow. Buggers are always hungry. Go on, heap a plate. Take a pot of coffee. Then it's out on patrol for us."

"Thanks, Mike."

"You poor fool."

He couldn't quench my feelings.

There isn't a lot more to tell. Oh, only the most consequential events of all.

How loving Conchita was! How deeply interested in me. I was her new life, and she needed to know everything about that life, both as regards Eugenia Mansion and our duties out here at the Lips. Her own background couldn't have been too vile, else she would hardly have learned our language so fluently. She had picked it up, so she said, from her father who had once been a servant in our house; hence her aspirations, hence her dreams. She didn't wish to dwell on that background.

How naïve all us guard boys were, at heart. Even Mike accepted Conchita for what she seemed. Invited to my tent, he met her and was captivated despite himself. Indeed, the strange thing was this: she *was* as she seemed. She was love and hope and joy.

She was also something else: a spy for the beggars, no less, an agent of their secret organization.

One night, worn out by garbage escort and deep penetration, I was loved to extinction by Conchita. Even so, in the midst of the night I was awoken. I think a mouse had run across my face, but I imagined that her fingers had tickled me.

'Conchita? Love?" Beside me, was emptiness. Silence. I lit my staff and found myself alone in the tent.

Dousing the light, I sat waiting cross-legged. Waiting and

waiting. Compelling myself to stay awake . . . until at last the canvas rustled and revealed a shape and stars before falling back. I brightened the staff and discovered her.

"Oh! I went out to relieve myself of water."

"No, you didn't. You've been gone much too long."

"A night patrol was about. I didn't wish them to . . . take me by mistake, you understand? So I hid a while. Shall we make love, *kay-reedo*?"

A veil lifted in my mind.

"You crossed the Lips, didn't you, Conchita? You went to talk to the buggers to tell them all you've learned."

Suddenly a knife was in her hand.

"Yet I care for you," she whispered. Or did she mean that she would take care of me, fatally so?

I staggered erect and leapt at her. We struggled. Did she seem to turn the blade away from me? She gasped. When I stepped back the blade was sticking in her heart. I'm sure that I had not forced the knife into her. Maybe, as our bodies collided? She stood a moment longer, gazing at me, and smiling – yes, smiling, as if with true love. Anguish distorted her face and she crumpled, fell. It was I who shrieked like a night owl.

That smile before death . . . I could not understand her foreign heart. After I buried her in the Lips she was ever on my mind. My mind could not plumb her depths even if my widowed body imagined that it had succeeded in this quest.

I grew careless on patrol – unless the buggers had become more cunning thanks to Conchita. I walked into a booby trap. An innocuous patch of leaves hid a cruel metal contraption cobbled together from scrap which we ourselves must have dumped. Jaws snapped my ankle, lacerated my shank.

While I lay feverish in my tent waiting for the bone to set I was sometimes haunted by an image of Conchita personally setting that trap. but at other times I saw her stepping upon it herself and being dragged down into the ground until she stifled hotly as if pinned under a heavy body.

Once I was well enough I was invalided back to our home

room in the mansion to complete my recovery. Dad grumbled at the standard of medical repair being carried out in the field and predicted that I would always walk with a limp. In wintertime and damp weather I must expect to feel twinges. Mom tried to cosset me, at which I rebelled. Thomas regarded my walking stick with contempt mingled with grudging enthusiasm – I was a bit of a hero, after all. Alicia visited and announced herself pregnant already. I would soon be an uncle, a prospect which made me feel as if my life was ending, not beginning. Complacently matronly, Alicia sat at the piano and played lullabies. I thought of my dark, fiery, dead love. Sam came and exhorted me to become an ambassador.

"I don't see what's in your heart, lad. But I know you need to get away."

I nodded. "You're right."

"You'll need some training first. I'll see to it myself. I'm sure you'll do our mansion proud."

"Peg-leg Eugene," muttered Thomas. "Our greatest ambassador ever."

"Why not, boy?" barked Sam. "He might be remembered like – like Diamond Jim."

When I first flew up and away over the mansion in one of Ed's machines, at the very start of our journey we passed above the Lips. Fleetingly I glimpsed how far the situation had worsened in a few short months. Trenches disfigured our rear lawn. Beyond, patches of wilderness were on fire.

A hideous thought occurred to me. What if, during my absence, Eugenia Mansion was overwhelmed by the beggars? I imagined hand-to-hand fighting from room to room, from sector to sector. I saw our library gutted by fire, bodies in corridors, looting and rape, staffs broken or discharged, wealth-stars squandered. Might our servants betray us too?

Exposed to so many fine rooms, such furnishings, such a treasury of wealth-stars, would the beggars not feel overwhelmed by our worth? By what we had wrought in the years gone by? Would their spirits not be moved to generosity? Or might they only smash and ruin and drive the surviving

Eugenias out to till the wilderness, reduced to the same circumstances as themselves?

I remembered Conchita's last expression but one. No shadow of doubt lingered in my mind. Hers had been a radiant smile of genuine – though postponed – love. The love that taketh away. The love that strips naked . . . the clothes, the skin, the soul.

From the Annals of the Onomastic Society

Melvin Twelves surveyed his audience there in the library of Hardley Hall, emitted a few throat-clearing coughs as if in imitation of Lady Hessleforth's poodle, and commenced.

"New names. *New names*," he said portentously. Picking up a phone book from a nearby bureau, he thumped it down on to the lectern.

"Ablitt, Abolins, Aburto, Aindow, Ainscough," he declaimed, then gripped both sides of the reading stand. If the fat, fussy fellow hadn't been dressed in a loudly-checked suit and mulberry bow tie – his notion of a posh lecturer – he would have resembled some vicar of old, invited to preach before her Ladyship in her own home, and who had chosen for his text interminable lists from *Chronicles* in the Bible. ("And the sons of Ram the firstborn of Jerahmeel were Maaz, and Jamin, and Eker . . ." *Et cetera, et cetera*.)

Melvin riffed through the wafer-thin pages.

"Breukelman, Brevetor, Brimacombe, Bumpsteed!" he proclaimed. "Oh the endless wealth of names!"

Already several members of our society were eyeing him quizzically. The Reverend Pendlebury was pursing his thin lips as if detecting a parody of his own Sunday morning performances. Chubby Sally Wigton, who actually worked for Telecom, compiling the phone book, wore a frown.

"These particular examples might not truly be unusual names," allowed Melvin, "though I suspect they are, I suspect they are. My point, my thesis, is simple. And I think it is revolutionary."

Elegant, silver-haired Lady Hessleforth smiled tolerantly. She was wearing a powder-blue silk gown and a discreet diamond necklace. Generations of her kin had lived in Hardley Hall. She could chart her own ancestry back, with only a hiccup or two, via William the Conqueror to the seventh century. Compared with which, revolutions were such trivialities.

"The Spontaneous Emergence of Names," said our speaker. "There's my title, there's my theory. How come there are so many weird names in the world, as well as all the ordinary ones? New names must be emerging spontaneously; that's how. Indeed I believe this is a key to the so-called population explosion – "

With a sinking feeling, and to avoid accusing eyes, I let my gaze rove round the library, taking in all those volumes bound in brown, golden, and red leather, or yellow calf; the rosewood furnishings and panelling, the red and gold Indian carpets, the gilt-framed ancestral portraits. Overwhelmingly this was a golden room, though some chairs were of black leather.

Mr Twelves proceeded to talk dross.

No, not dross. Lunacy would be the more rigorous description; eccentricity, a polite term.

"A new name sprouts – and bingo, here's another family on the scene. God, for want of a better name, is creating new persons complete with phoney backgrounds. Society swallows these new individuals as if they're real. Indeed, they *are* real; they firmly believe in themselves. Reality, my Lady, ladies, and gentlemen, is being adjusted to allow this situation – "

Haldane Smythe, one of our professional genealogists, had stuck up a hand in protest but the speaker ignored him.

"Twaites, Tweddle, Twemlow, *Twelves*: when you come across such a name, you're coming across someone who only came into existence recently, someone who is equipped with a whole false history which fits into the newest crack in reality. *Not*, I hasten to add, in such a way as will distort the major currents of history. For when did a Tweddle or a Bumpsteed or a Twelves ever feature in the history books? Such persons trickle into existence in the corners of the world, simply fattening out the population somewhat, enriching the host of names.

"I, my Lady, ladies, and gents, believe that *I* am such a person who has spontaneously emerged in the wake of my name. Let me explain my thesis in some detail – "

He twiddled his bow tie. This was Mr Twelves' hour of crackpot glory. I, God help me, had allowed it.

Lady Hessleforth inclined her head at me and winked. *Not to worry*. Well, maybe we should regard this occasion as a cabaret act, entertainment by a clown . . . Our lady president and patron could be fun as well as generous. She wasn't notably prissy or snooty.

It's really incredible, the wrong assumptions some people will make.

"Onomastic," of course, means "pertaining to proper names." From the Greek, *onoma*. In the ranks of our Onomastic Society we numbered several genealogists, half a dozen amateur tracers of family trees, a topographer – who was interested in place names, from which family names so often derive. Then there were a linguist and a historian from the university, which is home to the Surnames Survey; some teachers, a couple of librarians (myself included), not to mention Jim Abbott who compiled computerized mailing lists, Harry Wise who supervised the electoral register at the council offices; and sundry other devotees of names. Principally, names of people: origin, meaning, distribution.

Melvin Twelves, a fairly recent recruit, worked in the town museum in a humble capacity.

As a group we weren't stuffy or threadbare. Thanks to Lady Hessleforth's sponsorship we didn't need to meet at some room in the College of Further Education, or the like. We hired a plush private suite in the Grand Hotel, conveniently close to a rather decent bar, where we would let our hair down somewhat afterwards.

Perhaps this touch of luxury led to misconceptions.

We'd chosen a name for our society which we thought had a certain eighteenth-century cachet to it. During the first few months of our existence I was approached by one chap who was convinced we must be a gourmet dining club, dedicated to mastication.

Another well-heeled enquirer implied that we might perhaps be practitioners of – how shall I put it? – the sin of Onan in the Bible. Perhaps we were interested in masturb . . . no, I shall not write that word. Say rather: mutual bodily self-expression. This . . . connoisseur . . . appeared to envisage medically safe manual orgies in our hotel suite.

A young coin collector contacted me too; one of those treasure-hunting vandals equipped with a metal detector. Sorry, lad, that's numismatism.

What we enjoyed once a month at the Grand were lectures followed by question time; and I should have thought that by now Melvin Twelves would have gleaned some of the fundamentals of the name-game. Apparently not.

Melvin Twelves was one of two enthusiasts who joined at our meeting back in April. The other was Mr Chang, who had learned of us through the Surnames Survey and contacted me beforehand, as did Twelves. I had taken to screening new recruits by means of a little interview, though this wasn't exactly out of forelock-tugging deference to Lady Hessleforth. Not at all. She laughed merrily when I related, in the bar, the stories of the coin collector, the gourmet, and yes, yes, even of the onanist who imagined he had discovered a sensual salon to suit his taste in safe but perhaps exhibitionist sex. (Naturally, I phrased this euphemistically.) No, I simply didn't wish our meetings to be disrupted by the ridiculous, any more than I would have wished to see Superman comics shelved next to Shelley. A secretary has duties.

Melvin Twelves was under no misapprehensions as to what onomastic meant; his peculiarity only emerged subsequently.

Mr Chang, on the other hand, remained a bit of an enigma. Possessing a Chinese name, nevertheless he didn't look especially oriental. What race did he belong to, or what mixture of races? I really couldn't tell. His bland sallow face hinted at a medley of origins. When he spoke, his English was slightly slurred though verbally precise. Mr Chang claimed he was in exporting – though the exporting of what? And why should this lead him to the office of the Surname Survey? He would sit silently in our meetings and would hardly chat much afterwards in the bar, where he only drank fruit juice; but he would smile benevolently. For a while I had him figured as someone who was waiting for our real purpose to announce itself – for us to produce a snuff-box of cocaine or whatever – as if all our talk of names was merely code. Before long I decided that he was simply lonely, shy, and enjoyed our company, so I mostly forgot about this witness in our midst . . .

Melvin was going his ends, linking everything possible together in true conspiracy-theory fashion.

"The eminent scientist Fred Hoyle has stated that atoms of hydrogen come into existence spontaneously in the depths of space – in a sufficient number to fill up the gaps as the universe expands. What's more, the whole original universe may have emerged out of nothing at all. This phenomenon is known as a vacuum fluctuation . . .

"The Creation Scientists in America explain that if God indeed made the world a few thousand years ago, He surely placed all those fossils in the rocks at the same time, so as to give the world a consistent history – "

I noticed Chase Daniels, our Mormon genealogist from Utah, nodding and wincing simultaneously. Probably wondered whether he was being satirized.

"God named things," said Melvin, "and those things duly appeared. *And God said, Let there be light; and there was light.* The word caused the event. Why shouldn't the creative force name new *people*? Why shouldn't these people appear like lots of hydrogen atoms – we're mostly water, aren't we? H_2O. Why shouldn't this force provide fossil memories and records to back up these new people? Obviously these people would possess rare and weird-seeming names – "

Disgruntlement warred with waning courtesy on the faces of his audience. Lady Hessleforth, for her part, looked vastly amused, to my relief. Her Ladyship possessed a centuries-old pedigree. Well, everybody does! But, unlike her, the majority of people have no idea what it consists of. Whereas our Melvin was demonstrating remorselessly that he could claim no pedigree whatsoever; that he had sprouted up like a mushroom overnight . . . through a crack in reality.

It was Melvin who was cracked.

An orphan? Brought up by a succession of foster parents? Heavy feeling of alienation? Impaired sense of reality? No doubt! And now at last the stupendous rationalization by this cuckoo: he was *unique*.

As he took pains to explain, thousands of other people must fit into his category. However he, uniquely, had decided that individuals with odd names were being created out of nothing, along with their appellations.

Did Lady Hessleforth anticipate some such fiasco? It was her suggestion that for this special anniversary gathering at Hardley Hall our keynote speaker should be eager Melvin, a member with no obvious onomastic qualifications beyond his unusual name and his enthusiasm. How democratic this evening would be; more of a celebration.

Was Lady H playing with us, laughing behind her slender, ageing hand?

All previous lectures at the Grand had been much more strictly onomastic. Though not without humour and brio! Have I said that Chase Daniels was assigned to the Surnames Survey from the Family History Library in Salt Lake City? Chase told us all about the massive project by the Genealogical Society of Utah to microfilm records of names worldwide. Parish records, crumbling Hindu shrine registers, elegant Chinese *fang-chih*, oral recitations by Pacific islanders and West African *griots* . . . He described the atom-bomb-proof granite vault in the Utah desert. He enlarged on the "extraction" of names, the auditing process, the baptisms of the dead by proxy in batches, the pressures from the Mormon "Maoists" who wished to save as many souls as possible as quickly as could be, lest their names and their souls were lost forever . . .

Our historian, Jack Brakespear, spoke about the ways in which new names were adopted in the past (and Melvin definitely could *not* have been listening). In Britain the Norman Conquest stimulated the use of hereditary surnames.

Mainly these were borrowed from birthplaces or job descriptions or might be nicknames or even insults. Since most people were illiterate, such surnames soon mutated wildly. In Japan the Tokugawa Shoguns, in their amiable wisdom, prohibited any mere peasants from owning surnames for two hundred years on pain of swift decapitation by a samurai blade. After Commodore Perry had elbowed his way in, millions of farmers vigorously invented surnames at random, resulting in over a hundred thousand such, the biggest bonanza of any nation. From the 1780s or so European governments compelled Jews to adopt surnames rather than patronymics. Often wistfully, Jews took their names from animals, towns, or nature. The first Mr Rosenblum probably lived in a dingy urban ghetto. That was Jack's spiel.

"But," explained Jane Chapman on a subsequent evening, "names also die out . . ."

Perhaps this was dodgy territory. Lady Alice Penelope Diane Hessleforth had presented his Lordship, now deceased, with two daughters but no son; her adolescent grandchildren did not bear the Hessleforth name.

The De Montfort Suite was richly curtained, with a peacock motif. The carpet was mock-Chinese, with dragons; the seating upholstered in brown leather. On one wall hung a huge dingy oil painting of cows grazing a water meadow while a thunderstorm brewed. A Swiss cheese plant did its Jack-and-the-beanstalk business from out of a terracotta urn. The atmosphere was more that of clubland than a conference room. Most of us nursed a glass of something sustaining.

"By 1974," said portly, tweed-clad Jane, "the American Social Security rolls listed one and a quarter million different names. Yet of this wealth, nearly half a million were held by single individuals!" Her glossy black hair was tied in a bun. Like a beauteous barge was she, to coin a phrase.

"People marry – and a name dies out." (Her Ladyship fanned herself.) "Or else people fail to marry, with the same result. But the principal mechanism for extinction is known as *pedigree collapse* . . .

"Every pedigree is shaped like a diamond. Going back in

time, this expands to embrace thousands of individuals. However, more and more common ancestors crop up on the different lines of descent, for the simple reason that cousins close or distant mate; I mean, marry. Thus the pedigree narrows again . . .

"These diamonds move through history, overlapping and fusing, merging. Why, if one single nomad from Asia visited Africa in the ninth century, today every Chinaman must be closer than fiftieth cousin to every living African!"

Providing that said nomad had mated.

It must have been round this time (not the ninth century but during Jane's lecture) that Melvin, quite disregarding the creativity of Jews and Japanese and British peasants, conceived or misconceived his theory about the spontaneous emergence of names.

I spotted Lady H speaking democratically to Melvin afterwards in the bar. At the next month's meeting she made her hospitable offer regarding our up-coming anniversary; and Melvin's eyes lit up. With, I now thought in retrospect, the light of lunacy.

I had arrived at Hardley Hall in my old green Volkswagen, giving a lift to Chase Daniels. A solo Mr Chang was paying off a taxi as we drove up. Also arriving, chauffeuring a beaming Melvin, was Lady Hessleforth's Jaguar. Guest of Honour treatment indeed; Lady H was gracious. The gravel forecourt already housed half a dozen vehicles belonging to our members. The August sun was painting clouds as it sank slowly, gilding parkland, casting long shadows from oak trees.

In spite of its name, Hardley Hall had nothing scanty about it. An original quadrangular medieval manor had grown into a Tudor, then a Georgian mansion. The east wing edged against a lake. To the rear, lawn and topiary gardens led to an adventure playground and nature walk. The converted stable block was home to a vintage bicycle museum and tea rooms. Ten miles from the city, Hardley Hall was open to the public, and even hosted hoverboat championships attracting competitors from as far away as Sweden.

Lady H hadn't exactly fallen on hard times. The surrender of a single Rembrandt had settled the death duties when her husband died. Simply, any stately home in its right mind soaked the admiring public for all it was worth. A modern version of peasant tithes, perhaps!

Inside, was opulence: oil paintings, tapestries, marble staircases, a great hall with hammer-beams of sweet chestnut, chinoiserie mirrors, ormolu candelabra . . . and a butler, Rogers, waiting with a tray of sherries. A white poodle yapped at us.

"Gosh," said Melvin, ignoring the dog. He wasn't so overwhelmed that he wasn't gearing up to overwhelm us.

"Gee," agreed Chase. "Reeks of history, right?"

Mr Chang smiled faintly, and indicated the great chandelier illuminating the entrance hall. A hundred diamond-shaped lustres sparkled in concentric skirts of crystal.

I remembered Lady H relating how Hardley Hall had been electrified back in the 1890s. Essential to replace the oil lamps and candles, but the then-Lord was loath to rip up fine floorboards. So therefore . . .

"He bored holes at either end of each room." Her voice had tinkled when she told the tale. "He tied flex to the collar of a ferret, and popped it down one hole. A groom placed a piece of rotting rabbit by the far hole – and hey presto, we were wired up so quickly."

Had I detected a subtle callousness in this anecdote? Did she view our earnest study of names and lineages as an equivalent to the gawping of the unaristocratic crowds at art works and furnishings which they could not possibly possess, yet which their ticket money helped subsidize?

"The separate pedigree diamonds dangle down," said Mr Chang. "Yet the same electricity unites them into one incandescent mass."

Was this some foreign proverb? If so, it hardly made sense, since numerous light bulbs were mounted in the array, nor did the lustres melt together.

"So many different diamonds," said Mr Chang, "and all the same."

Well, that was true enough, otherwise the chandelier would have looked a right mess. His revised proverb made rather more sense, but what was he driving at?

"Thus," concluded Melvin in the golden library, "I am what I am." How philosophical. But was this the philosophy of Wittgenstein – or Popeye? Or Sartre – or Loony Tunes?

"I have no pre-cendents." He grinned daftly, perspiring. "I am unprecedented. How many more are there like me, filling up the world with their new names?"

So at last he ended his crazy speech and sat down, expecting applause.

Lady H obliged, which obliged me likewise. Many felt under no obligation. Jack Brakespear looked furious, Chase sad, Haldane Smythe disgusted.

Then Mr Chang rose to his feet; he who had never so much as raised his hand before to ask a question.

"I have a statement to make, your Ladyship, my friends . . . With respect, Mr Twelves is not only wrong. He is so far wrong that you can hardly imagine how wrong."

"Oh no?" called out Jane Chapman, eyebrows hoisted.

Mr Chang eyed her. "Mrs Chapman, you once spoke on the subject of names dying out . . . the pedigree diamond, marriage of cousins, the inter-relatedness of everyone on Earth. Names are doomed to die out faster than any new names are coined. All diamonds will converge – just as the races of humankind will converge physically. Only one surname will survive; which of course will be Chinese."

"Eh?" from Jim Abbott.

"Why Chinese? Even now there are a billion Chinese people – a sixth of the world's population or so – and they only share a meagre five hundred surnames between them. Ultimately these surnames must swamp all other surnames, and then drown one another – until the last Miss Wu weds a Mister Chang, and everyone on Earth is named Chang for ever and ever."

"Come off it," growled Harry Wise. Oh he'd be mindful of the horrors of compiling a register consisting entirely of the same name repeated thousands of times. "I thought *marriage* was supposedly becoming obsolete? More and more people keep their own names these days, don't they? Specially in America, hmm?" He glanced at Chase – who fidgeted. What price the future of the genealogy project and the salvation of unique souls under Chang's scenario?

"Children of any union generally only bear *one* surname," said Chang. "If they do take a double-surname, this process of hyphenation can hardly be extended to their own offspring without absurdity. Thus fashions in marriage make no difference."

First, Melvin had told us that he was spontaneously created from out of a void. Now Mr Chang claimed to possess the only name in the world – of the future. Lady H looked bemused. She couldn't possibly be responsible for this new twist of the screw of buffoonery.

"The history of a thousand years is as nothing at all," Chang went on. "Nor the history of a thousand generations, either. Think of a quarter of a million years, think of a million generations."

Lady H's eyes hardened. How could a thousand and more years of proven pedigree be swept away so glibly?

"Why Chang?" Her voice was brittle. "Why your very own name, *Mister* Chang?"

"Because, your Ladyship, I come from that future a quarter of a million years ahead. I am from the *mono*-onomastic society where everyone is a Chang. There's no one who isn't Chang. We are the Chang Race, we are Changkind!"

"Whatever next?" sneered Jane.

"Preposterous!" cried Jack.

However, others seemed inclined to play along with this latest foible. Oddly, after Melvin's parody this afforded some relief.

"Does everyone look exactly like you?" asked Sally merrily.

Chang pivoted. "No, there are still variations: of size, of hue, of body type. We are not all clones of one Chang, be clear about that. We are as various as the cows in a herd. Ask any of your farmers on that score! We are Mary Chang and

Abdul Chang and Heinrich Chang and Yukio Chang and
Natasha Chang. A world of ten billion Changs. Ten thousand
million."

"I guess you needed a vacation," joked Chase.

"You have a mission, Mr Daniels. So do I." Chang patted
the pockets of his suit. "I came back in time to gather a million
true surnames. For yours is the epoch where the diamond of
names is widest. I have these names now on microleaves."
(*What were they?*) On my return I shall liberate these names.
We will rename ourselves. We shall be free from the psycho-
social uniformity of Chang. The mono-onomastic society will
fracture fruitfully – "

"Hang on a minute," protested Harry. "Why didn't all you
Changs merely consult past records? Archives? Registers?"

"Old phone books?" suggested Sally. "Though maybe you
don't use phones . . ."

"Old mailing lists?" chipped in Jim Abbott, getting into the
spirit.

"Cultures rise and fall," Chang told them. "Data buries
data. Records are lost, erased, obliterated. I speak of a quarter
of a million years. Nothing survives from your time: no
pyramids, no Parthenon, no works of Plato or Shakespeare,
no memory of your days, no history. I have plunged far into
the past to find this hoard of names."

Jim asked, "I suppose you'll be taking the works of the
Bard home with you too?"

Chang shook his head. "All his references are incomprehensible in my time. I take names, only names."

"But you can understand Shakespeare."

"No one else would, in my world. After long and special
psychological preparation, I have been able to assimilate
amongst you. And I thank you for your hospitality, one and
all. Ladies. Gentlemen. And Lady Hessleforth." He sketched
a bow, then moved towards the French windows. Outside, the
lawn had grown grey with dusk.

I had been watching Lady H from the corner of my eye all
this while. Affronted surprise had given way to amusement,
then to something resembling shock.

"Wait," she quavered, "is my name one of those you are taking home?"

Chang grinned. "Perhaps."

"Seems a whole lot of trouble to go to," said Jim. "If it's new names you want, why not just invent a barrelful? Make 'em up?"

"Not the same," said Chang. "No pedigree."

High time to conclude this farce. I stood and clapped for attention. "Friends, friends, your Ladyship, members of the Onomastic Society: this has been a wonderful charade. It's All Fools' Day in August. It's Hallowe'en. It's masquerade time. But really . . . nobody can travel a quarter of a million years through time – any more", and I directed a cautionary glare at the wilted Melvin, "than they can pop into existence from out of nowhere. So let us laugh, and call this little carnival to a close. Well done, Mr Chang! Well done, Mr Twelves. At our next meeting in the Grand on September sixteenth we shall have the pleasure of a visit by William Monkton, author of the acclaimed *French Nicknames* . . ."

Chang opened the french windows on to the stone-flagged terrace. A flight of steps led down to the glooming well-shaved grass. Illumination from the library diffused so far, no further. He crossed that terrace, descended those steps, walked out across the darkening turf . . . And vanished.

Surely he had simply put on a spurt of awesome speed and sprinted off into the topiary, which hid the adventure playground beyond . . .

He would have needed to streak like the fastest greyhound ever, to flit like a hummingbird, one moment there, one moment gone.

"Bloody well disappeared into thin air, he did," said Sally. "I swear it. Pardon my language."

Nearly all of us had crowded to the open windows.

"He's gotta be out there," said Chase.

"Manifestly he *isn't*," said Lady H.

"Hiding in the hedges," I suggested.

"You know that he couldn't possibly have reached them."

Who was I to argue with her Ladyship?

"What Mr Chang said . . . it was *true*," marvelled Sally.

"It was all *true*." A chorus.

To his credit, our Melvin took this up-staging in his stride. Maybe the derision which greeted his own performance had finally sunk in.

"I suspected him all along," said he. "And I jolly well flushed him out, didn't I? Chang just couldn't resist contradicting me."

Lady H relapsed into the nearest seat. She surveyed the gilded portraits of her ancestors, and murmured:

"Did he really take my name with him?"

Melvin bustled to her and vulgarly patted her slim, well-bred hand.

"I'm sure he did, your Ladyship. I'm sure he took all our names, Hessleforth, Twelves, Brakespear . . . They'll all spontaneously emerge quarter of a million years in the future. Fair's fair. Only right and proper. There'll be, ooh – " he was performing a computation in his head: ten British billions divided by one million – "there'll be ten thousand Hessleforths scattered across that future globe, in Europe, in Africa, in Asia – "

Lady H shuddered. Ashen, she jerked her hand away.

"That isn't *pedigree*, Mr Twelves. Don't you understand anything? I was asking Mr Chang because I *didn't* wish my name to be . . . taken . . . in vain!"

Fearing for the future funding of our meetings at the Grand, I hastened to raise my sherry glass in which a few drops remained.

"On this our anniversary, may I propose a toast? To the Onomastic Society!"

Lady H fixed me with a beady stare.

"Which one? Ours – or theirs?" However, she gestured for the decanter which Rogers had left on a rosewood writing desk. Melvin hurriedly obliged. Lady H needed that sherry to steady her nerves.

She drank. We all drank. A bond was re-affirmed; a promise renewed.

When we foregathered in the De Montfort Suite a month

later, her Ladyship was present as usual. And so our society listened to Mr Monkton discoursing upon French knickers. *Nicknames*, damn it. Nicknames. Sobriquets not soubrettes. Lady Alice Penelope Diana wore an attentive smile throughout.

I always say there's resilience in the old blood.

Lambert, Lambert

You must be finding your present situation pretty odd, eh? Bear up, pal! Chin up. There's company awaiting you further on inside.

Why *me*? you're wondering. I took pity on you, see. Yes, pity! I decided to save you.

'Course, once I started doing this trick of mine I developed a certain appetite for it, as you might say. I won't go so far as to call it a craving. If I craved, could I control myself, could I choose my customers? Could I ration myself sensibly? Whatever my girth, I'm no glutton. No addict, me. I feel a definite *relish*; that's about it.

Listen up, lad, and you'll understand. *What's in a name?* asked the Bard. Quite a lot, I do believe. To a greater extent than chance can explain, people's names can be unusually fitting. I'd go so far as to say that in a good many cases the name maketh the man.

Take me, Bert Brown. Blunt and solid, eh? Bert Brown could hardly be a violinist or a philosopher. He could be a bus driver or a postman. In my case, a prison camp guard. Right? You agree? Only my pals inside know differently.

Oh you'll meet them just as soon as I do my trick the next time, and you get squeezed within. Interesting company! Your sort. The people they put in these camps are usually interesting, at least when they arrive and for a few months afterwards. Then they stop being so interesting. Lack of the old brainfood, eh? Gruel and thin soup, scabby veg and stale bread wears them down.

You're still able to peep out. When that stops, you'll meet the others. Oh I can talk to them or just listen to them nattering but you can't yet.

By "inside" I'm not of course referring to the electrified fences, the rows of huts. I'm talking about *me*. This here is my standard orientation lecture. How thoughtful of me to provide one! Well, it calms you down. Otherwise you might thrash around and give me a spot of indigestion, as 'twere. You might unbalance me a bit; though for a fact that would take some doing! I'm carrying ballast, chum. You need to appreciate what a kindness I'm doing you. I'm sure you're catching on, you're getting there.

Where were we? Oh yes, my name. Bert's a useful sort of moniker to have these days. Doesn't attract attention; doesn't mark a fellow out. That's how I see it. It's a name, if you'll excuse my humour, lacking any colour.

But thirty years gone by, my Mum and Dad named me *Lambert*. Lambert Brown. That's what Mum always called me when I was a nipper. "My little lamb, Lambert!" "Lambkin Lambert." "Where are you, Lambkin?" She stopped that caper as soon as I started fattening up. Problem with the glands, right? Soon I became bloated Bert, who got bullied at school. That's what makes me sensitive; that's how I can sympathize with people like you. Then I got a bit too big to bully.

Mum actually took the name from an old encyclopedia that was lying around. Chap called Lambert Simnel attempted to seize the throne of Britain back in the time of Henry the Seventh; he got chopped for his pains. Lambert Simnel was named after a Saint Lambert, a Billy Graham type who also got the chop. Belgium has lots of churches in his honour. Belgium: mayonnaise and chips. I know things, see. It's the company I keep.

Not a very good track record so far for Lamberts? Mum didn't care much about history; it was the little lamb aspect that appealed to her. She was like that: of diminished I.Q. Dad too, I suppose, though he must have been a bit brighter because he pissed off. Presumably I get my brains from him. Simnel's some kind of kraut cake. *Very* fattening. I used to eat a fair whack of rich stodgy cake when I was a kid. I don't now. I'm very stringent about my diet.

Stop twitching, will you? Won't do any good. Think about the word *lam*. Means to thump, to trash. That's what goes on inside the wire. Beatings. My fellow goons like to cut a prisoner out of the herd now and then and work him over. At random, when the fancy takes them. Nothing systematic. If starving doesn't get you, a thumping might. You're finished after that.

Commander doesn't mind. Relieves the strain. They're all missing persons in there, to begin with. If someone becomes more missing, who cares? He certainly hasn't done a runner. No inmate gets through the high-voltage wire or the auto-guns. So, pal, you won't be missed. No one's looking for you.

I mean, that applies across the board to all the prisoners. They can forget any silly notion of help from some other country – which is where it would need to come from. From America or Russia. But every country's in a mess. Sea level, economic collapse, heat, famine; need I go on? We have this country sewed up tight for a long time to come. Count your blessings. I feel sorry for people like you.

"Lam" also means to escape, to beat it. You're on the lam now. Thanks to me.

All comes down to names, doesn't it?

I was working as a debt collector in Leicester. See, I could intimidate people. That's where I discovered about my name-sake and felt such a strong yen to join the penal service. Not surprising, huh? Best job these days. So many nuisances being rounded up. Pinkos. Greens. Poofters and wogs. Domeheads and arty-farties. All the stirrers. Got to belt up about stuff like freedom and politics and art if this country's going to survive the greenhouse. Doesn't really require as much exertion as sticking one's bod in some pensioner's doorway; not with all the control equipment at our disposal. If goons want to work up a sweat thrashing a detainee, that's their business. I don't join in. Other fish to fry. Not that I'm easily exhausted, by the way. I'm a tireless fellow.

Same as my namesake. My double! Right: chap name of Daniel Lambert. The fat man of Leicester.

Found out about him when a hailstorm chased me into the museum. Hail the size of bloody golf balls, shooting down at machine-gun rate, bouncing as high as a bus. Several people were killed that day. Old folk, babies in prams. Windows shattered all over. The climate's all screwed up and that's a fact. Anyway, the museum was showing Lambert's clothes and other memorabilia.

He was born in the year 1770, and his Dad ran the House of Correction, the Bridewell prison. This Bridewell wasn't for your murderers or forgers or thieves who were bound for the noose and the gibbet. No, it housed people who had committed what you might call moral offences against society. Debts, drunkenness, vagrancy, that type of thing. You ought to know about moral offences against society, hmm? They're what landed you in the camp.

In his earlier days Lambert's Dad was huntsman to the Earl of Stamford. His uncle was gamekeeper to the next Earl and his grandad on his mum's side was a famous cock-fighter. Thus young Daniel grew up real sporty. Swimming, fishing, riding to hounds, hunting otters, fighting cocks. 'Course, the countryside wasn't any distance from the heart of the city back then. Oh he loved the sporting life. Pinkos like you did your damnedest to spoil all that. Still, what does it matter nowadays?

With all that exercise, our Dan became a powerful fellow. Could carry quarter of a ton without any fuss. Could kick seven feet high, standing on one leg. Once he thumped a whopping dancing bear owned by some Froggy entertainers. You see, they were performing in the street outside the gaol when the gaol dog went for the bear, and this Froggy in charge unmuzzled Ursa Major to let her kill the dog. Felled her with one blow to the skull, did our Dan. The bear threw in the sponge.

Dan's folks apprenticed him to the button trade in Birmingham. To learn die-sinking and engraving. Must have seemed a bright idea at the time. A few years later, fashion turned topsy-turvy. Out went buckles and fancy buttons. And it was a time of unrest: the factory burned down in a riot. So Dan returned to Leicester, Dad resigned from the Bridewell, and his boy took over as keeper.

Boy, am I saying? Dan started putting on weight at a swingeing pace. (Could it have been the lack of sporty exercise, running a prison? Not to mention the glands?) Wasn't too long before he weighed in at nearly fifty-three stone. Measured three feet round each leg, and nine feet round the body. When he was sitting down, his belly buried his thighs to the knees. His legs were pillows almost smothering his feet. The flap of his waistcoat pocket stretched a foot across. Special clothes for him, special chairs more like sofas.

One remarkable fact was how healthy our Dan was. When he finally died, most likely of a heart attack, at the Waggon and Horses in Stamford where he'd gone for the races, they needed to demolish a wall of the inn to get him out in his coffin – he was putrefying fast. But up until then, not a whisper of frailty! Dan could fair trot upstairs. He could outwalk most fellows. He'd teach kids to swim in the river Soar – he could float with two grown men on his back. Never caught a cold in his life, even when he used to come in soaking wet and sleep with his window open then don the same damp clothes in the morning. He never snored. Never panted. Perfect bronchials. His voice was a sweet, strong tenor.

I'm a lot like our Dan Lambert with regard to health and vigour. Additionally, he was a very *nice* bloke. So am I – as you must agree – saving you from slow starvation! Really considerate to the guests in his lock-up, he was. Humane? Benevolent? Why, he was a byword. Departing prisoners sometimes wept with gratitude.

But in 1805 the magistrates decided that such prisoners as those would be better employed labouring in the town's factories. So Daniel's job came to an end; though not without an annuity of fifty pounds a year for life for him, freely granted as a mark of esteem.

Alas, fifty pounds proved insufficient to his needs. That's why our man-mountain began to exhibit himself to the curious. Either that, or hide in his house! Such was the fame of his bulk, people would knock on the door on any pretext.

In the main, the exhibiting down in London went off really well, since our Dan was such a damn decent fellow. More like a king of men holding gracious court than a freak. Thus there was nothing ludicrous about the occasion when the largest man in the world met the smallest man – a Polish dwarf named Count Borulawski, whose missus used to pop him on the mantelshelf as a punishment when she was feeling peeved with him. A single one of Dan's sleeves could easily have provided a whole suit of clothes for the Count. This was a meeting of two civilized prodigies. Ah, civilization's taken a downturn since those days, hasn't it just?

Dan's head was perfectly proportioned, by the way. No bloating or grossness about his face! A normal, handsome head was simply dwarfed by a giant body.

Do I hear you enquire as to his diet? Simplicity itself! Quite Spartan. A single dish at a meal, and he only ever drank water. A little like the menu in the camps.

I can tell you, how little he ate came as a revelation to me. Did he convert the whole of his modest intake of food into flesh, a hundred per cent? Didn't he ever crap or pee? Seems as how all of his bodily secretions were quite normal! So where did all of his bulk come from? Out of thin air?

You've heard the old saying as to how inside every fat man there's a thin man crying to get out. Do I hear you crying right now? Don't bother. Wipe your sobs away. Adjust to circumstances, that's the ticket.

Let's put two and two together tentatively. Soon as our Dan becomes boss of the gaol he puts on stones and stones of extra weight without any evidence of gluttony. And he liked his prisoners; he was good to them.

Could he have been so kindly disposed that he *liberated* his favourites – by engulfing them? By absorbing them into himself? Now there's a fine way to solve overcrowding in prisons! The gaoler becomers his own private gaol.

Ah, but magistrates back in those days were finickety. They kept count. Had ledgers and lists. Families enquired after prisoners. Creditors bore them in mind. Prisoners didn't merely disappear, as nowadays. Once you're behind the wire now, it's do-as-you-please.

Let me tell you, it pleased me very much when I absorbed my first prisoner. (Pleased me for his sake too! I was saving him.)

Dan Lambert inspired me. But it was me myself, Bert Brown, who cottoned on to the trick. The cottoning-on was a leap such as bloody Einstein made. Fourth dimension and all that. That's where you all are: stacked behind each other in another dimension inside of me. Soon as I cottoned on, I could do it.

Quite a party's going on in here. You're busy debating, arguing, telling your life stories. Making friends and quarrelling. Comforting and entertaining one another. Drawing up manifestos, playing games, composing poems. And not worrying at all about starving or thumpings. All courtesy of big Bert Brown. Lambert Brown.

Naw, not *you* yet. I've told you, you need to wait till I absorb someone new; that's how it works. I grab one of you spindly types, one that I fancy, take him somewhere quiet. I wrap myself around him, I engulf, I crush. And into me goes the personality – after the ritual. Eating some liver, heart, and brain; right. Fair's fair; gives me a spot of extra nourishment to fuel the procedure, very like what I gather savages in the South Seas used to get up to. Only, I do it properly seeing as how I understand about the fourth dimension I'm putting you into.

I'm sure Dan Lambert didn't do my trick, but I think there must have been *something* a bit four-dimensional about him, don't you? Four dimensions squashed into three. If everything possesses four dimensions the way Einstein said, then that includes food and drink. Your ordinary run of geezer only uses three dimensions; that's all he can take. A Dan Lambert could digest the fourth dimension of food too – that's how he got so big on so little. There's the explanation.

Me, I'm a step beyond our Dan, aren't I? Good thing for you I am! Welcome to the family. I'm really expanding wonderfully within. It's an education, all these new persons inside me. Henry and Crispin and Alec and Mohammed and Rasta and Lucian and Tony, ooh a good thirty lodgers by now with plenty of room for expansion. More customers pouring into the camp every day.

I wouldn't have thought I had it in me! But I do. I can contain multitudes; could be my very own prison camp.

Actually, so as not to keep you on tenterhooks, I think I'll take another stroll inside the wire pretty soon, stomp into a hut, haul out a nice face; then it's off to somewhere special and get down to business. My fellow goons don't know what they're missing.

All this hard graft of *thinking at you* is fair working me up an appetite.

Tales from Weston Willow

The line-up of ales in the Wheatsheaf Inn wasn't too impressive, so I settled for a bottle of Satzenbrau. Nor was the decor much to speak of. Outside, the pub was old stone, but inside it was tatty modern. Over the bar hung a joke "Texas flyswatter" fully three feet long. Beside the darts board dangled a nude pin-up calendar from the local garage. A joke clock ticked off the time backwards, its numerals arranged in reverse order. Polished brass shell cases lined one window ledge, darts' and skittles' trophies another.

More congenially, the Wheatsheaf resembled a large living room for an extended, garrulous family of villagers. I soon found myself in conversation with a stout, grey-haired woman in her late fifties. She wore dark glasses. A harnessed labrador lay snoozing by her seat.

All *I* had said to her was, "May I share this table?"

"You'll be Mr Campbell from Manor Cottage?" was the reply. She chuckled as if she could see my surprise. "Anyone can hear the Scots in your voice. So who else could it be?"

"Word travels fast. We've hardly been here a week, Mrs, er . . .?"

"It's Prestidge. Mrs Prestidge. I hear you're an author as well as being a history teacher."

"Well, I've done a couple of detective stories set in the eighteenth century. The last one was about a jewel theft: *The Rape of the Rock*."

"What name do you write under?"

I sighed silently. "My own."

"You'll find our village *interesting*, Mr Campbell."

Ominous words. I noticed how some of the locals were watching us with interest. One hairy fellow grinned at me. Nodding in Mrs Prestidge's direction, he tapped his head; signifying that she was wise, or that she was a bit batty?

"Let me tell you about Charlie and his wife Ann, who moved here from the city."

I didn't wish to be rude. Quite soon I was riveted . . .

FOXED

"Charlie was a jogger. Now, you don't see too many pavements here in the countryside, and the roads can be a bit narrow and twisty, but Charlie kept up his jogging. Every evening throughout the summer, and on Saturday and Sunday mornings too, he could be seen in his russet tracksuit completing his six miles. He would head out of the village by the road to Briarley, then cut across a field footpath and down the rutted green lane to the edge of Red Ditch Farm. From the farm he trotted along a ride through Neapton Wood owned by the Forestry Commission, all flanked by firs, to Thumpton Pool where a girl once drowned herself, but that's another matter. From Thumpton Pool a bridleway took him back into the village for a welcome shower. His trainers were usually filthy by then. He needed to buy several pairs.

"In the autumn, the darkening of the evenings forced him to limit his running activities to weekends. We don't have many street lights, you'll have noticed. To compensate, Charlie would get in a game of squash most afternoons before driving home. An accountant for the Heritage Hotels group, that's what he was. Of a Saturday and Sunday he sometimes went round his familiar course twice. Winter brought a bonus. The ground hardened. Running was much easier now along the formerly muddy stretches.

"With winter, too, came the Hunt. They meet at different likely villages around the county, not more than twice at any one place during the season, though that's not to say you don't see huntsmen and women passing through on horseback more often, or pulling their horseboxes behind their Range Rovers if they're from further off. When they meet here, it's in the car park outside. The girls from the Grange serve the trays of sherry. Oh, the crisply jacketed fellows and ladies on their expensive hunters with tightly plaited crests and tails! Young girls on ponies too.

"Neither Charlie nor Ann cared for hunting, nor thought it picturesque. It was with a sense of righteous annoyance at the tetchy pomp of many of the riders that Charlie watched the Hunt set off from the village that Saturday morning, then himself set out at ninety degrees to the route of the hunt for his customary run.

"Charlie had passed by Briarley and was jogging along the green lane when he heard faint halloos coming closer. He saw hunters leaping a distant hedge, the dogs racing ahead of them across the bare brown soil of Red Ditch Farm. In the next field which was a pasture, sheep were panicking, and maybe one or two of the silly muttons would stifle to death in a ditch; but the Hunt would pay up. Did you know it costs the price of a smart car to kill a single fox by hunting, and often as not it gets away? Though sometimes it's broken-breathed, a shadow of itself. You always pay for what you do, Mr Campbell.

"As the dogs neared the barns there came a check and a casting about. Presently, as Charlie jogged on, the quarry itself popped through a gap in the hedge along the green lane. Charlie paused. The animal halted in the middle of the lane. It flicked a glance at Charlie as though he was an irrelevance to it that day – but he wasn't – then stared sharply back the way it had come, panting. Its tongue hung right out. As though the animal had all the time in the world, it squatted and loosed some droppings. Maybe it did so out of fear, or to lighten the load. Or maybe for another reason! Huntsmen admire the patience and pluck and quick wits of the fox. I heard one tell a farmer he could no more shoot a fox than he could strike a woman. Another saw a vixen bring her cubs on to his lawn, and the huntsman put out food for them. In fact he gave the fox family the choice of a dead kitten, a dead pigeon, and a stale loaf. Would you believe, they all went for the loaf? Oh yes, hunting folk feel affection for their clever quarry.

"This particular quarry darted away through the opposite hedge. Not wishing to be trampled by hunters crashing across the lane, Charlie picked up speed to a full sprint. As he was rounding a bend he glanced back and spotted foxhounds wriggling through the first hedge. These checked again. For some unaccountable reason the lead dog gave tongue and began to lope his way. The other dogs followed, yapping.

"Charlie realized that he must have trodden in those fresh fox droppings and was now laying down a strong fresh scent. This amused him. He was in no danger, being recognizable to any foxhound for what he was. He could give their poor prey a head start – if the idiots followed him far enough!

"Running as fast as he could into Neapton Wood, he diverted from his usual route down another ride. Behind, the dogs cried. He could hear the muffled pounding of horses along the green lane. Beyond the Forestry plantings was the parkland of Marston Hall, a great undulating sward where mature oaks, sycamores, and chestnuts grew. Charlie didn't know, but Marston Hall is the home of the Master of Foxhounds, the Honourable Jeremy Brett. Scaling a five-bar gate, Charlie ran for the nearest trees. He fancied that their leafless lower branches might knock a few unwary riders off. Pausing briefly, he saw the dogs fanning out behind. The Master's horse took the gate in its stride, followed by others. Of course, the Master saw Charlie – the man pointed with his whip.

"The foxhounds checked again. They snuffled and clawed at a hole in the ground between tree roots. Could it be another den, with a new scent? While the dogs stooped, and one younger hound tried to squirm into the earth, Charlie took the chance to put more distance between himself and the Hunt, though by now his heart was pounding. But for the fact that he was gasping through an open mouth, he would probably have gritted his teeth with determination.

"As he breasted a rise, a horn blew, and riders pointed to where he was. They gestured at him, seeing him for what he was, yet now urging the hounds on. The riders drummed on their saddles and shouted. Hounds raised their muzzles to proclaim a deep, throaty music.

"As the pack flooded down the rise behind him in full cry, Charlie spotted a tree which he could scramble into.

"He pulled himself up, from branch to branch.

"Moments later, the pack reached the tree and bayed around the base, rearing, scratching.

"Recovering his breath, Charlie laughed at them.

"The core of the Hunt – those horses which had stayed the obstacle course – soon arrived at the tree. The flushed faces of the riders remained curiously blank, as though Charlie wasn't there at all. Some riders patted and slapped their steaming mounts, but no one said anything. No one quite looked him in the eye.

"Then the red-coated Master stood up in his stirrups and, reaching, he grasped Charlie's ankle."

"Ann saw the Hunt return through the village. A young girl rode proudly beside the Master. Ann was disgusted to see blood smeared on the girl's cheeks. She had been blooded, a custom which Ann thought had died out.

"Instead of riding past, the Master dismounted at their gate. Doffing his riding cap, he strode up the front path.

"'Mrs Fox,' he said when she opened the door, 'I'm afraid there's been a terrible accident.'"

"Is Ann still living here, Mrs Prestidge?"

"What do you think? She moved away. There's others who haven't ever moved away."

"Wait a bit. Didn't Mrs Fox call the police?"

"No need. We have our own constable right here in the village, Mr Tate."

"Yes, but – "

"Poor Charlie died of a heart attack, didn't he? All that running wasn't good for him. That's why he tumbled out of the tree."

"But you said . . . And the blood on that girl's cheek!"

Mrs Prestidge chuckled. "If only the dogs could have known his name, what would they have thought?"

Her glass was empty. Likewise, mine.

"Can I buy you a drink, Mrs Prestidge?"

"Rum and black, please."

I elbowed through to the bar for her rum and blackcurrant and another bottle of the German lager for myself. The skinny, hyperthyroid landlady – I gathered her name was June – winked a bulgy eye at me.

"Having a good time, love?" As if I was in the process of picking up Mrs Prestidge, who was almost old enough to be my mother!

I contented myself with saying, "Fascinating."

I set the rum and black in front of my informant, who heard the clink of glass, and sniffed, and thought, then cautiously reached and captured the drink.

"Cheers, Mr Campbell." She sipped. "And some," she repeated, "did not leave here at all."

"Such as Charlie Fox?"

"Oh no, I was thinking of Paul and Ruth Andrews down at Centre Point, and of course their daughter Julia too . . ."

CENTRE POINT

"'I always thought that Centre Point was a building in London!' Ruth joked to the secretary of the Women's Institute, who had called round. Ruth and Paul were still in the midst of moving in to the huge old ex-vicarage; the last few tea-chests weren't yet cleared.

"The stone building dated back to Tudor times. With the departure of the most recent vicar, the Church Commissioners had put the unwieldy edifice on the market. When a new vicar arrived to take up his duties, he would live in a neat little bungalow. Until then, Archdeacon Hubble – who had retired to the village from Cambridgeshire, to an imposing rose-clad house in two acres – was taking services in St Mary's. Paul had grand ideas of converting the house to include a couple of independent luxury flats as well as their own domain.

"Mrs Armstrong had said to Ruth, 'Welcome to Centre Point.'

"'We're almost on the edge of the village,' Ruth pointed out.

"The visitor smiled, 'We have our centre point, too, and it's here.'

"'Oh, do you mean in the sense that the church is a centre of village life? So therefore the vicarage – '

"'Not really,' Mrs Armstrong said vaguely. She peered through open doors. The former vicarage had huge rooms with high ceilings and two enormous oak staircases front and back. To Ruth's eye one particular dark patch of ceiling above the rear stairwell looked almost perversely inaccessible.

"'What'll you be doing with this vast house then, Mrs Andrews, since you only have one child?'

"From the first moment that the Andrews arrived in the village they had become accustomed to friendly, though searching questions.

"'We'll probably split it into three, Mrs Armstrong. One part for us. We'll either sell or rent the others.'

"Mrs Armstrong frowned. 'You'd need to make a lot of alterations. This house is over three hundred years old.'

"Ruth took her remarks in good part. The other day she had dug up some raggy spiraea which was blocking the front path of the overgrown garden. Another neighbour had rushed across with a plate of scones an hour later and had spoken about the vicarage garden as though there was a preservation order on every single plant.

"Ruth grinned. 'All those weird old statues in the garden need a bit of rethinking. They're simply lost in the bushes – though, from the look of them, I don't know that they're worth finding.'

"'Those statues are loved in the village, Mrs Andrews. They belong here.'

"Oh yes, thought Ruth. The preservation order mentality again."

"Paul was in insurance. After he had come home and they'd had dinner and Julia was tucked up safely in bed, the couple did some more unpacking. At nine o'clock Paul left to wander along to the Wheatsheaf here, where he was already integrating beautifully, so he claimed.

"You'll have noticed what a lot of people drive to the pub, even if they're only coming quarter of a mile. But Paul, as I say, knew about risks – "

"Such as being nabbed by Constable Tate?" I interrupted.

"He wouldn't dream of it. Has to live here with his missus and nippers, doesn't he? Patrol car from town, maybe – lurking up a lane. Why, last month a fellow was driving back home at twelve down Marston Lane when a patrol car blazed up behind him, floodlights full on. He stopped, hitched himself up three inches taller, marched round and stared at the back of his van, just in case a light was out, which it wasn't, then he stepped up to the police and demanded, 'Do you think I stole this van? Do you think I have something stolen hidden in the back?' Actually he was carrying a computerized thingy for controlling crop spraying. The police took a look and said, 'What's that?' He said to them, 'You wouldn't bloody know if I told you.' But that's by the by.

"Paul returned home at eleven, seeming tipsy.

"'You know, Ruthy,' he said, 'I don't think we ought to shift any of those statues.'

"'They're so *ugly*,' she protested. 'Shapeless. They look like those people at Pompeii who were covered in slag. Mrs Armstrong was round today telling me what I shouldn't do. Have the chaps been getting at you in the pub? It's our garden, Paul. It's our house.'

"'They were telling me how this house got its nickname. It's because it *is* the centre of everything. The centre's in this very house.'

"'What nonsense. The centre of England is in Meriden, isn't it?'

"'No, not the centre of *England*. The centre of the universe, Ruthy. That's why the last vicar left. He couldn't compete. Having custody of that in his own house was too big for him.'

"'They're kidding you, Paul. They must be laughing their heads off. What do they know about the universe? Ever heard of Galileo? The earth moves – millions of miles around the

sun. If the universe had a centre, and goodness knows where
it might be, it can't possibly stay in one spot on earth.'

"'Maybe it can.' He grinned feebly. 'What do you know
about the universe?'

"'I know that a village is the centre of its own universe!
This is ridiculous. You've made a fool of yourself. Did they
slip something in your beer? Oh, it isn't ghosts or witchcraft
in villages nowadays. No yokels here! They've wised up.
They're going to try and control us by telling us we're sitting
on the centre of the whole damn universe! I wonder who
dreamed up this crazy joke. It *is* a joke, you know. Wise up,
Paul. Climb into bed, wake up tomorrow, watch the sun rise.'

"'I shouldn't have told you.'

"'They told you not to tell me? That's even richer. What
happened tonight? Was it the village boys' initiation ritual?
Did you all pull up your trouser legs? They were pulling *your*
leg, Paul.'

"'No one who didn't know would believe it . . .' He seemed
to be holding back some further foolishness. 'We aren't sitting
on the centre, Ruthy. It's up near the ceiling, over the back
staircase; that bit which you can't get to.'

"'I'll tell you one thing. You're going to get to it tomorrow
evening. You're going to bring the extending ladder inside,
and you're going to stick yourself up there to get rid of the
cobwebs – and out of your brains too.'

"'No! I can't.'

"'If you don't, husband mine, I'm leaving this house the
morning after and taking Julia with me. I am not living here,
to be manipulated by all and sundry.'"

Mrs Prestidge paused. "I was here in the 'sheaf that night.
Well, they weren't kidding him, not a bit. Not Fred and
John." She turned her head towards the bar as though she
could see. "Ah, but that was before . . . another event. Yes,
Paul was faced by a big risk now. Whether to act unwisely –
or to risk losing his wife. I think she might have meant that
threat. Don't you? Marriages are so much looser nowadays."

One thing I thought was that Mrs P was a dab hand at
imitating voices. But how did she know so intimately what

had happened inside the vicarage after Paul returned? Unless
Paul himself – or even Ruth – had later been her
informant . . .

"Paul passed a fairground on the way home from work, so as
a peace offering he brought back a gas ballon with a funny
face on it. Julia squealed with delight.

"Then he wrestled the ladder in through the back door and
extended it fully up the stairwell. His hands were shaking. It
was a very heavy ladder.

"The phone rang, for Paul. The doorbell, for Ruth. Mrs
Armstrong hovered outside with news about the Women's
Institute drama group. Has Mrs Armstrong been to see your
wife yet, Mr Campbell? Your Jill, isn't it? We do like people
to join in."

I shrugged, then remembering Mrs P's condition I said,
"I'm not sure. Jill hasn't said." I was starting to imagine more
than your usual WI of jam and Jerusalem – rather, a secret
society for village women! Did these villagers try to control
newcomers by separating husband from wife? If so, in our
case they wouldn't succeed.

"Mrs Armstrong'll be round," Mrs Prestidge assured me.
"I'll remind her." She resumed her story. "While Paul and
Ruth were both through at the front of the house, a cry of
'Look at me!' came from the rear. Excusing herself hastily,
Ruth ran back.

"The balloon had escaped up to the ceiling. Little Julia was
high up the ladder, reaching for the dangling string. She was
really at risk.

"'Don't move, Julia!' cried Ruth. 'Paul, leave the phone!
Come here!'

"Mrs Armstrong trotted through inquisitively behind Paul.

"'Oh Lord,' she exclaimed. 'Oh dear.'

"Julia caught, and lost, the string. The balloon bobbed
away. Ignoring her mother, the girl climbed even higher.

"A flash of light blinded the onlookers – as if Julia had
touched some exposed wiring!

"Their little girl no longer stood on the ladder. Up top only a mass of white slag perched, in her vague shape and size."

"The village takes care of its own. Constable Tate and Archdeacon Hubble both came. They both *knew*.

"'Whoever reaches the centre of the universe cannot move away in any direction,' the Archdeacon said wistfully. 'This is the centre of absolute motion. So they're trapped there. We can shift them, but they themselves can never move again. They're eternal.'

"'Nobody can prove as that's your little girl,' the Constable told the Andrews bluntly. 'Outsiders would assumme as you'd . . . got rid of her. We can sort this out with your co-operation. The last vicar didn't leave. He got reckless. Others too, over the centuries since the first happening while this place was being built. Vicar's in your garden along with the rest of them.'

"'What the hell *is* up there?' Paul demanded.

"'It's the centre of things,' Hubble repeated gently. 'Has to be somewhere, doesn't it? You're in charge of it now.'"

"With Tate's help, Paul moved the small new statue out into the shrubbery. It looked very ancient and worn out.

"Ruth would sit by the window, weeping. Outside, rain would fall on the blurred Pompeii cast of Julia. All the statues would seem to weep."

"If you like to, Mr Campbell, you can visit those statues. If you call on Mr and Mrs Andrews they'll show you round their garden. They won't leave each other now, nor leave Julia."

"Mm," I said.

"All newcomers to the village have the right to see, just the once, to satisfy theirselves."

"Has a new vicar arrived yet?"

"Ah, that can take a number of years. Our Archdeacon doesn't mind helping out. Besides, we hold joint benefice services with the parishes of Briarley and Marston."

Services, yes. Rituals. But what did these villagers truly believe?

"This Hubble must be a peculiar chap, considering what you say he knows." Not that I credited this latest offering from Mrs P, but she could tell a good yarn, and I had driven past the old vicarage; my eye had been caught by the shapeless objects vaguely visible here and there in the shrubbery.

"The Archdeacon's one of us," she said and tilted her empty glass. Mrs P could certainly sink a few drinks.

"Another one?" I asked. And another story?

She nodded. When I got to the bar, June was holding up eight fingers twice to tell a bald, weatherbeaten, middle-aged bloke how much two pints of Mild cost. He paid over a palmful of silver and was toasted by a moon-faced contemporary with an unruly grey thatch. This drinking companion said nothing as such, merely gesturing with his glass. The bald bloke bellowed back, "Cheers!" then he too fell silent. It was pretty noisy in the pub, what with everyone else chattering, piped pop songs playing, and a darts match in progress.

THREE MONKEYS

"Well, Mr Campbell, we decided that our little village of Weston Willow was going to walk off with the trophy in the County Inter-Village Quiz this year. Last year and the previous year we'd been knocked out in the first round.

"The questions are always fairly vicious. Can you say offhand who designed Nelson's Column? It was William Railton, in 1843. Do you know the collective noun for moles? It's a 'labour' of moles. Seems plausible enough once you know the answer.

"This year, thanks to our three monkeys, we were through to the final round . . ."

"Richard was the instigator of Project Monkey. He's the secretary of our village hall. You'll meet him – Richard's always on the look-out for new committee members. He has to organize our end of the quiz, get a team together, liaise with rival villages, contact the quizmasters. The Rural Community Council arranges the roster of teams and sets the questions; and Sterling Property Services sponsor it. The county newspaper hosts the grand final at the college in town.

"Richard had come across a pile of paperback quiz books in the secondhand bookshop and discovered to his delight that all the questions we had suffered from in previous years had been cannibalized from these. Naturally he bought the lot, imagining that our team could get some practice in.

"The flaw in this plan soon became obvious. Each book included approximately two thousand questions and answers, a total of ten thousand in all.

"One thing you soon learn in a village, Mr Campbell, is that there's always someone who can turn their hand to anything you want. This doesn't only apply to ordinary things, but to exotic items. I really do believe, if you wanted a small space rocket built in your back garden, someone would turn out to be, or have been, a guided missile engineer.

"At a meeting in the village hall we marshalled our collective talent.

"Richard works for a computer firm which is trying to sell home computers to farmers. He would provide a new prototype micro-memory. With all of us mucking in, we could load the tiny box for instant access to all ten thousand answers.

"Martin's company specializes in micro-electronics, including bugging devices. We weren't supposed to know about this aspect, but of course we all did. Martin could rig up a hearing aid to receive whispered radio messages from Richard. Unfortunately Martin could only gimmick one hearing aid. Stock security was tight at his company – and perhaps three deaf team members might have seemed excessive, don't you think?"

"We also had our three monkeys: Lucy, Fred, and John. For the purposes of the quiz they were going to become Blind Lucy, Dumb Fred, and Deaf John.

"Deaf John would wear the hearing aid, to receive the computer answers from Richard in the audience. Richard would be hidden amongst our supporters.

"According to the rules any unanswered question goes to the next team member before being passed over to the opposition. Here, we slyly hedged our bets. Dumb Fred would be printing his answers on one of those 'magic writing' slates which erases itself when you pull it out. If Blind Lucy didn't know the answer and Dumb Fred did, he would scrawl it on his slate under the table for Blind Lucy to squint at out of the side of her dark glasses. Those would hide the movements of her eyes.

"Naturally we didn't ever score *full* marks, but we won all the preliminary rounds. At last the night of the grand final came, in a lecture theatre at the college. Prizes were set out on a table midway between the tables of the two contending teams: a silver cup and souvenir pen sets. Of course there was particular interest in the fact that we had fielded three disabled candidates, who had done startlingly well so far.

"Blind Lucy was guided to her seat by Dumb Fred, who gestured Deaf John to his.

"The question master summarized the rules; and battle commenced. We were up against Milton Langford. Their team were hot shots: a headmistress, a bank manager, and an estate agent. They had won the quiz in the two previous years, and now they stared across at our disadvantaged trio with a mixture of sympathy and amusement.

"The questions rolled on.

"'Who was the highest scorer for England against Australia in the first innings at Lords in 1909?'

"Deaf John fielded that one easily. 'J. H. King.'

"'What is Kepler's Third Law?'

"Dumb Fred didn't know, so Deaf John trotted out: 'The squares of the periodic times of planetary orbits vary as the cubes of the semi-major axes.' Right!

"'In which county does the River Itchen reach the sea?'

"This was tricky. Blind Lucy had no idea of the answer, but most happily Dumb Fred genuinely did. Squinting, Blind Lucy read from his writing tablet, 'Hampshire'.

"Milton Langford didn't do badly at all, but they could hardly match our performance. We won by 115 points to 98,

and all the while Blind Lucy managed to remain convincingly
blank, and Dumb Fred suitably tongue-tied, and Deaf John
gratifyingly hard of hearing. During the presentations John
even added to the illusion by tapping his hearing aid, with a
puzzled look on his face."

"Afterwards Dumb Fred led Blind Lucy out to our rented
minibus which was in the college car park, waving Deaf John
along with sweeps of his other arm. The doors were slammed,
and off we drove.

"As soon as we were safely isolated out on the dark highway,
Richard – who was driving – began to laugh triumphantly. Or
to cackle triumphantly; it was that kind of laugh.

"But as he laughed, Blind Lucy cried out in a strangled
voice, 'Don't you understand? I can't *see*! I can't see a thing.
I'm blind!' She tore off her black glasses. 'There's nothing!
Nothing.'

"Deaf John shouted. 'Eh? Eh?'

"Dumb Fred mouthed at his fellow passengers, noiselessly."

The moon-faced chap and his drinking companion had edged
up close to our table. The former was listening keenly. His
bald friend stared blankly at Mrs Prestidge.

"You're Blind Lucy, aren't you?" I cried at her.

"That I am, Mr Campbell." She laid her spectacles carefully
on the table and gazed at me with sightless, whitened eyes.
"And here is Deaf John and that's Dumb Fred. Weston
Willow's a special village, you see, being so close to the centre
of you-know-what. Mostly our village *appears* like anywhere
else. Just you look out of the corner of your eye, though!
Hereabouts things are given, and things are taken away, if you
follow me. We shouldn't have drawn attention to ourselves
outside the village. The village didn't like that. That's what
went wrong. That's why something was taken away from us."

"Look here," I protested, while John and Fred crowded
closer, "you used *technology* to cheat in the quiz. You didn't
use magic or something!"

"Weston Willow doesn't wish any attention drawn to itself;

that's the simplest I can say. I could tell all kinds of tales, Mr Campbell. These three tonight are just the icing on the cake. Odd things happen here, and that's a fact. You'd hear the stories soon enough. You tell stories, don't you, being a writer?"

"Detective," I mumbled. "Eighteenth century."

"We had an eighteenth century here too, same as everywhere else. Soon enough you'd be sending your eighteenth century investigator here to try to plumb a mystery." Her hand snaked out unerringly and caught my wrist. "You mustn't tell on us, must you?"

I felt paralysed by her clutch. My eyes glazed with tears. For a few moments I couldn't see a thing; everything went blank.

"I can see through your eyes, Mr Campbell," I heard Mrs Prestidge whisper.

My vision snapped back into focus. A man's hand gripped my shoulder.

"I can hear through your ears," murmured John. Music had died in the room. Conversation, too. The locals were all looking at me.

No sooner did John release me than my shoulder was seized.

"I can talk through your mouth," I said. This was my own voice – but those weren't my words!

The pressure subsided. Lucy Prestidge reclaimed her dark glasses and hid those eyes like glass baubles filled with ashes.

The piped music and the chatter both resumed, the locals once again engrossed in each other's lives. Lucy Prestidge smiled at me. Her eyes were invisible, but her mouth stretched, her cheeks swelled and creased into a smile.

"Shall I tell you another tale, Mr Campbell? Not to be told elsewhere ever, in any form, do you promise?"

I nodded.

Promises. Ten-year-old promises. It's already half a decade since Jill and I moved away from Weston Willow. We came all the way to Edinburgh, where I'd been born. Surely far enough away in time and space!

Nowadays I'm head of history in a large comprehensive. I did manage to write one further novel about my eighteenth-century detective, Montague Hamilton, but it was the novel for which I already had ideas when we moved to Weston Willow. After that the drought in my imagination commenced – while simultaneously a forbidden reservoir was filling up.

No more novels. I was sure, and Jill too was sure, that I should have been able to break through to become a full-time writer, quitting teaching forever. Indeed the mystery novel which might have propelled me over this threshold was waiting inside me, blocked only by my promise to Lucy Prestidge. It in turn blocked the possibility of any other different novel. The frozen embryo within me prevented any other fertilization. The visit of Montague Hamilton to the Manor House of Weston Willow for a hunting party, the mysterious disappearances, the events at the vicarage, a distillation and transmutation of everything I picked up from Blind Lucy and the other locals during five years' residence; if only I dared to tackle this material. I knew I would be free. If only I could break the seal upon my lips – or upon my typing fingers.

Surely the seal existed only in my imagination. So far as publicity went, didn't I now live in Edinburgh, in another country, Scotland? Wouldn't I faithfully change the name of Weston Willow to Milton Mandeville, or Chipping Charlford, or whatever?

A week ago the school holidays started, and I began to type *The Undeserted Village*. Just as I had echoed Alexander Pope in the case of the jewel theft, now I echoed Oliver Goldsmith. And the story flowed, how it flowed.

Three nights ago I woke in the early hours to find that my left forearm and hand were paralysed. That arm lay on top of the bedspread like a lump of rubber. I needed no Montague Hamilton to deduce that I had not squeezed the blood flow by sleeping upon the arm. Nor was the night air cold; I had not chilled my exposed flesh. It was as if part of my body had died.

Bemused, I used my right hand to lift the dead limb and shook it about. A dentist might have needled it full of novocaine. No demon dentist prowled the darkened bedroom, where only Jill and I lay. I listened to Jill's breathing; she sounded deeply asleep.

Sensation returned suddenly. Feeling flooded back fully and immediately without any prickling interval of pins and needles. One moment dead meat, the next living flesh. Something had slipped a sleeve over my arm which blocked off all feeling, which nullified the nerves. Suddenly the sleeve was snatched away. Puzzled, I drifted back to sleep.

Two nights ago, after writing some more, I woke to find the whole of my right arm dead. After five minutes the limb came alive again.

Last night, after another five pages of *The Undeserted Village*, both my legs died. For ten minutes I lay in terror, paralysed from the waist down.

I consulted a medical book today. I did find a rare disorder known as periodic paralysis. Yet it didn't seem as though I ought to suffer from this. I also came across a reference to hysterical paralysis. Can it be that I'm doing this to myself?

I fear that isn't the case. Nor do I know whether the nightly symptoms would cease if I abandoned my book, if I deserted *The Undeserted Village*. How can I abandon it? What do I tell Jill? What do I tell myself? That I'm a failure? That I've found a perfect excuse to be a failure?

What I did today at my desk was to set those first chapters aside for the moment and to type up this brief account instead. Just in case.

I never told Jill all that I learned in Weston Willow – for instance the way in which Dumb Fred spoke through my own lips, that night in the Wheatsheaf. Jill's reaction would have been similar to Ruth Andrews' – before her daughter was turned into a shapeless statue. I'm sure that Fred did borrow my vocal chords, my tongue; that it wasn't just a trick. I'm sure that it happened. I wonder whether Jill knows any secrets that she never confided to me, through fear of . . . who can say what? Most of the time, of course, our life in the village was ordinary and normal.

This has taken till eleven-thirty. I shall leave the pages in full view. And now that I have done, I shall climb upstairs to join Jill in bed. She will be asleep. Soon I will also be asleep – until I waken up.

In Her Shoes

When David Latimer left school before going to art college, he took a job in the real world for a few weeks. His parents had not thought this such a good idea, yet David craved independence, which a job seemed to promise. He would be earning a wage: meagre enough though much to a schoolboy. After years as an only child who was quite protected, he wished to be his own person. Here was proof of his rebellious, artistic streak which he had nurtured quietly.

The year was 1960, the wage for such as David was four pounds per week. The job was as accounts clerk in a shipping company. Squabbling kittiwakes nested on the stone window ledges, streaking the riverside office block white with their droppings. Cargo vessels moaned and hooted on the foggy river. Sometimes the sun shone, heating the office like an oven. At lunchtime he walked through the city in company with other junior clerks, who seemed enrolled for life, to a cheap, clean restaurant for a businessman's lunch: cream of tomato soup, roast beef, jam pudding and custard. Senior accountants in the office talked endlessly about a pub they would pop into at night, the Balloon, and its luscious landlady.

The job was a form of imprisonment; and besides, David botched it. He couldn't understand the filing system. He was asked to tot up a portage account, to tally the thousands of pounds which a ship spends in a foreign port, and found five different answers. Unfortunately he had already inked in the first, and second, and third. His supervisor's only comment was a quiet, "Shit". After a month David quit, promising himself never to do an ordinary job again.

Nor did he; not that he avoided hard work in his lifetime. At art college he became a potter. Twenty-five years later he was master of his own pottery, run from a cottage and barn workshop in the Warwickshire countryside. David specialized in traditional rural spongeware: robust pots and plates crafted from local clay and hand-sponged with bird motifs, with paisley curlicues, with flowers and fruits. He had abandoned the old method of stamping with cuts of potato in favour of using shock absorbers, which held finer detail and lasted longer. David had also devised a crisper method of firing than the old copper oxide routine.

Early in his career he had won a scholarship to Japan, to follow in the footsteps of Bernard Leach and study with the master potters in Sendai for a year; not that David's work showed any traceable Japanese influence. He was too much his own man. Still, he sold his work to Tokyo and New York; though not so much in his native land. Local success and real prosperity eluded him; yet his fortunes ticked over, with a few missing heart beats, from year to year. His life was free, even if the freedom was constrained by the need to keep on designing and firing and stamping, and packaging his wares, by upkeep, by work. Holidays? Only brief working ones. Travel? Only with a purpose. His one-ton van was always several years old. As to the family car, the Latimers were always the final owners; afterwards it went for scrap or banger racing.

This family consisted of Meg whom he met during his first apprenticeship, in Wales, and daughter Gwen, now turned fifteen. Meg had waited for a child till she was thirty. David's mother had died of cancer the previous year; his father was ailing with heart trouble. Now forty-five, David began to think of death, particularly if he woke in the wee hours.

Meg had become stout. Gwen, chubby as a child, had grown up tall and slender. She had never cut her long black hair. Boys were beginning to show interest. How long until David became a grandfather, and died? Maybe he had been too bound up in himself and his work, too busy, too impatiently his own self. Yet now for the first time – with a sense of shock, and sympathy, and love – he fully noticed Gwen as *her* own person.

Had Gwen enjoyed a full, true life up until now?

"Shouldn't there have been a few real holidays?" he asked

Meg one Sunday night in bed. "Shouldn't there have been more experiences for our Gwen? Instead of us staying stuck in the country, lovely though it is?'

"You stuck us here, David," said his wife.

"We stuck ourselves here. Art stuck us here. Life did." A life which kept on promising, always hanging juicy carrots just out of reach.

"Shouldn't we have done more?" Meg said. "That's what you mean. Well, it's too late to wake up. Years have slipped by. Those could have been the best years. I feel tired, David. If we became rich tomorrow I couldn't handle it – no more than you can handle that little bit extra, the *giving* of yourself; that's the truth."

"It's never too late."

"Oh it is. If you could have given more of yourself, you might have become famous. What you give you get back."

Years sliding by, speeding up: had *he* enjoyed a full, true life up until now? He feared not. He feared, at night, the darkness at the end of life.

Perhaps they had raised Gwen the way in which he himself had been raised: as an only child, protected, yet never wholly connected with. Naturally Gwen would be going to art college in a few more years. She would probably do fashion and textiles, since she hadn't his feel for the clay. As she approached her first major exam hurdle – limping somewhat – her school had set up a work experience scheme.

This was the immediate trigger for his present bout of anxiety. For a week at the end of the summer term she would have to work in the real world, in Leambury, the nearest large town. She would catch the early works bus in from the village and do her nine-to-five stint in a small designer textile factory. Fending for herself.

The prospect terrified her.

"I'm not just *worried*," Gwen confided earlier that Sunday evening. She didn't call David "Daddy" and never had. Maybe she ought to have done, however David hadn't liked the hint of, well, obsolescence in the word Daddy, the sense of being on the way out. He had insisted on first names, which sounded more intimate, but wasn't really.

Gwen had her route mapped out, and her outfit ready for the morning: brown Indian cotton skirt, lace slip, green silk blouse, green tights, high heels. She knew the bus timetable. Her bag was packed, with enough pounds in her purse to buy lunch.

"I'm scared stiff," she said. "What if – ?" She raised a number of "What Ifs" which he deflected with a familiar family joke: "Rabid sheep!" What if a flock of rabid sheep attacks the bus? What if rabid sheep are loose in Leambury?

She seemed genuinely frightened. He made to hug her, and pat her – like a pet dog – but she deflected him.

"Put yourself in my shoes," she muttered.

"I was, once." He told her about his job at that shipping office long ago.

"That would be back in the Dark Ages when you were alive, you mean?" She shrugged. "You never told me any of that before."

Meg made a better job of reassuring Gwen.

Who could reassure David? Not Meg, that night. He woke at three in the morning and thought of generations and of his own death. Forty-five was over the hill, more than halfway through.

He thought of Gwen, lovely daughter, a separate independent consciousness with a lifetime still ahead. He thought death, he thought life. His own life was slowly fading, yet her life came alive to him then with a loving intensity which astonished him – so much so that he could almost feel what she had been feeling earlier, could almost see himself through her eyes, watch himself failing her, not so much intentionally as inadvertently.

"I'll die," he murmured. Meg wouldn't hear; she always slept like a rock. "Gwen'll live. In ten years' time she'll be leading a rich, full, adult life, fulfilling herself. She must! And in twenty years' time. Whereas me . . . should I last another twenty years . . . cancer, heart attack, who knows?" Dread possessed him. Fiercely he willed her to thrive and enjoy, to bloom and prosper.

Half awake, he plotted her footsteps to the bus stop next morning, her ride into town, her walk to the textiles place. How would people treat her? What would she eat for lunch? How would she fare?

After Gwen had left, David slapped clean wet clay on his wheel. He hoped to make fifty jugs that day, to be sponged another time with the print of a rooster. The first lump of clay rose up spinning between his fingers, much slimmer than he had intended. His fingers weren't moulding a jug at all. They were modelling a body. Female. A girl's.

True, the body showed no details. How could there be details when the clay was rotating? Legs were fused into one single large leg. But here was the in-curve of the knee, the out-swell of the thigh, the pinch of waist. Breasts formed a lip all around the chest. Arms? No arms. A neck; a featureless ellipsoid of a head.

Surely the clay would sag and collapse if he quit supporting it. He couldn't bear to cease connecting. It pirouetted like a ballerina, whirled like a dervish, around and around. His fingers were its arms, her arms.

He heard the purr of traffic, the click of high heels, the roar of a motorbike, hiss of air brakes, snatches of voices as people passed, as she walked past other people. Presently . . .

"Hullo, I'm Gwen Latimer – "

She had arrived at the factory.

Throughout the day, as he spun the same clay, keeping it wet, he eavesdropped with anxious love.

When Gwen arrived home at six-thirty she looked tired but thrilled.

"It went fine, just fine! I did learn a lot."

David nodded. He knew, though he couldn't put any faces to the voices.

"You must tell us everything right from the moment you

caught the bus!" insisted Meg. "No, wait, how about a cup of
tea? Or maybe a glass of ginger wine?"

"Oh, ginger wine, please. May I really?"

Yes, Gwen's day had gone just so.

That night David awoke and knew he was blind. He
couldn't see the pale shape of the window or the luminous dial
of the bedside clock. He was worse than blind. He couldn't
feel a thing. Sheet and blanket made no impression. His whole
body was without sensation, that of a corpse. No taste of
moisture in his mouth. No mouth. His spine might have
snapped. He was a corpse awaiting burial.

But then the voices began.

"Hello, I'm Gwen Latimer – "

And the sound of the factory. Loving relief overwhelmed
him.

When David woke the next morning he felt normal; until he
sat at his wheel and made the same wet clay rise up again into
the girl's smoothed, amputated body.

This time he not only heard but smelled the street which
Gwen took on her way to work: the whiffs of exhaust fumes,
lardy, bloody reek of a butcher's shop, a rich nutty pipe
tobacco, a hint of perfume, dust in the air, an open dustbin.

That night he awoke again, but he could hear and smell all
that she had heard and smelled.

On Wednesday, besides, he tasted her morning coffee and
ginger snap, and later her lunch of cheeseburger and chips
with tomato ketchup.

On Thursday he touched whatever she touched, while he
also touched the clay.

Thursday night – was it already Friday morning? – he woke
still sightless but could hear, feel, smell, and taste whatever
she had met with. Friday was to be Gwen's last session of
work experience; summer holidays thereafter. Nowadays it
wasn't nearly so easy to be accepted by an art college as had
been the case in David's time. Would Gwen perform well
enough in her exams, due the following June and July, to stay
on at school to take Advanced Level Art? Might she be better

advised to start straight in on a pre-diploma course at the local college in Leambury?

Worries, worries.

He put his whole heart into wishing her good fortune.

He placed his fingers on the clay, on Friday.

So strange to walk along Alfred Street in Leambury in an adolescent girl's body, smoother and softer than his own, long hair fussed by the breeze, breasts pressing at his white Angora sweater, worn because the weather had cooled, legs clad in tights rubbing together under the skirt as if naked. Yet so gratifying, so full of promise, so fresh, so perceptive. Glancing into the florist's window at the corner of Alfred and Peel Streets, he saw new hues in the vases of roses. Why, look at the terracotta mouldings on the upper storeys of that bank! Like a predator he smelled the aroma of life around him. Soon he would see those faces belonging to the voices at the factory. He was bound to make some mistakes and hoped he wouldn't seem too stupid all of a sudden. He hadn't Gwen's memories, only his own.

Gwen: where was she now? Why, here she was, mounting steep Peel Street. A glance at a mirror in the window of a furniture store proved this.

But where was her own independent self? Gone away, gone away. Lost. Dust to dust, clay to clay. Could it be that she was sitting at his potter's wheel right now, lovingly spinning the clay figure so that he could live in her shoes for a day? Why should she wish that? So as to tease him, to taunt him with new young life for a few hours?

That evening David stepped anxiously along the lane from the village bus stop. Cottage and barn came in view. Opening the garden gate, he was assaulted by the scent of the Madonna lilies raising their white trumpets high on thin stems, a hallelujah of angels. He touched his breasts, feeling sinful, an incestuous abuser.

As usual all that week, both parents were waiting to greet

him in the living room, its shelves and Welsh dresser crowded with pastel-stamped, biscuity pottery.

"So how was your last day?" asked Meg. She had a cup of tea waiting on the pine table. Mustn't make a habit of the ginger wine.

"Fine, simply fine!" he assured Meg in his girl's voice. He stared at David; stared at himself.

"Well done, Gwen," said the man. "I'm proud of you." After a moment, his face smiled. His tone had sounded so flat.

Gwen's father seemed like some animated waxwork, a working model. He was perfectly modelled in every respect – to the life! – yet some elusive ingredient was absent. What was it? Individuality? Personality?

It occurred – to the one who had returned home – that the Latimer spongeware business was doomed to fail slowly over the next few years. From this day on this man would only turn out copies of his previous work, nothing fresh or original. Presently buyers would cotton on that some spark had been extinguished. Enthusiasm would slacken. Reluctance would turn into rejection, while the man grew disheartened – but didn't really suffer! Nothing inside him could suffer. His would be a charade of sadness – and of failure, and perhaps finally suicide? The machine, at last, switching itself off?

Lean times lay ahead. The Latimers' daughter would barely have time to escape to a good art school, to London, to life, blessed by her new-found talent and persistence. She wouldn't study fashion and textiles now. No, she would become a sculptor.

The waxwork man didn't matter; he only possessed imitation feelings, but Meg would be bitterly unhappy. Meg wouldn't be able to understand. Could her daughter make it up to her?

David's daughter. How much worse this was than driving a daughter away from home in bitterness, losing her to teenage rebellion, or to a fatal road accident, a car crushing her bicycle.

"Poor dear Gwen," murmured the one who had come home.

Meg stared in puzzlement. "Why's that? Your week's over now. You said it went wonderfully."

He nodded Gwen's head, and her hair swung. He felt choked and swollen. Helplessly he burst into tears.

Meg hastened to hug him. "You were just pretending, weren't you? Was it so terrible?"

The man stood incapable, a lump.

"No," he managed to say through his helpless sobbing, "it . . . wasn't terrible. Not at all, it was fine. It was fun."

"Must have been a strain," said Meg. "I didn't realize how brave you were being. Never mind! Silly darling, you're back here now. It's the holidays, the whole summer." She looked at the man. "I'm sure they expect too much of the young these days, too soon – forcing them to grow up at fifteen! I expect she'll be all right about staying away from home when she's a few years older."

"I will be," he promised, scared at how much he needed to learn if he was to succeed: about Gwen's schoolwork, her school friends, dress, make-up, periods, the whole pretence, always knowing that he was an abuser, a murderer, all the while living in the same house as the waxwork man.

What if Gwen were to return, from wherever? In what style would she return? In dreams, vengefully or piteously? As a furious, imp-like creature? As a walking, living corpse? Or simply a disembodied voice crying from far away to let out of whatever cruel confinement held her captive? He sent out all his love to her, wherever she was, so as to calm her and keep her away from him.

That night, in her room, he woke and heard the boards on the landing squeaking as footsteps slowly approached. Shivering, goose bumps roughing his soft skin, he switched on Gwen's bedside lamp. A fumbling at the door . . . the handle began to turn. He held her mouth so as not to scream. The door opened gradually.

The waxwork man stood there.

"Gwen, my darling," said the man in that same flat voice.

"Go back to your bed, David," he begged. "Go back to bed with Meg, Daddy."

And this was the first time she had called the man Daddy.

The Human Chicken

Molly and Joe lived on the narrow-boat *Meadowsweet*, chugging along the English canals, mooring wherever they chose for as long as they chose. They rejoiced in the good, free life. They'd been together for the seven years since they left art school, at which time Molly's parents were killed in a plane crash in Saudi. This was bitter news. However, Molly's share of inheritance and insurance bought her and Joe the *Meadowsweet*. Molly's roots were cut – she wasn't too close to her older brothers, one of whom was an accountant, the other a junior solicitor. Why shouldn't she and Joe cast off their moorings entirely from the mundane world? They felt special and different, as the boat-folk of old had felt with their melodeons and Measham teapots and ribbon-ware plates, their rose-and-castle decorations painted on doors and walls and utensils, their private rituals and traditions as to how to dress or how to knot the rope buffer for the fender of a butty boat; those were a breed apart.

Actually, the water-gypsy life had been forced upon those boat-folk of old by the arrival of the railways. During the great Canal Age preceding, narrow-boat men usually left their families ashore dwelling in proper houses. Compelled to cut costs, the canal carriers incorporated home and boat, family and crew; whereas Molly and Joe gained the freedom of the waters thanks to a little legacy. Nevertheless, Joe and Molly – who were both into naïve art – felt that they were carrying on a folk tradition alien to the modern world. Now they earned their modest living expenses by painting roses and castles upon water-cans and pots and pans for the tourist shops at boat-yards, as well as from sale of their own naïve-art canal-scapes; not that they ever hoped to be "discovered" by an art dealer. Nor by any form of authority.

Molly and Joe hadn't bothered with any wedding ritual, but

after six years afloat they trusted their life and the future well enough for Molly to become pregnant one midsummer. Come the drizzly, windswept start of March of the following year *Meadowsweet* was moored in open countryside a few miles north of Oxford when Molly's waters broke a fortnight early.

Though they hadn't consulted any doctors or gynaecologists, no more than the boat-folk would have done, they had both studied a book about pregnancy and childbirth. *Meadowsweet* was only a quick taxi or ambulance hop from Oxford's John Radcliffe hospital with its maternity wards. Yet labour occurred so suddenly and proceeded so rapidly that Joe didn't dare leave Molly to dash ashore to a phone. Within less than an hour – with the ease of a Third World delivery in the fields, or a wild creature's accouchement, *molto allegro* so as not to be pounced on and eaten – birth took place on board *Meadowsweet*.

Maybe it was fortunate that no third party was present to witness the event. Maybe it was *un*fortunate, since how now would anyone but Molly and Joe credit this? *They* were both very disconcerted, for Molly had given birth from between her legs, as most women do, not to a baby girl or a baby boy – but to a chicken.

This was a fully grown chicken, same size as a lusty newborn human baby, an eight- or nine-pounder with feathers of buff gold, still slicked and matted from birth. Already it was fluffing these out to dry, flapping the crooked arms which were its wings as it perched at the bottom of the bed. Their offspring's body was roomy, its head broad though refined. Its beady eyes shone bright and prominent as it gazed at its human parents.

Molly squealed a little but this set the chicken to squawking in reply.

"My God, what'll we *do*?" asked Joe. "It isn't as if it's a freak or a monster! It looks perfectly normal. It just isn't human, that's all. It's a blithering chicken. You just gave birth to it. We both made it together, didn't we? Of course we did. You didn't sneak ashore last summer and have an affair in a barnyard with a rooster."

"In that case it's a *human* chicken," gasped Molly. "It's our child. We're special, aren't we? We're different. This is the most special, different thing that ever happened to us!" She began to sob, then dried her eyes on the sheet.

Should they try to register the birth? *Could* they? Hardly! Who had known that Molly was pregnant, in any case? Only casual acquaintances along the waterways. No one was likely to think it odd that there was, or wasn't, a baby.

Molly recalled the book on childbirth they had read. "Do you think it might have jaundice?" Newborn babies often developed a mild touch of jaundice during the first few days.

"Bit hard to tell, with feathers that colour!" said Joe. "I mean, it's sort of yellow anyway. But its hair . . . can't call it *that* . . . the stuff on its head, and the flap under its beak . . ."

"The comb," she told him, "and the wattles." Molly had included poultry in her paintings (though she didn't make a thing of it) so she had found out the names of the parts, and what went where.

"Those look a bit blue, don't they? As if there isn't enough oxygen in the blood. Maybe it isn't breathing properly."

Indeed the chicken's wattles and comb were bluish, shrunken and scurfy; they looked cold not warm.

"I think," said Molly, "those only turn red and smooth, and swell up when birds are laying. I think they ought to look like that."

"You think," repeated Joe, "our baby ought to look like that: feathers and claws and a beak?"

"Why not?" cried Molly, defending her offspring now that she was more used to the idea.

Their child began to squawk again. Head bobbing, it pecked at the blanket.

"It's hungry. We should feed it." She patted her breasts but these did not feel damp or full or sore, and already she suspected that milk had no intention of coming. "Run to that farm over the field and ask them what you give chickens to eat. They can sell you some food. Or we might already have the right stuff on board! Don't worry about me; I'm not tired.

I'm not even hurting. While you're away I'll start getting to know it."

"Er, Molly, should I ask how to feed a baby chicken – or a fully-grown one?"

They both stared at their feathered child.

"Well, it's newly born," allowed Molly, "though on the other hand – "

"It's full-size already, isn't it?"

She shook her head. "I don't think so, not if it's a *human* chicken. It's still only a baby. Might need a grown-up chicken diet, though."

"Yeah, let's offer it everything the farmer says. It'll know what it needs."

She smiled. "*It* needs a name. You'd better ask the farmer how to tell a chicken's sex."

"Yeah. Then we'd best shift the boat before he gets nosey."

Their chicken proved to be female so they called her Arabella, only reflecting later how this hinted at the word "crops", thereby suggesting both farmyards and the first organ of their feathered daughter's digestive system. Thus does the subconscious refuse to forget whatever disconcerts it. On a conscious level Joe and Molly had quickly decided that Arabella was a beautiful and unusual name, with a hint of Spain about it, and therefore of gypsies, rumoured (no doubt incorrectly) to be the source of those rose-and-castle motifs which adorned *Meadowsweet* and other narrow-boats.

As to food, Arabella's diet was soon sorted out. In common with a human baby she lacked any teeth in her mouth, and in her case probably always would. Thus a mash of rice and grains formed a good basis, though Joe and Molly needed to be wary of which grains, since nutritious barley proved not very palatable to Arabella and rye she rejected outright.

To this mash they must add protein such as white-fish meal, meat-and-bone meal, and skim milk; and let them not forget her mineral requirements. Steamed bone flour provided her with calcium and phosphate, while in their marble mortar acquired years earlier from a kitchen reject shop they were able to crush oyster shell and limestone chips for her calcium. They had long regarded common salt as a poison, causing bloating and high blood pressure, not to mention ruining the fine discrimination of the palate so that most people could only ever taste a meal if they first emptied a salt cellar over it. In large doses salt would indeed poison Arabella, yet she did require a moderate sprinkle.

Vitamins were essential, with the exception of vitamin C which she ought to be able to synthesize herself. Thus: vitamin A from greens, vitamin B from wheat-germ, and vitamin D from cod-liver oil. Lacking D, she might grow up weak in the legs, and precious little sunlight – source of D – entered the windows of *Meadowsweet* during that dull wet spring. What sunlight did fall upon Arabella as she explored the inside of the boat was robbed of its precious ultra-violet component by passage through panes of glass.

Much of this nutritional fuss could have been circumvented by buying a proprietory compound chicken feed in the form of meal or pellets, yet Molly felt this would be subtly demeaning of Arabella, ranking her as an absurd pet rather than a biologically wayward infant.

Of course Arabella did possess concealed teeth, after a fashion. Her "back teeth" were located in her gizzard, the strong muscular organ deep in her which milled her meal and crushed grains before sending them to the intestine, the walls of which absorbed the nutrients. To fuel her gizzard she required grit. Daily Joe gathered a fresh bowlful from along the towpath, or else he ground up flints in the mortar. He also cleaned up Arabella's moist, smelly squit from the floor and from their now tarpaulin-covered bed. Yet they were happy together; and their child was thriving on her diet. Within a month, fulfilling Molly's prophecy of growth, Arabella was a twenty-four pounder, a giant of a chicken; for that matter, a giant of a human infant of similar age. They began keeping the curtains closed across the windows in case any impertinent passer-by looked in.

Enough of her diet. What of her psychological development?

To what extent did she relate to her parents as a human infant might?

Rather more so than any human baby! A very young human is fully employed in simply getting its mental and bodily act togther. It'll be a long haul through the stages, so it spends much of its time asleep and wakes to squall for more food; whereas Arabella was brightly alert most of the day and could certainly forage. No insects long survived being on board *Meadowsweet*.

Arabella certainly knew Molly and Joe. They weren't simply detachable extensions of her own body to be smiled at if compliant, screamed at if recalcitrant. She would readily feed from their hands – though this might draw blood – and roost on their laps, crooning. At such times of family affection she seemed inclined to control her loose bowels, a feat which became easier for her to accomplish once her parents realized they should cut out the bran and fibre from her mashes. Aside from laxative properties (which Joe and Molly might value, but not she) fibre and bran bulked Arabella out without nourishing her. She would feel she was spuriously full. Once fibre was drastically reduced, she grew apace. Ultimately her comb and wattles swelled red and smooth, hot to the touch.

Enough about her diet, enough! We speak of her person-ality: which was clucky, warm, inquisitive, perhaps a shade scatterbrained, though nervous only to the extent of her not trying to flap her way up on deck in the absence of specific parental encouragement.

Soon lusty, busty May arrived, when new-sprung leaves first cloaked bushes and trees overhanging the waterways. Green, floral June followed. Arabella was almost three feet high, from claws to the top of her comb.

By now *Meadowsweet* was on the lower Leicester leg of the Grand Union canal. Joe and Molly intended to keep on the move a little a day rather than settling in a favourite spot for a month or more. Since Arabella's birth neither parent had managed much by way of art work. A turn at the tiller allowed each a rest from supervising their child, wiping up her squits, dealing with spilled grain and grits and water.

Molly popped up on deck, shutting Arabella below, to join Joe.

"I've been thinking," she announced. "We oughtn't to bother tidying the grain and grits all the time. And why put it all in bowls? Why not scatter her food on the floor? We want her to be free-range, don't we? We want her to fend for herself, not be cared for like a poor spastic."

Was Molly fraught? On the contrary! She sounded quite a jolly Molly as she went on, "Now that Arabella's growing up she needs more experience, don't you think? Otherwise she'll believe the world is a long, curtained box we live in with her!"

These words stirred several lines of thought in Joe. Yet he kept his counsel, and she hers, while they were passing alongside another narrow-boat, its roof laden with girls in bikinis, a couple of young chaps in yachting caps chattering at the helm. Third boat in the last half-hour. Tourists were infesting the waterways.

"Maybe we're feeling a bit crowded." He jerked a thumb at the receding holiday-makers. "It'll be okay once we pass Market Harborough. We'll be on broad waterway then."

Molly gestured at the cow-grazed meadows, the rolling grassy hills around which the weedy, reed-lined canal was wending, the steeple-poke of a village in the distance; none of the scattered villages actually lay on this stretch of canal, though you could walk to them, a mile away or more. "I'd have thought we're okay now."

A warbler flew by.

"How about letting Arabella out this evening to see the world?" she said. "Let her peck ashore? Tourists will all have moored near some pub. We can't carry on as if we're ashamed of her."

"Still, we ought to be discreet, don't you think? It isn't everyone who has a child-sized chicken on their boat."

"*Unlucky* them. And we mustn't worry about not getting much work done to sell."

"I'm not worrying!"

"We can call this our holiday year. Remember," and she giggled, "we do have a bit of a nest-egg."

True enough, not all of her inheritance had been sunk in acquiring *Meadowsweet*. Joe and Molly still kept some money tucked away in the Post Office Girobank. Their needs were simple; perhaps a shade more complicated of late in view of Arabella's eager appetite for her own special diet, of which enough, enough.

Our holiday year, he thought. Arabella was shooting up fast towards, presumably, full-size maturity as a human chicken, whatever size that might be. Might she, not so much "outgrow her strength", as possess the same brief life span as an ordinary chicken? Did Molly fear that this year – and maybe one or two more – might be their only alloted time with their chicken daughter before she grew scraggy, lacklustre, and died of old age?

How long *could* an ordinary chicken live naturally, if left to its own devices and not slaughtered? Joe had no information on the subject. Farmers didn't maintain retirement wings in their sheds for grandma chickens, for pensioner poultry.

If the worst came to the worst, how would one dispose of the corpse of a giant chicken? Hide it behind a hedge, hoping that foxes would home in? God no! Bury her decently in a field at least.

The prospect, and the puzzle, sickened him momentarily. Arabella would not, must not, die after a brief span on earth. Yet could she plausibly continue living with them year in, year out? Hidden in the boat by day? She herself might wish to leave home. Maybe she already did, though they couldn't interpret her cluckings. The notion that she was akin to a disabled child offended him. Here was a healthy human chicken, perfectly formed, with no sign of lice, mites, worms, or salmonella – she hadn't grubbed with other infested poultry. Yet in regard to her human aspect, did the chicken suit she wore spell a species of disablement? If so, might Arabella one day learn to read and write and by dextrous use of her claws or beak might she scratch or tap out her autobiography, which might win a literary prize to reward her courage in overcoming the obstacles of whimsical nature? To which end, she must surely need more experience of the big wide world to write about, including encounters – perhaps unsettling and feather-ruffling – with human beings other than her parents. Joe shied away from the implications.

However, he agreed with Molly. "Yes, let's take her ashore this evening, if we're moored alone. It *is* quite like paradise here. It'll be as though she's emerging from her shell, pecking her way out, seeing the sky and the hilltops – "

Or was their daughter short-sighted? Birds of the air such as the warbler must enjoy excellent distance-vision. How about fowl, which had to spot tiny specks of food on the ground at close quarters? Yet hens could flap aloft, could they not? Could, after a fashion, fly. Unless Arabella's wings grew disproportionately to pteranodon size, how would they ever buoy up her body weight? His mind was drifting again. Joy had entered their life, accompanied by doubts and anxieties such as they had not suspected the year before.

Yet maybe here was an encounter with *reality* – neglected (temporarily) by those bikini-clad girlfriends and their boy-friends who were pretending to be the Captain Cooks of the waterways. In spite of the rose and castle image, canal life in the olden days had not been an idyll for everybody. Only a few days earlier, *Meadowsweet* had navigated the bat-infested Braunston tunnel. During the nineteenth century "Ben the Legger" had spent the fifty years of his working life lying there in Stygian darkness with his back on a board a foot wide and a yard long, while he legged one boat after another through the two thousand yards of the tunnel to and fro all day. He legged his way the equivalent of twice round the world, till his thighs must have been as plumply proportioned as those of a chicken, no less, from gross excess of muscle.

Just today, *Meadowsweet* had passed the village of Crick, home in his later years of George Smith, ex-brickworker from Coalville, Staffordshire, who had first crusaded on behalf of under-age labour, issuing his *Cry of the Children from the Brickyards of England*, and who had finally exposed the plight of pre-legislation canal folk, slaving in wretched immoral misery, hot, soaked, stinking, drunken, and bug-ridden, tens of thousands of their kids illegitimate and illiterate . . .

"Let reality be transfigured!" Joe exclaimed to Molly; and she nodded her full-hearted agreement.

So, that evening, as the golden sun melted behind the hills under crimson banks of cloud, as a kingfisher darted from bank to bank, wings vibrating like a humming-bird's, as cows settled in their meadow perhaps anticipating rain, Joe heaved Arabella – squawking and flapping somewhat – up the steep steps into the open cockpit to parade herself aloft and blink over the side, raw, at a deserted towpath and at the wide world.

Out went the gangway on to land. While Molly went ahead to receive and encourage, Joe hoisted his daughter on to that narrow plank ribbed with shoe-grips.

As if trained to the occasion, Arabella waltzed ashore to be preened proudly by her mother. Guarded by Molly and Joe, Arabella pecked her way happily hither and thither till it was time for bed.

Later, in the curtained and grain-strewn cabin, Joe recollected his earlier vision of a chicken authoress receiving a literary laureate, and at last he took out from a cupboard the small pile of illustrated children's books which they had rashly, prematurely, far-sightedly bought during the later months of Molly's pregnancy. Two of these books seemed appropriate to Arabella: *The Little Red Hen* and *Chicken Little*, stirring tales – realistically anthropomorphic – of humanistic hens, chickens of articulate consciousness in full control of their affairs, with which she might identify or empathize.

"It's time to read stories to her," said Joe. With a minimum of struggle he settled Arabella's fussy bulk upon his lap, using both hands to keep her steady. Molly sat opposite, holding out the large-print *The Little Red Hen* in front of Arabella (and Joe), and the first bedtime story commenced.

Alas – how should Arabella know any better? – their daughter apparently mistook the black marks, the regular printed letters on the page, for some line-up of unusual insects, at which she pecked vigorously. Her beak was big now and she tore the page again and again till Joe desisted, and Molly withdrew the gashed, punctured volume. Clucking vigorously,

Arabella insisted on being let down on to her own legs on the floor where she set to, desultorily, at a drift of grain before turning to the boiled potato, a recent favourite of hers.

"Perhaps she's trying to tell us something?" said Joe. "She mightn't identify with chickens – she mightn't wish to! Maybe we're insulting her. Maybe she'd prefer stories about little boys and girls."

Though disappointed, Molly adopted a more practical approach. "I think the old grain and grit's getting a bit small for her to deal with, don't you? I think she'd prefer nuts, and little pebbles for her gizzard."

By July they were on the not-so-frequented Macclesfield canal. Arabella was the size of a ten-year-old schoolgirl – fat-bodied and seemingly stout-necked in her sumptuous fancy dress of feathers, her diminutive head bonneted and a-dangle with rubbery adornments of a garish, blood-red lipstick hue. When Arabella bobbed her head zestfully, they sometimes heard pebbles tumble in her gizzard deep inside, rattling faintly like muted maracas. By now she was accustomed to stepping ashore of an evening when the coast was clear – of which they made certain – and she would return aboard when told. The gleam in her eye indicated that she saw eye to eye with them and understood not only the general sense but the very words they uttered, even if her own vocabulary of *tuck-tuck-tuck* remained opaque to her Mum and Dad.

Late one afternoon, when Joe had just hammered home the steel mooring stakes fore and aft and tied up with half-hitches before rejoining Molly in the cockpit, a barrage of concerned cluckings erupted from below. As if a fox had sneaked into the cabin! Surely Arabella was well beyond any vulpine mugging. She could have kicked a hungry fox to kingdom come, trampled it, pecked holes in it; though hitherto she had shown no signs of aggression.

They hastened below to find Arabella flapping in a fine flummox upon their bed; and behind her tail . . .

"She's laid an egg!" cried Molly. "There, there, Arabella dear, don't fuss on, poor thing. This must be like her first period. She doesn't know what's what, or where it came from. Fine parents we are! We ought to have prepared her, we ought to have told her."

"I suppose it was bound to happen," agreed Joe. "Looks like a big egg. I wonder if it hurt her."

Bigger than any normal size-one egg! Bigger than any goose egg, though in proportion to Arabella's body-size the egg was probably no prodigy. It might have slipped out easily. Their daughter had simply been . . . taken aback by the event. The egg was russet brown with sepia speckles; warm to the touch, of course.

Arabella had calmed. Perhaps she had known what was due to occur and when she laid her egg had simply been proud of her achievement and wished to draw immediate attention to it.

"I wonder if we should let her keep it, to sit on?" mused Molly.

"Use our bed as a *nest-box*? Look, that egg can't be fertile. She hasn't met a cock. I don't know it would be much use if she ever did! Like a golden retriever with a chihuahua. Anyhow, she's too heavy. She'd burst the egg, she'd flatten it. Splootch, all over the bed. Terribly disappointing, that could be."

"What I meant was, keep it as a sort of souvenir. For us too! We could hard-boil it . . . I guess it would go off. Or else pickle it in a jar! Or blow out the contents and keep the shell."

"Sort of like baby's first shoe? She isn't a baby any more; and here's our proof! Parents don't exactly hang up their daughter's first sanitary towel, do they, eh?"

"*Tuck-tuck*," said Arabella; or was it "tut-tut"?

"Hmm. Maybe we should ask her." Molly crouched to face Arabella. "Darlingest, what shall we do with your lovely egg?"

Cumbersomely Arabella squirmed around upon the bed to scrutinize her product. Her beak descended and she tapped it gently a few times, rolling it in Joe's direction.

"I think", said Joe, "she's saying we can eat it. It's her gift to us. And why not? She can eat some too. We can all share it. Is that all right with you, Arabella?"

"*Cluck.*"

"Whip up an omelette? There's three eggs-worth, I'd say."

"*Cluuuuckk.*" With its rising intonation assuredly this was a different word from "cluck" – maybe it was a whole sentence, of approval.

"An omelette, it is!"

Which is what they made; and Arabella pecked her portion with gusto from a plate of her own.

Duly encouraged – no doubt she had little *choice* in the matter – Arabella went on to lay another egg a couple of days later. Presently she was producing an egg a day, and they were enjoying not only regular omelettes but for variety scrambled egg, fried egg – some of her offerings were triple-yolked and divided up nicely – not to mention egg en cocotte, bacon and egg pie, egg à la florentine, egg fritura, egg à la maison, and archiduchesse.

They felt they were enjoying a kind of holy loving communion with their daughter, part of her substance transubstantiated into yolk and albumen – a sort of suckling of the parents by the child. Arabella could hardly be regarded as indulging in auto-cannibalism any more than a cow that licks up its own milk. What a clever trick, to create some of your own food from out of your own body, thus recycling what you ate.

"Weirdest thing Oy ever did see," declared a voice across the bar of the Sunrising Inn at Claydon. "Oy tell you, Bert, it were like a massive great yellow *turkey* struttin' about over by the old railway line, only that weren't no turkey. The sheep was scatterin'."

"Dusk light plays tricks when you've had one too many, Harry."

"Talk sense. How could Oy have one too many by dusk?"

"By havin' one too many at lunch to start with, eh, same as today?"

"That's for me nerves."

"Maybe your monster came out of a yoofo, eh Harry?"

Joe took a nervous swig of his Hook Norton ale, which tasted buttery. By now it was well into autumn, the tourist trade was slackening, and *Meadowsweet* was heading slowly southwards again. In this northernmost of all Oxfordshire villages, goats roamed the churchyard and the church clock might strike the hour but it lacked a face. The canal skirted the village itself – yet Arabella, now the height of a fifteen-year-old, had been spotted.

"We'd best head down beyond Cropredy this afternoon," Joe murmured to Molly. They supped up and sneaked away from the Sunrising.

Fortunately, with the decrease in sunlight, Arabella had grown a tad broody so she wasn't restless for her nightly jaunts in the open air. Still, she needed exercise; now there was more of her than ever to exercise, and to be seen. She had also quit laying and was moulting, which Molly and Joe at first feared was a disease – her feathers littered the floor of the cabin.

The acceleration of Arabella's childhood – the fact of their child maturing at the same speed as a barnyard chicken – made Molly and Joe feel prematurely middle-aged, as if in the course of a single summer fifteen summers had flown by. Surely Molly's body incorporated some growth hormone which could prove of inestimable value to science, though possibly only in the rearing neither of persons nor of poultry but of the hybrid, a human chicken – product perhaps of some game of cat's cradle played with Molly's genes and Joe's at the behest of some narrowly focused though happenstance bombardment by cosmic rays at the time of conception, so that Arabella, their creation, was "midwifed" by the explosion of some distant sun.

Should her vigorous form be a response to a tight beam of radiation rather than to, say, pollutants in the environment which must surely have affected other parents' offspring too – and neither the *Sun* nor the *Star*, those luminaries of the gutter press, had said a word about this to the best of Joe's knowledge – might military scientists be even more interested in Arabella as an ideal post-nuclear survivor?

Suppose that a nuclear war swept away civilization and humankind, clans of Arabellas might well rove and forage the irradiated, mutating landscape, carrying forward into a faceless future submerged within themselves a protected germ of humanity which might one day in a cleaner, fresher world a thousand years hence give birth once again to Homo – the cat's cradle unknotting, the DNA string pulling out straight and true – though goodness knows how those future human chickens would rear their slow, helpless, featherless, maggot-like babies when born, or hatched. Possibly those future parents, appalled and forgetful of human history, would peck their offspring to pieces or simply suffocate them undeɪ their feather-pillow rumps whilst squatting upon those babies in an effort to keep them warm.

The prospect of Arabella being spirited away for study – in a manner possibly insensitive to her feelings – did not appeal. Yet should not the world know *something* of Arabella, if only for the sake of her own liberty and fulfilment? She did appear to be developing her own opinions and desires, in so far as they could interpret these.

What's more, if Molly and Joe were in a sense growing prematurely "old" – emotionally, psychologically – due to their rushed experience of her childhood, who would care *for them* – care about them – when Arabella was fully adult? Who but her? Yet how?

Joe and Molly had distanced themselves from the workaday world, and the birth not of a child but a chicken had at first seemed to increase that distance. No longer! Arabella's presence, blessing that it was, now began to thrust them back towards the world they had left, both for her sake and for theirs.

Without settling on any plan whatsoever nor having in any way resolved the ambiguities attendant upon their prodigy and wonder, they were heading back down the South Oxford canal towards Arabella's birthplace, and beyond.

Locking into the River Isis – the baby Thames – through Duke's Cut (yes, *Meadowsweet* did carry a licence from the Thames Water Authority) they moored abutting the common land of Port Meadow, Oxford, on the opposite shore from the footpath commonly used. Herds of cattle roved a mile and a half north and south from Medley to Wolvercote and back. Horses galloped. Geese honked. A mile away to the southeast, the spires of the university dreamed. Being autumn, every evening dense white mist sublimed from the sods of the huge meadow, veiling the view to a height of eight or nine feet. Though the city was close by, Arabella, restored to full plumage, eager and boisterous and five feet tall, could sprint about the wide midlands of the meadow, deserted except for beasts, herself unseen, clucking, gizzard rattling, wings flapping as if here at last was a runway long enough to lift her jumbo body from, even though visibility was atrocious beneath the moon-lit mist bank which hid her.

Unseen . . . till one night around eleven, when against the advice of her parents – did she fully comprehend? – she deserted those safe midlands for the southern neck of the meadow where the rough path crossed from Fiddler's Island over to the railway bridge and canal bridge, thus to Walton Well Road and into town.

Intuiting something amiss, Joe and Molly were already out searching for Arabella in the chilly mist when they heard discordant singing from a group of undergraduates staggering back drunk from the Perch Inn at Binsey by way of Medley boat station and long, thin Fiddler's Island.

Before long, a series of screeches floated to their ears upon the mist, followed by cries of what sounded, at first, to be terror. Hearts in their mouths, their feet risking tussocks and hummocks and squidgy cow-pats, Joe and Molly hastened towards the source of commotion through the obscure fluffy murk. Had Arabella decided to prey upon travellers? Wooed by the sozzled songs, had she assaulted those beer-pickled undergraduates, racing down upon them from out of the mist and the night as if out of prehistory?

We must now pull back our focus and adopt a bird's eye view of events, as well as fitting an X-ray or infra-red lens to cope with the night and the mist. We must borrow Arabella's viewpoint.

Source of such squawks and cackles and crowings, these

undergraduates were interesting to her. She meant them no harm. After their initial surprise, they perceived this. They grew, well, intoxicated with Arabella. To take a five-foot-tall intelligent chicken back to their college with them struck them as the most splendid notion. She certainly appeared to be bright and willing. One student, Jeremy, offered his arm gallantly. Arabella stuck out her wing. Thus linked arm-in-wing Arabella and escort marched up over Walton Well Bridge. Destination: Worcester College, where cricket field, lake, and gardens backed on to the final cul-de-sac of the Oxford canal below Louse Lock.

Mist had infiltrated Walton Street yet not obliteratingly so. Would those undergraduates sneak Arabella through the maze of back streets known as Jericho, so as to enter their college via the cricket field, heaving Arabella over the gate if need be? Not at all. Adopting a full frontal approach, Jeremy and friends strode along past the University Press to the Porter's Lodge of Worcester and crowded through it. The long-suffering night porter eyed them sceptically yet he did not intervene. Oxford colleges had long since become co-educational. This couldn't be a scheme to smuggle a girlfriend in for the night. If a young gentleman, or lady, chose to costume themselves as a chicken, that was their problem.

Split screen: Joe and Molly had trailed Arabella and party, slinking along the misty pavement a couple of hundred yards to the rear. Thus far and no further; they weren't members of the university.

What to do? How to retrieve their daughter? Would she return of her own accord, clucking her way along Walton Street in the wee hours of the morning, and manage to steer herself all the way to the *Meadowsweet*? Molly and Joe returned to their boat and waited sleeplessly in vain.

Next morning, they untied *Meadowsweet* and chugged onward down the Isis to Louse Lock, locked through, and moored opposite the gardens of Worcester to keep vigil, by now praying that Arabella would not try to retrace her route to her vanished base in Port Meadow.

Through the autumn-denuded branches they watched a few

undergraduates jog along to the tennis court for an unseasonal foursome. Water hens trod the dying lily pads on the lake. A few Canada geese squabbled on shore. No sign of any dramatically larger bird. Down at the gut-end of the canal, up against Hythe Bridge, some vagrant alcoholics were stirring amidst a litter of empty cider flagons. Locking up their boat, which Arabella would surely spy if she and her hosts decided to take a turn in the gardens, Joe and Molly headed along the towpath to Hythe Bridge, declining the privilege of providing the raggy gentry with the price of a cup of tea. They mounted Hythe Bridge – by now it was late morning – and hurried round to the front of Worcester College . . . in time to see Arabella and her escorts of the previous night setting out boldly garbed in gowns.

"Arabella!" Molly cried, distressed by her daughter's exposure in full daylight. Actually, Arabella had been lent a long black scholar's gown which she wore with panache, her wings jutting through the short capacious sleeves – her friends were walking her to a lecture! Well, she would hardly have been able to ride a bicycle to one, would she? Thus the others walked too. Distances are short enough in Oxford.

Their daughter eyed her parents, and clucked reassuringly.

"Excuse me," Joe addressed blond, fresh-faced, bleary-eyed Jeremy. "She's . . . I mean to say, we're her . . . She's our . . . You can't!"

Yet they could, and they would, those frolicsome undergraduates: all the way through the centre of town, even by way of the covered market with its rows of gutted, plucked chickens hanging upended from butchers' hooks, down to the Examination School at the end of the High Street where lectures were held, admittance to anyone wearing a gown, even including a human chicken. Arabella's new friends were reading English. The lecture that day was on Shelley, which seemed appropriate.

Of course, Arabella's progress through town and her return attracted attention. Though it was clear that she was *different*, acceptance of her was remarkable (perhaps less remarkable, this being Oxford). Many people must have supposed she was

a dwarfish person – perhaps a thalidomide victim of genius –
whose eccentricity it was to dress up in a chicken suit. Others
better appreciated her absolute uniqueness but they kept mum.

And so time passed. No zoologists or brigadiers arrived to
distress her. She fast became a mascot, an honorary member
of college. Its esteem sky-rocketed as much as if its crew of
oarsmen had bumped ten rival boats on the river. The Provost
and Fellows of Worcester more than condoned her presence.

Nor were Joe and Molly exiled from their daughter. Moored
by Louse Lock, they could visit her in college where she
shared rooms with Jeremy, who tipped his college servant
handsomely to adjust to new circumstances. Each morning
Arabella would trot around Worcester gardens as far as the
tennis court, flapping her wings to Molly and Joe across the
water and clucking, horrifying the Canada geese but gladden-
ing her parents, who felt at last, through her, a sense of
belonging.

Oh yes, Arabella had taken to college life. Although largely
unschooled – apart from her abortive encounter with the tale
of *The Little Red Hen* – she who had raced through her
childhood had now gone straight to university. Could she
possibly have capsuled not only her tender years but her whole
educational career, proceeding directly from *The Little Red
Hen* to a degree in English Literature? Could it be, mused
Molly, that their daughter might actually become Arabella,
BA (Oxon) – by an honorary nod, such as was bestowed on
public figures who received doctorates of law without the strict
requirement of passing an exam?

Not exactly. Fate had a rarer destiny in store. In this
universe ruled by caprice, where the award of a fellowship at
All Souls was rumoured to hang ultimately upon how well the
candidates dealt at dinner with a dish of cherries for dessert –
did they spoon the cherry stones out of their mouths on to the
side of the dish? Or use their fingers to extract the stones? Did
they *swallow* those embarrassing mini-marbles? Or did they
nonchalantly spit them upon the floor? Here, the honorary
office of Chancellor of the University was newly vacant. For
the first time in history the election was being hotly contested,

tooth and claw, by several politician-alumni representing doctrinaire Tory, moderate Tory, and the splintering wings of the hectic, power-hungry minority party known as the "Alliance". What happened in the Oxford election might well be writ large upon the land.

Electors consisted of all Masters of Arts of the university, who must vote in person on election day. Many potential electors did not very much appreciate this once sedate, geriatric ceremony being turned into a political rumpus, a cock fight with substantial sums of money spent upon mailing propaganda leaflets to all living MAs of Oxford, whether they were currently residing in Manchester or Madagascar, to enthuse them to make the trip to Oxford.

Consequently, once Jeremy wittily persuaded sufficient senior members of the university – mainly wayward Fellows of Worcester College – to sign a proposal form for Arabella, who was by now a famous sight of Oxford, a campaign on her behalf rapidly gained momentum by sheer word by mouth.

Dons and graduates of the university, in their black gowns and other academic finery, had always somewhat resembled processions of penguins, had they not? Why not elect as their Chancellor . . . a giant chicken? (What's more, a female chicken – Arabella could surely rely on the feminist vote.) The formal duties of the Chancellor were slight: a Latin oration to be pronounced once a year, which only two or three people in the audience ever understood – with coaching, surely Arabella could cluck her way through this?

Election Day in early December was crisp and cloudless. Joe and Molly were out in Broad Street most of the morning and afternoon to watch long queues of penguins, young and old, tailing back from the Divinity School, the ancient stone polling station. Tucked behind the Sheldonian Theatre guarded by its semi-circle of bearded stone heads, the Divinity School was part of the Bodleian.

Several colleges including Worcester had laid on a buffet lunch with wine for any old members returning to Oxford to vote. Late into the afternoon many voters were still trying to recognize, and hail, former acquaintances, often with little success. Some electors drank champagne as they shuffled towards the polling station; others concentrated on their walking sticks. Coachloads of vicars had arrived from the countryside, their transport paid for by the Liberal-Democrat candidate, or was it the Democratic-Liberal? These vicars would vote as the fancy took them, and as Arabella paraded back and forth along Broad Street she must have reminded them of eggs and chicks and Easter, high point of their calendar.

Some doddery voters seemed to be arriving by bathchair, invalid carriage, even perhaps by hearse as if disinterred for the occasion, almost resurrected.

The wintry sun gilded spires and roofs and gargoyles. The line inched along. The university police, the bulldogs in their bowler hats, stood sentinel by the door to the Divinity School, as in filed the MAs to bow to an exhausted Vice-Chancellor and to be bowed to by him before receiving their ballot paper . . .

At eighty-thirty that evening, from the steps of the Sheldonian, the result was declared to a still-thronged Broad Street, brightly lit. Applause broke out.

What a night for Joe and Molly.

Almost Log-cabin-to-White-House! Well . . . narrow-boat-to-ivory-tower. What might the future not hold for their daughter now?

"Rejoice!" cried Molly.

Jeremy popped open a bottle of champagne.

"The human chicken! The human chicken!" chanted Arabella's supporters.

She fluffed herself up. She did not cackle. For the first time in her life, quite rooster-like, she crowed a resounding doodle-do.

The human chicken had been elected Chancellor of Oxford University.

The Case of the Glass Slipper

Outside the heavy chintz curtains of those famous rooms in Baker Street the London fog, yellowed by gaslight, crept and probed for entry and hid the world from view.

To Sherlock Holmes, seated within, the fog always seemed to afford a paradoxical image of his own relationship with the world of crime. That world sought to conceal its malignant, insinuating activities from view; activities which he by subtle probing would reveal. It sought to conceal, yet its very smoke-screen betrayed its position. This fog was an organism which carried the seeds of its own unmasking, as did any crime of lesser rank than the hypothetical "perfect crime" – which, Holmes reasoned, would be no crime at all, since crime must necessarily be imperfect. Did not crime represent a flaw in the logical structure of society?

His thought processes were interrupted – if not disarrayed – when the visitor whom he had been expecting was ushered in.

"Your Highness," Holmes said, rising.

The Prince was strikingly handsome despite the muffler he wore to guard his lungs from the fog, and to preserve his incognito. Nodding, he glanced around the room, taking in the roaring fire, the music stand, the leather-bound volumes on pharmacology.

"My colleague Watson has been called away to the bedside of an old friend," Holmes explained. He had immediately detected the missing element which puzzled the Prince.

"Excellent! Then there will be no record of this visit, nor of my dilemma." When the Prince unwound his muffler, Holmes noted a very slight scar on the side of the Prince's chin compatible either with an old hunting accident or with a boyhood fall from a tree. The poised dancer's – but not duellist's – grace with which the Prince moved ruled out the second, maladroit alternative.

"I can assure you of Watson's entire discretion," said Holmes mildly.

The Prince waved this equivocation aside, politely so.

"Mr Holmes, I come from a neighbouring kingdom. Yet my kingdom does not neighbour Her Britannic Majesty's realm in any ordinary sense . . ."

"In my experience the extraordinary usually yields to logical scrutiny."

"Which is why I have come to you. I believe myself to be the victim of a monstrous imposture, though I cannot put my finger upon the betraying detail."

"Pray proceed."

"At a Grand Ball in my palace I fell in love with the most beautiful girl in all the world. She danced with me till midnight; then, as the chimes of twelve sounded, she ran off without telling me her name."

"What of her appearance, Sire?"

"Delightful, delicate, wonderful! She wore the most elegant gown. On her dainty feet were a pair of glass slippers, not quite size three and a half."

Holmes temporarily dismissed the question of shoe size and of how the dancing Prince had determined this feature of his partner. Such a fellow might well have drunk champagne from the girl's slipper. Indeed such a slipper, made of glass, was the only suitable receptacle for the legendary, chivalrous pouring of bubbly into a partner's footwear.

"She danced in *glass* slippers all night long?"

"Certainly. Ah, how we tripped the light fantastic! Then, so suddenly, she fled from my arms!"

"Of *glass*, Your Highness? Were they not fragile? If not fragile, how could her tender young feet . . .?"

The Prince dismissed these suspicions of the sage of Baker Street. "It is nothing unusual in my kingdom to dance in glass slippers. As she fled down the steps of the Royal Palace in apparent panic and disarray she left one of those slippers behind her on the steps. Thus I was able to trace my beloved runaway. I sent heralds through all the kingdom to accompany that slipper. It fitted the foot of only one person: Cinderella, a poor oppressed maiden who I believe must have been a changeling for some royal princess. She confessed. She told me how her fairy godmother changed a pumpkin into a fine coach, and white mice into footmen. We married joyously. And yet – "

"And yet?"

"We have only been married for a year and a day. Her temper grows sharp. She shows signs of becoming a shrew. She is constantly indisposed. I cannot think but that my own true Cinderella has been stolen away, abducted from my palace, and that a simulacrum, a golem of her, has been substituted. This imitation will gradually sour my whole life, thus too the life of the kingdom whose well-being – as you know – is intimately connected with the well-being of its prince."

At this point Holmes took up his pipe and placed it in his mouth – though out of deference to his royal visitor he did not actually light the tobacco. Holmes paced to the window and back a few times. Presently he placed the pipe on a walnut table.

"Your Highness, I must know: prior to that last midnight dance, did you by any chance drink champagne from your partner's slipper?"

"Why do you ask?" marvelled the Prince. "I did not. But why do you ask?"

"Champagne may have made your partner's slipper *slippery*. Consequently it fell off when she fled down the steps."

"A slippery slipper? I did nothing to cause such a thing! I believe the consequence of spilt, drying champagne would be stickiness rather than a slippery condition."

Holmes glanced momentarily at his volumes of pharmacology, his memory searching for a reference in those texts, then he nodded slowly.

"Without intruding too far upon the privacy of the royal bed – "

Gallantly the Prince took the lead. "I may add that Cinderella does not have . . . lubricious feet, delightful though they are to behold."

Holmes admired the discretion of the Prince, for he had told Holmes what he needed to know without invoking the vulgar word "sweaty".

"In that case, Your Highness, there is only one possible answer. We arrive at it logically. Cinderella's slipper slipped off as she ran, yet when your heralds visited her home that slipper fitted her exactly and perfectly. Is that not singular? She did not deliberately kick the slipper off in order to run more swiftly, otherwise she would have kicked off *both* slippers. Therefore, on the night of the Ball that slipper did not in fact fit Cinderella exactly! It almost fitted her; it was slightly too large. Consequently, the Cinderella who lost her slipper at the Ball and the Cinderella whom your heralds visited are not one and the same."

The Prince held his brow, aghast.

"How can that be? The one Cinderella and the other exactly resemble each other!"

"Except in the matter of temper," Holmes reminded the Prince. "And except as regards foot size. You yourself have already harboured the suspicion of a simulacrum, substituted recently, but the true state of affairs is more serious. The Cinderella whom you have married, Your Highness, is either an identical twin of the Cinderella who attended the Ball – or much more likely she is a *clone*. Not a golem, no, a clone. There may be a number of Cinderellas. Your Cinderella fled from the Ball because of her lack of uniqueness. She fled to save you – and herself – from the revelation of that shame."

"I do not care if she is what you call a clone. I love her. Where is she now? That is all I desire to know." The Prince slapped his brow. "Stap me, but I have married the other, and bedded her. A shrew in the making."

"If so," Holmes pursued sadly, though logically, "she must have a genetic predisposition to shrewishness." He carried on remorselessly. "You have already said that her Godmother can transform mice into footmen. I can only conclude that, in addition to the clandestine cloning of at least one of your subjects, experiments in recombinant DNA technology are proceeding secretly in your kingdom. Enticingly beautiful and gracious maidens are being created by the Godmother, with a whole range of specific *animal* characteristics. Shrewishness may only be one such!"

"This is a vile conspiracy!"

"Quite so, Your Highness. It is a conspiracy of monsters in beauteous human female form: identical, innocently seductive people with a coding for some bestial characteristic in their very make-up. She will pass this shrewishness on to your offspring, Your Highness."

"Oh, but my bride is expecting a child even now!"

"When she has given birth to a prince or princess of the blood – and of her blood too – a child who is partly a beast . . . I warrant that this Cinderella whom you innocently married will slip away back to the Godmother. She will not be missed, for another almost identical Cinderella will slip secretly into the palace to take her place, possessing other implanted characteristics which she will pass on to your next child. This new Cinderella may be foxy, a veritable vixen. She will present you with a whore of a daughter. The Cinderella who follows her might present you with a *mouse* who will never win any neighbouring prince's hand. Your household, Your Highness, will become a menagerie of subtle evil: a zoo very like our own Regents Park – of the Beast *inserted into* Man. The Godmother's plans are even more cunning and poisonous than those of the evil Moriarty."

Holmes deeply pitied the stricken Prince.

"All this," the Prince said quietly, "proceeds from a slipper which fell off . . ."

"By elementary logic, Your Highness."

"What shall I do, Mr Holmes?"

"I am only an investigator, Your Highness. My final recourse is always to the justice of the law. In your land – "

"In my land I am the Law. The love of my subjects for me is the whole of the social contract."

"In your bed, through the agency of love, the state will be brought low through the machinations of the Godmother!"

"Must I kill Cinderella, then? Must I stifle my own child, new born? Must I emasculate myself so that my subjects shall not know evil? How can I? The destruction of the capacity for love would destroy the social contract."

"How devious this plot is! How ingenious the Godmother!" Holmes paced the room in anger. "It is as well that the good Watson is not present to hear this. As a medical man he would be stricken to the core by this foul misuse of recombinant DNA and embryology. You are involved in a struggle, Your Highness, against the direst evil in the person of this Godmother. She possesses technology far in advance of your own. Yet she must have some weakness, some flaw. It is my experience that crime always carries the seeds of its own destruction!"

"In the same way that Cinderella carries the ova of my destruction?"

"Indeed. Perhaps here is the key to the eradication of this beastly crime – " Holmes drew out a key from his fob pocket and opened a locked cabinet. Amidst phials of reagents, bottles of laudanum, hypodermic syringes, and antidotes to poison, there reposed a beautiful tortoiseshell comb with a silver handle. This rested across a brandy goblet containing a red apple with bite marks in one side, pickled in clear alcohol. Next to this glass lay a spindle from a spinning wheel, with a springblade needle recessed into it. Carefully Holmes removed the comb.

"Your Highness, I have retained this comb as a memento from a previous case. The worthy Dr Watson was able to ascertain in his small laboratory that this was treated with a certain nerve agent. When the comb is drawn through the hair so that it touches the scalp, it will induce paralysis. Not death, but a suspension of the faculties for at least a century. You must make a present of this to Cinderella. Once she uses it, she will fall into a deep sleep akin to a cryogenic trance. Likewise, the child in her womb. That child which she bears must not be born until you have searched out and found the secret laboratory of the Godmother; until you have compelled her – aye, upon pain of dancing on molten glass – to develop a viral DNA agent which will usurp the shrewish traits in your wife and unborn child! This viral DNA will eject the beastliness from all the cells of Cinderella's body, and from those cells gestating in her womb. *Then* you may revive her. *Then* the joyous birth of your heir may proceed."

From the same cabinet Holmes produced a tiny jar of red salve.

"Here is an antidote to the nerve agent. The good Watson was obliged to develop this to revive the victim in the case I mentioned. It may be applied by means of your own lips. It is a binary agent. In contact with human saliva it becomes effective."

Carefully Holmes wrapped the comb and the jar before presenting them to the Prince. Modestly he acknowledged that nobleman's thanks.

"As to the other Cinderella clones whom you will discover, you must compel the Godmother to inject them also with the viral DNA anti-agent. There will probably be seven Cinderellas in all. Bring the others back to your palace and lock them in the attics. If discreet, you can found a great dynasty – and who will be the wiser? As to your first love, let the glass slipper always be by your bed as a sure way of distinguishing her."

Half an hour after the Prince's departure, Dr Watson returned. Coughing on account of the fog, he gratefully accepted a medicinal glass of whisky.

"How is Hodgkinson, poor fellow?" Holmes enquired solicitously.

"Failing fast." Holmes' faithful scribe cleared his throat. "Did anything of note occur during my absence?"

"I received one visitor – whose identity I may not reveal, even to your good self. His was a problem which I could solve by simple deduction without leaving this room." Holmes reached in his fob pocket and displayed an emerald ring. "I may only say that he was suitably grateful."

"Can you say nothing else, Holmes?"

"My dear fellow, it concerned matters of state." The sage of Baker Street reached for his Stradivarius, and began to play.

The Pharaoh and the Mademoiselle

A river of aether flowed from God's empty skull to his feet, then back again. Its route took it along the left side of the spine, through the pelvis, down the narrow valley between the legs. The river was in two layers. The upper one journeyed towards the feet; the lower layer returned in the opposite direction. So we built a boat of carved bone to ply back and forth. Hull and steering oars rested in the understream; linen sails flew in the upper. Judicious use of sails and oars propelled the boat from skull to heel, from heel to skull.

We built the vessel because Ho and Emtep were boatmen, and what else could they do but sail? Even though our world was only the length of all seventy of us lying head to toe.

Yet the opening of the river to navigation seemed to broaden our horizons. In the old days when God's dead body occupied most of the space in our world, life was much tighter.

That was before we snipped and burrowed and dug and sawed, converting God's substance to other uses. We made tunnels then caverns then quite emptied him out. We mined him, accumulating wealth in the process. What we didn't need we tossed into the stream, which dissolved loose soft substances. Of course all this activity took a long while – more than sixty million turnings of the sand-glass of Ote the Timekeeper.

The boat would not dissolve. It was sawed from God's shoulder-blade, which was hard. Besides, Otem the Priest had laid a binding spell upon the vessel by carving God's name on the hull. (That was before Otem took a revulsion against the boat and began to loathe it.)

Let me list our wealth; for was I not Tep the Treasurer?

We gained many things from God. From his scalp: hair to braid into rope. From his jaw: the ivory of a false tooth together with the gold wire holding it. From up his rectum we extracted cedar oil and honey; from inside his head other oils and balms. Body fats, wax, carbon, black paste, oil of turpentine, bitumen, mercury: all these things from his flesh, and many more.

Sheets of leather lay upon his shoulders. Rugs of gazelle skin hid God's ulcer scars. From his wrappings we gained cotton and saffron cloth and linen.

When we first became aware of our existence, we were all enmeshed in that linen and could hardly move. It took unmeasurable time to bite and claw our way free. And cut; fortunately some of us clutched sharp tools in our hands.

We also obtained glass, lapis lazuli, and silex; gold and silver and copper; jewels and rare iron.

From God's chest and belly we excavated straw and wadding and salts. We threw most of the straw and wadding into the river. God was spacious to live in after that.

We disposed of most of God's flesh likewise, but we left the muscles of one arm and thigh intact. On the arm we grew the little mushrooms which glowed with so bright a light. Whenever we felt hungry, which was very seldom, we ate some mushroom. We absorbed it into our faces. Its light entered us, letting us see clearly into the deepest nook.

On the thigh we nurtured a few beetles and mosquito eggs and pupae which – just as seldom – we ate. We cut the wings off the two adult mosquitoes of each generation which we allowed to mature. We hamstrung the beetles by breaking their legs.

We drank by bathing in the aether stream.

But enough of this bragging of our wealth! I did not let it obsess me merely because I was the Treasurer. (In the way that Ho and Emtep were obsessed by the need for a boat to sail.)

God's name was Hotemtep. We knew this because his name was carved on every one of us. According to Otem we were supposed to serve the God after his death. It seemed to me that Hotemtep served us instead; we were his maggots.

We were all black of body. All of us, with the exception of Em the Musician, had the same face – which must have been the face of the God Hotemtep, though his own huge countenance had been burned away by an excess of caustic unguents. Our eyes were small, close-set; our cheekbones prominent; our noses thin and long and slightly hooked. Our jaws were strong and powerful. Our lips were thick. Our ears protruded.

As for Em, her countenance was a smooth blank. Maybe the God forgot to give her a face before he died. Maybe a musician did not need a face, since her character was manifest in her music. She had ears, and experienced no difficulty in hearing her way around our world.

I loved Em in her scanty lutist's costume. I loved her music, which was voice enough. On my abacus I tallied her golden notes. On her lute she plucked the tally of our treasure. To me her facelessness suggested wax craving the impress of my own face: my nose, my lips, the orbits of my eyes, my tongue. But of course *my* face was just like anyone else's.

We people weren't meant to recognize each other by our faces. What distinguished us was the cut of our clothes and the kind of implements we bore, announcing our function: the stonemason's mallet, the weaver's bobbin, the smith's hammer.

But we learned to put our tools down. We discovered how to detach them from our hands. So to avoid confusion we adopted personal names, which we took from the lexicon of Hotemtep's own name as inscribed upon us. Priest Otem said that since each of us was only part of Hotemtep it was fitting that we should each bear only part of his name.

When I met someone I announced who I was. "I am Tep," I said. In reply he or she announced their name. Consequently our sense of being different individuals was reinforced.

When we saw each other's faces with our own selves reflected so many times over, surely we were meant to reflect that we were all the same – that we were all parts of another, who was dead and torn apart by us. Instead we felt that we were all unique.

We grew apart and altered. We found love and hate. We learned rage and laughter. We smiled and frowned. We helped one another; sometimes we conspired or argued or deceived.

Generally we had work to keep us occupied, but we also had leisure. Leisure gives the opportunity to cultivate oneself. That's because in leisure you find yourself to be a mystery, a taunt, a hollow demanding to be filled.

Otem, as Priest, was our source of secret knowledge. He it was who first taught us to read God's name. Even so, his knowledge was limited – as became obvious.

One time a number of us were sitting perched on the phalange bones of Hotemtep's right hand. I was there, and Otem, and Te the Mason and Carpenter Hote, and Em with her lute, and Timekeeper Ote forever turning his sand-glass, recording within him the number of turns since time began.

Otem announced that our world was a wooden box.

"Beyond the box is the land of *life*. But not immediately. The land of life is too far away for us to reach, unless we first die like the God."

"How can we die?" I asked. "What is dying?"

Otem frowned.

"*We've* no idea," said Timekeeper Ote, "and neither have you."

"It is the long sleep," said Otem.

"What is sleep?" asked Ote.

Otem made no reply.

But if sleep and dying were a puzzle, we certainly knew what a box was! Carpenter Hote had built boxes to store treasure in. And Hote was fast becoming a humourist.

"If our world's a box," he said, "it has two sides."

"No, boxes have six sides," said Te.

"Aha! I mean an inside – and an outside."

"If the land of life isn't immediately outside the box," I asked Otem, "then what is?"

"Another box," replied Otem. "A bigger wooden box enclosing the first box."

"And beyond that?"

"A third box, and maybe a fourth box."

"Oh yes? And beyond?"

"A box made of stone not wood."

"I see. After which, we find a still bigger stone box?"

"Made of granite, the hardest stone of all."

Te tapped out a rhythm with a chisel on God's finger-bone. He matched the strummings of Em's lute, and this made me feel a surge of resentment at him, which I named *jealousy*.

"Hmm," he said. "Even the hardest stone can be split by lighting a fire against it then quenching the fire suddenly with moisture – and repeating the process many times. I know that because I'm a mason. Silex struck on stone will make a spark. The spark will inflame wadding soaked in oil; be thankful we saved some wadding. And if the idea of moisture is inside me, then so is moisture itself. I could spill it from my eyes, *weeping*. I could spit it from my lips, in *contempt* at the granite."

Otem seemed put out by this display of knowledge to which he wasn't privy. He began lecturing us.

"Our world is a hollow concealed within increasingly hard shells!"

Te spat. A blob of moisture stained God's bone, though it soon dried. This was an example of contempt.

"Beyond the hardest shell is the land of life where the demons dwell!"

"What are demons?" demanded Te.

"Demons are terrible beings. Appalling, abominable, abhorrent. Cruel, vile and wicked. We must not rouse those demons. If we do, we'll be destroyed. Within our hollow here we are safe. Yet every time that boat's prow bumps the wall before turning, a tiny noise travels forth through shell after shell." (This was when Otem first became consumed with hatred of the boat.) "One time a demon might notice. And tear the shells apart!"

"According to you," Te reminded him, "the outer granite shell is ever so hard."

"Demons are strong beyond belief! Hotemtep died so that he could protect us here within; so that he would be a world unto us."

"Then Hotemtep must have been a demon." Te struck a

glancing blow with his chisel at the finger-bone, breaking free a flake.

"Hotemtep was a God, you fool! Gods are not demons." And Otem strode off angrily.

I tugged Em by the hand. "Come with me. I'm Tep. I've had an idea."

We walked together under the femur of God's unfleshed thigh till we reached the pelvic arch by the side of the river.

My idea concerned two things. One was the blob of moisture which Te had produced from out of his mouth. The other was the way we absorbed food into ourselves. Perhaps something could pass between Em and me.

"Lie down, Em." She lay; and I lay down upon her. "I love you," I said.

As I rested on top of Em I felt a swelling and glowing sensation deep down in me, and began to squirm. The hot swelling intensified into a fire – a blaze which must somehow be quenched. Yet the fire didn't hurt; or if so, the hurt was a pleasure.

Em must have felt similarly. She was writhing and tearing at her lute with polished nails, twanging the strings loudly, making wild music.

Of a sudden I felt a boiling release, of part of my own being which was absorbed into Em.

We lay still a while then I helped her to stand. Briefly she cradled her blank face against my shoulder. Softly, as though we might melt into one another.

"I name this *sex*," I said. "It is the finest treasure of our treasury. It is the diamond."

We both went on our way, she to strum about our discovery, I to speak.

Soon many people were enjoying sex together in their leisure time. But now that our world had become so well organized, leisure was on the increase. Sex generally occupied no more than fifteen or twenty turns of the sand-glass; and we discovered that we had to wait several hundred turns before our diamond was sharp and bright again. Thus there was still leisure time to fill – otherwise the dispute between Otem and

Te and me (and by extension the boatmen) might have been forgotten.

It certainly wasn't forgotten by Otem, who in his pride didn't know when to leave well alone. Some time later when the boat was tied up to one of God's ribs and Ho and Emtep had just swum ashore, Otem arrived and denounced the boatmen. He accused them of urinating over the side of their boat. This would pollute the aether, said he.

This accusation was a lie. True, some of us had begun to urinate – though seldom. Whenever we did so, our beads of urine were trapped in our robes, there to dry sweetly. But Otem had conceived a loathing for the boat, which suggested the possibility of travel to some place else. So he who had once blessed the vessel now sought a scapegoat in its crew.

"Pissers! Polluters!" he shouted.

Emtep wasn't to be browbeaten. "We did no such thing," he asserted stoutly.

Otem stamped his foot. He pounded his rod of office on the ground.

Emtep wouldn't back down. Emtep clenched and unclenched his fists. Suddenly Otem lashed out with his rod, catching Emtep a violent blow across the shoulder.

Amazingly, Emtep's arm snapped off. His right arm sheared away cleanly and dryly at the shoulder and tumbled, tunic sleeve and all. It lay on the ground with the fist still opening and closing. Many eyes stared from the scar to the arm, from the arm to the Priest's cruel rod.

Then Emtep's partner, Ho, howled and launched himself at Otem. He wrested the rod from the Priest's grasp and beat Otem fiercely with it. Ho's labours on the river had made his muscles mighty. His first blow smashed off Otem's right arm. The second blow, his left arm. A third blow cracked the Priest's head off at the neck. Blow followed blow. Ho belaboured Otem till he had demolished him into a dozen large pieces. Still the boatman wasn't satisfied. He thrashed the pieces of Otem as they lay on the ground, reducing them still further.

Finally Emtep stayed his partner's hand. "Enough. I name this *fury*. You'll wear yourself out."

Discarding the rod, Ho picked up Emtep's severed limb. He was careful how he held it in case the flexing fingers closed blindly on his own hand, trapping it. Ho fitted the top of the arm to Emtep's scar and held the two together for a good few turns, but the arm stayed loose and unjoined. Ho sighed deep in his chest.

"I'm Te," said Te. "A mason joins stones by chipping till two blocks fit perfectly." He flourished his chisel.

"The join is already perfect," said Ho. "Can't you see?"

"Simpler buildings use mud to bind the straw bricks together. Maybe some of God's mud would help?"

Carpenter Hote pushed forward. "I could drive a nail through but the sharp point might shatter the hard flesh."

"I know mud," said Gardener Hoë. "Spittle may be better."

"Wait," I cried. "We must call for Ep the Nurse, with her salves!"

"Of course!" chorused everyone. Now that I had pointed this out, it was obvious. The situation had simply never arisen before.

Immediately a loud call went out for Ep. In the silence which ensued I was the first to notice the squeaking of many tiny voices. Stooping and cupping a hand to my ear, I stepped among the scattered ruins of the Priest.

"Beware demons!" squealed a toe.

"The land of life," piped a nose.

"Boxes within boxes," muttered an ankle.

All the pieces of the Priest were talking, with a noise in proportion to their size. From ear and shoulder-chunk and elbow, Otem continued to nag and curse and instruct us.

"It seems to me," said I, "that our voice isn't of our lips alone, even though it sounds that way. It is of our whole being. Ho hasn't rid us of Otem – he has multiplied the nuisance."

"Aye, but at least I quietened him! And he can't wander around any more."

If our voice was of our whole being, why couldn't Em

speak? I resolved to ask her this. But meanwhile Nurse Ep had arrived bearing her tray of jars. No one had needed these, and Ep had put her tray down long ago and turned her hands to other things; but when the call came, Ep found the tray soon enough.

She assessed Emtep's injury competently then uncapped a jar.

"Sticky honey from the God is what's needed." She smeared the sweet thick ooze upon limb and scar alike then held both together for a while. Soon the honey set, and Emtep was healed.

"Thanks, Ep!" Gleefully Emtep clapped his hands. And we all discussed what to do with the Priest.

Ep said, "If you sort all his parts into the right order, I can fix him together."

Hote said mischievously, "What if we get him in the wrong order, so that his nose grows on his knee?"

"No!" Ho barked out. "I say we should throw his parts in the river like rubbish. The God's name, carved on him, is broken apart. So the aether may dissolve him. We'll be rid of him forever."

Mason Te spoke up, cunningly. "His being might flow through the end of the world."

"And betray our presence?" Emtep asked.

"I don't believe in demons. What would you give, Emtep, to be able to sail that boat of yours through the end of the world into the land of life, to explore?"

"If only . . . but it's impossible!"

"In a boat – quite. In that case we must creep."

"Creep?"

"Aye, creep through the tunnel which Hote and I will bore and drill through the shells of wood and stone. Of course, we'll need assistance."

Hote and Te must have been plotting privately. Never mind! As treasurer I was fully convinced that our time should be used to gain something of value. This scheme would certainly solve the problem of excess leisure.

"That's a good plan," I said. "I support it. We must invest our time and treasure."

"But this might take millions of turns," said Timekeeper Ote.

"So what?" I countered. "It's a bold and excellent plan. And a fine insult to our cringing, bullying Priest."

"What about his parts?" Nurse Ep reminded us.

"I could build a box to store them in," said Hote. "O the Soldier could guard it with his spear."

"We must keep them separate," said Emtep, "otherwise they might join up of their own accord, honey or no honey."

"Let's not forget," said Te, "that Otem taught us to read words. And he told us of the boxes, and the land of life. He might possess more information. He could be valuable. The difference is, now we can control him." The Mason grinned. "How many bits is he broken into?"

I scanned the ground and strummed my abacus. "About seventy, I'd say."

"That's one for each of us. I propose that we all carry a piece of him round with us, in case we need to hear his voice. Emt the Smith can fix loops of God's gold wire to each part. We can hang them from our necks as amulets. If they're a nuisance we can take them off. If he's disobedient we can scorch him or smear foul black paste on him."

"Yes!" cried many voices. So the proposal was adopted.

I hurried to find Em the Musician so that we could enjoy sex together. All the excitement had inflamed me.

However, Em was already lying with someone else. I felt jealousy mount in me as I watched them – but then I restrained myself. Blows struck in anger could break an arm off. Blows could smash a person to pieces.

As soon as Em's lover stood up and saw me, he said, "I am Temte the Manservant."

"Is Emep the Maidservant busy, then?" Temte usually lay with Emep.

"Why yes, Treasurer."

"I see. Well, we shall all be busy soon. We're going to

burrow out through the end of the world. This will be a great task."

"I'll serve gladly," vowed Temte; and I knew that I had made a loyal friend, where I might rashly have made an enemy.

When he had gone I sank down by Em. "Surely you have a voice," I said.

By way of answer she played music at me, and in my heart I clearly understood the tune to mean: "A voice I will have, when I have lips and a face."

Heedless of the fact that Em had just had sex, I fell upon her lovingly. But gently, lest she break. Or lest I break a part of myself. It was then that I found that woman's sexual diamond can be sharp and bright again immediately; unlike man's. I decided to keep this information to myself; since men outnumbered women by a factor of two and additional sexual opportunity might interfere with our work schedule.

Within a few hundred thousand sand-turns Carpenter Hote and helpers had carved a tunnel all the way through the wall just beyond God's feet. This tunnel was ample enough for two people to crawl along in comfort side by side. It led to a second wooden wall which was similar but distinct – between the two there was a narrow fissure.

I had crawled to inspect the gap, but the tips of my fingers would hardly fit into it. I was wearing the upper right section of Otem's head, including one eye and one protruding ear; so I pressed his eye to the crack.

"Look! Tell me what you see."

Silence.

I bit Otem's ear-lobe harshly. "Look!"

"Ouch!" squeaked the Priest's voice. "I *am* looking. It's very dark between the walls. The crevice is as narrow as can be. That's all. Give up this madness while you're still safe. Plug the tunnel with wax."

"Never! Shut up again." I withdrew; and soon Hote was scraping away at the second wall with his tools.

I met Musician Em. She looked different to my eyes. She

stroked her belly, which was swollen. She played music which I found hard to understand. Meanwhile Maidservant Emep approached as if called by the strings of Em's lute.

She too stroked her belly. "I am Emep, and I'm swelling. Something is growing in Em and me."

"Is any other woman swelling?"

"No, just us two."

Emep wore most of Otem's left foot around her neck. I reached and twisted a toe. "What grows in her, Otem?"

"Can a foot see into a belly?"

Em herself wore a shapeless piece of Otem's insides. I didn't know whether this had any feelings but I jabbed a finger into it. "What grows in Em?"

"The energy of your loins, Tep," said a chunk of guts.

Hote and helpers experienced greater difficulty with the second wall. Diffuse aether was flowing into the slight gap between the shells. Just as it's hard to pull a sheet of papyrus loose from the aether river – the papyrus sticks where it floats and feels heavier – so there was a tension across the fissure between the walls. It took effort to shoulder through, and gouge beyond. Otem's various parts mocked our efforts, but we punished them and doubled our exertions, working harder, shorter shifts in the tunnel. After several hundred thousand more sand-turns the second wall was fully tunnelled through – disclosing a third wooden wall. By now the tunnel was as long as three of us lying head to toe.

When Hote finally broke through the third wall, many hundreds of thousands of turns later, he uttered a great *Ha!* of triumph. Clustered round the tunnel entrance, we clamoured to know what he saw.

"I behold *stone!*" came the answer.

But his answer was almost drowned by other cries from nearby – cries of shock rather than acclaim. O the Soldier came running.

"Treasurer! Em the Musician and Maidservant Emep – they're splitting."

"What?" Yet my wits did not desert me. "Find Ep the Nurse, O! Tell her to bring honey."

I hurried in the direction of some of those shocked voices; and found Em lying on the ground upon her back. Her lute was cast aside, as if useless to express her predicament. Her legs were spread apart. A broad crack had appeared on her scant skirt and belly.

Even as I watched, this crack yawned much wider – and a glistening green ball rolled out of Em's belly.

The ball unfolded itself; it sprouted a number of legs and staggered erect. The thing was kin to one of our captive beetles, though considerably larger.

I yanked Otem's ear-lobe, directing his eye at the creature.

"What is its name, Otem?"

"Ah, yes," whispered that hated but at times useful voice, "the knowledge comes. *Scarab*: its name is scarab."

O the Soldier trotted up, with Nurse Ep following at slower pace so as not to drop her tray. The scarab jerked its head about and clashed its jaws.

"Slay it with your spear!" I ordered O. And in that moment I named something which was beyond Otem's knowledge. I named the possibility of killing something, of rendering it dead. Otem had been smashed to pieces but he had neither died nor slept.

Immediately I had second thoughts. What if the scarab was something godly or demonish which had entered our lives? Was it wise to kill it impetuously?

"No, no, do not slay," I countermanded. "Capture it. Crack its legs with your spear shaft. Cut off its wings, if any, with your blade. Bind it with rope from God's hair. No, with wire! With golden wire. Drag it to pasture on Hotemtep's thigh. Peg it securely. And O – beware its jaws."

This was done.

"Aren't you clever?" sneered my Otem amulet.

Ep smeared honey into the crack in Em and pressed her together. Then she went away to tend likewise to Emep – for shouts told us that she too had produced a scarab.

After a good many turns Em stood up, took her lute, and played a wailing melody.

Scarcely had the two hamstrung scarabs been pegged on what remained of the God's thigh-flesh, than Carpenter Hote approached.

"My job's almost done. Stone is Mason Te's province. But listen to this, Treasurer. As soon as I began enlarging the hole, my Otem started babbling."

Hote's share of the Priest had been a knee. Out of the hollow of that knee Otem's voice ranted quietly, thus:

"I name the tiny light at the end of blackness, a *star*. I name the blazing brighter, golden fire, the *sun*. Sun and star shine upon the land of life!"

"Did you see any star or sun, Hote?"

"I only saw stone."

"Is there a lot of resistance from the aether?"

"Yes. Te will have a hard time of it. But it isn't insuperable."

Otem's knee said, "When the final granite shell is pierced, much aether will escape. You will see the sun by night, the star by day. Or the other way round; I'm not sure."

"What is day?" I asked the knee. "What is night?"

It giggled. "Who cares? A mountain of stone sits on top of all the shells. It's tremendous. No one could ever cut through it."

"Then how do we see the star and the sun?"

The knee simply resumed its litany. "We'll still be safe from demons, I pray. Unless they hear us scrabbling. Unless they smell the aether that escapes. Beware!"

I hit the knee just below the kneecap, making it jerk. "How do you know about day and night, and sun and star?"

"When the final wood was pierced the aether shifted, and a veil fell from me; I knew. Beware day and night."

"How can we beware what we don't know?" snarled Hote. Wisely Otem fell silent.

*

Te and helpers began to drill and scrape to open tiny wounds in the stone. Into these holes he smeared oil which he then set alight with silex sparks – and quenched with cups of spit. As though to escape this punishment by flame and moisture the wounds wriggled deeper into the stone. Hammer and chisel could break off flakes and chunks and even little boulders.

The work was hard and dangerous. One labourer suffered from smoke. Another was charred by flame. A third lost an eye – gouged out when his chisel flew askew; but Nurse Ep was able to fix the eye back with honey. Gardener Hoë had her left foot crushed by a tumbling boulder. Since nothing was actually broken off, Ep couldn't help Hoë. So Hoë limped thereafter, dragging her bad foot behind her.

Timekeeper Ote turned his sand-glass a myriad times, but slowly the tunnel lengthened.

Meanwhile the two scarabs were causing trouble. Their appetites were huge. They devoured all within reach. The once-fat pasture of God's flesh was fast becoming mere scraps and tatters attached to the bone. Though the scarabs were hamstrung they often wrenched their tether-pegs free and squirmed to attack and eat our beetles and mosquitoes. O had to stand guard almost permanently, ready to bludgeon them.

"Theirs is a hunger typical of life," Otem's head-part told me. "Beware of life."

Otem had also claimed that the energy of my loins was what had swollen Musician Em. After the emergency of the scarab from her belly Em avoided sex with me. Emep likewise spurned Temte; and soon other women were following their example. Imagine my astonishment when one time I surprised Em and Emep snuggled away together inside the empty jaw of God. The two women were having sex with each other. Both were using their hands a great deal. Em was plucking music from Emep's body, causing a moaning song to issue from deep inside the Maidservant. Emep was moving her mouth on Em's legs and loins and fingering her, playing her like a flute.

I wondered at first, angrily, whether to beat the two of them apart with Otem's rod. Yet after I had watched for a while I found myself pleasurably excited. Stepping closer and crouching down, I enquired whether I might join them; and if so, in what style?

Emep panted. "So that no scarab is conceived!"

"You might be wise. Their hunger's ravenous. Tell me how."

"Lie upon my behind while we squeeze together," said Emep. "Then lie upon Em's."

I did so. I enjoyed. Up to a point. I don't know for sure if the two women enjoyed, but afterwards Em pressed her blank face gently to mine, rubbing softly against my visage.

Eventually the stone wall was tunnelled right through. Beyond the usual narrow fissure, rose a wall of sparkling granite. Granite was the hardest wall of all to tunnel. Mason Te and helpers (of whom I was one, of course) finally had to resort to polishing the granite away by using jewels from our treasury. You crouched in the tunnel with a jewel held full in your fist, sometimes in both fists, depending on size. You leaned your weight forward and scrubbed around and around.

Diamonds were best for the purpose. Amethysts rubbed away too rapidly, staining your hands a prickly mauve. Rubies and sapphires also wore away, more slowly, coating you with sharp dust, deep red, azure. Another myriad of turns passed by.

Why were we striving so? In despair at ever rubbing through the granite, and depressed by the tension of aether in the gaps, I asked myself this question more than once. No doubt we all suffered the same crisis of confidence, but nobody voiced such doubts aloud. The pieces of Otem performed that service for us vociferously enough (if hushedly).

Yet the answer was obvious. The answer had been shown us by the scarabs. Until we could burrow out into the land of life, sex and joy must be unnatural to us.

At long last we had all but tunnelled through. How did we know that our work was nearly at an end? Why, our method had polished the granite to a surface like glass. When that surface became very thin we began to see a hint of what lay beyond through the sparkle-specks embedded in the rock. We polished more gently. We did not lean our weight forward at all. Eventually we could stare through what was virtually a window.

An enormous volume of darkness gloomed beyond. In the darkness several large motionless things loomed. In turn we all took a trip down the tunnel to stare through that window. Even Em went to listen to the echoes of her lute returning from beyond.

When we had all gathered outside again, I asked Oëp the Surveyor, "What do you make of it?" Oëp had the keenest eyesight of us all.

"Hmm. I saw four giant jars, each with the head of a beast as a stopper."

"Are the beasts alive?"

"No."

"And what else?"

"There's a vast wall of rock with a wooden door in it – a door as tall as the God himself. Overhead there's a roof of rock. I didn't see any sun or star, though."

"Beware, beware!" said part of Otem. "You haven't stuck your head into the chamber yet."

"Then we shall do so," I said. "Mason Te, take hammer and chisel – and smash the window."

"Yes, Treasurer." Te crawled back inside.

A couple of turns later we all heard the window break. Immediately aether streamed past us fiercely into the tunnel. There was a great wind, a turbulence. I heard a scream – and thought that Te was screaming. In fact this was the sound of aether escaping out of the hole he had broken, as he later told us. Right now he shouted back to reassure us – he had nearly been swept over the edge.

Two other events clamoured for attention.

"Look up the river!" howled Boatman Emtep. "Our boat sinks! It sinks!"

O the Soldier roared, "Look to God's thigh! The scarabs are free!"

I quit the tunnel mouth and ran. So did O and the boatmen

and a good many others. When we reached the river side of God's thigh, we were astonished. Most of the aether had drained from the river. The boat no longer floated; it lay grounded on the bottom, tilted over. Ho and Emtep clung to each other and wailed with grief. But more amazing still was the sight of the scarabs. The two creatures were devouring one another.

One scarab's jaws had expanded to gobble the whole body of the other scarab. The victim in turn was consuming its attacker from within. Imagine two bubbles on the aether river merging into a single bubble which then shrinks away. That's how it was. One scarab ate the other; the other ate the one. O had no way to prise them apart with his spearshaft. The mingled mass got smaller – till presently nothing remained of the scarabs but a green stain on God's thigh bone.

Truly this was a time of horrid marvels; for now other voices back at the tunnel were calling out, "The star! The star!"

I hastened back there. O followed me, spear at the ready.

People milled around the tunnel entrance, several looking dazed. I saw Surveyor Oëp force his way within and followed him. Soon we were both clinging to the edge of the portal which Te had opened. A granite cliff yawned sheer below, dropping to a plain of dusty stone. Above our heads the precipice continued upward – then there was empty space, then a stone sky.

"Look that way, Treasurer – near where the sky meets the wall."

I did as Oëp showed, craning my neck and tilting my head. A twinkling white light assailed my sight.

"The star, the star," I said stupidly.

Oëp crowded his head against mine. "Whatever it is, it's a long way off."

"Re-mote!" cackled Otem's neck, which Oëp wore.

"We're viewing it through a shaft bored upward at a slant through the stone sky. That shaft must be the length of our world, oh, thirty times over!"

"Just as well it's there," said I. "Is it wide enough to crawl up?"

"Yes. But how do we reach the mouth?"

"No way!" said Otem's neck. "You'll never do it. And you can forget all about the wooden door. Even if you cut your way through that, oh the blockages and barriers beyond! The granite portcullises, the pits as deep as valleys!"

"Shut up," I said. "That star is our signal-lamp. If we hang ropes tied to ropes down this cliff, we can descend. We can walk to the wall. Emt the Smith will make nails to drive into the cracks in the stone. He'll build a ladder of nails all the way up to the sky. Once a few of us reach the mouth of the star-shaft, we can help the others up by pulling. We'll leave by way of the sky-tunnel."

"Folly, folly," said Otem.

The next moments were ones of total terror.

The giant wooden door began to groan and shake. With great grindings and screechings slowly it started to open outward! Blinding light flooded around the edges. From beyond, deafening sounds boomed; voices of thunder! My heart hammered and my limbs quaked.

I nearly became insensible. Somehow I managed to haul myself – and Oëp by the scruff – back to the mouth of the tunnel. Even there, all present were stunned, dazzled, and terrified. Still, I hadn't taken leave of myself – as witness my rescue of Oëp. So I had the wit not to say anything about Priest Otem having been right. What I said was this:

"Listen, everyone: there are giant creatures outside. Spread the word quickly and quietly. After that, be silent. Do *nothing*."

I departed in the direction of God's thigh, with Oëp accompanying me tamely as though my hand was still attached to his neck. Soldier O bravely stayed to guard the tunnel mouth, his spear aimed at the fateful hole we'd cut. I hadn't told him to defend it, but no matter. He stood quite motionless. What else could he do but guard? He was a soldier.

By now Ho and Emtep were sitting disconsolately on the bank. Quickly I advised them to get back on board. Voices chirruped near and far in warning – not as quietly as I would have liked – but soon all fell silent, even including Otem's pieces, though thunderous giants could hardly have heard these.

For hundreds of turns we stayed as we were – doing nothing, saying nothing. All this while, strange fearful noises came intermittently from outside. Vast bumpings and draggings. Godly or demonish speech – perhaps! Who could comprehend such sounds? They made no sense.

Finally the culminating horror occurred.

High up, all around the roof, our world cracked open – screeching in protest. Showers of dust fell and billowed about us. Slowly the whole top of our world was lifted off.

Light drenched down through the dust. Sounds drummed at us.

I let myself be paralysed.

Cast of Demons

HARRY, EARL OF DUNDALK
THEODORE PECK
PROF. DANIEL POULSON, *of the Egyptian Antiquities
        Service*
MLLE. YVONNE BIZOT
TOM KEEVES, *HARRY's "man"*
MME. MARIANNE BIZOT, *of the Louvre*
ALI BEY
IBRAHIM, *a cook*
GAMAL, *a servant*

Act I

(Inside a large tent a table is set for dinner. Candles burn brightly. IBRAHIM and GAMAL wait at table; the others sit around it.)
HARRY: How ill-fated we seemed until today;
    Nothing was going our way.
    All Theodore's dollars doled out for dust.
    How his beef-baron Dad would have fussed.

(*He raises a glass of Perrier water.*)

THEODORE: I'd sure like to know what you think
    Is so damn special – pardon me, ladies –
    About old Hotemtep's tomb!

HARRY: The new Lord Carnarvon Ted would be
    Paying the check for immortality.

THEODORE: Don't blame me if I have the cash
    And you're a penniless Earl.
    Have you been sneaking gin into that glass?

HARRY: It isn't my country which prohibited
    Alcohol – and created Al Capone.

THEODORE: We repealed the Volstead Act
    Three years ago. I'm no puritan.

HARRY: And a poet is never penniless.
    Riches flourish in his heart.

DANIEL: And a sharp tongue in his head.

(*IBRAHIM carries round a soup tureen, and GAMAL serves from it.
Both men wear red tarbushes and white uniforms.*)

HARRY: Dear me. My only desire was to amuse.

YVONNE: Que vous êtes un bel esprit!

TOM:
(*He tears up a bread roll.*)
    What's that mean?

HARRY: It means, Tom,
    That the charming and ravishing Mam'selle
    Appreciates my wit.

(*MADAME BIZOT clears her throat.*)

YVONNE: You are charming yourself,
    Monsieur le Comte!

TOM   Oh ho,
    And maybe she's hunting a title.
    Wed Byron here; becomes Countess of Dundalk.

MARIANNE:
(*She clears her throat more loudly.*)
    In answer to your question, Mr Peck:
    Hotemtep's tomb presents a strange enigma
    – One which may become as notorious
    As any trove of treasure.

THEODORE: There's little enough of that commodity.
  A couple of sandals with gold buckles
  And a cofferful of earrings
  Spilled in the antechamber.
  The tomb was robbed, by hasty thieves.
MARIANNE: But absence is revealing in itself.
TOM: As on the *Marie Celeste*, do you mean?
MARIANNE: I refer to the absence of tampering
  With the seals on the burial chamber.
  The twine was still tied. The wax,
  Still stamped intactly with Hotemtep's sigil.
DANIEL: *Ergo*, the robbers did not break in there.
TOM : Ibrahim lad, this soup's boiling hot.
IBRAHIM: It will cool, Effendi, if you look at it.
HARRY: Better boiling hot than bubbling with typhoid!
MARIANNE: And yet inside the inner coffin
  We find ruination, total wreckage of the mummy.
  Explain that if you can.
THEODORE: I blame that mouse hole.
MARIANNE: Mice?
  Mice don't bite through granite!
HARRY: Maybe some malicious enemy of Hotemtep –
  Such as his mother-in-law – inserted beetles
  Down a readymade hole at the last moment
  To feast on his flesh? Dung-beetles.
  Scarabs. Or that other kind we found.
MARIANNE: The larder beetle, which feeds on dead flesh.
  No beetles could account for such damage.
DANIEL: If Hotemtep's mother-in-law had wished him ill,
  She would hardly have fed him to scarabs!
  The ancient Egyptians viewed the scarab
  As a symbol of eternal life. Deified as Khefri,
  The scarab is the God of Life ever renewing
  And ever transforming itself, forever reborn
  Out of its own substance. You'll recall
  We found glyphs for Khefri carved here and there,
  Hmm?

YVONNE:
(*She claps her hands.*)
      But we did find a treasure, didn't we?
  The little figures.
MARIANNE: The *Ushabti*. Yes indeed.
  What a wonderful model of society
  Three thousand years ago! The detail
  Of their faces, hands and tools: exquisite!
TOM: Their faces? You must be joking.
  They're all as alike as Chinamen.
MARIANNE: Well, they *are* made of china; almost.
TOM: They all look the same, is what I mean.
  Like Chinamen all look the same.
MARIANNE: But of course! That's because
  They're all modelled on dead Hotemtep.
  As well as being an entourage to serve him
  In the afterlife, they are different aspects
  Of his spirit. As a collection they're unique.
TOM: Box of toy soldiers, I'd say.
DANIEL: Only one
  Is a soldier.
THEODORE: Exactly *how* unique?
DANIEL: Madame Bizot isn't exaggerating.
  They're exemplary. In my view this alone
  Redeems the whole expedition. That's to say,
  Our efforts were worthwhile. All your, um,
  Generosity.
THEODORE: You're kidding.
DANIEL: I assure you,
  To a true Egyptologist these Ushabti
  Are as much treasure as any golden thrones.
MARIANNE: Oh absolutely.
YVONNE: I feel I could be
  A little girl again, and play with them
  In my nursery.
HARRY: You are eternal girl, Mam'selle,
  Fille éternelle! You will never age,
  Never lose – how would Ted phrase it –
  Your peachiness.

DANIEL: No touching!
HARRY: My dear Sir,
    I'm well aware we're at the dinner table.
DANIEL: No touching the Ushabti unnecessarily.
    No playing with them, that's to say.
HARRY: Are they as fragile as all that?
DANIEL: One of them got smashed to pieces
    And strung round the necks of the others
    With gold wire.
MARIANNE: Another enigma!
    One which opens a strange perspective
    Into the conscience of Old Egypt.
HARRY: The consciousness.
MARIANNE: Same thing.
HARRY: Not since psychoanalysis. I must glance
    At this new *Autobiography* of Freud's
    Some time, to see if he understands himself.
    Not that I care much for analysis –
    We murder to dissect – but I might find
    The prompting for a poem.
MARIANNE: The Ushabti
    Deserve to be staged in a worthy setting.
    A tableau. A special exhibit.
    They should be posed all together
    In a miniature reconstruction of ancient life,
    Not just lined up in any old glass case.
    Not these little marvels.
DANIEL: Hrumph.
HARRY: Ah, now there's poetry for you.
    How could the mother of such charm and beauty
    Not have poetry in her soul?
THEODORE: I get it:
    A sort of tableau vivant.
MARIANNE: Tableau *mort*.
    But you understand me. Failing the Louvre,
    Which could certainly do our Ushabti justice . . .
(*DANIEL POULSON shakes his head violently.*)
    The local museum might serve the purpose.

> Somehow I feel the figures should stay
> Near the tomb where we found them.
> Twenty kilometres is no great distance.

DANIEL:
(Brightening, he glances sidelong at THEODORE PECK.*)*
> If only our local museum had more space.
> Such as a new gallery.

THEODORE: I'll endow one.

ALI BEY: Your generosity is exceptional.

THEODORE: Yeah, well.

HARRY: Speaking of damage, did you notice
> How one of the Ushabti had lost its face?
> The lute-player. How poetically appropriate
> If it could wear a new face: namely that
> Of Theodore Peck of Chicago, USA,
> Discoverer, patron of Egyptology.
> Ah, but I'm forgetting: the lute-player
> Would be female. In which case
> Only one face could serve as a model
> Of eternal beauty and artistry.

(Plucking paper and pencil from his pocket, HARRY *starts sketching* YVONNE's *face.)*

TOM: Ladies and Gentlemen, I pronounce the soup
> Drinkable.

CURTAIN

Act 2

(Six months later; where desert sands meet tomb-pocked cliffs. A full moon shines bright. Holding HARRY's *fingers lightly,* YVONNE *peers closely into his proffered palm as though reading his fortune; or her own. Actually* HARRY *is showing her something tiny.)*

YVONNE: This is most mischievous of you, Harry.
> But I'm flattered.

HARRY: Oh, I was always
> As handy at this kind of thing

As a sailor carving scrimshaws.
My fingers are rather subtle –
In a number of ways I could mention.
YVONNE: I'm sure they are. Oh God, Harry,
I've been bored. How could it take so long
To erect one wretched gallery?
It was all right for you, lucky fellow,
You went hunting lions in the Sudan.
HARRY: Need I add that all that time
Your face burned in my mind.
Night after night in my tent
I worked at this face from memory.
YVONNE: Truly, a remarkable likeness!
In fact, it's *me*. I feel strange –
As though now magically you control
Part of me.
HARRY: Hmm. Now I only need
To fix this face on the little Ushabti
With tiny pins and strong glue.
I brought tools with me: a jeweller's drill
And such. The join will be imperceptible.
Do you know where your mother keeps her keys?
YVONNE: You are like Monsieur Raffles,
The gentleman cracksman! Whose crimes
Were never pinned at his door.
But won't this one be noticed immediately?
HARRY: Well, yes. Of course – by your mother,
And Dan Poulson and Ali Bey and Ted Peck.
But they'll all keep quiet as mice.
Just imagine the scandal there'd be
Supposing one of them cried foul
At tomorrow's opening ceremony
Before all those distinguished guests.
Such as the Director General of Antiquities,
The Queen of the Belgians, the Maharajah
Of Jaipur, the correspondents of *The Times*
And *Le Monde* and a *Zeitung* or two.
What dishonour. What disrepute.

And all observed by photographers
Eagerly popping off their flash bulbs.
Note how our beef millionaire insisted
No photos of the Ushabti should be released
For earlier publication – so that they
Should positively burst upon a moderately
Astonished world. I'll wager you
Our little lute-player captures the imagination.
She'll be the most pictured. The enigma!
The beauty! Then who'll dare denounce her?

YVONNE: Newsmen might remark on the fact
That I bear her a striking resemblance.

HARRY: The Egyptians believed in reincarnation!
You always felt strangely drawn
To an ancient destiny here by the Nile!
Hmm, perhaps that's a touch extravagant.
Why not just act surprised? If newsmen notice,
Protest! Then let them convert you
Oh so reluctantly.

YVONNE: I'm sure Maman
Won't be so reticent in private.

HARRY: Serves her right for marooning
A dashing spirit like you in the desert
To dine on donkey giblets for a year.

YVONNE: Ah yes, it has been a cruel exile.
So why did *you* ever come digging, Harry?

HARRY: In search of inspiration. Ancient passion.
Magic of antiquity – en route to the lions.

YVONNE: And in the absence of adventure
You invent it. As witness this face.

HARRY: That's how it is with poets.
I create. Though I also shoot.
Blood of death; blood of desire!
Did you read those poems I sent you?

YVONNE: Oh yes. Très passionant.

HARRY: You know their true meaning, Yvonne,
The meaning of the heart. If only
Our lute-player could set music to them

    To serenade you.
YVONNE: If only.
HARRY: I still need keys, though.
    Unlike Raffles, I can't cut and file my own.
    Will you fetch the keys for me?
YVONNE: Oh yes. But the night's still young.
HARRY: True. I shouldn't make my move too soon.
    The guard needs a few hours to get sleepy.
    Ah les clefs! Les clefs de mon coeur!
YVONNE: The keys to your heart?
HARRY: To yours too,
    Yvonne?
(*They embrace*)
YVONNE: Là là! I believe, ami,
    We are really speaking about another organ
    A little lower down the body than the heart.
    Let's touch on that, in the next hour or so.
(*They sink down together out of sight behind a dune.*
Enter ALI BEY, *clutching a rifle.*)
ALI BEY: First Muhammed quit. Today, Towfik.
    Let's hope the new man proves to be
    A less cowardly, superstitious peasant!
    Let's hope he just snores the night away
    And doesn't complain of hearing faint music
    Or spying tiny movements from the corner
    Of his eye – scurryings out of sight
    Which all turn out to be nothing.
    Sheer imagination! Or at most
    A scuttling spider or a scorpion
    Which a rifle butt could crush in a trice.
(*Exit* ALI BEY. *From behind the dune mild sounds of ecstasy are*
heard.)

CURTAIN

We were taken from our world and transported to a new one. What terrors and bewilderments we endured on the way. How hideous our existence once we arrived.

The new world was twice the size of the old, but its walls weren't of solid sheltering wood; they were of clear glass. Every now and then a giant demon would come to gape at us. That was during the bright time, time of the Sun. At first, stunned by such light and deafened by demon voices, we couldn't see or hear sensibly. But we adjusted. Somewhat. There was also a dark time of equal length, when we dared move around and discuss our predicament. The bright time and the dark time were *day* and *night*. Though even at night the demons could flood us with light, if they chose.

Could we continue to endure such an existence? Opinion was divided. Some of us said yes, others no. Otem's head-parts insisted that we must tolerate our fate; his heart and viscera argued otherwise.

We were in a mockery of a world. Formerly God's bones had sheltered us; now box-houses made of card and straw stood here and there meaninglessly. Oh the loss of God's bones! Sand shifted treacherously underfoot. Our boat was locked upright immovably in a false river of glass. Only a trace of aether remained. A thin thread was still attached to the prow; this snaked away through the glass wall. And oh, the loss of our treasure. We were robbed and ruined. Lucky that we had little appetite! There were only sand-mites to sustain us.

One night a dozen of us conferred.

"Are the demons really evil?" queried Carpenter Hote. "They didn't break us or crush us."

"Just as well," retorted Ep the Nurse, "since they stole all the honey that heals."

"Perhaps they are Gods like Hotemtep," said O the Soldier. "In which case maybe it is our duty to serve them by standing still wherever they put us."

"So *many* different Gods?" whispered Otem's loin. "I can comprehend a dozen Gods, or twenty. But these seem innumerable."

"Maybe they too live in a box," said Hote. "With the lamp of the sun crossing the roof by day; the stars and moon by night."

"No," said Otem's foot. "The land of life stretches forever."

"He's right about that," agreed Surveyor Oëp, "so far as I can see through that window over there."

"Could we appease the demons?" said Maidservant Emep. "Could we speak to them?"

Otem's mouth-part cackled. "Their words are not our words. And would you have sex with a demon's little finger?"

"We could attract them by moving about," she said. "By dancing and clashing our tools. Emtep could climb up and down the rigging. Em could play her lute by day, as she does by night."

"If they knew we could move they would destroy us," said Otem's mouth.

"How does our Priest know that? He even argues with himself."

"How does our Maidservant know that they *wouldn't* destroy us? Alternatively they might hamstring us, or bind us with iron stays."

"Iron!" Emt the Smith spat out. "The demons have so much of it. The little which we have is as nothing. So I am no one. Tep has no treasure left, so he is no one. Ep has no honey. Emtep's boat can never sail. We are all no one."

"No," I said fiercely. "Once we were nothing, with no existence. Now we possess existence. Our existence is equal to any other existence."

"Is it? Is it?" cried Emt. "Ask the parts of Otem their opinion on that score! Our existence is equal to that of a mite."

At that moment the giant distant door swung open. A sudden shaft of light swept across the white cliffs of the outer walls, towards us. We knew this searching light well. It sprang from an iron tube held in a demon's hand.

Immediately we scurried back to our given positions. I reached my own not a moment before the searching light turned night into day inside our world.

The light jerked and vanished. The giant door slammed shut again. The demon had withdrawn in haste. Demons, it seemed, were frightened by darkness.

Another night, a demon with a light tube came. It unlocked the glass lid of our world. This demon smelled of sex. It picked up the paralysed Musician Em, lifted her out, and bore her down along with the light to the hidden floor below. The sky stayed open.

Mason Te's position was close by me. Rashly he shuffled closer.

"Ho and Emtep are nimble climbers – "

"Fool! Get back!"

"If many of us go to the glass well and form a pyramid of bodies, Emtep might be able to – "

"To fall? To shatter on the floor far below?"

"He could take ropes from the rigging, to lower himself."

"He'd have to use *all* the rigging. And what if he did reach the floor? Where the demon is grunting! What then? Get back! Quickly."

Presently the demon rose up – too soon for Te's crazy scheme to have worked. Its hand descended. It put Em back into our world. Then away it went, having closed the lid on us. Within another turn our world was dark again; darkly visible.

We rushed to Em – and she faced us. Yes, faced us. For now she had a face!

It was a face quite unlike our own: with large eyes set well apart, with smoothly rounded cheeks. A nose more like a plump thumb than a thin crooked finger. Delicate lips. A firm little jaw. How strange, how alien. She explored her new face with her fingers – in particular feeling her eyeballs.

"I can see," she told us. Those were her first words, spoken in a lilting voice. "I'm still different from you all. So very different."

I caught hold of her hand. "Em, we're all of us different. We're all unique."

Nurse Ep asked to examine Em. She ran dextrous fingers

around the edges of the Musician's face. "Perfect," said Ep. "Strange but perfect."

"Do you call that a face?" exclaimed Timekeeper Ote. "It's the mask of a demon! Whose face will the demons ruin next? We must flee this terrible place!"

In wrath I hit Ote. He fell, dropping the sands of time. Immediately I felt remorse and helped him to stand. "This place *is* terrible," I said to him, "and you're right that we must escape. But Em's new face is a delight – do you understand? It's a treasure."

"If you say so."

Mason Te handed Ote back his sand-glass. Ote stared at it numbly.

"I've lost count . . . I've forgotten the number of turns! Even during the days while I couldn't move my hands I counted inside myself. I was still in touch with the sands. And now I've forgotten. You knocked the total out of my head. We've lost our history." He brandished the sands at me in blame.

I might well have deserved his blame, but I wasn't prepared to accept it. "We already lost our history!" I shouted. "We lost it when the demons took us from our home. Our real history starts now – with Em's new face, and with the resolve to escape. Is that clear? Turn your glass again, Ote. Count again, from *one*."

Ote hesitated; for a short while he looked about to oppose me.

"Ote has lost count," observed Smith Emt. "So now he is nobody, either."

Far from encouraging Ote in rebellion, Emt's sneer had the opposite effect. Ote glared at Emt. "I am Ote," he said. "I count time, that's what." And he did as I bid.

"If we *could* escape from here," said Surveyor Oëp briskly, "I believe we could follow the thread of aether all the way back to the God . . ."

Act 3. Scene One

(*Dusk, inside the Theodore Peck Gallery of the museum. White-washed walls, a chair, a stool; one window showing a desert of sand and stones. Waist-high on cast-iron supports stands the glass case containing the Ushabti tableau. Enter* ALI BEY *furtively, carrying a large matchbox in his hand.*)

ALI BEY: Maybe I'm not thinking straight.

But oh the insult to my dignity, as overseer!

There'll be no more funny tricks,

Once a scorpion shares the display case.

And just supposing there's a grain of truth

In what those credulous cowards

Towfik and Muhammed said on quitting,

From now on nothing will dare move.

(*He unlocks the lid, raises it. From the matchbox he tips a live scorpion into the case, closes the lid and hurries off. Presently* YVONNE *enters. Musing, she lingers by the door.*)

YVONNE: I'm drawn irresistibly; can't help myself.

Oh I'm not drawn to the Earl of Dundalk

Particularly. Maman's wrong on that score.

Harry's amusing, but it's clear to me now

That his seductive rigmarole was mostly

An excuse to delay the moment of truth,

To avoid erotic action; at which, frankly,

He isn't too expert. To begin with

He spilled his seed prematurely on the sand.

His second attempt was adequate.

Third time round, he couldn't perform

At all; lay limp. I'd rate him somewhere

On a scale between semi-competence

And impotence. If I married him

I'd certainly need to take a lover!

Though that doesn't mean he isn't amusing.

No, it's here that I'm irresistibly drawn

(Though I try to resist): to that glass case,

To the doll within who wears my face

And whose pictures will soon be in all the journals

Though not on the society pages.
Whilst I, as Maman suggested in pique,
Ought to wear a black veil
Like a Moslem woman, to avoid
Revelation of the scandal.
Oh but I can't resist another peep . . .
(*She tiptoes silently. She peers into the case – and gasps, wide-eyed with shock*).

CURTAIN

Emergency! Dire emergency! The armoured beast raced through our midst, scattering sand. The cruel claws of its arms snickered and snackered. Its tail writhed in twitching tension; a ball of poison flicked from its sting.

We stood paralysed; but this was no protection. The beast sensed what we were. It rushed at lame Hoë, seized her by her crippled foot, threw her this way and that way. It dashed at Manservant Temte and bowled him over. Its sting descended overhead. The sharp glistening tip stabbed Temte in the chest.

Poor Temte screamed and writhed. Then he convulsed and lay still. The beast's poison had destroyed him!

Now no one dared stay inert in its path. People blundered to hide in flimsy houses. Others skidded across the glass river, in haste to board the *Hotemtep*; which they did. From up the rigging Ho bellowed that they mustn't climb any higher. Unfortunately his voice attracted the monster, which rushed towards the river. Those on board cried out in fear and began to scramble up the rigging. The mast groaned alarmingly. However, as soon as the monster set foot on the river, its walking claws slid from under it. The beast drew back enraged, and charged elsewhere.

"Silence!" shouted O the Soldier. "Shut your mouths. Run soft-foot. Will any volunteers help me fight our enemy with tools?" That O needed help was a mighty admission; but it was realistic.

Emtep promptly shinned down from on high. He freed the

steering oar, dropped it clattering on to the river, disembarked. He and Ho were soon advancing shoreward, struggling to hold the great oar out ahead of them.

Hottep the Butcher brandished a long knife, though the blade had been blunted by tunnelling. Pto the Brewer-woman armed herself with lame Hoë's spade. O held our only real hope: his spear with the iron tip.

Soon, skirmish began. Pto and the boatmen tried to herd the monster while O jabbed and stabbed. But his spear only bounced off the armoured shell. Several times O danced aside from claws and sting, not a moment too soon.

From the fringes of the combat I called out, "I have an idea!" The monster leapt round to face me. "I'll lure it to the river. We'll try to make it lose its footing. O can spear it in the underbelly."

Hastily I fled riverwards – and the beast lumbered after me. On the deck of the *Hotemtep* I heard Em's lute-strings strumming. Her voice sang,

"Oh who will help us . . . ?"

Just then a great shadow loomed across our glass sky.

Act 3. Scene Two

(*Inside the gallery a powerful paraffin lamp burns, attracting insects in from the night. The door stands wide open; as does the lid of the Ushabti case. The stool lies broken to pieces.* ALI BEY, THEODORE, HARRY, TOM KEEVES, YVONNE *and* MARIANNE BIZOT *are arguing.*)

ALI BEY: Maybe I did put a scorpion in the case.

But that was to stop any more mischief.

HARRY: By stinging my hand? By killing me,

Whom the lions of the Sudan couldn't touch?

Hotter than fire, sharper than needles

Is the sting of the scorpion!

If you're stung you die in mindless agony.

You're sacked, Ali Bey.

MARIANNE: He isn't your man.

You don't employ him.

ALI BEY: The other reason
  Why I put a scorpion in there
  Was to keep the Ushabti in their places.
  May Allah have mercy on us all now,
  Even infidels. The Jinn are loose.
MARIANNE: Are you in your right mind, Ali Bey?
ALI BEY: Is your daughter in hers? Or is she
  Possessed?
MARIANNE: Insanity, insanity.
  This is another of your jokes, Dundalk.
  You heard how those wretched fellahin quit
  So you wanted to stir up some wild superstition
  Resembling the Curse of the Pharaoh.
  You corrupted my daughter, made her a thief.
  Where have you hidden the Ushabti?
  Return them promptly, and we'll say no more.
HARRY: *I* corrupted Yvonne? I assure you, Madame,
  She knows a lot more than me!
THEODORE: You ain't much of a gentleman.
HARRY: More about this incident, I mean.
YVONNE: I already *told* you all about it!
TOM: Why didn't you show us the dolls
  Busy dancing?
YVONNE: They were fighting so bravely.
  The scorpion was slaughtering them.
  I had to squash it with the stool leg.
THEODORE: Fine, fine; I can appreciate that.
  But did you have to pick them all up
  Afterwards and show them the exit?
  There are a damn sight more scorpions
  Outdoors than indoors, any day.
YVONNE: It was her voice, her eyes . . .
HARRY: Her eyes.
  Enchanting eyes. I'm so in love
  With what I made. I made her.
THEODORE: You oughtn't to talk about making
  Young ladies. That's vulgar.
HARRY: One face is in my heart, one face alone.

YVONNE: Not mine; but mine in miniature – on her.
　　That's safer, isn't it, Harry?
　　You can love her because she's so small;
　　Too small to make real love to, ever.
HARRY: Now I've lost her. She's gone.
YVONNE: Perhaps a lost love is preferable?
　　A poet's kind of love! Needing fantasy
　　To magnify it. If that's the size of the muse
　　These days, poetry has sunk somewhat low.
HARRY: It doesn't matter what size . . .
　　But oh her voice, and her eyes!
　　At least there's something we agree on.
　　Which way do you suppose they'll head?
YVONNE: I've no idea. Why do you ask?
　　Do you want to give chase to your new love
　　The way you pursue lions? In that case
　　You'd best proceed humbly on hands and knees
　　Otherwise you might destroy her
　　In the moment of finding her.
　　I beg you, leave them alone!
ALI BEY: In God's name, I agree!
　　Once the Jinn are out of the bottle
　　It's hard to cork the neck again.
HARRY: The tomb's too far for tiny legs:
　　Twelve miles as the crow flies
　　Even if they could find the way.
　　Besides, there's nothing left there;
　　Not even a bone.
TOM: 　　　　　　　　Speaking of bones,
　　The boat you took from the coffin –
　　The one in this case here – is carved
　　Out of bone, now isn't it? Right,
　　Mrs Bizot? I'm the first to admit
　　I'm no archeologist; but a bone boat
　　Always struck me as queer . . .
MARIANNE: Another enigma; I quite agree.
　　What's the point of this, Mr Keeves?
TOM: The boat's the missing shoulder-blade

Of old What's-his-name.

MARIANNE: Perhaps.

TOM: So when was it carved into a boat?
  And who carved it? Did that happen
  After Hottentot was in his coffin,
  All buried and sealed? Maybe it's true
  About these Ushabti people, hmm?

THEODORE: Gee, you're right, Keeves. Oh wow,
  I do believe you are. Here's me moaning
  About a slap in the face to my generosity,
  About fame suddenly becoming farce –
  And all along I'm missing the main chance.
  These Ushabti would be a million times better
  At pulling the crowds in, than any flea circus.

MARIANNE: The Ushabti aren't your private property,
  Mr Peck. They don't belong to you.

THEODORE: If they've run off, they surely
  Aren't antiquities. They ain't your province,
  Madame. Finders, keepers. Ali Bey:
  Do you have men who know the desert?
  Men who can track like bloodhounds?

ALI BEY: It's in my very blood. My own father –
  May Allah smile upon his memory –
  Escorted black gold from Cameroon to Arabia.

YVONNE: This is obscene. You're speaking
  Of slavery – of the slave trade!

THEODORE: The Ushabti ain't human, honey,
  Any more than a troupe of monkeys.
  They're a freak of nature, that's what.

TOM: If you catch them, what makes you think
  They'll dance and sing? Till the scorpion
  Tickled them, they stood like statues.

THEODORE: I'm sure I could ginger them into action.

YVONNE: Using scorpions? Or cattle prods?

THEODORE: No, that's plainly unacceptable.
  I'd find a kinder, more efficient way,
  Such as mutual advantage. I offer protection;
  They perform.

YVONNE: Freedom's what they want.
    Sacred liberty.
THEODORE: Is a steer free on the range?
    Yes, but in the long run, no.
    Are people free in a score of countries
    I could name? Such as France's colonies?
    Or Britain's? The blacks are protected –
    For their own sake. And in return
    They deliver the goods. That's the way
    The world goes round; and always has.
    Maybe the Ushabti will think I'm a sort
    Of God.
YVONNE: You? A God? What an ego!
THEODORE: I'll be magnanimous – great-souled –
    Towards them. And who says *they* have egos?
    How can they, when they're all the same?
HARRY: Save for the lute-player. She at least
    Has gained a soul.
THEODORE: Yvonne's soul?
YVONNE:
(*She rubs her brow.*)
    I think I have a migraine.
HARRY: I *created*
    A soul for the little musician
    When I created a face for her.
TOM: A black face, to be sure.
HARRY: A white face on a black body
    Would have looked rather silly.
THEODORE: Incidentally, Ali Bey, the Ushabti
    Don't know the tomb's empty, robbed utterly
    For the second time in history, by archeology.
ALI BEY: In the desert the little Jinn will face –
THEODORE: A long walk. An Odyssey.
ALI BEY: *Enemies.*
    Such as other scorpions. And wild dogs.
    Black-tailed vipers and horned adders.
    Overhead, ready to pounce, there'll be
    Sparrow-hawks, owls, kites, buzzards,

And falcons – not to mention small eagles.

THEODORE: So we'll be doing the Ushabti a favour
  By finding them, ultra-fast.

CURTAIN

It was black night, with stars spilt all across the sky. The ground creaked and groaned, releasing the day's heat. Lumps of rock got in our way, ranging from little chunks the size of a body to boulders like hills. Yet threading our way through the stony regions was easier than wading across tracts of sand.

Easier as regards our footing. But in sandy areas we could almost pull ourselves along the aether thread as though it was a rope. When tumbles of rock forced us off course we had to cast around afterwards to regain the line where it snaked over the terrain; and who was to say for sure that it was the same aether cord which we latched on to? Thrice already other aether lines had cut our path crosswise.

"This way," squeaked Otem's neck.

"That way," insisted his foot.

"Left," said one hand.

"Right," said the other.

Fortunately for us Surveyor Oëp was navigating – with help from Ho, who had found he had skill in following stars.

We'd halted to count our numbers and gather in any stragglers. It was the three hundredth turn of the sands since the demon with Em's face had set us free on the wild barren land.

"Why did she do it, Em?" I asked.

Em thought a while then answered, "She did it out of love. But demon-love is like madness. The demons search for lost parts of themselves which they imagine are hidden in the hearts or bodies of others; thus they can never find what they seek. This drives them to wild excess and fantasies – unlike us, who are all one at heart."

"So they are sick, and we are sane? Then why did the scarab come out of you?"

"The aether-energy was roused, and had to create something. It wasn't the right time or place."

"How do you know these things, Em?"

"As to the aether, maybe my lute could play the answer . . . As to the motives of demons, the lips of my new face shape my reply for me. Hear me, Tep: we have all forgotten something of great importance. Its name is ever on our lips, but we don't hear."

"Hmm," I said. I tallied our numbers on my abacus. Ho had finally joined us, helping twice-lamed Hoë along. Only Temte the Manservant was missing. He would always be missing . . .

"Hmm, that doesn't help us discover our way."

Otem's head-part spoke up: "Find a pool where many aether streams meet. Join me together there; then we'll remember what we need to know."

"Join you *how*?" asked Ep the Nurse. "We have no honey."

Different pieces of Otem answered.

"Use mud."

"Use dung."

"Use the blood of a hot beast. Use its belly juices and its spittle, and its anal slime and the drooling of its eyes."

"Kill a beast the size of a mountain?" asked O sarcastically.

"We're all here," I announced. "Let's continue. We'll march till the sun rises, then we must hide under stones."

"Why?" asked Emt the Smith. "I favour heat."

"So you might, but the sun's heat could crack us the way it cracks these rocks into sand; and as Ep said, we have no honey. Besides, we'll need shadows to hide us from hungry, hunting beasts. And by day the demons might hunt us. They might quarrel about our liberation."

"You are wise," said O.

We proceeded through boulders, then over shifting sand, and then across a plain of pebbles. When we were mid-way across that plain, the moon rose. That night, however, the moon was only a thin silver sickle. The moonlight did not search us out. One time, a monstrous long snake with horns and a flickering forked tongue reared at our approach. But it was sluggish, so we all escaped.

Towards dawn, the brightening horizon silhouetted two masses swaying ever so slightly against the fading stars. One was a square, the other a pyramid. From their direction wafted the memory of fire-embers, and a rank stench of beasts. But we had cover. Dry spears of grass rose around us, and bushes of wire sprawled higher and higher. Ahead, grass and bush became an arid forest, with the roofs of those shapes looming above. Our view wasn't wholly blocked by the forest, though.

Surveyor Oëp called a halt. "I name those two soft buildings *tents*," he said. "The tents of demons. We must avoid them. We'll have to circle right round and pick up the aether-thread on the far side."

Emt objected. "That's an enormous detour you're proposing! It's as long as our whole journey already."

"And Hoë can only hobble," said Pto, who was currently supporting our gardener.

"We'll have to hide soon," said O. "Tomorrow night perhaps we could slip stealthily between the tents? I could scout ahead."

"March right on!" urged part of Otem's head (with nose). "I smell an aether pool beyond those tents. Powerful aether streams converge. My nostrils twitch like a hare's. That's why so many plants grow hereabouts."

"Yes, we'll stop here all day," I said. "We'll scoop holes under stones and hide ourselves; and we'll spy on that, that . . ."

"That *camp*," said O.

"Then this evening we'll decide whether to detour."

Everyone agreed. So we burrowed in under boulders, scooped sand over ourselves, and lay still.

Swiftly a golden gong of fire heaved itself up over the forested horizon, hurling light everywhere but also casting deep shadows. I say "gong" because the sun did indeed sound the day. Soon bleats of hunger rose from the camp, nasal but strident: beast voices crying the emotions of their churning tyrant bellies. Four beasts, perhaps five.

"I name those animals, *goats*," muttered Otep the Herdsman who had crowded in with me. "Goats'll gobble anything: rags, sandals, knobs of dung. You hobble 'em by night, loose 'em by day. By night they'll have stripped everything. Demons'll up their tents and shift away. Our way'll be clear, come the dark. You'll see."

By the evening, however, our path was still blocked. Maybe the secret presence of the aether pool caused the demons to linger, unawares of why. Maybe there was a more sinister reason.

I'd chosen a hiding place from which I could keep watch. Depending on my line of sight through the bushes, from time to time I saw the hairy monstrous goats wander about, cropping, ripping, chewing. A raggy boy with a big stick supervised them; but he never herded them in our direction, where the vegetation must have looked paltry to his eyes.

Before long, two male demons approached the tents. Both were familiar to me. One was white-faced. The other, with a swarthy face, was the demon who had put the monster in our world with us! This time the swarthy monster held a box big enough to fit us all in. He shouted at the boy; and a demon in dirty robes emerged from the square tent. Demon words were spoken. Circles of metal were held up, which I recognized as coins though they weren't of gold or silver; and thin rectangles of papyrus. A few pieces of metal were presented; most were put away together with the papyrus. And the visiting demons departed.

Morning wore on; then afternoon. Frequently the boy ignored his goats and ranged far and wide poking the ground with his staff, jabbing down holes, flipping boulders over. He came close, but never discovered any of us.

The sun descended the far side of the sky and slipped redly out of sight. Dusk swiftly darkened; stars revived. We crawled out of hiding and formed up in a double line.

"We'll detour," I said, "however long it takes."

"Go straight to the aether pool!" squeaked Otem.

"Shut up, you."

Herdsman Otep had been right about one thing: the goats had indeed stripped much of the ground we were to cross. Oëp took the lead, with Ho sighting the stars. I brought up the rear, just in case anyone listened to their Otem amulet and was tempted to take a short cut.

We had only been marching for twenty turns when thunder drummed; when boulders flew from under the hooves of a hairy mountain – when a great goat loomed over us, horned and bearded! A broken chain hung from its neck.

The first to be seized and gobbled was Oëp. Ho, a moment later.

Some of us were shocked into immediate paralysis where we stood. Others – me among them – first threw themselves flat, then froze. Perhaps a dozen fled; but the goat pranced after the fugitives and easily snatched them. Then it picked up those who were standing stock-still, and gulped them. Finally, it ate those who lay – one by one. Within a turn or two I, who had been at the rear of the column, was the only person left.

The goat's lips and tongue reached down for me, and

The goat isn't sated. It wanders past the two tents, out in the direction of the little secret aether pool, which even it hardly knows is there. Arriving, it browses around – till it begins to feel unwell. Kicking up its heels, it races away in the dark and the starlight to escape the sensations inside it. A goat possessed, it flees along the strongest stream of aether far far out into the desert till eventually, exhausted, it plunges into a deep invisible aether pool down in a rocky depression near where some ancient inscribed stones rise, worn by time and sandy winds.

Here the goat lies down thumpingly upon its side, flanks quaking, breathing heavily. Soon it slumps unconscious.

During the remainder of the night the goat's whole body writhes as though it is a sack of maggots, a big bag of worms. Although it's hard to see what's going on down there in the dark, the goat seems to be steadily losing its original goat shape.

When dawn comes

I am alive again. Alive!

I name myself. I am Hotemtep.

The Priest didn't lie. Old Hatshep-Siptah told me the truth. The aether has borne me down the stream of years and washed me ashore at last. Hatshep-Siptah alone in the double kingdom had honed his senses to know the aether; no one else. In his youth Hatshep-Siptah sailed to Ind and Chin. He met sages, secret lords of power. He brought back the abacus, too, in which he instructed Henet-Taa my treasurer.

Yet Hatshep-Siptah made no special preparations for his own death. Did he not fully believe in the method? Did he feel fulfilled in life, content with one existence? Or couldn't he afford the cost of secure burial, till the Ushabti could begin their work? Aye yes, the cost! But I paid Hatshep-Siptah handsomely. Surely he had enough money?

I never asked him. Or if I did ask, I've forgotten.

Why am I thinking about Hatshep-Siptah? He isn't here. The Sun is rising, showing me the stony dent in the desert where I have awoken. Hereabouts must be a powerful aether pool, though I can't sense it with these wits of mine. Hatshep-Siptah alone . . .

What did he advise me to do on waking?

Check yourself, Lord Hotemtep. Contemplate yourself. Consolidate yourself.

Let me rise and behold myself in the morning sun. Let me stamp my legs and hold up my arms.

Ach, part of my left hand is missing. The hand is narrow – thumb and two fingers only – as though it has been chopped in half down the centre. Ach!

I'm wearing ill-cured goatskin. Hastily I lift and search beneath. Penis, yes. Scrotal sacks, aye. Shall I urinate or jerk seed to celebrate this new life of mine?

A goatskin . . . Suddenly the memory of all my shattered age-long dreams assails me. And I know that many things went wrong.

I was robbed; the golden wealth in my antechamber was all stolen.

My Ushabti didn't scale the air-shaft. Instead, they were stolen away, as well.

The lute-player's music could bewitch. Her face was left blank so that it could grow the face of the host chosen for me. But my Ushabti didn't enchant a human being, then climb down the throat into belly and lungs. They entered the body of a goat!

Things have gone badly wrong. Yet how bad is badly? – compared with the fact that I am alive? The goat's body has become human.

Its body . . . How about my head? Let me feel it carefully. A goatee beard sprouts from the nub of my chin; perhaps that's just as well, since my jaw recedes . . . Above my mouth: a huge nose. My ears are high and pointy. Two cranial bumps stud the sides of my skull like the buds of a kid's horns . . . Yet undoubtedly it is a human face; so my fingers tell me.

Does it matter if there is some goat in me? Did not Anubis wear the head of jackal? Did not Khnum bear the head of a ram?

Afar off down the desert I spy a couple of tents. Beyond, are buildings of some sort. My eyes are keen. I feel strong and nimble.

And a young woman's face – exotic, foreign – is painted in my heart.

Act 4 Scene One

(*The desert. Enter* MARIANNE *and* YVONNE *with parasols,* TOM
KEEVES *carrying a cardboard box, and* HARRY *in a Panama hat
with a hunting rifle.*)

MARIANNE: Fool's errand. Madness. Absurd. A jape.
    I've come for one reason alone:
    So that you can show me where you hid them!
    Ah no, *two* reasons . . . also to chaperone
    My rash daughter, since she insists
    On accompanying you – which you may say
    Is definitely a case of locking the door
    After the burglars have broken in.

But I'm not prudish, understand!
I sympathize with all true lovers.
If only that's what you were!
I hope to forestall some even greater folly.

YVONNE: You needn't worry about Harry and me.
. Maman. That's over and done with . . .

TOM: Now that Lord Harry's in love with a real doll;
As Mr Peck might phrase it. But Mam'selle
Wants Lord Harry to leave that doll alone –
Can she be jealous?

YVONNE: Harry's pursuit
Is the lesser of two evils; that's all.
If *he* finds the Ushabti (second day lucky)
At least he won't force them to become
A side show at a circus. Will you, Harry?

TOM: Orfully vulgar idea.

HARRY: Never! I shall . . .
I shall apotheosize her in verse.

TOM: So she'll be seated there on your desk
Playing her lute to inspire you –
Like that Frenchie, Colette, with her cat?
Sure, we'll transport the whole bunch
Back to the old ancestral sod in Ulster.
Plenty of the little people there already!
Sure, they'll skip like fairy folk
Across his pages, won't they now?
Though these'll be the first nigger leprechauns.

MARIANNE: Hotemtep may have had negro blood.
There was nothing odd about being black
In ancient Egypt, nothing disreputable.
No more than in France's African colonies
Where at least *our* negroes learn to speak
Parisian French – not the English of pigeons.
But that isn't why the Ushabti are black,
Tom Keeves. It's normal and traditional.

TOM: Is pigeon English what's spoken in Trafalgar Square
Where Nelson's Column stands; who sunk
The French fleet, even though he was blind?

HARRY: Shut up, Tom.
TOM: Or you'll horsewhip me?
    Sure, let the blood flow, as at school
    On the whipping block.
HARRY: I have *no* interest . . . !
YVONNE: Why do you tolerate this person, Harry?
MARIANNE: Dear child, you have a lot to learn
    About the English. Their public schools,
    So called, where only rich boys go,
    Mark a man for life, as surely as if
    His buttocks had been thrashed till scarred.
HARRY: I was *never once* . . .
MARIANNE: Sensitive poets
    Are specially marked by such experiences.
    Which is why they become such poor ones.
    Their imagery, suspect. Their view of woman,
    False: a mixture of ignorant fear and lust
    And soulful idealization. Their performance
    In bed, less than perfect. Do you know
    That their slang word for a young schoolboy
    Who serves the older boys, is a "fag"?
    The very same word is used for a catamite!
    Of course, they need to make love to women
    Since property has to be inherited properly.
    Their king seems to have the right approach,
    To his Mrs Simpson; but mark my word,
    Hypocrites will soon chase him from the throne.
    And oh the educational standards, là là!
    The English only stumble in a foreign tongue,
    Just as they stumble in love. Moi-même,
    As well as French I speak fluent English
    And German and Italian and Old Egyptian –
    Though there's no one to speak Egyptian to.
    In sum, my dear, our Lord Harry *needs*
    The roughness of his man Tom, as his foil.
    And Tom Keeves plays up to the part.
TOM: Do I just? In my humble opinion
    Most French poets were perverts,

    Like that chap Rimbaud who grew lice
    In his hair. Or Bawdy Liar, poxed
    And wallowing in Filth. Disgusting.
MARIANNE: Actually they were alchemists
    Making golden music out of dirt.
    I do mistrust the English respect –
TOM: I'm Irish, all be it from the north!
MARIANNE: The English respect for hygiene,
    Particularly when they don't know
    What a bidet's used for.
TOM: A what?
MARIANNE: This comes from having to defecate fast
    In public school toilets deprived of doors
    So the boys can be caught if they play
    With themselves, or with each other.
    Hurrying to get your pants back on
    Becomes a habit. Perverted hygiene
    Finds a Freudian sublimation in English cookery.
    Thou shall not eat the slimy snail
    Or the thighs of frogs, or such.
    Thou shall boil all vegetables
    Until they're safely dead. Thy beef
    Shall wear no disguises. Thy sauces –
    If any – shall consist of boiled white milk
    And flour.
YVONNE: Maman! All of you, stop it!
(*Enter* HOTEMTEP. *Barefoot, and dressed in an off-the-shoulder
goat skin which just covers his upper thighs, he resembles one of
those anchorites or pole-squatters who infested the Egyptian desert
in early Christian days, starving and scourging themselves, consequently seeing angelic visions and suffering devilish temptations.
He is of middle height and swarthy skinned. Short dun-coloured
hair coats his skull. Goatee beard, receding chin, big muzzle of a
nose. His resemblance to a shabby madman is, however, super-
ficial. His eyes gleam with vital energy. He holds himself proudly,
with great self-possession.*)
HOTEMTEP: (*To Yvonne.*) It is thou, without a doubt,
    Whose face is painted on my heart!

YVONNE: Qu'est-ce-qu'il dit, Maman?

MARIANNE: Whatever did I say? That no one
   Speaks Old Egyptian? But this man does!

(*In somewhat broken ancient Egyptian.*)
   How is it you speak language?

HOTEMTEP: With my lips; and tongue. Which are also
   The organs of love's preliminaries.

MARIANNE: True. But I mean: how do you talk
   That language?

HOTEMTEP: Why, I drank it with milk
   From my nursemaid's nipples. It is – it *was* –
   The language of the double kingdom here.
   I suppose words have changed since last I lived.
   Hatshep-Siptah warned me of such a possibility.
   You shall be my interpreter, strange woman.
   I once had need of an interpreter
   To converse with the Babylonians.

MARIANNE: Since you last lived, did you say?

TOM: Madame Bizot never told us she talks Arabic
   Amongst her many other foreign talents.

HARRY: I've never seen anyone remotely as queer
   As this chap, in the Sudan or anywhere else!
   Why does he stare at Yvonne like that?
   Has he stumbled upon the Ushabti?
   Has he come across the lute-player?

YVONNE: I'm strangely drawn to this person,
   God knows why. He's hardly personable.
   Yet there's a vigour about him, a clarity
   (Despite his smelly goat skin),
   A new kind of fire – as though
   He's a freshly discovered element of nature,
   Radioactive, whose rays strip me naked
   To the bone. Admittedly he's a bit
   Disgusting . . . Pity about his hand,
   More like a crab's claw. Yet I fancy
   It could grip firmly and caress softly.
   Monsieur! Effendi! How do I address him?

HOTEMTEP: She speaks to me. She knows me.

(*HOTEMTEP's virile member lifts the goat skin somewhat.*)
   It must be an age since last I knew
   A woman, except in my shattered dreams.
   My body cries out; it points.

HARRY:
(*He grips the rifle at the ready.*)
   Good Lord! Upon my word! I say!

TOM: Positively indecent! Next thing we know,
   This weird wallah will expose himself.
   I bet he isn't wearing underpants,
   No more than those Masai warriors
   We met outside Nairobi three seasons back,
   Who laughed at us for bottling our farts up
   In our breeches.

YVONNE: He's a force of nature;
   Yet also he is a man. So maybe we have met
   Some desert nature-deity, a Pan of the sands?
   His garments are certainly loose enough;
   And he bears a resemblance to a capricorn.
   I pray Harry doesn't go *pan! pan!* with his gun
   In defence of modesty and repression.

MARIANNE: Tell me! What did you mean by saying
   "Since you were last alive"?

HOTEMTEP: I was dead.
   The sands have turned twenty million times
   Since then; and now I am alive. I, Hotemtep.

MARIANNE: Do I have a fever, or sunstroke?
   Am I hallucinating? How on earth
   Can a dead man come back to life?
   He wasn't even a whole corpse.
   Just a ravaged, gutted mummy!

HARRY:
(*He lowers his gun.*)
   I heard him say Hotemtep. Why?

MARIANNE: That's who he says he is: the pharaoh,
   Resurrected and reborn.

HOTEMTEP: My Ushabti
   Served me well; they found me a new body.

HARRY: What's that about the Ushabti, eh?

MARIANNE: Where *are* the Ushabti, Hotemtep?

HOTEMTEP:

(*He strikes his chest.*)

Within the new me; their duty done.

MARIANNE:

(*She wipes her brow.*)

But how? I don't understand.

HOTEMTEP: Truly, it is the greatest of secrets.

I shall share it on receipt of a great sum

In gold – of which I have been robbed –

To provide for me adequately in my new life.

(*He plucks disdainfully at his goat skin; while Marianne proceeds at some length to explain the situation to the others . . .*)

CURTAIN

How amazed we were still to exist! Admittedly we were all lodged in different parts of Hotemtep's new body: Musician Em in his windpipe, Ote in his heart beating time, Stonemason Te in one of his kidneys, myself in the purse of his scrotum; and so forth. We had no way to walk around and meet each other face to face. Nevertheless we could still call out and hear each other. Hotemtep's nerves carried our voices along their subtle wires. The assorted bodily clamours – the pumping of the blood, the gurgling of the stomach, the gassy oozing of the guts – didn't drown out reception.

To Gardener Hoë, lodged in the intestines, our present circumstances were a fulfilment, a blissful return to an innocent paradise of which the dead God, lying in his boxes of wood, then stone, inside the tomb had only been a shell, a husk. Now the living flesh of God was encysting us.

To Maidservant Emep, within God's stomach, we were all serving at a noble banquet, all of us contributing to a grand communal task; sustaining the new life of Hotemtep.

Others – the majority – weren't so satisfied.

From the brain-stem an angry rebel cry came down from Soldier O:

"Does Hotemtep know or care that we exist? He does not! Like mindless tools we rebuilt this body for him. And now we give up all our freedom to sustain him. By our presence we power his heart and lungs and loins. We are uttermost slaves! I can say this now that Manservant Temte is no longer with us. He was the soul of servility."

"No, he was not!" cried Emep, from the belly. "He knew his place – and now we all know ours. The God was with us all along. Each of us was always part of him; and now we have simply restored him to himself. Where were we going, I ask you, but back to the tomb of boxes? What other desire or ambition did we have? But we had forgotten how to accomplish it. You should be guarding against any mutiny or desertion of God's parts; not saying such things, O."

Surveyor Oëp kept watch behind Hotemtep's eyes. From that high eminence he could see what was happening outside.

"Friend O is right," he said. "We need to look out for ourselves. This bondage is worse than the glass world, worse than the wooden world. What future is there for us? I should have sought a place for us to dwell on our own – in the empty burrow of some desert beast, perhaps."

My part of Otem spoke to me. "What future, he asks. Well, I'm the Priest. And I'm the Oracle. I'm the part of God who can guide, not through deserts but through destinies. If I'm put back together I can answer Oëp's question."

It transpired that all around God's body other Otem-parts were telling the same story.

"Was I not right about the star and the sun?" Otem went on. "What a mess you made of things on your own, without my guidance. True, I forgot much. I made mistakes. But if I'm put back together here inside Hotemtep all my skill will be restored."

"Aye," said I, "and maybe our independence of thought will be at an end."

"I'm one of you. Believe me!"

Nurse Ep spoke out, from the cleansing liver. "How do we put our Priest together, when we can't meet each other? Not even O can travel. He can only jab nerves with his spear if he wants to discipline us. Isn't that so?"

O confirmed that it was so.

"Release me from your necks," pleaded Otem. "Loose me all at once. My parts will enter the blood and lodge in the heart, where they'll clot together."

We discussed this proposal for a long time, some assenting, some dissenting. In the end it was Musician Em's vocal support for the plan to reconstruct Otem which swayed the doubters. She had talked at length to Surveyor Oëp about what he saw outside. She, who wore a face and eyes which were not Hotemtep's, was willing to trust to Otem's superior vision.

Act 4. Scene Two

(*The same.*)

HARRY: What, the Ushabti are inside him?
    Including my beauty, with Yvonne's face?

HOTEMTEP: Failing gold, then diamonds will do.
    Diamonds are lighter to carry around.

HARRY: What did he say?

MARIANNE: That he'll settle for
    A fortune in diamonds to stake his new life;
    In exchange for which: the secret
    Of Resurrection. But what kind of life
    Can a pharaoh ever lead in Nineteen-Thirty-Six?

TOM: Maybe the new king Farouk has a rival?

MARIANNE: There are already enough pharaohs
    In the world, with Hitler and Mussolini
    And that Franco creature clawing his way
    Through Spain!

TOM: What's wrong with old Adolf
    And Benito? Apart from them being foreign?
    You just said you speak German and Italian.

MARIANNE: I speak the German of Goethe and Schiller
    Not of these new uniformed barbarians
    And book burners; who don't much like Jews

And Gypsies.

TOM: Oh, so *that's* it!
     You and your daughter are French Jews
     Out in Egypt to dig up the pharaohs
     Who enslaved you? Well, well, well.

HARRY:
(*To Yvonne.*)
     Are you Jewish?

YVONNE: Yes. What of it?

HARRY: Oh nothing. Good heavens.

TOM: And your Pharaoh here's a gypsy.

HARRY: What?

TOM: "The Dukes of Egypt" is what
     The travelling people call themselves.
     And their boss man is the "Pharaoh" of the band.
     You don't know much about words, for a poet.
     The name "gypsy" comes from "Egyptian".

MARIANNE: What to do? He has to survive.

YVONNE: I shall teach him French, Maman.
     We must take him home secretly to Paris.
     His education should begin at once.

TOM: What kind of education would that be?
     A sentimental one, I'm thinking . . .
     Let's hark back for a moment
     From matters of morality
     To the business of immortality!
     The golden path to living again.
     I'd say we're on to a winner, wouldn't you?

HARRY: Oh but my lovely lost lute-playing muse!

YVONNE: Forget her. She's done. Digested.
     Swallowed up, incorporated, fused.

MARIANNE: The Ushabti bundled all together
     Don't add up to a single kilogram.
     They must have *stolen* a body; invaded it.

HARRY: Odd sort of body to find wandering round.

YVONNE: Remarkable! Full of animal magnetism!

MARIANNE: Hotemtep, whose body did your Ushabti
     Take? Who did they kidnap for you?

HOTEMTEP: *That* is part of the great secret.

MARIANNE: He won't say.

TOM: I'm wondering if Jesus
    Had Ushabti disciples – or angels –
    With him in his tomb? After all his Dad
    Did visit Egypt not long after the Magi
    Brought three boxes of rare gifts.

YVONNE: We'll find out the truth in Paris.
    We can hide him in our apartment
    Till he's fit to stroll the boulevards.

TOM: Unless your concierge gossips!

YVONNE: Madame Laval?
    Maman and her are two peas in a pod.

TOM: Laval, indeed, And might she be
    Any relation to Prime Minister Laval?

YVONNE: No fear! Maman despises that man.

MARIANNE: So should any Jew with sense.
    Laval encouraged fascists and Nazis.
    Oh the rumours that are leaking out of Germany!
    It's no world for Jews, I fear. Or Gypsies.

HOTEMTEP:
(*To* MARIANNE)
    I'm waiting;
(*To* YVONNE)
             face of my heart.

CURTAIN

I cast loose my part of Otem's head. Throughout Hotemtep's body everyone did likewise with their amulets. These were quickly swept away by the processes of the body. Timekeeper Ote, who was stationed at the heart, counted the pieces as they arrived there and began to congregate.

Within a dozen or so turns Otem was complete again, save for the part which scorpion-slain Temte had worn: half of the priest's left hand.

Soon Otem spoke.

"Brothers and Sisters," he called out, "I foresee terrible

things for Hotemtep, even worse than any *we* have known! I see him travelling to a city which is a hundred times the size of Thebes or Memphis. I see him hidden in the top storey of a huge house, while he learns to speak a new language. Then for a time there is happiness. Exploration of the city, love, drunkenness on wines the like of which he never imagined, meals such as he never dreamed could exist; though not too much wealth. I see him becoming a local character, consorting in cafés with painters, poets, philosophers and clowns. I see a painting by one Pic-As-So called *Man with Goat's Head*. I see a book written later by one Jon-Pol-Sart called *Monsieur Hotemtep, Pharaoh and Faker*.

"Then I see *war*. I see iron birds dropping eggs of death from the sky. I see iron bulls goring fields and cities. I see armies of men with iron helmets riding narrow iron chariots which bound forth tirelessly like hunting dogs.

"I see Hotemtep hiding again at the top of that house, hiding from the iron men wearing the sign of the crooked cross and from the men in long leather coats, who smash on doors. I see his mistress and his mistress' mother hiding with him.

"I see the iron and leather men, find them and drag them away, and crush them into a great closed wooden chariot packed with people wearing yellow stars. A dozen such chariots are chained together in a line, and pulled by a long iron chariot belching smoke; tugged by the wheels along iron tracks away from the city, through fields and towns for day after day while the people starve and cry for water. Then the chariots enter iron fences with high towers surrounding a hundred barracks of wood that stink of living death and of greasy smoke from high chimneys.

"I see worse! I see Hotemtep cry to a cruel commander dressed in black that he hides in him a great golden secret which the two women also share: the secret of Resurrection.

"The black commander is mad with faith in wizardry. He has heard rumours of the streams and pools of aether. He and his brethren of the crooked cross have sent spies to Ind and Chin to hunt the source of this knowledge; in vain. He tries to discover the golden secret of Hatshep-Siptah through harsh experiments and tortures.

"But Hotemtep does not know the whole of the secret. When the scorpion destroyed Temte the keystone was lost.

"Finally the torn body of Hotemtep is tossed into an oven; and burnt. We are all burnt with him, utterly consumed. That is what I see, Brothers and Sisters. And beyond that, *nothing*, forever."

So saying, Otem fell silent.

"What can we do?" Hoë called from the intestines. Many other voices took up this refrain.

"Hotemtep does not know us," said Otem, "so he cannot hear my guidance. We could perhaps warn him in dreams, which Em could sing to him; but he would ignore his dreams, as unbelievable, until they came true. Thus we must stop him. We must stop him in the only way he can be stopped, and pray that later when the world has changed we can start again. We are the Ushabti! What we have done, we can undo!"

"We are the Ushabti!" we all cried.

"Let me tell you how," said Otem, our true priest of wisdom once again.

Act 5. Scene One

(*The lofty lounge of a suite in Shepheard's Hotel, Cairo. Bamboo furniture – the chairs with lace antimacassars; potted palms; an Empire sofa the size of a bed. A huge brown oil painting of shaggy Highland cattle amid rainy Scottish crags. Electric lightbulbs scintillate in a crystal chandelier. From the dark balcony, through veils of mosquito netting, step HOTEMTEP, MARIANNE, and YVONNE. HOTEMTEP is now wearing an off-the-peg creamy tropical suit, white shirt, brown tie, and patent leather shoes.*)

HOTEMTEP:

(*He discards his jacket and unknots his tie.*)

Why do all men of importance
Wear nooses round their necks?
Is it a symbol of humility?
A sign that anyone can strangle them?

MARIANNE: How can I explain that a necktie
    Is de rigueur in good society
    Such as one meets at Shepheard's?
    Ah, what bourgeois hypocrisy!
    He's perfectly right. A necktie is really
    A symbol of strangulation, by convention.
YVONNE: How refreshing he is! How natural.
    Who cares about the Bourgeoisie? Not I.
MARIANNE: We all disguise ourselves, my dear.
    We hide our feelings and our origins.
    A Jew wears the guise of a citizen of France
    Till something like the Dreyfus case occurs.
YVONNE: I shall not hide my feelings much longer.
    Maman, it is time for his next lesson.
MARIANNE: And I must find Harry, whose title
    Certainly oils the wheels of authority
    Notwithstanding the scandal of the "robbery"
    Of the Theodore Peck Gallery.
    I hope we didn't rouse Ted Peck's suspicions
    By hastening off to Cairo . . . Take care, Yvonne.
(*She opens the door to a corridor which could probably accommodate a train; departs.*)
YVONNE: Sit down, Monsieur Hotemtep. Stand up.
    Shut your eyes. Open them. Good.
    What is this called?
HOTEMTEP: Your nose.
YVONNE: And these?
HOTEMTEP: Your ears. And those, your lips.
    Below: your breast. Oh face of my heart,
    I must kiss you.
YVONNE: To kiss lips,
    Which haven't kissed a woman
    For the last three thousand years!
HOTEMTEP: My tongue will speak more smoothly
    After it touches yours.
YVONNE: Indeed? Why not?
(*They embrace. But after a few moments* YVONNE *pulls away in puzzlement. For* HOTEMTEP *stands paralysed . . .*)

What's wrong? Why don't you move?
Stop pretending to be a statue!

CURTAIN

Act 5. Scene Two

(The same, except that YVONNE *is now apparently alone. On the carpet Hotemtep's shirt, trousers, and shoes lie mixed up in a pile of debris prominent among which are many bones.* YVONNE *bites her lip and digs her fingernails into her palms to ward off hysteria. Enter, from the corridor,* MARIANNE *and* HARRY.*)*

YVONNE: He kissed me, and he fell to pieces.

HARRY: *What?*

MARIANNE: My child!

YVONNE: It's true.
  As soon as we kissed, he stiffened.
  He froze. Not icily. More like stone
  Or marble. Suddenly cracks ran across him . . .
  And he crumbled – into this heap, my Hotemtep.

HARRY: Femme fatale, eh? That didn't happen
  When *we* kissed . . . ! You *are* joking,
  Of course.

YVONNE: No, no, no, no, no!

HARRY: Oh.

MARIANNE:
(She kneels to sift the rubble.)
  Here's one Ushabti. Here's another.
  Three, four, more.

HARRY: *(Helping).*   They're dead.
  Inanimate. Just figurines of clay.

(As MARIANNE *disinters still more,* HARRY *lays them out in a line on the carpet.)*

YVONNE: Maman . . . Harry . . . He was alive,
  And now he's dust.

HARRY: His golden secret
  Must have been fool's gold.

YVONNE: I'm shattered.

HARRY: (*Grimly.*) Nothing compared to him!

MARIANNE: But what do we do now?

HARRY: A bag:
    I'll fetch a bag, and we'll pop them in.

(*He dashes to the bedroom, to return with a leather travelling bag
and a couple of newspapers.*)

MARIANNE:

(*She counts hastily as she sorts.*)
    . . . Sixty-six, sixty-seven, sixty-eight,
    And here's the lute-player at long last.
    That's sixty-nine.

YVONNE: Show me her!
    Yes, it's me; still me . . . But look:
    She isn't wearing anything round her neck.
    Nor are any of them!

MARIANNE: You're right . . .
    Their amulets have all disappeared:
    Those broken chips stuck to gold thread.

HARRY: Sixty-*nine*, did you say? That's odd.
    There were sixty-nine to start with,
    Weren't there?

YVONNE: Oui, soixante-neuf.

HARRY: But one of them got left behind
    In the exodus: the one the scorpion stung,
    Which disintegrated subsequently
    In Ted Peck's beefy grasp.

MARIANNE: I must have counted one of them twice.

HARRY: You must have done.

(*Kneeling, he tears off squares of newspaper, wraps each Ushabti
up individually in a paper twist, and lays them in the bag.*)
                                Hmm, like boiled sweets.
    But beware of swallowing. Who knows
    What effect they might have on a fellow's
    Constitution! I'll get Tom to dispose
    Of the rags and bones and dust.

(*He reaches for the lute-player, which* YVONNE *has taken from her
mother and still holds.*)
    Please?

YVONNE: You arid Anglo-Saxon pragmatist,
    You stiff upper lip. He just kissed me,
    A moment ago.
HARRY: I know. And *I* loved
    Her – impractically, after my fashion.
    Frankly, of a sudden I feel cured
    Of that particular intoxication.
(*YVONNE releases the tiny figure; HARRY wraps it.*)
MARIANNE: What do we do next? Take them
    Back to the museum?
YVONNE: No! Ted Peck would stop
    At nothing, to make them move again.
HARRY: And obviously they never will.
    I wonder . . . I'm sure a psychoanalyst
    Would tell us that everything was caused
    By guilt and sex and infantile repressions . . .
    I wonder, did we all hallucinate?
    Did we three together steal the Ushabti
    Unconsciously, and bring them here
    In a sack full of bones and stuff –
    Then suddenly become sane again?
MARIANNE: When a poet becomes sane, he's finished.
HARRY: Or else he matures.
YVONNE: To administer
    His estate? To take his rightful seat
    In that House of Nobles at Westminster?
    Why do you say with such certainty
    That they'll never move again?
HARRY: The secret was fool's gold. Dross.
    It fell apart. Thanks to a kiss,
    From reality. Just like the Sleeping Beauty,
    In reverse. And you are my reality, Yvonne;
    Reality is you. Will you be my wife?
    Will you be the Lady of Castle Dundalk?
    The Countess?
YVONNE: Me? But I'm a Jew.
HARRY: Who cares about Hitler's prejudices?
MARIANNE: You ought to!

HARRY: I should let Adolf Hitler
    Rule my life? Not likely. Listen, Yvonne,
    You *must* marry me. We have to be
    The custodians of the Ushabti, you and I.
(He picks up the travelling bag for a moment, then sets it down.)
    The guardians of Pandora's box.
MARIANNE: Also in reverse.
HARRY: How's that?
YVONNE: Yes, how?
MARIANNE: Hotemtep has fallen apart. The Ushabti
    Let him crack up – I'm sure of it.
    They have hidden away inside themselves,
    Unlike Pandora's imps. But why?
    What prompted them? Surely not a kiss.
    Maybe *I* should be lucky to hide away
    For the next hundred years or so.
    Maybe millions of people would be lucky.
HARRY: Don't worry, there'll never be another war
    In Europe – not while the British Empire
    Lasts. *(Gallantly.)* And the French Empire too.
MARIANNE: At least Yvonne will be safely
    Out of it. Perhaps. For a while.
    He's right, Yvonne, you ought to wed him,
    And take the Ushabti with you.
    Why shouldn't you build them a tomb
    In Ireland, like the one they came from?
    Milord the Duke of Hamilton did so
    On his estate, in Eighteen-Fifty or about.
    When he died he had himself embalmed
    And placed in a genuine sarcophagus.
    Have a copy of a sarcophagus made,
    Harry. Lay them to rest in it.
HARRY: Along with a copy of a mummy?
    Or should it be the corpse
    Of a faithful Irish wolf-hound
    To puzzle future archeologists?
    Ah, there won't be any of those.
MARIANNE: There won't?

HARRY: Unless civilization ends!
  And that can't happen nowadays.
MARIANNE: Egypt fell; Carthage fell; Rome fell.
HARRY: Yes, but those were isolated places.
  There may be a few more wars to endure
  Here and there, but believe me
  From now on the whole world's continuous,
  All one from Tasmania to Timbuctoo,
  From Madras to Marseilles to Mexico.
  As are you and I, Yvonne. Continuous.
YVONNE: Really?
HARRY: Yes. I'll get Tom to clear up.
YVONNE: No. *I* shall do it. With my own hands.
HARRY: There's enough to fill a suitcase or two.
YVONNE: Fetch two. We'll buy new ones.
  We'll take his remains and drop them
  Into the Nile. Together, shall we, Harry?
HARRY: Yes, but we'll sink them from a houseboat
  Off Gezira. I'll hire a houseboat
  For our engagement party. Fireworks
  And champagne and dancing – we'll waltz
  And lancer! There'll be photographers.
  We'll release a hundred white doves
  With streamers bearing good-will greetings.
MARIANNE: Won't guests be puzzled about the suitcases?
HARRY: We'll say . . . what shall we say? We'll say
  That we're throwing our old lives overboard.
YVONNE: Bravo! At last you're learning to be
  A poet – of life.
HARRY: Thanks, Yvonne.
  Incidentally, I think I'll never shoot
  A lion again. I've lost the need, I fancy.
  I'll never shoulder another gun –
  Not if I live to be as old as Hotemtep.
MARIANNE: Hitler and Mussolini . . .
HARRY: Champagne and fireworks!

FINAL CURTAIN

The Eye of the Ayatollah

Three years earlier Ali lost his right eye and part of his face during one of the battles against Iraq. Which battle? Where? He didn't know. His cloaked, hood-clad mother had joyfully seen him off en route to paradise on the back of a fume-coughing truck packed with trainee revolutionary guards, all of about his own age, which was sixteen. Blood from Mother's finger adorned his forehead; she had cut herself deep with a kitchen knife.

What did Mother look like? Almond eyes, broad nose, big creamy cheeks, generous lips. The only time Ali ever saw more of her body was briefly when he was born, an incident which he neither understood at the time nor subsequently remembered. Her blood on his forehead was sacramental.

The truck drove all day and all night through dust – towards, latterly, the dawning thud and *crump* of heavy artillery. The recruits chanted and sang themselves hoarse and prayed for death, the door to paradise.

Arriving at a shattered moonscape masked by smoke, Ali and his companions were issued with hand grenades and sent out across a mine-field in the direction of the thunder. Ahead, a torrent of boulders could have been tumbling from the sky – as though here he stepped close to the very heartbeat of God, the compassionate, the merciful. The land-mine which blew his neighbour apart, arms and legs flying separately in the direction of heaven, tore off the side of Ali's face.

The next few weeks were nebulous for Ali. He himself existed inside a black, mute thunder-cloud occasionally riven by the red lightning of pain. Finally the crowded hospital released him, since he could walk and his mattress was needed; and hidden Mother welcomed half a martyr home. Neighbours admired Ali's scars and the remains of his empty eye socket.

Yet the war ended inconclusively.

Ali often visited the Fountain of Blood downtown to gape at the plumes of red-dyed water spurting as though from severed arteries. Part of a host half a million strong, he screamed for the death of the Satan-author, blasphemous apostate lurking in that Western devil-land.

Yet it wasn't the Satan-author who died; it was the Ayatollah, father of truth, beloved of God, the merciful, the compassionate.

Grief racked Ali, grief wrenched a million hearts, five million. Ali burrowed like a mole through the dense conglomerate of one of the hugest crowds in history, millions of pebbles of flesh cemented by the sand of rageful sorrow – through into the Beshte Zahar Cemetery. No, not so much cemented as surging, *churning* like the ballast and cement and liquid in some giant, horizontal concrete-mixer. Fainting, shrieking, reaching, clawing, crazed with bitter woe: a million locusts, and only one leaf to feed at – the coffin, soon to arrive. He fought his way into the inner square built of freight containers. Thousands of mourners were beating their heads with their fists in unison. Mystics were harvesting bowls of earth from the bottom of the grave, and passing these out – the crowd ate the precious soil.

A helicopter landed. Moments later, a tumult of young men hauled the shrouded body from its coffin. Hands tore the shroud to pieces, each scrap a precious relic. "Ya Ali, Ya Hussein," cried ten thousand voices. The thin white legs of the holy man jutted aloft like bare sticks, as his corpse slumped.

Ali, clawing, was in the forefront but his defective vision foxed him. As he fought his way to the rear through the tide of bodies he puzzled at what his right hand clutched, something resembling a slippery ping-pong ball. Panting, he paused long enough to glance. His palm cupped a glazed, naked eye. With a tail of optic nerve: a kind of plump, ocular tadpole.

Had a miracle happened? Had a piece of the shroud transmuted itself into Ali's own lost eye, now restored to him? Was he not himself named in honour of the martyr Ali, who founded the true school of Islam?

At last his brain caught up with what his fingers and their nails had done: he, Ali the half-faced, had torn out one of the Ayatollah's eyes.

Behind him, shots rang out. The helicopter landed once more . . .

Later, Ali heard how the corpse eventually entered its hole in the ground, to be covered by flagstones heaved hand over hand, and how a dozen of the cargo containers were piled across the grave. No one would or could say what state the body had been in finally.

The eye sat on a shelf by Ali's bed, staring unblinkingly at him. (For, lacking eyelids, how could an eye blink?) Its gaze appeared to track him about the little room, the pupil stretching into a squint to follow him.

Ali prayed. He thought about preservatives. He wondered what best to do. How could he possibly plunge that holy eye into alcohol even of the medicinal variety? So he visited a pharmacy to ask advice about – so he said – pickling a dead frog; he returned with a jar of formalin. Once afloat in that solution of formaldehyde, the eyeball definitely swung from side to side keeping an eye on him.

On *him*, on mere Ali the half-face? Oh no. Simply alert, awaiting, on the look-out. Ali prayed. Ali dreamed. A vision visited him. The holy man had been a hawk. What was that hawk's eye hunting for? Why, it was surveying all of the Earth, searching for the hiding place of the Satan-author.

Events deployed as the will of God decreed. Truly dreams were troubled in Tehran during those days. Angels guided Ali to the office of Dr Omar Hafiz, doyen of the country's ballistic missile programme, who for his part had dreamt originally of exploding a nuclear weapon on Tel Aviv to free the Palestinians. Those high-explosive birds aimed at Baghdad were a side-show. Alas, lack of a warhead derailed the project. So next, Dr Hafiz dreamed of a reconnaissance satellite to spy on Iraqi army positions; but peace had been declared. Lately

Hafiz dreamt of using the prototype rocket to put a communications satellite into orbit to criss-cross the whole face of the Earth: the *Voice of God*, broadcasting the truth . . .

An angel had also visited Dr Hafiz.

"We *can* fly your hawk," he assured Ali. "The cold of space will preserve the eye from corruption. It will look down on Europe, America, Africa. That Satan-author may have hidden anywhere. He may have bought plastic surgery. The eye will find him. With its miraculous perception it will recognize him. He is what it seeks; for fifty years, if need be."

"And I, the half-face," said Ali, "need to be on hand when our hawk finds its prey, do I not? For the eye was given into my hand, was it not?"

Events unfolded like a fragrant rose from a bud. Surgeons renovated Ali's face, rebuilt his orbital bone, gave him a glass eye. Tutors nurtured his smattering of English and French into something resembling fluency. Commandos offered him the sort of weapons training he'd sorely lacked when he rode to war. His forged passport identified him as a naturalized Australian.

Soon his country launched its first earth satellite named the *Eye of the Ayatollah*, and announced to the world (as well as to the Satan-author, wherever he was) that the orbiting instrument package did indeed contain exactly that. Benighted infidels outside the harbour of Islam laughed – uneasily. Corrupted souls within the harbour of Islam glanced askance at the night sky.

No one beyond the inner hierarchy knew the whole truth about Ali. Whenever Ali shut his left eye, he looked down through his artificial eye upon the countries of the earth from space. For his glass eye was more than a bauble. Through it, miraculously, the youth could see whatever the holy man's searching eye could see through the zoom-lenses of the satellite; as had been promised in the vision confided to Dr Hafiz . . .

*

In the cold void above the topmost air, the *Eye of the Ayatollah* orbited for a year, two years, five years . . . Disguised as a dinkum Aussie immigrant on holiday, Ali wandered the world as frugally as he could, financed by an American Express gold card. Universally acceptable; he still regretted the expedient.

The orbiting eye seemed to twitch as it was passing over Pakistan, and there went Ali; a solar flare must have been responsible. Again, over Nicaragua, it spasmed; thus Ali went to that strife-torn land. Perhaps a cosmic ray had hit the eye.

He found himself in Sweden, in Ireland, in America, England, France. Always keeping watch. From his hiding place the Satan-author published another book, redoubling Ali's fervour.

Seven years passed. The eye watched. Ali watched.

At long last the eye throbbed. It was gazing down upon an island off the south-west coast of Scotland; upon a tiny isle that nestled against a bay of its parent island like a newborn baby whale beside its leviathan of a mother. The eye passed over, but not before imprinting Ali vividly.

He flew to London, collected a gun and grenades from a certain embassy, and caught a train to Glasgow.

He would need to wait there for some weeks till the satellite would be poised to pass over the same part of Scotland again. Buying maps and guides, he soon learned that the name of the mother island was Arran, and of the islet: Holy Island, a title which set his teeth on edge.

As the time approached, Ali took a bus to the coast then a ferry to Arran. Renting a modest car, he reconnoitred this pinnacled island of granite bens and fells, glens of bracken and frisky streams rushing amidst great boulders, mounds of moraine, dark conifers, and wild red deer – suddenly giving way in the south to rolling heathery hills, calm pastures, sandy beaches with a few palm trees.

Ali checked in to a hotel in the small seaside town of Lamlash opposite Holy Island. He had brought a hammer, and was pretending to be an enthusiastic amateur geologist. Binoculars too; he was an eager bird-watcher.

How that islet dominated the shore. Its two-mile stretch of jagged cliffs and rugged moorland sheltered wild goats, long-legged diminutive Soay sheep, shaggy Highland cattle; and birds, birds. Holy Island was a nature reserve, a field study centre. From its southernmost tip a lighthouse beaconed across the Firth of Clyde.

Unholy island, thought Ali.

Apparently a Christian saint called Molaise lived on the isle in the time of the prophet Mohammed, bless his name. The saint's cell could still be visited; Vikings had defaced it with runic inscriptions. The Satan-author also skulked in a kind of cell. Did he think he could walk free in safety upon those moors amongst the goats? The bars of his cell were the eye-beams of an authentic holy man, whose organ of vision lived on.

But first the instrument package enshrining that organ of vision must re-enter the atmosphere and parachute down to earth; for such had been Dr Hafiz's design. Thus the hawk would pounce.

Studying his maps, Ali chose a glen leading to a ben. He telephoned a cover number in Australia, to alert Tehran. Next evening, the important part of the *Eye of the Ayatollah* descended and soft-landed in the bonnie upland heather.

The following morning, Ali took the ferry over to Holy Island in company with half a dozen ornithologists. The sea was choppy, the breeze was brisk, so spindrift soon coated the lens-studded box that held the eye, which Ali wore around his neck like some gold-plated camera. Already that camera-that-wasn't had attracted a few curious glances. Was Ali some aviphile oil sheikh travelling incognito who couldn't forsake at least one token of ostentation?

"Ah," he told himself, "I'm but the humblest servant."

Fortunately the crossing did not coincide with a time for prayer; however he found that his vision was fogging. Ducking down out of sight behind some cargo, he opened the golden box and cradled the holy eyeball naked in his palm once more.

The soft ball seemed to burn icily as though still frozen. Inspired, the Half-Face popped his glass prosthetic from its rebuilt orbit and replaced it with the Ayatollah's own.

His vision swam. He saw two scenes at once: the hellishly gaunt, approaching cliffs licked by sea-spume, and what he could only interpret as a glimpse of paradise, the slope of a verdant valley where fountains of milk gushed, spilling down in streams, where all manner of jewels glittered – a landscape girt with a dance of scintillating pastel auroras like diaphanous rose-and-pink veils of maidens, though minus the maidens. Ahead was a curiously imprecise promise of ecstasies without substance, as if he was seeing this terrain in some warmer Eden of the past, courtesy of an angel.

Some such subconscious, submerged vista must always have lurked in his inner gaze, as a cynosure, a focus. In this mystical moment he appeared to remember the lost object of all his buried desires. The whole island swelled with the light of joyful creation, the conjuring of mischievous beauty. Honey flowed like lava from one hilltop.

He shut the eye that was his own; and through that other, holy eye he saw only the sternness of cliffs again, their stark authenticity. Gulls screamed battlecries. The sun was an ulcer of yellow pus, its afterimage a ball of blood. The impact of waves faintly echoed that torrent of boulders he had heard on a previous occasion at the battlefront.

"Why, Satan-author," Ali said to himself in surprise, "you are in hell already."

When he closed his holy right eye to regard the scenery with his left eye, heavenly auras sparkled again, interference patterns between two modes of vision, awakening deeply hidden memories of a time when he had perceived the world freshly with wonder, long ago; of a time when he had been born and had had to create a universe around himself.

"In hell indeed," he added, "unless your eyes see otherwise."

After he left the ferry to mount the island, he hiked with either his right eye open or his left, the holy eye mapping out barren geometries of rock and sky and grass, the other eye teasing the tastebuds of his soul with that shimmer of scanty pastel veils behind which raw beauty beckoned.

He stepped out, he halted, he stepped out. The holy eye led him along a stony track towards what had once been a crofter's cottage and was now a sprawling homestead with mirror-glass windows surrounded by a high wire fence, supposedly to deter goats. The only guards these days were gulls.

The Satan-author sat at a desk. Haggard, yes. A nervous twitch in one eye; almost totally bald. Yet as he looked at this intruder who pointed a pistol as though out of habit, the author smiled.

"So it has come at last."

That damnable smile, of sanity still sustained!

Ali shut his holy eye. Seen through his left eye, a nimbus surrounded the author's head. Ali reverted to his right eye, tightening his grip on the gun as he scanned the despicable face. A moment later he looked with his left eye too, and his vision swam again dizzyingly, so he closed the left eye.

"You look like a human traffic light," remarked the author as though choosing wry last words for posterity, fit for some future dictionary of quotations.

Ali's holy attention was caught by a paper-knife used to open the author's voluminous, redirected correspondence, all his envelopes full of cheques paying him lavishly for his blasphemy in the currencies of Satan, dollars, pounds, francs, marks.

Now Ali's left eye also noted the knife with the sharp point. A roseate halo stained the blade with diluted blood. The handle was iridescent mother-of-pearl. Ali remembered the battle against Iraq and suddenly felt cheated. Strange desire surged within him.

"Which," he asked, as if this was a riddle, "which is my real eye? My true eye?"

Perhaps amazed at the idiosyncrasy of human nature, the author stared at this man who opened one eye then the other turn by turn, squinting at him. Was he really being offered a choice as though in a fairy tale? A choice between life and death – or only a choice between types of death?

He hesitated, then spoke at random. "The left eye."

"An angel guides your words." Ali snatched up the knife, opened both eyes at once, and pointed the steel tip at the holy one.

The author tensed, imagining that he had chosen wrongly – perhaps could never have chosen correctly! – but Ali skewered the eye of the Ayatollah, drew it forth dripping humours, and stabbed the knife and its jelly burden down upon the desk.

"This," said Ali, "is the eye that sees hell."

A weight of years-long possession drained away from Ali's heart; and for the first time since he could recall, his own left eye leaked tears.